LIFE ON LONG ISLAND WAS
AN X-RATED FILM.
BUT JUDITH NEVER GOT TO STAR . . .

Thirty-four, bright and bored, Judith Singer knew something intriguing was going on in Shorehaven. After ten years, she was sure it wasn't her marriage.

What was going on was a crime . . .

The victim: Dr. Bruce Fleckstein, gum specialist and stud—who kissed the girls and made them smile for his camera.

Now their faces were red. The movies were blue. The dentist was dead.

And solving the murder became Judith's hobby— then her passion . . . when she met Sharpe, the sexy lieutenant . . . and when her deep-buried, dazzling, sensuous self burst into the light, breaking out of her own . . .

Compromising Positions

SUSAN ISAACS

A JOVE BOOK

This Jove book contains the complete
text of the original hardcover edition.
It has been completely reset in a typeface
designed for easy reading, and was printed
from new film.

COMPROMISING POSITIONS

A Jove Book / published by arrangement with
Time Books, a division of Quadrangle/
The New York Times Book Co., Inc.

PRINTING HISTORY
Times book edition published 1978
Jove edition / January 1979
Tenth printing / March 1985

ISBN: 0-515-08089-6

Library of Congress Catalog Card Number: 77-13896

Jove books are published by The Berkley Publishing Group,
200 Madison Avenue, New York, N.Y. 10016.
The words "A JOVE BOOK" and the "J" with sunburst
are trademarks belonging to Jove Publications, Inc.

PRINTED IN THE UNITED STATES OF AMERICA

TO
Elkan Abramowitz
the best person in the world

AUTHOR'S NOTE   *I sought advice and encouragement from the people listed below. They gave it freely and cheerfully. I want to thank them—and to apologize if I may have twisted the facts to fit my fiction.*

Jonathan Dolger, Robert B. Fiske, Jr., Esq., Mary FitzPatrick, Ph.D., Fred Hafetz, Esq., Carol Harris, Helen Isaacs, Morton Isaacs, Robert Jupiter, Esq., Leonard S. Klein, David Mendelsohn, Edith Mendelsohn, Herbert Mendelsohn, Catherine Morvillo, Lawrence Pedowitz, Esq., Mary Rooney, Paul G. Tolins, M.D., William Wald, D.D.S., Fred Watts, Esq., Jay Zises, and Susan Zises.

And a special thanks to my editor, Marcia Magill, for her intelligence, perspicacity, and niceness.

S. I.

Chapter One

As they would murmur at his funeral, Dr. M. Bruce Fleckstein was one of the finest periodontists on Long Island. And so good-looking. But as he turned his muscular, white-coated back for the last time, he had no notion that he had shot his final wad of Novocaine, probed his ultimate gum. No, he simply turned for an instant, perhaps out of boredom, perhaps to hide the slight smirk that passed over his thin, firm lips. It was an unfortunate turn; his companion seized the moment to withdraw a thin, sharp weapon and plunge it into the base of Fleckstein's skull.

That was on the evening of Valentine's Day. My children lay on the floor of the den, watching television, unusually amicable; they were probably too engorged, too leaden, with the day's excess of Valentine's confections to raise even a whimper, much less a clenched fist. I sat alone, waiting for my husband, my finger tracing hearts pierced with nonlethal arrows on the frosted window near the kitchen table.

Fleckstein lay on the floor of his office. It must have been quiet there too, for his murderer stayed only ten minutes, taking time to make sure there was no tell-tale twitch of life, to grab a few tissues to wipe off the weapon and to search the office. Of course, even if

Fleckstein had been able to give one last shriek of protest, one last howl of dismay, I would not have heard him. His office, Suite 305 in the Shorehaven Colonial Professional Building, was ten minutes from my house, a ten-room Tudor in Shorehaven Acres. Actually, Shorehaven Half-Acres would be more precise, but the developers of Nassau County's North Shore insist on perpetuating the area's reputation as the Gold Coast, the Playland of the Robber Barons. So, minutes from F. Scott Fitzgerald's East Egg, we have Shorehaven Estates, split-levels on sixty by one hundred foot plots; Shorecastle, a red-brick sprawl of upper-middle-income garden apartments on the once-lush grounds of a nineteenth-century railroad tycoon; Shorehaven Mansions, a group of forty colonials, aluminum-sided mini-Taras, competing with a few sparse junipers for a place in the sun.

I learned of Fleckstein's death about two hours after it happened, as I listened to an all-news radio station broadcasting from Manhattan, thirty miles away.

"We have a report from Duke Gray, our Long Island correspondent," the voice said. I listened. Bob's train might be late, the switches might have frozen.

"Yes, Jim," came a second voice, crackling over the wire like Edward R. Murrow reporting the Battle of Britain. "I'm speaking to you from the suburb of Shorehaven, where a little more than an hour ago, the body of Dr. Marvin Bruce Fleckstein, a dentist, was discovered, brutally murdered, on the floor of his office." The voice droned on, reporting that there seemed to be no definite leads, but that an official from the Nassau County Police Department would try to issue a statement later in the evening. "And that's it for now from Shorehaven, Jim."

"Thanks, Duke."

"God," I thought, turning off the radio. "I knew him." I had seen Fleckstein in line waiting for a movie and at Parents Night at school. I had even consulted with him once, about six months into my pregnancy with Joey. I had been peering into the mirror, studying my face, the only part of my body not bloated, gazing into my slightly almond-shaped eyes, staring at my high cheekbones, mementos, doubtless, of a Mongol invader who had passed through my great-great-grandmother's *shtetl* en route to besiege Minsk. I smiled at my reflection and saw it: tiny rivulets of blood oozing out of puffy gums. My dentist told me to see a periodontist like Dr. Fleckstein. I did.

He gave me a friendly greeting. "Hi, Judy."

"Judith," I replied automatically.

"Okay, Judith it is." By that time, I realized I had lost the opportunity to be brilliantly assertive, to establish my adult credentials. I could have said coolly, "Mrs. Singer," or, better still, "Ms. Singer," or even "Ms. Bernstein-Singer." Instead, I sat passively, mouth agape, a napkin resting under my chin, a bib to soak up my infantile dribble. My eyes darted from the word "Castle" on Fleckstein's adjustable light to his princely, large-featured face. He probed, he scraped with one of those ghastly pointed metal dental picks, stopping at intervals so I could rinse my bloodied mouth with Lavoris and water.

"You haven't been using unwaxed dental floss, have you?" he asked, although he knew the answer.

"No, but I will."

"You really should. Do you have a Water Pik?"

"Yes," I muttered, the draining tube making crude slurping noises in the bottom of my mouth.

"Well, use it. It doesn't do you any good sitting on the sink, does it, Judith?" He sounded sad and weary, a prophet unheeded by a decadent, self-indulgent people.

"No, I guess not." I felt humiliated, as I always do with professionals who catch me in my sloppy, unroutinized ways. Periodically, I remind myself that I haven't taken my vitamin-mineral supplement, that my toenails have grown curved and jagged, that another month has passed without a self-examination of my breasts.

But Fleckstein wasn't too bad. He gave me some medicine for my gums and told me to massage them regularly. Then, looking at my belly, he said: "Good luck."

"Thank you."

"Is this your first?"

"No, my second. We have a three-year-old daughter, Katherine. We call her Kate."

"Very nice. Well, good seeing you. Good luck."

"Dr. Fleckstein," I said, "about your fee. How much . . .?"

"Speak to my nurse about it." He smiled and left the room.

Not exactly an "I-thou" relationship, but sufficient to leave me shaken at the news of his murder. Almost unconsciously, I twisted the knobs of the three doors to the house, front, back, and garage. They were locked. I turned on the outside floodlights. The grass, encrusted with a brittle February frost, was blanketed by a pale, eerie mist, but no crazed killers seemed to be lurking behind the swings or under the denuded rose bushes.

"Kate! Joey!" I called, and waited an uneasy moment until they tramped up the stairs. "Time for bed."

"Can't we wait up for Daddy? *Star Trek* isn't over. It's still early. It isn't fair." They protested, alternating sentences, whining louder each time.

"Shh," I hissed, and marched them upstairs to their rooms, where I tenderly smoothed back their hair to kiss their foreheads, tucked them into bed, and half-closed their doors. Then I tiptoed downstairs, accelerating as I moved through the hallway into the kitchen, straight for the telephone.

"Nancy," I breathed as she answered after five rings. "It's me." Nancy MacLaren Miller, whom I'd met fifteen years before in a Colonial American History class at the University of Wisconsin, was one of the best reasons for living in Shorehaven. Her house was about two miles from mine, and I saw her, needed to see her, at least once a week. "Did you hear the news?"

"Apparently not," she answered, her deep, husky voice thickened by a Georgia drawl, although she hadn't been back to Valdosta for nearly twenty years. "What happened?"

Taking a deep breath, I recounted what I had heard on the newscast, inhaled again briefly and asked: "Did you know him?"

"My Lord, no. But I've heard about him. Anyway, Judith, who could possibly have done it?"

I suggested a junkie, which Nancy rejected as being either unlikely or boring, or an irate patient, whose gums were still bleeding after years of treatment.

"No, no, no," she insisted. "Look, he was what my mother would have called a bounder. Most likely, it was someone he was fucking." Southern women, I've noticed, can say the most outrageous things, and even the most straight-laced listener will smile wanly, as if to say, "Isn't she cute?"

"Really?" I asked. "I mean, he didn't seem the Don Juan type."

"Judith, you wouldn't recognize it if you fell over it. You think that every guy who talks to you wants to establish a meaningful dialogue." Her voice rose. "Men do not want dialogues. What do you want them to do? Hang their dickies out of their trousers and wave them at you? Would you understand then?"

"That would be a fair indication," I conceded. "But listen, Nancy, why would one of his women want to kill him?"

"Maybe he wouldn't go down on her."

"She could have stoned him or thrown lye in his face. Don't you think murder is a little excessive?"

"No," she said firmly. "I most certainly do not."

We chatted a few minutes longer. At my urging,

Nancy recalled that she had heard rumors linking Fleckstein with a couple of the local ladies, but she couldn't remember the details. "How do you think his wife will take it?" I mused. "What's her name?"

"Let me see now. Norma. Norma Fleckstein."

"Norma. That's right." She had been pointed out to me once or twice, although we had never been introduced. Tall and slender, with short frosted hair brushed back to frame her oblong-shaped face. Not pretty, but aggressively attractive, she was one of those Long Island tough-ladies, brittle and magnificently groomed, wafting a sweet cloud of Norell or Estée. With three or four silver rings on each hand. Dressed in designer jumpsuits unzipped low enough to establish the existence of cleavage, toting an outsize Louis Vuitton handbag or clutching a Gucci under a thin arm. I cannot seem to comprehend the meaning of these flawless women, why they're here.

Are they divine messengers or mother surrogates, here to remind the rest of us to do our isometrics and polish our nails? Are they the ultimate threat, a warning that if we neglect to slather on body cream and blow-dry our hair every day, our husbands will abandon us and our children will mock us? I eavesdrop on their conversations in restaurants and department stores; they're consistently discussing clothes, vacations, or who did what to whom, in the most conventional, adulterous, heterosexual manner imaginable. Yet they seem so strange, alien almost.

"I don't know how she'll take it," Nancy said. "But I'll just bet she'll open her closet and find the perfect little black dress to wear to the funeral."

We said goodbye, vowing to call each other if we heard anything new. I sat at the kitchen table, running my finger over the ridges in the polyester tablecloth that was meant to approximate burlap, pondering the fact that the body of a near contemporary—I was thirty-four, Fleckstein couldn't have been more than six or

14

seven years older—was right then lying on a slab in the police morgue. Why had it happened? Who could have done it?

Then, hearing Bob's car in the driveway, I leapt up to stick the steak under the broiler. If we sipped our tomato juice slowly enough, the meat would be done before he noticed that the entire dinner was not arrayed before him, steaming and juicy, after he handed me his coat and dashed to the dining room table. I strolled to the front door and opened it, knowing that Bob would still be fumbling with his key ring, as if trying to locate the key to some obscure filing cabinet instead of the one to his house.

"Thanks," he said, stepping inside. "And how was your day today?" He leaned forward, aiming his lips toward my cheek for their usual greeting, but I must have moved slightly, because he kissed my right eye. He didn't seem to notice. "Boy," he breathed, "did I have a bitch of a day."

"Happy Valentine's Day," I replied. I reached into the closet and took his present from the top shelf, a book, complete with maps and illustrations, on life in medieval France.

"Thanks," he said. "I'll open it after dinner. Look, Judith, I didn't have a chance to get you anything, and I really don't know what you need. Go out tomorrow and buy yourself something nice. Okay? Jesus," he added, "am I exhausted."

"Well, you look great." He did. Bob had just enough character in his face for him to be judged as good-looking, rather than handsome. A tall, slender man, slightly over six feet, with curly light brown hair, a long straight nose, and crinkly laugh lines in the outer corners of his pale blue eyes—which actually came from squinting—he rarely looked fatigued. His shoulders might slump a bit, his beard might apear a little scratchy, but he always looked scrubbed, fresh, healthy. Clear, bright American looks, like a Kellogg's Corn

15

Flakes ad, contrasted to my darkness, a face in the crowd in a documentary called "New York City: Melting Pot." When his ancestors chose exogamy, they obviously went in for Aryans. "Anyway," I asked, "what happened this afternoon that was so hideous?"

"Nothing. A meeting with some new clients. A toy company. I don't even want to talk about it." Bob is vice-president of his family's public relations firm. When we met, eleven years before, he was about to begin his doctoral dissertation in comparative literature. A year later, about two months after our wedding, he opted for Singer Associates.

"What's for dinner?"

"Steak," I said, hanging up his heavy blue overcoat. Why did I do that? "Let me just turn it."

"It's not ready yet?"

"No."

"All right. I might as well go upstairs and wash up."

We sat at the long, oval dining room table a few minutes later, he at the head of the table, me on his left, facing a large painting his mother had given us, a pink and mauve and gray arrangement of rectangles painted by an artist friend of hers. It was still recognizable as the standard Manhattan skyline.

I offered him a baked potato. "Did you hear about it?"

"About what?" he asked, shaking his head, refusing the potato.

"Remember when I was pregnant with Joey, I went to a periodontist, Dr. Fleckstein?" He nodded. "Well, he was murdered."

"Jesus, a dentist. Who'd want to kill a dentist?"

I gave him my synopsis of the radio report and repeated Nancy's theory that the murderer was one of the women he had been sleeping with. "What do you think?" I asked.

"I dunno," he replied. This from a man once equally comfortable speaking French, Spanish, Italian, German, and Russian, a man who had once possessed a reading knowledge of Latin, ancient Greek, and Hebrew. He leaned back in his chair, a signal that he was ready for coffee. As I walked into the kitchen, he called after me: "You know, I heard something about Fleckstein recently."

I did a rapid about-face. "What?"

"I'll think while you get the coffee." I returned and poured the coffee, watching him as he twisted the lobe of his ear between his fingers. "I know," he finally responded. "I had lunch with Clay last week, and he said one of his partners had a neighbor of ours for a client." Claymore Katz, who had been Bob's roommate at Columbia, was a criminal lawyer who specialized in white-collar crime—securities fraud, tax evasion, bribery.

"Was it a criminal thing? Did Claymore say what it was about?"

"It must have been something criminal, but he didn't go into detail. Look, it had to be something interesting if he bothered to mention it to me. I'm sure he was trying to see if I knew anything about the guy." He pushed his coffee cup back an inch and stood up. "I'll meet you upstairs," he said, giving me his knowing look. "Hurry up with the dishes."

I worked slowly, patiently scraping the gristle and the remaining green beans into the garbage, carefully rinsing the dishes before stacking them in the dishwasher. Why should a suburban dentist need a high-priced criminal lawyer? Some sort of Medicaid fraud? Not likely. Fleckstein's patients were drawn from the Shorehaven community, and the community could pay its own way.

"Judith," Bob called in a hoarse whisper from the top of the stairs. "I'm waiting for you." I finished hurriedly, leaving the broiling pan to soak overnight. He was indeed waiting, I saw, as I passed through the hallway to the stairs. His Valentine present lay on the shelf where he had left it, unopened. I walked up the stairs to him. "Hi," he said softly, standing slim and naked and erect.

He didn't like to waste time. "Ready?" He asked me that three nights a week.

"Bob, could you call Claymore tomorrow and try to find out some more information? Please?"

"Come on, Judith. Who cares?"

"I care. It's interesting."

"Clay probably doesn't know anything."

"But maybe he does. Or he could speak to his lawyer friend."

"How would that look?" he demanded.

"It would look like you're curious. Tell him I asked you to find out what's going on. Clay likes me. He'd do it for me."

"I don't have to bring you into it," he snapped. "Come on, Judith, it's getting late and I want to get to the office early." I stepped toward him and ran my hands over his chest and stomach, firm from his daily prelunch workout, hairy and warm. "Come on," he urged. "Let's do it in bed. Okay?"

We did, finishing neatly in our usual twenty minutes. It was fine; one hundred watts of sexual incandescence discharged, a baked potato's worth of calories consumed, a faint aura of warmth and friendliness established that lasted through the night and into the first few minutes of the morning.

At seven-thirty the next day I even smiled, then glanced out the living room window and noticed the *Times* on my driveway, practically pulsating with what I knew to be a major story on the Fleckstein case. But my path was blocked by Kate and Joey, having their first skirmish of the day.

"Dumbhead." Her dark brown eyes narrowed.

"Chicken-doody-faggot," he retaliated.

Then Bob came downstairs, wondering aloud why I couldn't find two extra minutes to roll his socks into nice little balls instead of stuffing them all into his drawer. By nine o'clock, they were finally dispatched to their respective first grade, nursery school, and office.

Pulling a sheepskin jacket over my bathrobe, I scurried down the front path toward the driveway to retrieve the newspaper. The air was warmer than I had expected, the deceptive hint of spring before the end of February and the whole of March dump their final icy insults. Nothing in the index about the murder, I noted, reading as I walked back into the house. But I found a short squib on the third page of the second section, "Dentist Found Slain," datelined Shorehaven.

The body of Marvin Bruce Fleckstein, 42, a periodontist, was discovered in his office last evening in this affluent community on Long Island's North Shore. According to a police spokesman, death was probably caused by a wound in the base of the skull. Investigators in charge of the case refused further comment, although they said a report from the Nassau County Medical Examiner's office was due in a day or two.

The *Times* had failed me. During elections, monetary crises, Congressional scandals, it had always come through. Throughout Watergate, there was always something to wallow in with my second cup of coffee, something enough even for me, a once-promising doctoral candidate in American political history. But today there was nothing to mull over. Not a blonde hair twirled around a button of Fleckstein's jacket, not even a medicine cabinet tampered with. No mention, of course, that M. Bruce had found other orifices to probe. I sat slumped on a straight-backed kitchen chair, debating who would be the most fascinating person to call and discuss the case with. Nancy would be unavailable; a free-lance writer, she works from nine to one every day and takes her phone off the hook. Well, I thought, I could call . . . And the doorbell rang.

I dashed out of the kitchen and yanked open the door with sheer joy at having human contact. But it was a strange man. I took him in at one glance: average height, bushy eyebrows, a small smile on his wide mouth. Quickly, I pushed the door shut so it was left open just a crack. He could be the Shorehaven Slayer and I was his next victim, selected with insane randomness.

"Mrs. Singer? I'm Sergeant Ramirez of the Nassau County Police." He held up an identification card to the glass of the storm door. It had his picture and a raised seal. It was official. "I'm investigating the murder of Dr. M. Bruce Fleckstein. Would it be all right for me to ask you a few questions?"

I grinned and held the door wide open.

Chapter Two

"Did you hear about the murder?" he inquired as he stepped into the hallway. He glanced away from me, his eyes darting about the hallway toward the kitchen, into the living room, perhaps out of curiosity, perhaps in the mild hope that he might find a blood-stained weapon lying casually on an armchair.

"I heard about it on the radio last night. Awful. Absolutely awful." His eyes were focused on the far end of the living room, examining the empty log basket by the fireplace. I stepped into his line of vision. "Would you like a cup of coffee?"

"No. Don't bother."

"No trouble. It's already made."

"All right. Light, two sugars."

I strolled into the kitchen, fixed two mugs of coffee, and returned, offering him one. "We can sit in the living room," I suggested. He followed me and perched on the edge of a wing chair. I sat a couple of feet away on the couch. Peering at the coffee, a bit suspiciously I thought, he pursed his lips and took a delicate sip. I smiled, trying to appear sincere and cooperative.

"Did you happen to notice what time your neighbor, Mrs. Tuccio, came in last night?"

"Why do you ask?" Now that we were friends, drinking coffee together, I could afford to revert to my usual perverseness.

"Well, it's nothing serious," he said crisply. Ramirez had assimilated with high honors. No trace of an accent, demeanor as open, as briskly friendly, as a WASP car salesman. "It's just that Mrs. Tuccio was his last patient yesterday, probably the last person to see Dr. Fleckstein alive."

"Except for the murderer."

"Oh. Right. Anyway, did you happen to notice what time she came home last evening?"

"Is Marilyn Tuccio a suspect?" Is the Pope an atheist?

"We just have to check every possible fact, Mrs. Singer." Ramirez, despite my excellent coffee, seemed mildly annoyed.

"I'm sorry. I didn't notice. I was busy with the children and getting dinner ready."

"I see," he said slowly. "Do you know Mrs. Tuccio well?"

"We're friendly."

"Did she ever happen to mention anything to you about Dr. Fleckstein?"

"No."

"Well, thanks anyway. If you remember anything, give me a call. I'll jot down the number." He took a pen from his coat pocket and extracted a small green-covered notebook from his jacket. He wrote down the number and tore out the page. "Here," he offered it to me. "And thanks for the coffee. It was strong, but I like it that way."

I escorted him to the front door, waved goodbye, and plodded back inside. Could they suspect Marilyn Tuccio of anything? The Saint of Oaktree Street? Absurd. Then why was Ramirez checking? And if he was so interested, why hadn't he asked any probing questions about her? Was she stable? Any homicidal tendencies? Did she keep any dangerous weapons in her bread box, between the oatmeal cookies and the home-made cracked wheat rolls?

With an explosion of energy that is rarely visited upon me before noon, I jammed the breakfast dishes into the dishwasher, ran upstairs and made the beds, then quickly drew on a pair of jeans and my favorite blue denim work shirt. Finally, lifting the receiver of a beige Princess phone that I had ordered in a long-forgotten moment of frivolity, I called Marilyn.

"Marilyn? It's me, Judith. Can I come over for a few minutes?"

"Judith, I'm a little busy now . . ."

"Look, the police were just here asking questions about you."

"Oh. What did they say?"

"Marilyn, I'd rather not talk about it over the phone. Anyway, you sound as though you could use some company." Actually, she sounded as though she were aching for solitude.

"Well, sure. Come right over. Would you like coffee?"

"Always. See you."

Marilyn O'Connor Tuccio is one of those wispy Irish redheads who look as though they were born to be taken advantage of: tiny, delicate, you could imagine her exhaustedly carrying an enormous pot of stew to the parish house "for Father Sweeny, Mrs. Mallory" or lugging home cases of beer for a beefy, veiny-nosed husband who made certain she was pregnant every year. Fragile and petite, with pale blue veins shimmering under the lightly freckled white skin of her hands, she should, according to stereotype, whisper hello to you and then lower those long, pale eyelashes, astonished at her own brazenness. Instead, she is unfailingly assertive, competent, and almost violently energetic, the only housewife I know who doesn't, even secretly, feel she got shafted. Marilyn sews all the clothes for herself and her four children, cans all her fruits and vegetables, drives endless car pools and, in her spare time, is president of the junior high PTA and a Republican County Committeewoman.

I trotted across the street and, when I got to the door, noticed that she had taken down her Valentine wreath and put up her Presidents decoration, a crewel-work double portrait of Lincoln and Washington, simply framed with flowers she had dried herself. Next month there would be an adorable stuffed lion and lamb hanging from the door, and for April, I recalled, a fluffy crocheted Easter bunny clutching a bouquet of crepe-paper daffodils.

I rang the bell and Marilyn called out: "The door's open." I stepped into a massive room that took up the entire first floor of her house, a combination kitchen, dining room, living room, and playroom, paneled in a light wood and dominated by a large brick fireplace. A room for a family, she had called it two years before, when she ran across the street to show me her architect's drawings.

"Marilyn," I said, seeing her sitting at the end of her long refectory table, "I'm sorry to disturb you, but the police came over and started asking me questions, and I didn't want you to think . . ."

"Judith, this is unbelievable. A police detective was here last night asking me questions for over two hours."

"Unbelievable," I concurred. Her small, pointed chin jutted out angrily. "Ridiculous."

"I told him I was busy going through my voter registration lists, but he just kept asking the same questions over and over."

I liked that. Marilyn was a politician after all, probably letting the detective know she was a committeewoman, well-connected in this congenitally Republican county.

"What did he ask you?"

"The usual," she replied. Twenty years from *Dragnet* to *Kojak* and we're all experts. "Whether Dr. Fleckstein seemed upset about anything. Did he get any phone

24

calls. What time Lorna Lewis, you know, his nurse, left. Did he seem in a hurry to get me out of the office. Did I see anybody hanging around. Things like that."

"What did you tell him?"

"You take your coffee with a Sweet 'n Low and a little milk?"

"Yes. Thanks. Were you able to tell the police anything?"

"Well, you have to understand that I was absolutely numb from the Novocaine and that nearly the whole time I had that gas thing on and was floating over the clouds somewhere. I wonder if that's what marijuana is like."

"Were there any phone calls or anything?" I sipped my coffee. Excellent. Marilyn had ground her own beans.

"No, I don't think so."

"And what about people? Any other patients waiting?"

"No. In fact, I felt a little uncomfortable being alone in the office with him after his nurse left."

"Really?"

"Yes. And that's why when I opened the door to leave, I was glad to see a couple of people in the hall."

"Who?" I demanded.

"I forget. Some doctor, I think, in a white coat, and maybe one or two others." She ran her hand over her red hair, as if making sure she looked presentable enough for those strangers.

"Did he seem different to you in any way?"

"No. Well, Judith, you know what a complete lecher he is."

"Was. I'd heard."

"Well, he started flirting when I came in, just like always."

"Like how?" Men like Fleckstein, who wear gold chains around their necks and have manicures, tend to ignore me. I seem to attract hypercerebral types,

25

chubby astrophysicists in wire-rimmed glasses who tell me I have a first-rate mind while they stare at my breasts.

"Oh, the usual come-on. That there was only one way for me to prove that I'm a natural redhead. And didn't I know that dentists were better than doctors?" Marilyn's husband, Mike, was a pediatric surgeon.

"What did you say?" Things like that never happened to me. Once, an advertising copywriter whom I'd met at a dinner party took me aside and said: "If you ever get into the city, give me a buzz. We'll have lunch."

"What did you say?" I repeated.

"Nothing. I just laughed, although I told Lorna, his nurse, her daughter was in Kevin's class, that her boss had himself one heck of a reputation and that someday he was going to get himself in big trouble."

I stared at her. "When did you say that?"

"Yesterday. She came to tell him she was leaving, and he stepped out for a minute, so we chatted a bit."

"Terrific, Marilyn."

"What do you mean?"

"I mean that Lorna probably told the police that you said her boss was going to get himself into big trouble."

"That's absolutely idiotic."

"Of course, it's idiotic. But, look, Marilyn, you know the police. And that Lorna looked like she had a stick up her ass; she was probably whooping it up with him between patients. Those super-neat, prissy types are kind of sneaky. I mean, they look like they don't even have vaginas and then all of a sudden you hear they . . ."

"I don't know," she interrupted. "Maybe." It occurred to me at that moment that Marilyn, when she wasn't baking bread or drafting nominating petitions, taught confraternity class; I had been more forthright with her than I usually was.

"Sorry about my choice of words," I said.

"That's okay." She stood and walked to the refrigerator and extracted a large plastic bag of green baking apples. "I'm making apple crisp," she explained. "What do you think I should do?"

"I assume you're not asking me for a recipe."

"No," she responded softly.

"Well, it can't hurt to talk to a lawyer."

"If they were crazy enough to consider me a suspect, wouldn't they tell me to get a lawyer?"

"I don't know. That's why you need one." I paused and watched her take a paring knife and peel the apple. The skin came off in one long, thin strip. I leaned on the table and told her about Ramirez, that all he seemed interested in was the time she returned home.

"This is Lorna Lewis's second marriage," said Marilyn. She wanted to change the subject.

"I didn't know that. I only saw her briefly, when I had some work done in his office."

"She and her first husband had three children, and then one day, out of the clear blue sky, she told him to pack up and move out. She didn't feel fulfilled." Marilyn said "fulfilled" with great contempt. Despite her wide circle of friends, her sophistication, and the legions of divorced women scurrying about Shorehaven, she was still appalled at the breakup of any marriage. She was, above all, a devout Catholic. "Then she married George Lewis, but I gather she doesn't find him fulfilling either."

"Do you think Lorna was having an adulterous affair with Dr. Fleckstein?" I asked, adjusting my diction to suit my audience.

"Yes." She was already on her fourth apple.

"What makes you think so?"

"Because I saw them."

"Saw them?"

She laughed. "Not doing it, Judith. But a few months ago I was pulling into that Chinese restaurant, the one that's right next door to the Tudor Rose Motor Inn. I was meeting my sister-in-law Cathy for lunch. Well, who should I see sitting in a car in front of the motel

27

but Lorna Lewis. And not ten seconds later, guess who saunters back to the car? Dr. Fleckstein!"

"What did you do?"

"Pretended I didn't see."

"Did they see you?"

"No, I don't think so."

"Marilyn, did you tell this to the police?"

"No. I don't like to spread rumors."

She was upset. She left her apples, walked to a cabinet and took out a bag of sugar to transfer into a cannister. Then she sat next to me, peering into my cup to see if I needed more coffee. I didn't, so she stood and paced about the huge room, walking aimlessly from microwave oven to stove to refrigerator to freezer. It was disturbing. Marilyn rarely wasted a moment. If she's having coffee with you, she's stitching up a hem between sips, or snapping off the ends of green beans, or making little red checks on voter registration lists. But now she was perturbed. If someone had forced me to choose, I would have said she was only mildly concerned over the police involvement; what really bothered her was that she was being dragged into a matter that was potentially so sordid. But Marilyn was a private person, and I couldn't be sure. I simply guessed that whatever portion of her enormous energy was sexual, it was expended behind closed doors of her bedroom with her husband, in complete conformity with Church doctrine. To her, the proscription against adultery was just one of ten commandments to be obeyed, unquestioningly. She would no more flit around with a Bruce Fleckstein than kill or take the Lord's name in vain or covet her neighbor's ass.

But she was uncomfortable, anxious even, so I guided the conversation onto safer ground, Nassau County politics. Finally, I gave her my let-me-know-if-I-can-do-anything speech and left to meet Joey, due home from nursery school, at his bus stop on the corner.

He ran to me, heels kicking out at awkward angles to his body; at four, he still retained a trace of the toddler's stance, stomach preceding the rest of the body, which gave his movements a touchingly clumsy appearance.

"A man got deaded with a knife in his head." His light brown eyebrows were drawn together, his small, round face full of concern.

"That's terrible. Where did you hear that?" I held his hand as we walked to the house.

"I want peanut butter and grape jelly cut in triangles."

"Where did you hear about the man who was killed?"

"Can I have peanut butter and . . . ?"

"Sure. Who told you . . . ?"

"I forget."

We sat over lunch at the kitchen table, Joey studying me and the peanut butter sandwich with equal intensity. Can all the kryptonite in the world kill Superman? How many infinities do I love him? When am I going to die? If you smash an ant with your shoe, will it go to heaven? Joey, under a patina of cuteness and whimsy, has a core of profound seriousness. He posed question after question, all with the hope of getting a commitment that I would not die—at least not until he was old enough to be an astronaut and a fireman and have monkey bars in his back yard.

"Joey, I won't die until I'm very, very old, and by that time you'll be a grown-up." I was not unaware of airplane crashes and cancer, but I decided to go with the odds; a four-year-old needs security, continuity. Somewhat reassured, he dashed to his room to play records. I sat at the table, pushing bread crumbs into a small mound. The phone, seeming to sense my plight, decided to ring.

"Hello," I said hopefully.

"Where were you all morning? I kept trying to get you." It was Bob. Where was I? Having a quickie double-header with Jean-Paul Belmondo and Saul Bellow and completing my dissertation in time to have lunch at Lutèce with David Halberstam.

"Over at Marilyn's."

"Oh. I asked because you wanted me to talk with Clay Katz."

"Bob! Tell me."

"Are you still interested?"

"No. Goodbye."

"Okay. Don't be so touchy, Judith. I have a very heavy schedule today and I took time out . . ."

"What did he say?" I persisted.

"Well, you know that under normal circumstances he wouldn't say anything at all. It wouldn't be ethical."

"I know. I know."

"But a reporter from *Newsday* was up to talk to his partner, the other criminal lawyer, and this guy gave Clay the story; it's going to be in the paper tomorrow."

"What?" *Newsday* is a Long Island daily, an excellent newspaper, but not above publishing minute details of a really good murder.

"Bruce Fleckstein was in big trouble," Bob said, pausing for an ominous effect.

"How big?" I demanded, abandoning all pretense of being just casually interested.

"Big. Big. He was called in front of a Grand Jury, and he was almost definitely going to be indicted."

"What for?"

"Tax evasion."

"Tax evasion? What kind of dentist gets indicted for tax evasion?"

"A dentist who's a partner in a porno film distributorship. A dentist doing business with the Mafia and pocketing a pile of cash. That's what kind of dentist gets indicted." Bob's Darrowesque delivery was superb; if he hadn't insisted on being so soulfully literary at twenty-one, he would have made a fine lawyer.

"I can't believe it," I said, although I could. "How did *Newsday* find out about it?"

"Clay thinks someone in the IRS blabbed the whole thing to the reporter. That's the Internal Revenue Service, Judith."

"Thank you." I'd only studied American government for nine years. "Anyhow," I continued, "how did the authorities find out about Fleckstein being involved in a pornography ring?"

"Clay says that a federal Grand Jury was looking into some mob business, and Fleckstein's name came up. He thinks that someone involved in the mess was cooperating with the U.S. Attorney's office and was testifying against Fleckstein."

"I thought Mafia people don't talk."

"They're not supposed to. Clay says it was probably someone on the periphery, but he really didn't know the details."

"How would a suburban dentist get involved with the Mafia?"

"Judith, I really don't know. I told you everything Clay told me. Why are you so interested in this?"

"I don't know. It's exciting, I guess. Having someone you know get murdered without being close enough to see it as a tragedy."

"But it's very sordid. I mean, Fleckstein sounds like a really slimy guy."

"I know. That's what makes it fun."

"Judith!"

"Well, it's a change from *Sesame Street* and chicken pot pies."

"Is that what we're having for dinner?" he asked, his voice filled with dread.

"No," I sighed, "lamb chops." Stretching the telephone cord, I opened the freezer and took out a package of lamb chops.

31

"Look, I have to run. I'm having lunch with Charlie Leboyer." Charles Leboyer, a hockey player of great renown, if one cared about hockey, is a client of Bob's firm. They see that he endorses the right aftershave lotion. They cover up his violent, sadistic treatment of his girlfriends by planting newspaper articles about his warm family life.

I hung up the phone and concentrated on the Fleckstein case. I really didn't understand it. The Mafia is simply not one of my areas of expertise. American political history, of course. Some macroeconomics. A little Shakespeare. Bette Davis movies. But the Mafia? A group of tight-lipped men with diamond pinky rings and white-on-white shirts who paid off legions of equally tacky politicians and distributed heroin by remote control.

Something sounded wrong. I called Bob on his private line.

"Me. If Fleckstein was going to be indicted, it means he wasn't testifying against the Mafia."

"Judith, I have a lunch date and I have to get to the club for a quick workout first."

"Come on."

"Well, I don't know. I guess you're right. Let me try to remember what Clay said." I waited. "From what he said, it sounded like Fleckstein was in pretty thick; he wasn't talking or anything."

"So if he wasn't testifying against the Mafia, why would they kill him?"

"I don't know. Judith . . ."

"And they don't stab people. They'd gun him down. They would have booby-trapped his car. Or cut off his balls and carved a black hand on his chest and left him on his front doorstep."

"Maybe. But what's so important about this? He's dead."

"I don't know. It's not so nice to kill. It offends me."

"People are starving to death in Africa and you don't ask me to make phone calls."

"That's unfair. And I sent a check to CARE. It's just that this is close to home."

"Not close to my home," he declared. "Now, look, you know he was involved in a nasty business, and people who get involved in nasty businesses get into trouble. Right?"

"Yes."

"Good. I have to run now. I'll see you for dinner."

At least he hadn't told me not to worry my pretty little head about other people's dirty laundry. Although in reality that's exactly what he had said. Bob only wanted me to worry about his dirty laundry. And his dinner. And to make sure his children were carefully tended. It's not that he wanted a robot, a smiling automaton to make his bed and giggle on cue; he enjoyed what he called my "intellect." I could comprehend his business problems, appreciate his latest press release, savor with him the courtship of a new client. And I could be trotted out to dinner with a wide range of business contacts and never make an ass of myself. During political conventions, I could remind him who were the two vice-presidential candidates in 1956. In short, a pleasure to have around, a housekeeper of reasonably pleasing countenance guaranteed not to steal, an accomplished lover with hips as fast as lightning.

"Mommy, the doorbell." Joey tugged the leg of my jeans.

"Coming," I called, and strolled to the door. Kate wasn't due home for another fifteen minutes.

"Mrs. Judith Singer?" the man on my doorstep asked. I gripped the knob and peered at him. Blue-eyed, about my age, with crisply cut short hair. He smiled with a mouth full of bright, white teeth. Very good-looking. Totally unappealing.

"Yes, I'm Judith Singer."

"Sorry to bother you, ma'am, but we're investigating

the murder of Bruce Fleckstein. Dr. Fleckstein. I know Sergeant Ramirez spoke to you, but there are just a couple of things we'd like cleared up." He showed me his ID: Detective Steven Christopher Smith. "I'd like to ask you a few questions. Is this a convenient time for you?"

"Of course. Please come in."

Chapter Three

Smith stepped into the house. "Do you happen to know where Mrs. Tuccio does her shopping?" His voice was gentle, soothing, like a doctor on a TV show about to give the family some sad news about their loved one.

"Shopping?"

"For groceries, ma'am."

"I don't know. I guess Waldbaum's or the A&P. They're the closest."

"Mrs. Tuccio never mentioned where she shops?"

My relationship with Marilyn was obviously less intimate than the police had assumed. "No, she never did."

"I see. Well, ma'am, would you happen to know the time of day Mrs. Tuccio went shopping?"

"No." I paused, concentrating on Smith's plump, pink cheeks. "Are you trying to establish some sort of alibi?"

"I really can't say, Mrs. Singer."

"Look, this is silly. Marilyn Tuccio wouldn't be interested in a man like Dr. Fleckstein. It was a professional relationship. I went to see him a few years ago and all he was interested in was my gums. I'm sure it was the same with Marilyn."

"We're just going through his patient file. Could I ask you a few more questions, now that I'm here?" I nodded. "During your visits, did you ever see Dr. Fleckstein in angry conversation with anyone?"

"No," I said apologetically. I wished I could help him.

"Well, do you recall seeing him answering the telephone and becoming upset?"

"No."

"Did he say anything significant to you?"

"He told me to use unwaxed dental floss."

"I see," Smith said. "Mrs. Singer, when we investigate a murder, we have to look at all aspects of the deceased's life. Do you have any reason to believe that Dr. Fleckstein was keeping company with other women?" I must have looked startled, because he explained: "It's just a routine question, but it's important."

I stepped back a few inches and cleared my throat. "Well, I've heard some rumors about him."

"Would you mind going into detail, ma'am?"

"I can't. I just heard he was quite a ladies' man."

"Ma'am, I want to assure you that this is a confidential investigation. We just want to get to the bottom of this." He was wearing a navy peacoat, and a thin line of perspiration had appeared on his upper lip.

"Would you like to take your coat off?"

"No, thank you. Did you happen to hear who Dr. Fleckstein was having an affair with?"

"I don't like to spread rumors."

"We'll check everything out very discreetly, ma'am. We don't want anybody to get hurt."

"I heard he was carrying on with his nurse, Lorna Lewis. But it's pure, unadulterated gossip and I have no way of knowing if it's true." Not a flicker of interest; his blond eyelashes didn't even blink. "I see you've already heard that," I observed.

The perspiration moved up to his forehead. "I can't really comment on that, Mrs. Singer."

"Okay. Anything else?"

"To the best of your recollection, have you heard any

36

other information about Dr. Fleckstein or his associates or family?"

I pondered that for a minute, debating whether to mention Fleckstein's Mafia link. But the police must have known, and it would be in *Newsday* the next morning. "No, I can't think of anything. As I said, I saw him years ago, and only for one visit."

Smith thanked me. I went to open the door for him and noticed Joey, leaning against the wall, observing us both.

"Do you want to be a policeman when you grow up?" Smith asked.

"No," Joey snapped back. "No way."

"Joey," I said aghast. "What kind of way is that to talk?"

"That's all right, ma'am," Smith said softly. "Goodbye," he said to me. "Goodbye, son." Joey turned his back and stomped up the stairs.

Kate came in a few minutes later, her overalls covered with green paint, traces of it on her nose and cheeks. "I was painting today," she explained.

"I see that."

"It's really a mess," she observed cheerfully. "Where's Joey?"

"In his room, playing records." She considered that for a moment, entwining a stubby, green-tipped finger in her smooth, dark braid. "Would you like a glass of milk?" I asked.

"No. I'll see if Joey wants some company. Thanks anyway."

I smiled as she pranced upstairs, hoping that they could spend the afternoon together in relative peace. Two minutes passed without any screams of protest, no sound of toys or bodies being hurled against the door. I walked into the living room and curled up on the couch, and tried to put things in order.

The police would be interviewing hundreds of puffy-gummed people. A few of the women would say that

37

Fleckstein propositioned them. A few of the men might say he liked the Jets or that he seemed fascinated by wheat futures. But I couldn't imagine any patient having solid information on Fleckstein. He was one of those professionals clever enough to make small conversation with a patient, so you'd feel comfortable enough to return instead of going elsewhere to have your gums deflated. But my instincts were that he had no depth, no substance, the type who could play tennis with a man for eight years and never ask where the man grew up.

"Great stuff, honey," he'd say to a woman he'd just slept with; he'd call her "honey" because he couldn't quite remember whether her name was Joan or Jean or Jane. And he didn't want to offend. Fleckstein wanted her to feel comfortable enough to come back again.

But there had to be more to Marvin Bruce than this, because men just like him live until seventy-six and keel over on the fourteenth hole of a Florida golf course. Even though I had barely known him, he didn't seem the sort to get involved enough with someone so that she would care enough to kill him. A forty-two-year-old man still slim enough to wear tight, streaky, French-cut jean suits and a gold ID bracelet on a hairy wrist would normally grow old gracefully, metamorphosing into khaki leisure outfits and ultimately into navy blazers with silk ascots to hide his crepey neck.

The more I considered, the more certain I became that Fleckstein had a secret life. Not a hot little blond number tucked away in an apartment in Queens. Certainly not a cool, secret connection with the CIA or FBI. Men like Fleckstein, bourgeois to the soul, lack moral and physical courage; their patriotism extends to standing for "The Star-Spangled Banner" at a baseball game.

But from what Bob had gleaned from Claymore Katz, Fleckstein had become involved in a very dirty business with some very dirty people. A normal suburbanite will take certain risks, especially for money. But why would a man like Fleckstein find himself so deeply enmeshed? Why would a dentist with a practice good for over a hundred thousand a year find himself, on the verge of a criminal indictment, with a fatal wound in the base of his skull?

He seemed so ordinary, just another thread in the community fabric. We ate at the same restaurants, sent our children to the same schools, probably used the same plumber. But he was dead.

Bathing Joey: Did Fleckstein die for his sins? The moment he felt the murder weapon piercing the soft skin covering his medulla, did he regret trying to become a mogul of the porno pix biz? Bathing Kate: Did he see who killed him? Was it one of his women? Did he have one last pang that somehow he hadn't satisfied her completely? Making dinner: Had it hurt? At the table: trying to discuss my musings with Bob.

"Judith, can we please change the subject?"

"Why? This is interesting."

"The children are here."

I looked at them, Kate peering at Bob and me, intent on our conversation, Joey rummaging through the fruit bowl, a large bunch of grapes on his plate, untouched. "Don't you want to watch television? Maybe *I Love Lucy* is on?" Joey bolted and ran for the den. Kate looked at me quizzically, knowing that I must be truly desperate to allow them this boon.

"But, Mommy, you said that *I Love Lucy* rots your mind."

"Only if you watch it all the time. Once a month is okay." She clutched her half-eaten pear and shuffled out of the dining room.

A great tactical coup, but now the enemy was on the alert. There would be no way, short of swinging a machete near his groin, that I could get Bob to discuss the Fleckstein case with me. I had been too animated. I hadn't asked him about his day. I hadn't told him about mine, about wallowing in the joys of hearth and home.

39

"Enough about this murder business. You don't mind that I sent the children downstairs? I just wanted some time alone together."

He gave me his cute little self-effacing smile, where he cocks his head to one side and lowers his eyes. He always smiles like that when caught in the midst of a triumph, like when he told his parents that the Turner Ammunition and Armaments account just fell into his lap, or when he informed me that the thousand dollars I hadn't wanted him to invest in Vitachill Cryonics was, at that very moment, worth five thousand.

"Tell me about your day," he said graciously.

"Oh. It was nice." I smiled at him. "Marilyn Tuccio has a great new recipe for apple crisp."

He nodded and squeezed a section of the orange he was eating. A pit slid out onto his plate. "That's nice." We smiled warmly at each other. Bob said: "A wonderful dinner—as always." He'd eat pigeon droppings if they were surrounded by watercress and served with a dry white wine. The phone rang. "I'll get it," he said wearily. "It's probably for me." He stood and sauntered into the kitchen. "Hello," he said. "Oh, fine. Great. How are you doing? Yes. Judith's right here. Nice speaking with you." He covered the mouthpiece with his hand and made a sour face. "It's Malice."

Mary Alice Mahoney is the most excruciatingly boring human being I know. One of those dormitory acquaintances whom you forget within minutes of graduation, she had moved to Shorehaven two years before. It took her only a month to discover that Nancy and I were living in town. "Nancy! Judith!" she squealed across the high school auditorium during a particularly vituperative meeting over a proposed sewage disposal bond. "You live here!"

We nodded wearily and watched as she squeezed past a row of rigid knees and dashed up the aisle to greet us. Her thin, boyish body and blond pixie haircut had not changed since 1963. Only her clothing had altered, from knee socks and pleated skirts to the suburban alphabet potpourri—entwined Gs on her handbag, Ys on the vamps of her shoes, double Bs on her sweater. She offered a cheek for each of us to kiss. "Old friends are the best friends. Right? Right, Judith? Right, Nancy?"

Mary Alice thought nothing of arriving uninvited for a "little chat." She would ring my doorbell on the average of once every two weeks and invariably ask the same question: "Busy?" Unlike Nancy, I never had the courage to say yes.

She had the gift of reducing every subject to its tritest common denominator. Once, Nancy and I were discussing a mutual college friend, a woman who had left her husband and was now living in Manhattan with another woman; she had made the transition from Wisconsin farm girl to faculty wife to radical lesbian with what appeared to be extreme ease, and Nancy and I were wondering if this could possibly be so.

"Lucy Anderson is a lesbian?" Mary Alice asked. We nodded. "Well, homosexuality is not an evil." We agreed. "They just can't help themselves." Before we had a chance to moan with boredom, we received a fervent defense of Mary Alice's hairdresser, whom we'd never even dreamed of attacking, a list of Gay People in the Seven Lively Arts, plus the collected experiences of her three sisters, Mary Elizabeth, Mary Therese, and Mary Jeanne, and their dealings with gays. When Nancy delicately pointed out that her sisters, saints though they may be, were not germane to the subject being discussed, Mary Alice smiled a small, sad smile and said: "I think you're being very judgmental. My sisters are relevant to me."

Bob, who generally likes my friends in direct proportion to their resemblance to the Platonic ideal of the happy homemaker, had detested her within five minutes. This was because when he offered to shake hands with her, she asked: "Are you doing this as one human being to another or because you think it's what I, as a

41

liberated woman, expect?" He handed me the phone as if a moist, green fungus had sprouted on the receiver.

"Hi, Mary Alice," I said, trying not to sound too encouraging.

"Judith, I've just got to talk to you." She still had a midwestern accent and pronounced each word separately, as though each was a distinct idea in itself. "Please."

"Sure."

"Not on the phone. It's very personal. Do you possibly have a free minute tomorrow?"

By Mary Alice's standards, it was probably something momentous. Maybe her son's gym teacher, with whom she had been exchanging meaningful glances for a year and a half, had told her she looked cute. Should she tell him he looked cute? And was the next move up to her? But don't men wait for a signal from women?

"I'm really busy, Mary Alice."

"I know you are. You're so bright. But this is very urgent. It's about the murder."

"The murder?" I sounded incredulous because I couldn't believe that Mary Alice could be even remotely connected with anything interesting.

"Please, Judith."

"Oh, of course. Sure. What time do you want to come over?"

"Could you possibly come over here?" Tedious, limited, vacuous, but endowed with a great, manipulative genius.

"All right. I'll be over about nine-fifteen."

"Could you make it nine-thirty?" she asked. "I meditate till nine-twenty."

I agreed. For a moment, I considered being cool and hanging up with a quick "See you tomorrow." But the pressure of curiosity forced me to continue. "Did you know Fleckstein?"

"Yes, Judith, you might say I knew him." She lowered her voice. "In the Biblical sense, if you know what I mean."

Stunned, I looked around the dining room, trying to reestablish some sense of reality. Bob had gone downstairs to play in his darkroom. I stared at a very real-looking lamb chop bone. Mary Alice and Fleckstein? How could Mary Alice, for whom the postman's visit is an opportunity for an intimate discussion, how could she have even met Bruce Fleckstein and withheld her knowledge from Nancy and me?

"And I'm going to ask you a personal favor, Judith. Please call Nancy and tell her to come with you. I'd call her myself, but I know she doesn't like me."

"Oh, come on, Mary Alice," I said, embarrassed by being confronted with the truth.

"No, it's true. But I think we have a great deal of respect for each other's intelligence, and I would appreciate her comments on the situation."

"What situation?"

"Judith, I can't speak on the phone. I'll see you tomorrow."

Probably she just wants to play the grief-stricken lover, to sob in silence—in front of me and Nancy—or to spend an hour or two ruminating on the plight of the other woman. I considered this as I scoured the pots, but couldn't really accept it. Mary Alice had been unnaturally cogent, hadn't digressed even once. Not a whimper, not a sniffle during the entire conversation.

"Bob," I said later that evening, "I think Mary Alice was having an affair with Dr. Fleckstein."

"That's ridiculous." He was lying on his side in bed pummeling his pillow into a perfect mound.

"Why is it ridiculous?"

"She's sexless. You can see the bones on her chest."

"Well, she may not be your type, but she wants to talk to me tomorrow about Fleckstein."

"Judith," he said patiently, "why waste your time? You know you can't stand her."

"I know. But I'm dying to hear how she got involved with Fleckstein."

"Why? Who cares?"

"Aren't you curious about other people?" I demanded. "Don't you want to know what's going on behind the facade?"

"Maybe," he said, and yawned. "I mean, if they're intrinsically interesting. But not Mary Alice or this Fleckstein character."

I sat on the bed in a silky red nightgown, decorously draped in front and cut to a low "V" in the back. Bob seemed to be studying the stitching on the quilt. "Look," I said, "doesn't it surprise you how varied people are? I mean, everyone in Shorehaven seems to conform to the same blueprint. Okay, so there are variations in religion, higher education, number of kids. But when you meet anyone living in this community, you meet on common ground. You go to an office, all the other guys go to an office. I drive two car pools a week, someone else may drive three. There's a sameness, right?"

"So?" he asked.

"So, beneath the sameness, all sorts of things are going on. Affairs. Crime."

"Well, what do you expect? People are individuals." He was right, of course. What intrigued me was that the vast substratum of activity that everyone seemed to be enmeshed in seemed much more exciting than anything going on beneath my surface. I was what I seemed to be. "Why waste your time?" he continued. "Stay home, relax, read the paper, read a book. Enjoy your leisure."

"Speaking of books," I said, getting under the quilt, "you never opened your Valentine's Day gift."

"I'm sorry," he said. I didn't reply. "Judith, come on. I said I was sorry. Don't make me out to be some kind of insensitive stinker. I'll open it first thing tomorrow morning, okay?" I nodded. "Where is it?" he asked.

"On the shelf in the hall."

"Goòd. Let me thank you in advance." He leaned over, kissed my cheek, turned out his light, and went to sleep.

Chapter Four

"It's painful enough that I have to listen to that suban-thropoidal horse's ass whenever she manages to stick her skinny foot in my door before I can slam it shut." Nancy's perfectly shaped mouth, shimmering slightly with lip gloss, closed in a pout. Concentrating on the road, she drove expertly through the back streets of Shorehaven toward Mary Alice's, neatly guiding her gray Jaguar around tight turns with a light hand on the wheel. "Really, Judith, why do you insist on subjecting me to that fool's inane babbling?"

"She specifically asked to see you."

"The only reason she asked to see me is that she cannot bear to play to an audience of one."

"Look, just put it down as a personal favor to me," I said.

"Oh, I will indeed." She raised her finely plucked eyebrows and glanced at me for a moment. "You know I'm missing a morning's work for this circus."

"Well, you could have said no, Nancy." She seemed only mildly annoyed; her face, with its even, classical features, relaxed. She brushed a long strand of auburn hair behind her ear, then sighed. "Are you working on anything now?" I asked.

"Nothing special," she admitted. "But I damn well could have come up with ideas for at least ten marvel-

47

ous articles this morning instead of listening to that white trash moaning and groaning."

"Actually, she was pretty much to the point when she called. Maybe it won't be that bad."

"Fat chance," Nancy grumbled.·

We spent the next few minutes in silence, passing increasingly larger houses on increasingly larger acreage. Nancy pulled the car into Mary Alice's driveway, slammed on the brakes, and switched off the ignition, all while resuming her pout. The house was a three-story monstrosity of stucco, red tile, and wrought iron, which might have made sense in California, but was simply silly in New York.

"Isn't this just lovely?" Nancy demanded. "Casa Mahoney." Mary Alice's husband, Keith, was reputed to be "big in construction." He and Mary Alice had spared nothing in building their dream house. We stood in front of a massive carved wood door and rang the bell. "So understated," Nancy whispered, looking at the large brass doorknob. The housekeeper, a tall, heavy West Indian woman, let us in and told us that Mrs. Mahoney would meet us in the sunroom.

"Just charming," cooed Nancy. "Sala del sol. So adorably Andalusian. She even has a Moor."

"Shh," I hissed as we walked across the dark tiled floor of the living room. "Just behave yourself for the next half hour."

Mary Alice stood on the threshold of the sunroom to greet us. "Hello, hello," she said, pecking each of us on the cheek. "I can't thank you both enough for coming today. Truly, you are sisters in every sense of the word." She was dressed in a pale yellow wool jumpsuit with the zipper opened to mid-torso. Although she had the body of a malnourished ten-year-old boy, Mary Alice often dressed as if she were so magnificently endowed with breasts and hips that she had to share her bounty with the world.

We declined her offer of rose hip tea, sat down on her elaborate wicker chairs, and watched as she tiptoed to the door to close it, first peering out to make sure her housekeeper wasn't lurking about, steno pad in hand, to report to Keith.

"All right," she said, rubbing her tiny, childlike hands together, "this isn't going to be easy, ladies."

"Try," suggested Nancy in her deep voice.

"Yes, yes. But where shall I begin? There's so much to say."

"I'd begin at the beginning," I said firmly. "It's the best place, isn't it?"

"Good choice," murmured Nancy.

Mary Alice took a flowered cushion from one of the chairs and placed it on the floor, equidistant between Nancy and me. "Well," she said, sitting down Indian fashion, "I first met Bruce, Dr. Fleckstein, at a party at the Wagners' house. You know him, Nancy, Rick Wagner, he belongs to your club. He's in real estate."

"I'm so pleased for him," Nancy said.

"Anyway," continued Mary Alice, "I knew instantly that there was something between us, something very strong and very powerful. He was standing in front of the fireplace talking to Christy Wagner and Nicki Rubin, but for some reason he happened to glance in my direction and our eyes met. I was wearing my black Halston. Did you ever have that? That electricity with a man where you're the only two people in the world, even though you're in a crowd? Anyhow, it took him about a half hour to get himself away from the two of them, and he came over to where I was standing and said hi. So I said hi back and we introduced ourselves. He said 'I'm Bruce Fleckstein' and I said . . ."

"It's a quarter to ten, Mary Alice, and I have to leave at ten-thirty, even if you're in the middle of your first soul kiss," said Nancy.

"All right. But I want to give you a feeling of exactly

49

what the relationship was like, so you can comprehend everything."

"Tell us," I suggested. "Nancy," I added, "please relax." She complied, after peering contemptuously at Mary Alice and flaring her nostrils at me.

Mary Alice cleared her throat. "Thank you, Judith. Well, to make a long story short, he called me on Monday. The party had been on Saturday night. Anyway, he said he'd really enjoyed talking with me, that I had a lot of personality and substance, and asked if I could meet him for lunch. Well, I wasn't sure at that point whether or not to go, but I said to myself, well, it's just lunch and I don't have to commit myself to anything if I don't want to. So I met him at one o'clock at Wong Foo's."

"Right next door to the Tudor Rose Motor Inn," interrupted Nancy, a cold, stiff smile on her face.

"Yes. But it never occurred to me that anything would happen that day. Anyhow, he looked so handsome. Very tight jeans with a Gucci belt and a yellow body shirt. And that dark Jewish complexion. Oh, I'm sorry, Judith."

"It happens. You know, I once was second runner-up in the Susie Semite Pageant for dark-skinned beauties."

"Really? Are you teasing me, Judith?"

"Yes. Go on, Mary Alice."

"All right. Where was I? I can't believe he's dead. Anyway, we just talked for a while, and then after we finished our soup, he looked me right in the eye and said, 'You turn me on.' So I said 'Oh, come on,' and he said that no, really, it was true and he put his hand on my thigh. He said I was adorable.

"Well, one thing led to another, and I felt very attracted to him. So before we'd even had dessert, he said, 'Let's go,' and put twelve dollars down on the table. He didn't even wait for the waiter to bring him change. We just walked out."

"And nipped right next door to the motel?" asked Nancy.

"Yes."

"And then what happened?" I inquired.

"Nothing. We did it. That's all."

"Just that one time?" I demanded.

"No. We met every Tuesday."

Nancy gazed at her. "At Wong Foo's?"

"No. At the motel. Bruce said if we skipped lunch we'd have more time together."

It made sense to me. If I were having an affair, I'd rather be rolling about on a rough motel sheet, sweaty body to sweaty body, than lunching in a second-rate Chinese restaurant. But it didn't make sense for Mary Alice. She never struck me as a highly sexed person, one who could feel her underpants getting damp over Moo Shoo pork. She was generally vague about her sex life, although she had confided in me that she wished her husband's "thing" were bigger; but I never thought she'd go out of her way to search for one that was. She was so wrapped up in herself that it was difficult to imagine her focusing on someone long enough to become interested, much less aroused. Most of all, I couldn't understand why she had never alluded to the affair before.

"How come you never mentioned this before, Mary Alice?" Nancy asked.

"I was going to, but then I couldn't. I just couldn't."

My turn. "Why not?"

"I don't know. I'm not sure. It was a very complex relationship, and I guess I felt I couldn't really give an outsider the realities of it."

Nancy crossed her long legs and glanced at her watch. I looked at mine. It was after ten and I knew I didn't have time to listen to Mary Alice meandering down her usual path of self-actualization through interpersonal give-and-take meaningful relationships.

"Why are you telling us now?" I asked.

"I don't know," she answered, somewhat uncomfortably. She picked at the dark brownish red nail polish on her left hand.

"Come on, Mary Alice. Something's bothering you," I insisted. I hoped something was, or I'd never hear the end of it from Nancy. "I mean," I continued, "you don't seem horribly broken up about the fact that he's dead. And you told me it was important. Come on."

"He took some pictures," she mumbled to the tiled floor.

"Holy shit!" Nancy exclaimed.

"What kind of pictures?" An unnecessary question, I suppose, but Mary Alice seemed to want to cut off the entire conversation.

"Pictures of me," she said, and began to cry.

"Naked?" I asked.

She nodded and took a tissue out of her sleeve. She had obviously been anticipating a scene. "Yes, naked." She wiped her eyes and dropped the tissue into an ashtray. Then, without thinking, she drew the back of her hand across her nose, and a pearly trail of pale green mucous spread from her upper lip to her cheek. "Naked," she sniffled. "And more."

"More?" breathed Nancy. "More what?"

She whispered something I couldn't hear. "What?" I asked.

"Bound."

"Bound?" I forced myself to look at her, knowing that if I did, I probably wouldn't giggle. "You mean, like S and M?"

"We had just been doing it regular. You know. But then he said since our relationship was based on mutual trust, we should feel free to act out our fantasies. So a couple of times he brought rope and tied me up and did things."

"Like what?" asked Nancy. She didn't seem at all surprised, merely curious, like a mechanic examining the engine of a new foreign car.

"I can't. I can't," she sobbed, drawing in huge

breaths and making loud noises in the back of her throat.

"Mary Alice," I said softly, "did he hurt you?"

"Not too much," she whispered, looking past me. "And he was always careful not to make any marks that Keith would see."

"What about the pictures?" I asked. Her breathing became more normal, but she still couldn't look at me. Nancy was sitting back comfortably in her chair. I leaned forward toward Mary Alice. "The pictures. Tell us about them."

"Oh, he said that these were sacred moments that showed our mutual trust and he wanted to preserve them. He got this new Polaroid camera for his birthday and he took a few photographs. He said he'd burn them after he looked at them a few times."

"Why would he burn them if he wanted to preserve your sacred moments?" Nancy demanded.

She began crying again. "I don't know, Nancy. Oh, Jesus God, I'm so scared," she wailed. "What if someone finds them? What if the police find them? What if someone shows Keith?"

She was terribly frightened, like a tiny fieldmouse that had somehow found itself in the midst of the annual American Pest Control Convention. I felt sick for her. "Did you ever ask him what he did with them?"

"No."

"Okay. Calm down. We'll think of something." But what? I wondered. A complete confession? Suicide? A quiet little arson job on Fleckstein's office and home?

"I can't think of anything," Nancy announced.

We sat silently for a moment. I looked at Nancy, but she avoided my glance. She played with her long hair, rolling it into a chignon and then letting it fall back to her shoulders. Mary Alice didn't want me to look at her either. We usually shape our confidences to fit our audience's taste. This time, though, it couldn't be done and they were embarrassed—Nancy because Mary Alice had made it so painfully personal, not a tale to be smiled at from a distance, and Mary Alice because she had once again made herself vulnerable by letting the outside world peep into her fantasy life.

"Mary Alice," I said. They both turned and looked at me. "Are you positive he never said anything about the pictures?"

"No. Nothing. Not really."

"What do you mean, 'not really'?" Nancy barked.

"I mean, I once asked him if he still had the pictures he took."

"And what did he say?" Nancy demanded, her voice low and tough, like a small-town southern sheriff.

"Nothing. Just what did I think he was doing with them, using them for blackmail, and that I shouldn't be so neurotic."

Again we were quiet, but this time more from impotence than discomfort. If the police found the pictures and showed them to anyone involved in the Fleckstein case, there would be two results; one, word would flash through Shorehaven about Mary Alice's hobby and, two, she would instantly be deemed a suspect. If the police could seriously consider Marilyn Tuccio, they would leap with joy at the prospect of Mary Alice. In either case, Keith would kill her and use her body as a cornerstone for his next shopping center.

"I'll tell you why I asked you both here today," said Mary Alice in a voice that startled us. It had great force and clarity, with none of her usual simpering, ingratiating tones. "First, Judith, I know you have a friend who's a criminal lawyer. Right?"

"Yes, Claymore Katz. He was Bob's college roommate."

"Well, I'd like you to ask him what I should do. I mean, just describe the situation. You don't have to mention any names."

"Look, Mary Alice, I'll be glad to try, but Claymore doesn't seem the type to go for hypothetical situations.

Why don't you call him so you can give him all the details?"

"No, Judith, please. I don't want to get involved. Please do it for me. Please."

In a moment, I thought, she'd grab my hand and cover it with kisses and say "Pretty please." So I nodded and said: "Sure. No problem." She bestowed one last smile on me and turned to Nancy. "Now, Nancy, you're a writer. You investigate things. Right?"

"Wrong, Mary Alice. I do articles on personalities, a little pop sociology. I can barely find my own Tampax without a road map. So don't think I can investigate . . ."

"But you used to work for *Time*," Mary Alice insisted.

"Sure. But I was a researcher. I looked things up in books. I made phone calls. I smiled a lot. But an investigative reporter is something else and . . ."

"Nancy, I've thought this whole thing out. All you have to do is pretend you're a reporter and call up the police and try to find out what they have. That's all."

"Impossible," Nancy said. She glanced at me, looking for support. I looked away, back at Mary Alice. "Absolutely impossible."

"What do you mean, 'impossible'?" Mary Alice demanded.

"The police aren't going to give out that kind of information. Even if they were going to give something away, they'd give it to some reporter they know. Lord, I don't even have any credentials. What should I do, call and say, 'Hi, I'm Nancy Miller and did you happen to find any pictures of a nude blond in Dr. Fleckstein's files? They'd probably be under M for Mahoney. And would you mind giving all the pictures to me because I think they'd make a peachy bonfire?' "

"Wait a second," I said. "Look, you free-lance, Nancy."

"So what?" she challenged.

"Well, couldn't you call one of the magazines you

work for and ask them if they'd like a story on this case? That way, you could get credentials."

"That's a great idea, Judith," Mary Alice enthused. "Isn't that a good idea, Nancy?"

Nancy glared at both of us and put her head down and peered at her lap. "Quiet. Let me think. All right now," she breathed, "*Newsday* will have their own reporters on it. Maybe *New York* would take a piece on the ninnies who abandoned the city because they were afraid of crime but got it up the ass in the suburbs. Or maybe the Sunday *Times Magazine* would take a police procedural, but they're the biggest skinflints in town."

Mary Alice smiled at her eagerly. "I'll pay you the difference between whatever they pay and your usual fee."

"God, Nancy," I chimed in, "it's not just another article. You're doing a favor for a friend."

"Blow it out your twat," she responded. "Oh, all right. I'll try. But don't expect anything."

We left a few minutes later, with Mary Alice still murmuring thank yous. She seemed relieved, although I couldn't be sure why. What could a criminal lawyer do for her? Tell her that in the future she should keep her fantasies to herself? Hold her hand? And what could Nancy dig up? That M. Bruce did, indeed, have a swell photo album? That Mary Alice was a suspect? That she was just one of Fleckstein's bevy of beauties?

Maybe she seemed relieved, I mused to Nancy in the car, because someone else was helping to shoulder the burden.

"Maybe," she responded, "but it's so pathetic. I mean, she's built up this whole fantasy that you and I are going to pull off a couple of miracles and save her virtue." Nancy braked the car at a stop sign and looked at me. "How could she be such a fool? Did you hear that line of crap he gave her? About her having substance. And she believed it! My Lord, that broad is proof positive of the decline of the West."

"Do you think," I asked slowly, "that she believed him because he zeroed right in on what she wanted to hear? I mean, deep down she really thinks she's a fascinating, adorable human being."

"All I know is if some guy who barely knew me called me up and told me how much substance I had, I'd hang up the phone before he could finish the sentence."

"But you have substance," I said to her.

"I know that. But how could a guy—who's spent a grand total of fifteen minutes with me, fourteen of them staring at my crotch—how could he possibly know that?"

"I don't know," I replied, trying to adjust the seat belt so it wouldn't cut off my circulation. "Do you think maybe he did get rid of the pictures?"

"Do you think so?"

"No," I conceded, and paused. "You know what really gets me?"

"The seething lust?"

"No. Seriously. The fact that she wanted you for your talents. The only reason she wanted me was because I know a good criminal lawyer."

"Touchy, touchy."

"No, I'm being honest."

"Judith, if she didn't have faith in your diplomatic ability, would she have confided in you? Listen, I know plants with higher IQs than Mary Alice's, so why do you care about her opinion anyway? Let's get this thing over. We have better things to do."

"Like what?" I demanded.

We drove back to my house for lunch. Peanut butter and jelly on white for Joey and friend, who arrived from nursery school famished. Tuna and tomato on rye for me. A slice of Swiss cheese and a bottle of Chablis for Nancy. Ever since we met, Nancy has been a very selective wino. While everyone else at school was guzzling Purple Passions, a cloying concoction of grape juice and domestic vodka, Nancy would pour glass after glass from her own bottle of wine. Always French, always dry. She would never share it. And throughout the years, I had never seen it affect her. Her personality was consistently caustic, her intellect sharp, her figure slim, tight, and perfect—even though she drank at least a bottle a day. But I never felt comfortable about her drinking. I worried about her liver, about her need to anesthetize herself, about the effect it would have on her children when she became pregnant.

And yet nothing seemed to happen. She wrote her articles, had healthy babies, played a superior game of chess, and slept with every third man she met, provided he had a high school education or less. Her three children found her delightful. Her husband, Larry, an architect, adored her and smilingly assumed their faithfulness was mutual.

I built a fire in the living room and we sat on the floor, going over our meeting with Mary Alice. Because I seemed so interested, Nancy patiently helped me review nearly every word. "Well," she said at last, "that's it. What did it say in the paper?"

"My God! The paper!" Without putting on my coat, I raced out to the driveway and picked up the *Newsday,* slightly sodden from the damp air. And there it was, front page. "Slain Dentist Linked to Pornography Ring." And two pictures. One, a body, covered with a white sheet, being lifted into an ambulance by two men who looked slightly annoyed, as though their coffee break had been interrupted. And the other, a smiling head shot, Bruce at the beach, handsome, sleek, his curly brown hair styled into a perfect helmet around his fine head.

"Anything new?" asked Nancy when I ran back into the room.

"Look!"

58

"I'll read it when you're finished."

"I'll read it out loud." I cleared my throat.

"Dr. M. Bruce Fleckstein, a periodontist (gum specialist) who was found slain in his plush Shorehaven office two days ago, was about to be indicted for federal income tax evasion. According to law enforcement sources, Dr. Fleckstein was involved in a pornographic film distributorship that had long been the object of federal investigators' scrutiny.

"Dr. Fleckstein was reputed to be the silent partner in an operation that had been grossing over a quarter of a million dollars a month, much of it in cash. His alleged partners included Ira Spiegel of Great Neck, an accountant, and Carmine ('Cookie Browneyes') Lombardi, a reputed member of the organized crime family of Peter Gambollo. Mr. Lombardi, who resides in Lido Beach, once served six months of an eighteen-month sentence for extortion.

"According to *Newsday*'s sources, Dr. Fleckstein had not been cooperating with the investigation, and thus his death is not believed to be a typical Mafia hit. However, since the murder does not seem to be the result of random violence or robbery (Fleckstein's wallet, containing over three hundred dollars, was discovered on his body), investigators are pursuing the theory that the slaying was somehow linked with the pending indictment.

"According to Lt. Nelson Sharpe, the officer in charge of the case, an autopsy will be performed on Dr. Fleckstein to determine the precise cause of death. A small wound was found in the base of the skull.

"The Long Island Dental Society has offered a reward of $5,000 for information leading to the arrest of the murderer. Dr. Fleckstein's family has offered an additional $5,000.

"Dr. Fleckstein's widow, the former Norma Dunck, refused to answer reporters' questions about . . ."

"That's right. I forgot," Nancy interjected.

"Forgot what?" I asked sharply.

"Fleckstein's wife is Dicky Dunck's sister."

"Who in God's name is Dicky Dunck?"

"You've seen him. He belongs to Larry's club. They took in a token Jew and a token black, remember? Well, he's the token Jew. He's completely bald and wears a goatee."

"Him?" Dicky Dunck wasn't easy to miss, especially at Larry's club, where all the men looked like they were competing in the National Blondness Sweepstakes. Dunck was an ordinary looking man who had shaved what remained of his hair and grown a wispy brown goatee; he looked silly rather than sophisticated.

"He's awful," said Nancy. "An unmitigated creep. But everybody tries to be nice to him to prove how liberal they are. Lord, they make me want to puke, the whole damned lot of them."

"But what about Dicky Dunck," I persisted. "Was he involved with Fleckstein?"

"Oh, no. In fact, they were on the outs. Something about Dicky's father's will."

"What about it?"

"Nothing fascinating, so don't get your hopes up. I think his father left the bulk of his estate to Norma—Fleckstein's wife—and Dicky was contesting the will. Just a normal, ugly family fight over money. Nothing unusual."

"Was Dunck really angry?" I asked.

"Not *that* angry. Cool it, Judith. He just went around the club saying what a prick Brucie was and that he was proud to be a member of Shelter Cove and that he'd never belong to a flashy club like Green Trees, where people like Brucie hung out."

"And that's it?"

"That's all, folks."

"All right," I said, stretching out my legs and picking

up the newspaper again. "Let me finish. Norma refused to answer the reporters' questions. Oh, here."

"She is said to be in seclusion.

"The funeral is scheduled for tomorrow at the Baum Brothers' Funeral Home in Great Neck. Interment will follow at the Shalom Cemetery in Flushing, Queens.

"Police have requested that anyone with information about the crime call a special number: (516) 689-2104. All replies will be treated confidentially."

"Oh," breathed Nancy, "the possibilities simply boggle the mind. Let's call and tell them all about Mary Alice."

"Are you crazy? You've got to be kidding."

"Of course, I'm kidding. Lord, Judith, don't take this so seriously. Nothing's going to happen to Mary Alice. She's a born survivor; nothing really touches her."

"Bruce Fleckstein did," I commented.

"Come on, we've been through that. All he did was confirm her own high opinion of herself."

I ran my hand through my hair, thick and short and slightly kinky from the humidity. "Let me give you a for instance, Nancy."

"Go ahead."

"For instance, when you're having an affair with someone, do you suspend your normal intellectual processes and allow yourself to believe a line of blatant bullshit?"

"No. But I never trust a guy, even if all he says is hello. Listen, it's really an unfair question. I can't compare myself to Mary Alice. She has no normal intellectual processes." She stood and looked down at me. "I'm going. I have to make a few phone calls and see if anyone wants an article on this drivel."

"Okay. I'll call you tomorrow. Are you all right to

61

drive home?" If I had consumed that quantity of wine, I wouldn't be able to find the ignition.

"Judith, stop busting my chops."

A few minutes after Nancy pulled her Jaguar out of the driveway, a large beige station wagon pulled in. It was Prescott Hughes, call-me-Scotty, the mother of Joey's friend from nursery school.

"Hi, there. Is North ready?" she asked. The child was Northrop Collier Hughes, and in forty years, with the combined clout of his three names, he would be director of the CIA or president of Yale. This didn't disturb me very greatly; North was a bright, self-assured four-year-old and would no doubt carry on admirably.

"Hi, Scotty." I walked to the foot of the stairs and called softly, "North, your mother is here." Normally, I would have bellowed out the child's name, in tones worthy of my Lower East Side great-grandparents, but somehow Scotty's calm, slightly nasal, upper-class voice had a tranquilizing effect. North came careening down the stairs. I watched with respect as he put on his own coat and buttoned it with no help from his mother. She didn't even praise him; he was merely fulfilling a minor expectation.

"Nasty business, this murder," said Scotty, her eyes on the opened copy of *Newsday*. Her lips, momentarily covering her large rectangular teeth, were drawn tightly together. I felt faintly uncomfortable, as if I had a share in bringing this unpleasant notoriety to Shorehaven.

"It's terrible," I agreed. "Shocking."

Scotty tightened the belt of her camel-hair coat. "Are you going to the funeral tomorrow?" she asked.

"Well," I said, trying to appear thoughtful while I whizzed through a list of possible replies, "I really hadn't thought about it."

"I feel I ought to go. I worked with his sister-in-law, Brenda Dunck, on the anti-sewer campaign."

Now I knew exactly whom to blame whenever my

septic tank backed up into my laundry room sink. "Oh, yes, Brenda," I reflected, still pondering the possibilities.

"I hope this doesn't sound naive," she said, "but what do you do at a Jewish funeral?"

"Well, you don't laugh."

She allowed herself a small smile. "Thank you, Judith."

"You're welcome," I grinned back at her. "Look, why don't I go with you?"

"Would you, Judith? I'd really appreciate that." She paused. "But I don't want to put you out."

"No problem," I assured her, trying to sound warm and gracious. "Anyway, I think I should pay my respects to the family."

"Well, thanks." Her long, bony face softened a little. "Can I pick you up? About a quarter to ten? The funeral is at ten."

"Make it nine-thirty. Ten is when the service starts, and you generally say all your 'I'm so sorrys' before that."

"Yes, of course. And Judith . . ." I looked at her. "You're a brick. Thanks."

She turned up the collar of her coat and left, followed by destiny's darling, North. As she walked down the path to the driveway, I tried to consider exactly why I have always been so intimidated by that class of WASP, the ones who always seem to dress in thick, rich tweeds no matter what the season and never perspire. It's not a matter of pedigree. Nancy's family probably became Anglicans the same day as Henry VIII and she's a descendant of Oglethorpe, but she is real. Her periods are painful and she thinks Woody Allen is funny and she has a passion for Italian salami. But there's something so unfailingly correct about people like Scotty, as though they've been programmed to be eternally vigilant in order to avoid a social gaffe. Scotty's shirts never rumple, her children say "thank you" without prompting. I'm sure she never had wax in her ears. And when I'm with her, I feel she expects something more of me. But I don't know what.

At least tomorrow, I thought gratefully, I'll be on my own turf. At a wet-eyed, damp-palmed Jewish funeral. And maybe a sneaky-looking murderer, paring his or her fingernails with a pointed instrument. Well, maybe not. But better than facing two weeks' accumulation of laundry.

Chapter Five

Baum Brothers occupies a large building, a white brick cube, with a blue canopy stretcher out in front and space for three hundred cars in the rear. It could easily pass for a catering hall, except, as you enter, you are greeted by one of several good-looking young men, doubtless young Baums or Baums-in-law, dressed in black suits, white shirts, and narrow, somber, striped ties. When they ask, "May I help you?" they sound sad but somehow reassuring, as if they recognize their responsibility to mute their grief and carry on.

"The Fleckstein funeral?"

"Second floor. The elevator will take you up."

I followed Scotty, observing that the short, almost mincing steps seemed incongruous for such a tall, long-legged woman—as though as a girl she had been embarrassed by her height and had mimicked the walk of a petite classmate. She was perfectly dressed though: a simple gray dress with a white collar and cuffs. Everyone would know she was truly sorry but not one of the prime bereaved, not one of the family. My black sweater and plaid skirt seemed wrong, and I began to sweat under my arms.

"It's chilly in here," she remarked, as we paused by the brass elevator door. "Or maybe it's just that I don't like funerals."

I nodded and swallowed hard. Although I was fully

aware that no one would challenge me, that no one would point a finger and demand, "Why are you here? Who do you know in the family?" I felt terribly uncomfortable. And with Scotty around, I'd have to keep a stiff upper lip; I could not change my mind and bolt.

When we got upstairs, we stepped into the room where the family waited. About half the faces, about a hundred people, looked faintly familiar to me. They were faces I saw in Shorehaven, in the supermarket, the bakery, the playground, PTA meetings. But I felt my eyes drawn to a beige leather couch. There was Norma Fleckstein, surrounded by men and women with sad expressions. I couldn't gauge hers because she was wearing large sunglasses, although she seemed not to be crying. As I inched closer, I heard her say, "Thank you," and, "I don't think it's hit me yet."

"That's his wife," I said softly to Scotty. "Do you want to say something to her?"

"No," she responded abruptly, staring, it seemed to me, at Norma's long, thin legs, which were covered in translucent black stockings. "I mean," Scotty added, turning to me, "I've never met her. I don't think it would be appropriate."

"Okay," I said, a little regretfully. I had thought to test my courage by going over to Norma and offering my condolences.

Scotty touched my arm and whispered, "There's Brenda Dunck." She lifted her head in the direction of another beige leather couch across the room, near a coat rack.

So that was Brenda, Dicky Dunck's wife. I knew her. At least I had seen her half a dozen times. She belonged to the health club where I swam occasionally, when I felt my body going from merely soft to mushy. She was fairly short, about five foot three, and slim but very buxom, with a beautiful head of black hair, which she wore in a tight chignon at the base of her neck. Her face was not at all pretty; she had small, hazel eyes and a rather sallow complexion, but at least her small, sharply hooked nose and square chin gave it some character. Now, though, she looked wretched. Her eyes were bloodshot and there were red blotches on the sides of her face, darker than the rouge on her cheeks.

"Brenda, I'm very sorry," said Scotty, offering her right hand.

"Scotty, how nice of you to come. Thank you so very much." Brenda seemed to perk up a bit at our arrival. Maybe she liked Scotty. Maybe she felt comforted by her presence. Maybe she felt hysterics would be unacceptable and sobbing a wee bit overdone.

"Brenda, you remember Judith Singer."

"Yes, of course. Thank you for coming." Clearly, she had no idea who I was. But because I was attached to Scotty Hughes, I must be a person she should have remembered.

I blinked. I swallowed. "Brenda, I'm sorry. This must be a hideous shock to all of you." I felt I sounded wonderfully sincere.

"Oh, yes," she said. "It's been a horror. An absolute horror. And of course for Norma and the children. A nightmare." I don't know why, but her voice seemed to have a pretentious ladylike quality. I wanted to poke my elbow in her ribs and say, "Aw, come on, Brenda. Talk regular."

She turned to the man next to her, her husband, Dicky Dunck. "Dicky dear, you remember Scotty Hughes. And Judith Srrg."

"Yes. Yes. How are you ladies?" His goatee was too long and untrimmed. He looked like a billy goat.

"I'm fine, thanks," said Scotty.

"Fine," I echoed.

"I hope the next time we meet it's on a happier occasion," said Dicky. "A great guy, taken in the prime of life."

We all nodded and Brenda started to cry. "It's a loss, a loss to all of us," she sobbed. Scotty drew a handker-

67

chief out of her pocketbook and offered it to her. "Oh, I don't want to ruin your handkerchief."

"That's all right," Scotty reassured her.

"Who could have done it?" Dicky demanded. "A homicidal maniac. Nobody's safe these days. He was like a brother to me."

We nodded, and Brenda sniffled delicately into Scotty's handkerchief, rubbing the soft Irish linen between her fingers.

A black-suited Baum emerged from a door a few feet away and announced: "Would everybody except for the immediate family kindly step into the chapel?"

The chapel was a high-ceilinged room, paneled in maple. The casket, unadorned and in a slightly darker wood, stood front and center. A small lamp, the Eternal Light, was suspended above it. When everybody was seated, still another Baum walked noiselessly to the side of the casket and asked: "Would you please rise?"

We rose and the family walked through a door at the front of the chapel. First Norma, in a clingy black wool wrap dress, relieved only by a long strand of large, luminescent pearls. Very simple and quiet, befitting a widow not yet merry. An older woman clung to her arm, obviously Mrs. Fleckstein the elder; she had her son's generous nose and wide mouth with thin lips. She looked like the one who had been embalmed: one of those women well past middle age who, through dieting and plastic surgery, managed to look about forty from a distance, but who, as you get closer, have the dry, brittle look of a mummy. They were followed by a girl of about ten. According to the obituary, there were three young Flecksteins, two boys and a girl. This was obviously the eldest, Nicole Kimberly. A momentary break in the procession and then came the Duncks, Brenda listing against Dicky and Dicky peering intently into the chapel, as if taking a head count. And, finally, a short man in a long black robe and the wrap-around aviator glasses that were popular a few years ago. He motioned us to be seated.

"Who do you think he is?" Scotty whispered.

"The rabbi."

"But he's not wearing a hat."

"He's Reformed," I explained.

"What?"

"Norma, Nicole, Mrs. Fleckstein, Brenda, Dicky," began the rabbi, "family and friends. What can we say about Bruce Fleckstein?"

Let me up on the pulpit and I'll tell you, I thought. Scotty looked at me, then, strangely, blushed and looked away.

"We can, of course, say what a tragedy it is, a fine man taken from us in the prime of his years. And we can mourn the loss to our community of a dedicated professional. But the loss of Bruce, or Marvin, as his beloved mother adoringly called him, is the loss of the hub of the Fleckstein family wheel, the center of their world. As Yeats so aptly put it, 'The center will not hold.' "

Obviously not, as Norma, with a great noise, took in a huge breath of air and started sobbing. "I'm glad she's finally letting it out," the woman in front of me said to her husband. The woman looked about forty-five and had exactly the same streaky colored hair as Norma. They must have met at the beauty parlor.

"And what can we say to Bruce's wife, to his three fine children, to his mother, his family, his friends?" pondered the rabbi.

You can say that whichever one of them gave him a Polaroid for his birthday made a big mistake. As he went on, I peered around the chapel. Everyone seemed to be concentrating intently, possibly because at this funeral of a contemporary, they might hear a preview of how their own eulogies would sound. They all seemed serious, but not suspiciously so. Could any of these ordinary, predictable people have ended Fleckstein's career as the Don Juan of dentists?

The rabbi banged his fist down on the pulpit, as if remonstrating me for losing interest in his sermon. "We may be deluged with rumors, besieged by innuendo," he continued, "nearly strangled by the half truths and smears the media call journalism. But we all know the sort of man Bruce Fleckstein was. We know . . ."

I sensed, more than felt, a shudder and glanced at Scotty. Her eyes were filled with tears and she opened them wide so the tears wouldn't run down her cheeks.

"Scotty," I said softly, "are you okay?" She nodded, staring at the rabbi. "Scotty?"

"I'm fine," she snapped. At first I was bewildered. The combination of Scotty Hughes crying and irritable was barely believable. She was such a controlled person that normally the most emotion she could show was a big round of applause at a tennis match.

Then I knew. "Scotty," I murmured, "were you having an affair with Bruce Fleckstein?" She whipped her head around to stare at me and then turned away. I knew I had committed a gross breach of etiquette, but I persisted. "Scotty, this is important," I whispered. "Did he take any pictures of you?" This time, her whole body turned toward me.

"You?" she whispered.

"No. A friend of mine." I watched as she rummaged through her pocketbook, obviously looking for the handkerchief she had given to Brenda. I reached into mine and handed her a clean but linty tissue. She pressed it against her eyes.

"Scotty," I began again.

"I think enough has been said, Judith," and she turned from me, offering me a bit more of her back than was polite. There was no way I could pressure Scotty, as I had Mary Alice, to give me information.

Mary Alice was so easily manipulated, and Scotty was a bright, self-possessed woman. But Bruce had gotten to her too.

". . . that Bruce Fleckstein was a man, a fine man with a fine family, and the memory of his warmth, his humor, his thousand little kindnesses will be our record of his life, our inheritance." I tuned out the rabbi again and looked around. In a pew across the aisle, I saw my dentist, Dr. Burns. He was a soothing sort, small and quiet, who had Chopin piped into his office.

A few rows in front of him sat a friend of mine, Fay Jacobs. I was startled. How could she know the Fleck-steins? Fay and I had met three years before at a NOW conference, where I had led a seminar on women in the New Deal. We began chatting and discovered we lived no more than a mile apart. Fay was in her fifties, short, stocky, and as muscular as a longshoreman, with chopped-off gray hair. She wore no makeup except for bright red lipstick, which invariably became smudged, giving her mouth a kind of pleasing, undefined generousness. She had been teaching history at Shorehaven High School since the late nineteen forties and was totally dedicated to her subject and her students. I adored her.

"As Wordsworth so aptly put it . . ." the rabbi was saying. Certain that the quotation would not be apt, I glanced away from Fay back to Scotty. Her large, bony hands gripped the arms of her seat, and her eyes were locked on the Eternal Light in a red-rimmed, unblinking stare. Had she come to Baum Brothers for a short goodbye, for a last moment with a lover who had brought passion and spontaneity into her placid, correct life? Or was she simply making sure the corrupt, manipulative son of a bitch was dead?

" 'The Lord is my shepherd,' " I heard dimly. How many women had followed him to the Tudor Rose Motor Inn, bleating with excitement? Would I have? If

Marvin Bruce had told me how substantive I was, how thrillingly intelligent, would I have allowed myself to be led to an afternoon's frolic?

The mourner's Kaddish, the benediction, and then a brief announcement: "The family will be sitting *shiva* at the home of Mrs. Norma Fleckstein. The address is number fourteen, Fieldstone Road, Shorehaven North." The "North" added about seventy-five thousand dollars to the price of the house. Every home there had, minimally, a "water vw, central AC, and over 2 acs of beaut. wooded property."

The frosted-haired woman in front of me turned to her husband: "The home of Mrs. Norma Fleckstein. I can't believe it."

"Can't believe what?" he asked. He was about fifty, with adolescent-length gray hair, dressed in a tan corduroy sport jacket with suede elbow patches. They clashed. She was with it, a Bloomingdale's lady in a gray cashmere dress and heavy bracelets. He should have complemented her with a snug body shirt and Cardin suit, but instead, as if to emphasize the gulf between them— or to hide his paunch—he had opted for the sincere, professional look. He probably misquoted Buber to his nineteen-year-old girlfriends.

"I mean, I can't believe that just a few days ago it was Bruce and Norma's house and now it's the home of Mrs. Norma Fleckstein. That's what I can't believe."

A Baum entered from the wings and asked us to rise again. We did, and the family began to trudge out.

I turned to ask Scotty if she was ready to go. But she had already left. I could see her weaving through the crowd, heading along the side of the chapel to the rear exit. People poured into the aisles, a few looking dazed, a few waving eagerly to friends and neighbors across the chapel. A swelling wave of voices rose after the funereal silence. "How've you been?" "God, I hate funerals." "How was Martinique?" I pushed my way past them and over to Fay Jacobs.

72

"Judith. How are you?" she asked, beaming at me and adjusting her bra strap. She explained my presence to the woman standing next to her: "Judith is my favorite historian since Commager." The woman looked a little confused and then decided Fay had told a joke. She laughed and then quickly excused herself.

"Fay, it's good to see you. It's been months."

"I know. Why don't we have lunch? Come on, Judith, don't refuse me. I took a personal day and I have all afternoon."

I thought for a second. "Sure. But I have to pick Joey up at a friend's house at two-thirty."

"No problem," she said. "I feel like pampering myself today. Let's go some place very quiet and luxurious."

"How about Quelle Crêpe? They have a decent salade niçoise." She put on a too-long red plaid coat and buttoned it slowly. Her knuckles were swollen with arthritis and even that simple task was painful for her.

We walked outside, blinking from the bright sunlight, and stood under the canopy, watching the hearse and its escort of limousines and cars. "I didn't know you knew them," Fay declared. "They weren't friends of yours, were they?"

"No. Not really."

"Then why did you come?"

"I don't know, Fay. I just shaved my legs and I wanted to wear a skirt and show them off."

"Judith," she smiled, "come on. Why?"

"I really don't know, Fay. The mother of one of Joey's friends said she was going and I volunteered to keep her company. Just a whim. Curiosity. I don't know."

We walked to the parking lot, Fay waving to every other person. She had lived in Shorehaven for so long that she seemed to know everyone. She patronized their stores, taught their children, worked with them at countless fairs and rummage sales.

73

"How did you know the Flecksteins?" I asked.

"Wouldn't you rather discuss the revisionist view of Kennedy?"

"No."

She opened her pocketbook and extracted her car keys. "He went to dental school with my nephew Roger. I suggested to Roger that he practice here, but his little boy had asthma, so they moved out West. But he told Bruce about Shorehaven, and when Norma and Bruce first moved here, I had them over to dinner a couple of times. Mainly to introduce them to some couples of their age."

"That was very thoughtful of you," I commented. She smiled and shrugged her shoulders. "Fay, what was he like? Really like?"

"Well, you wouldn't be able to comprehend him. You lead a decent, uncomplicated life." She opened the door to her car with some difficulty, unable to get a tight grip on the handle.

"For God's sake, Fay. What's this decent business? What are you going to do, explain the situation to me when I grow up?"

She looked up at me, coloring a bit. "I'm sorry. I really didn't mean to sound condescending. Look, let's get to the restaurant and I'll tell you everything I know about the Flecksteins. If you're interested."

"If I'm interested? Would I be here if I weren't interested?"

"All right," she sighed. "But it's not a pleasant story. And you'll see why Bruce didn't live happily ever after."

Chapter Six

"How many, s'il vous plaît?" asked the hostess, a heavy middle-aged woman dressed in a beribboned French provincial costume.

"Deux," I replied, and followed her across the dark red linoleum floor, embossed in a brick design, to a small table in a corner.

"Ees zees hokay?" she inquired. She had the inept French accent of Americans who have never studied the language.

"Oui," I answered, and she smiled warmly at us and departed, no doubt pleased because she had carried on a conversation in French.

Quelle Crêpe had opened in the early sixties, when masses of young couples, thousands of little Jacks and Jackies, moved to Long Island from Brooklyn and Queens. Refusing to adopt the suburban Eisenhower-esque style of their neighbors—the crew cut, the circle pin, and the barbecue—they served coq au vin to each other and spent Saturday nights in Manhattan at the theater or the opera. Their sons, it is true, joined the Little League, but physical fitness did have the Kennedy imprimatur. And the ladies—they weren't women then—marched right by the tea rooms of the Old Wave suburbanites and into Quelle Crêpe, where for a few dollars you could have a glass of wine and a crêpe with fromage or fromage et oeufs or fromage et oeufs et jambon or even fromage et oeufs et jambon et asperges, like a francophile's Dagwood sandwich.

We declined the proffered menus and ordered our salads and coffee. Fay ran her arthritic fingers through her massacred hairdo and smiled.

"So?" I asked.

"So? You want to know about the Flecksteins?"

"Everything."

"Well, Judith, 'everything' is a little beyond me. I made certain never to cross over the barrier of intimacy." Our salads arrived. Fay carefully picked out the anchovies and put them on the side of her plate. "Well, the most interesting thing was that there was nothing interesting about either of them." She paused.

"What do you mean?" I inquired.

"Well, they weren't uninteresting, in the sense of being stupid or dull. Bruce was quite pleasant really. The first time they came over, he chatted with everybody and even managed to sound interested in Lou Sherman—he's on the board of the North Shore Historical Society. Well, Bruce asked him a lot of questions about the history of Shorehaven, and Lou was quite voluble. But I don't know why, it wasn't anything Bruce actually said, but I knew he really wasn't interested in what Lou was saying."

"You mean he was just trying to make a good impression?"

"No. More than that. It was as if he felt that a little bit of local history might someday be useful to him. So he let Lou give him a short course, and he filed it somewhere in the back of his mind. I don't know, there was something about him . . ."

"What?"

"Wait a second." She speared a piece of lettuce and tuna fish. "It was as if he were programmed for niceness. He was pleasant to everyone, interested in everyone, to the same degree."

"Who else was there that evening?"

76

"It was so long ago. Let me think. The Shermans, the Burnses."

"The dentist?" I asked.

"Yes. And Joe and me. I think that was all." Joe, Fay's husband, a vice-president of a local bank, was such a quiet, pallid man that I often had to be reminded that he existed.

"All right," I said, "what about Norma? What's she like?"

"Nice."

"Nice? From what you said at the funeral home, I was expecting a little more than 'nice.' "

"Well, she was. She had the same sort of pleasantness he had, a kind of controlled friendliness to everyone. I remember thinking she was very attractive for a basically ordinary-looking woman. Very well groomed and beautifully dressed, and they didn't have much money then. But there's nothing more to tell about her. She asked all the right questions—about the schools, which temple to join, things like that. And she did all the right things."

"You mean she didn't pick her nose at the dinner table."

"No," Fay grinned. "Only over hors d'oeuvres. But you know what I mean. She brought me a nice little house gift. She talked with everyone. She sent me a thank you note."

"Do you think," I asked, holding a wrinkled black olive between my thumb and forefinger, "that she seemed a little bland because she was nervous or shy? Being new in the community?"

"I think that might have had something to do with it," Fay conceded. "But it was odd. Nothing else came through. Usually, like the first few days of school, when kids are on their best behavior, you can pick up a lot about them. Their quirks just seem to pop to the surface. I can always tell the intelligent ones and the ones who have personal problems and the ones who will spend the whole term just taking up space. But with Norma, well, she was what she was."

"And what was she?"

"Nice. Attractive. Polite. Reasonably intelligent."

"How did she relate to her husband?"

"She adored him. That was obvious. Every time he spoke, she would concentrate on every pearl that dropped from his lips. I mean, if he had announced he was going to the bathroom, she would have thought that was terribly clever and very profound."

"And how did he act toward her?"

"He seemed devoted to her, did all the things a model husband should do, smiled at her, lit her cigarettes."

Our coffee came and by tacit mutual consent we took a break, although I was still unclear why Fay was so disturbed by the Flecksteins; there had to be more. For a few minutes, we chatted about her honors class, a seminar of high school seniors studying the Civil War.

Then Fay asked: "Would you like more coffee?"

"Yes. And more about the Flecksteins." She looked at me and shifted uncomfortably in her chair. "If they were so terribly ordinary, why didn't you like them? What happened?"

"Well, it's hard to say when it started. Oh, I know. About a week after the party, Jean Burns called me, ostensibly to say thanks. But she started asking all sorts of questions about Bruce, and about his relationship with Norma." She stopped for a minute. "Judith, this is to go no further."

"It won't," I assured her, looking straight into her eyes.

"Well, by the time we finished talking, I was absolutely convinced that something was going on, or was about to go on, between Jean and Bruce."

"Did you ask her?"

"No. I couldn't. We're not particularly close." Remembering how I had behaved with Scotty, I realized

78

that Fay obviously had a great deal more discretion than I. "Anyway," she continued, "about a month later, we ran into the Burnses at a restaurant, and Dennis asked us if we had heard from Bruce. I said no, and he went on to tell us that he had referred a few patients to Bruce and that they all seemed very pleased. We were standing there, smiling and chatting, when I took a look at Jean; she looked like she wanted to crawl under a table and die. Nothing specific, but she was obviously terribly uncomfortable. And I remember thinking, what a nasty thing for Bruce to do. To cuckold a man who's gone out of his way to be decent to him. And really, Judith, I wasn't being unfair. I later heard rumors from two different sources that something was going on between Bruce and Jean."

"He sounds like a real sweetheart," I commented.

She took a deep breath. "That's not all."

Fay told me that over the years she had heard buzzing about Fleckstein's involvement with several women. Two or three of them were housewives, although she didn't mention their names. One was a successful real estate broker in town, another was—and she seemed surprised—an activist in the feminist movement. "He was bound to run into trouble sooner or later," she added.

"Is there any common denominator?" I asked, thinking about Mary Alice and Scotty. "Is Jean Burns Jewish?"

"Yes," Fay said. "But not all of them were." I knew that, but that blew my first theory, Ethnic Revenge or stick it to the *shiksa*. "They were all upper-middle-class women, all married."

"The husbands?"

"All successful, come to think of it. Doctors, dentists, lawyers, stockbrokers, businessmen."

"Men too busy to pay attention to their wives?" I theorized.

"Let me think. No, I don't think so. I mean, I can

think of at least two cases where the husbands were really genuinely devoted to their wives. Dennis Burns, for instance. It was as if Bruce only wanted to associate himself with success."

"And what about Norma?" I asked. "Do you think she knew?"

"Well, I don't think so. You know, Judith, I've seen several men with a pants problem, and I'm convinced their motive isn't sex. Usually, if you'll excuse me, they screw other women literally to screw their wives figuratively. But Bruce was different. He was always lovey-dovey with Norma, never flirted with anyone in front of her." She peered down into her coffee cup. "You know, I don't usually talk like this. About other people's private affairs. But there was something so threatening about Bruce."

"In what way?" I asked, my hushed tones matching hers.

"I know this sounds melodramatic, but I got the feeling he was pure evil, like the snake in Eden. Very smooth and very corrupt. Corrupting, really. Nothing blatant, like Hitler."

"Churchill called him 'this wicked man Hitler.' Remember?"

"Yes. But Bruce was more subtle, like Albert Speer. Wickedness was a choice, not a response."

"God," I breathed.

"Well, the opposite really; nothing godlike about the incredible Dr. Fleckstein. You know, I've always been fairly religious, a reasonably observant Jew, but for a long time I told myself that I just had to watch out for myself—and my family. That it was wrong to make moral judgments about others. But the longer I live and the more I study history, the more I believe that one has to take a moral stand. And Bruce Fleckstein was a bad man."

"You're certain the rumors were true, then?"

She smiled. "You're a truly just person. Yes, the rumors were true. I know. Because he tried to seduce me."

Fortunately, I restrained my impulse to blurt out, "You?" Any man getting to know Fay as a person would soon realize what a lovely human being she was, but she was not the type to light a fire in the loins of the average suburban Don Juan. "Tell me," I said.

Fay's colorless, ordinary face looked drawn. Her lipstick had disappeared with her lunch, so her mouth blended into the rest of her features, defined only by a few deep lines in the corners. She was terribly uneasy, though I couldn't tell if it was from her natural reticence or because her memory was still burdened by the weight of emotion. "Well, about a couple of months after they had been to our house, Norma called and invited us to dinner. We went, had a reasonably nice time, and that was that. At least I thought that was that. But the next Monday I had a call from Bruce about four o'clock, a few minutes after I came home from school." She hesitated. "This is so embarrassing."

"If you'd rather not," I began.

"No, it's okay. Well, he began by saying how much he enjoyed my company, how much he admired me. I had a good mind, I remember he said. And then he said: 'I find you very attractive.' "

"What did you say?"

"I said thank you and how was his lovely wife Norma? He just pretended he didn't hear and then asked me out for lunch." She paused for a minute and then made a noise, a cross between a snort and a nervous giggle. "Anyway, I told him I had forty-five minutes for lunch and thirty minutes of that time were spent grading papers."

"Did he take the hint?" I asked.

"Yes. He even managed to be very gallant. He said something to the effect that it's so rare to meet such an intelligent, sensitive woman and it's too bad we couldn't get together."

81

"Maybe he was being sincere, Fay."

"Judith, I know what I am. I'm reasonably bright, competent, and interesting. And just between us, I would be overjoyed if a handsome young man came and kneeled down before me and offered himself as my liege man—especially if he didn't want to admire me from afar. But I'm not pretty. I'm not, according to current usage, sexy. I was a good ten years older than he, and I just knew he was saying to himself, 'Here's a plain, dull, menopausal woman who would be pathetically grateful for my attention.' "

I shook my head. "You're not being fair to yourself, Fay."

"Maybe not fair, but honest." She toyed with a locket she was wearing and told me that at her husband's insistence, they had seen the Flecksteins a few more times. Joe, in his role as a bank officer, felt that Fleckstein had the smell of success—and had hoped some of the aroma would waft his way. Finally, Fay told him that she found the Flecksteins very dull and refused to socialize with them again. Joe acquiesced.

"So you never saw them again?"

"No, but Joe saw Bruce on business. That's why I came to the funeral; Joe had an appointment today and couldn't break it."

"You never said anything to him about Fleckstein's overture?"

"No. What good would it have done? Anyway, Joe finally became disillusioned with Bruce. Bruce's brother-in-law, Dicky Dunck, you know, asked Bruce to co-sign a loan about eight months ago. Joe says Dicky was good for the money, but had a cash-flow problem or some such thing, but it wouldn't have meant any risk to Bruce. But he wouldn't do it. In fact, he told *Joe* to call Dicky and tell him no. It was horribly awkward."

"What did Dicky need the loan for?" I asked.

"Oh, I think it was for some new equipment. Oh, wait, to meet his payroll. That's what it was. And Joe said that even if there had been a risk, ten thousand would have been pin money to a man in Bruce's position. The thing that got to Joe was the callousness." Fay ran a gnarled hand over her mouth. "I guess I shouldn't be talking like this about Joe's business. But it was so cruel, so upsetting."

We lingered over a second cup of coffee until the waitress came with the check. We both grabbed for it.

"Let me," Fay insisted. "I invited you to lunch."

"Come on. Let me be a sport," I argued back. "That way I can close my eyes and pretend I'm grown up with an expense account."

We split the check and walked slowly to the door, each of us nodding to various neighbors and acquaintances. "It's such a small town," Fay remarked.

She dropped me off at the house and I flopped down on the couch, grateful at the prospect of a half hour of silence. Off came my shoes, and I began playing with a thread on my pantyhose. Within seconds, I had a full-fledged run and a rush of adrenalin. You have deeds to do, obligations to meet, my body called out to me.

Naturally, I obeyed. I stood and marched purposefully into the kitchen—then stood there, confused. Just what was I supposed to do? Bruce? Norma? Fay? Scotty? Ah, Mary Alice. Mary Alice needs a good criminal lawyer. All right, I would call Claymore Katz. Surely Claymore would know what to do. He was, for an Ivy League-educated, upper-middle-class attorney, street-wise; he once told me that a client of his had had an accident. What happened? I asked. "His head got in the way of a bullet."

But if I called him, Bob would be annoyed. He would demand, coldly, just what was wrong with me. Why was I getting involved? Still, I could tell him the extent of Mary Alice's involvement, explain she needed a lawyer fast. And what would Bob say? "Fuck her. Her husband can pay for a lawyer. Just stay out of this."

I stood looking at the telephone. Why not call? Claymore was my friend too. He would swoop down on me at a dinner party and herd me into a corner. "Judith, my joy, my pleasure. Talk to me of life. Of history. If I hear one more word about tax shelters, I'm going to heave. God, what happened to them? How did they become so incredibly boring? How did we escape?"

Rather nervously, I looked up Claymore's number and dialed. The switchboard operator greeted me with a cheerful, "Burton, Furn, Ziss and Katz. Good afternoon."

"Mr. Katz's office," his secretary said, sounding even more cheerful than the switchboard operator. Should I disguise my voice, give a false name? Bob called Claymore frequently. What would the secretary think if *Mrs.* Singer called? But couldn't men and women be friends? Could they be? "Mr. Katz's office," she said again.

"Mr. Katz, please."

"Whom shall I say is calling?"

"Mrs. Singer."

"Hello." Claymore's voice was smooth and clear and deep. Hearing it, you'd imagine you were talking to God, or at least someone over six feet tall, instead of the short, pudgy man with a big nose and walrus mustache to whom it belonged.

"Hi, Clay. Judith Singer."

"Judith," he said, his voice full of warmth. "Why didn't you just say 'Judith?' When I heard 'Mrs. Singer,' I just assumed it would be some tedious functionary from the A.G.'s office. That's the Attorney General's office. How are you, you lovely, bright, human being?"

"Fine, Clay. Look, I have a major favor to ask you."

"Anything. Could Dante say no to Beatrice?"

"Clay, listen, there's something I want to talk to you about. Could we have lunch one day next week?"

"Yes. Sure. Is it something important?"

"Kind of. What's a good day for you?"

"Let me check my calendar. Monday I'll be downtown all day. Is Tuesday okay? I have a Bar Association committee meeting where everyone sits around clearing their throats to see who has accumulated the most phlegm, but I'd love to get out of that. About one o'clock? I'll meet you at my office and we'll go someplace painfully elegant."

I thought about it. Claymore's firm did all of Singer Associates' legal work. "Tuesday's fine, but could we meet in a restaurant? I don't want to run into my father-in-law or one of my brothers-in-law if they happen to be around your office."

Claymore paused for a minute. I could hear him swallow. "Sure. I assume you don't want Bob to know about this either?"

"Right. I'll explain at lunch."

"Fine. We can meet at Orsini's then. At one."

"Lovely, Clay." Maybe I'd see Jackie Onassis. Or at least Lee Radziwill. "Look, I really appreciate this."

"I'm looking forward to it, Judith."

I replaced the receiver gently and began worrying about what to wear. By electing to serve my sentence in Shorehaven, I had grown out of touch with Manhattan fashions, as well as ideas. I knew my pleated skirt was wrong, but I didn't know what was right. In desperation, I called Nancy, who told me to wear a plain dress; she'd fix it up with a scarf and a few strategically placed gold chains.

"Thanks," I said. "By the way, guess where I was today." She couldn't, so I filled her in on what I had observed at Baum Brothers.

"That's terrific, Judith. Going to funerals might catch on. All the ladies could give up tennis and pay condolence calls instead. Just think. You'd need a lot more clothes, and dresses are so much more interesting than tennis shorts. What a boon it would be to the garment industry. And you'd make so many families happy because the deceased was so popular and you could get a

85

real education listening to all those ministers and rabbis. And Judith, have you ever heard a requiem mass? It's magnificent."

"Did you do anything about getting magazine credentials?"

"Yes."

"Oh. Why didn't you tell me?"

"Why didn't you ask?" she inquired, using her sugary Melanie Wilkes voice. "Anyway, I made a few calls, and no one gives a hoot about Bruce Fleckstein. They've done suburban crime to death, and they're tired of pornography. Maybe I should have asked if they were interested in gum diseases."

"So you didn't get anywhere?" I asked.

"Of course, I got somewhere. I'm doing a piece for *New York* on the fleeing suburbanite, about all the folks who've had it up the old whazzoo with car pooling and who are moving back to the city."

I shifted the receiver to the other ear. Perhaps I just didn't understand. "But, Nancy, that has nothing to do with the murder."

"So what?"

"You promised Mary Alice you'd try to help her."

"Well, I tried and failed. Look, I don't give a crap about Mary Alice. I'm a writer, damn it. If she wants, she can try to get hold of those pictures and we can do a book. I'll write the text."

"So you're not going to help her?" I demanded, my voice rising in anger. "Goddamn it, can't you use your *New York* credentials with police? Just say one of the reasons people are leaving the suburbs is the increase in crime and use the Fleckstein murder as an example."

"It won't wash, dearie."

I realized then that from the beginning, she had wanted no part of Mary Alice and her problem. The only reason she had agreed to help was that it ensured a graceful exit. I fired my last shot. "You can't spend the rest of your life avoiding commitments. You can't just label a situation tacky and boring and make it go away."

"Take your psychoanalysis and ram it up your ass," she answered.

She slammed the phone down a split second before I did, only because her reflexes are sharper. I sat in a kitchen chair, feeling heavy and depressed, as I always do after an argument. She'd never speak to me again. I'd be all alone. All I'd have was Bob. My parents, happy and retired on their high school teachers' pensions in Arizona, could only love me from a distance. And now with Nancy gone too, I'd have to go it alone. She wouldn't lend me her gold chains. All my half-articulated hopes, all my well-considered dissatisfactions, would have to be confided to Bob.

With that thought, I called her back. "Peace at any price."

"Oh, Judith. Hi. Sorry I was such an old bitch." I mumbled that it hadn't bothered me. "Look," she said, "I just realized I have a source in the police department. He probably won't know anything, but I'll give him a call just the same."

"Who?" I asked, immensely relieved more about our truce than about her prospect.

"Remember Jim Hogan? Jim, from about two years ago. You know, Little Cupcake."

Of course I remembered. Little Cupcake had been a radio-car patrolman who had first met Nancy when her burglar alarm accidentally went off. To apologize, she invited him in for a glass of wine, and by the end of the bottle they had formed a relationship that had lasted for about six months. It had been wonderfully convenient. He would cruise her block, making sure no cars were in her driveway, and then pull his car in and drive around to the back. They'd make love on her screened porch, so he could listen for calls on his car radio. I was never certain whether she had broken off with him out of tedium or at the prospect of a long, cold winter on the porch.

"Are you still friendly enough with him to do it?" I asked.

"Well, I haven't seen him in ages, but I'm sure he'll be glad to hear from me." She said this with no self-consciousness, which I found absolutely remarkable. If I had ever had an affair, I would assume that after it was over I would either be forgotten, or if considered at all, it would be with a soupçon of contempt. But, then, Nancy had smooth, seemingly poreless skin and no stretch marks.

"Okay. Let me know what happens," I said.

"I'll call him first thing next week."

"Can't you do it today?"

"Judith, don't push your luck."

I took her suggestion and we said goodbye. If Little Cupcake was still assigned to the same precinct, he might have some information about the murder. I had no worry that Nancy would be able to extract whatever information he had. My only concern was that he was such a lousy cop that he wouldn't care enough to listen to the gossip about the case.

It was almost time for me to fetch Joey, and I walked into the living room to retrieve my shoes. As I did, I noticed a large station wagon in the driveway. Its door slammed shut. And marching up the path, looking very grim, was Scotty Hughes.

Chapter Seven

I pulled open the door before she could ring the bell.

"Hello," she said, trying unsuccessfully to smile. Her lips spread out, but her large teeth remained hidden behind them, as though she were doing an isometric facial exercise. "I'd like to apologize for walking out on you, leaving you without a lift home. It was rude. Inexcusable. I'm sorry."

"That's okay," I replied graciously. "Come in. Please."

"I can't. Really. I have to get some position papers in order. We're trying to save the wetlands."

"I see." I hadn't known we had wetlands. It felt reassuring to realize that people like Scotty existed to save them. "Look, Scotty, I know this is really awkward—for both of us. I'm sorry, and as far as I'm concerned our little exchange never occurred."

"I appreciate that," she said cautiously.

"Well, I have to pick up Joey."

"I see," she replied. "I really don't want to talk about Bruce Fleckstein. It was the one great mistake of my life."

"Well," I said reassuringly, "I've made some doozies in my life." She stood there, looking sad and awkward. "Let bygones be bygones. Water under the bridge," I murmured.

"He was so utterly charming at the beginning. And then so distant, so totally cold."

"Oh, " I said.

"I couldn't believe it was the same man. How could he act like that to me?"

"How did he act?" I asked.

"I really don't think it's any of your concern, Judith," she snapped, and turned and marched back to her station wagon.

"Oh, well," I sighed, and left to pick up Joey. The rest of the afternoon was serene enough. Bob called to say he'd be working late, so I took the children out for a pizza.

"You know what?" Kate demanded with a full mouth. "Mrs. Hamilton won't let Wendy eat pizza because it's junk food."

When we arrived home, I decided to reinforce my guilt by calling Marilyn Tuccio. At that very moment, I thought, she'd be serving her family a savory, low-cholesterol chicken cacciatore, simmered in the tomato paste she had canned the previous fall.

"Hi," I began, "I just wanted to check to see how you were. You had quite a day yesterday."

"Well, today was no pleasure either. The police were here twice. The first time they wanted to know if I had my supermarket check."

"What?"

"My supermarket check. I stopped off at the A&P after I went to Dr. Fleckstein's office."

"My God, Marilyn. Who the hell saves supermarket checks?"

"I do. I showed it to them."

"Oh." Someday I'll learn that my habits are not the standards by which to judge the rest of humanity. "What did they want the second time?"

"Well, this awful detective with eyebrows about a foot thick came and started asking a lot of silly questions." That must have been Ramirez. "Then he sort of

90

sneered and asked if my husband had any famous relatives. I couldn't figure out what he meant, so I told him no, but that Mike's Uncle John was chief of neurosurgery at St. Vincent's. Then all of a sudden I realized what this, this person, was asking me."

"What?" I asked eagerly.

"He was asking me if Mike was connected with the Mafia. Just because we have an Italian name."

"Wow." I was reduced to monosyllables, not by the detective's stupidity, but by the force of Marilyn's anger.

"So I told him that I was nauseated by his filthy smears and to go to hell. I said 'hell,' Judith, and told him to get out of my house and fast."

"Gee," I said. "By the way, did you speak with a lawyer?"

"Well, after that little scene I certainly did. Helen Fields. The Assemblywoman. She has a practice over in Mineola. She said if the police want to talk to me, they'll do it in her presence." Helen Fields was a tough old politician, a Republican who made William Howard Taft look like a knee-jerk liberal.

"Did you mention anything to her about seeing Fleckstein and his nurse at the motel?"

"Yes. And she told me to tell it to the police."

"And did you?"

"Not yet. But maybe I will."

"Marilyn, I think you should."

"This whole thing is ridiculous," she said. "It's not even worth thinking about."

"Yes, it is," I insisted, reaching over and opening a window. The air had become damp and frigid, a foreshadowing of snow to come. I took a deep breath and tried again. "Marilyn, if the police have it in their heads that you're some sort of avenging angel or that all those doctors in Mike's family are suddenly taking out contracts on Jewish dentists, you ought to realize they're serious. Stupid, maybe, but serious."

"I'll think about it. But the whole thing is so ugly."

"I know."

It started snowing that night and continued into Friday. Five inches of fat, puffy snowflakes, and we spent Saturday making snowpeople with the children on the front lawn. A great, rotund snowman, looking like a Victorian father, a somewhat smaller snowwoman, equipped with a kerchief, sunglasses, and two healthy snowbreasts, and two small snowchildren with eternally vigilant raisin eyes. Sunday, my in-laws visited, my mother-in-law catering dinner, walking into the house with two Bergdorf's shopping bags filled with foil-covered dishes, saying, "Judith, dear, today is your day to relax."

And all weekend long, I reviewed the Fleckstein play, envisioning the characters—Bruce, Norma, Mary Alice, Dicky, Brenda, Scotty, Fay, et al.—parading before me, the director. All they needed was a script to give coherence to their existences, lines and gestures to illuminate their inner lives.

"Judith," cooed Bob. "Judith. Come here." It was Sunday night and he hadn't put on his pajamas.

"What?" I asked.

"You were a thousand miles away," he observed.

"Oh," I said, realizing that having dimmed the bedroom lights, he was indeed serious. "I thought you were tired."

"Not any more," he whispered, his breath hot and damp in my ear. He grabbed my hand and placed it on his erection—in case I hadn't noticed. "Does that feel tired to you?" I conceded that it felt extremely alert. "Unless you're too tired," he added bravely.

"No, of course not." My usual I'm-not-in-the-mood signal is a mighty yawn as we ascend the stairs. At that moment, we achieve a tacit understanding and he heads for his pajama drawer. But that night, I was already at Orsini's with Claymore, examining some fine points of criminal law over an icy glass of Lillet. Bob began biting my lower lip. It worked. I put my hand on his chest and moved it slowly southward.

"Mmmmm. Judith. Hey, why did you stop?" I stopped, I declared silently, because what happens if someone sees me with Claymore Katz and mentions something to you? Automatically, I started my hand moving again. "It feels so good," he intoned. Would you think I was spending the afternoon making Claymore Katz feel good? That, of course, was patently ridiculous. Claymore had flabby thighs and a jiggly ass. But would that convince Bob? Or would he say, his blue eyes frosted with cold anger, "The lady doth protest too much, methinks." And pack up, leaving me in Shorehaven, and move to a lovely apartment in the East Sixties and fall in love with a thin blond biochemist who got her Ph.D. at twenty-four.

"Bob," I sighed. "I have to tell you something."

"I know. Oh, honey, I know."

He pushed me down onto the bed. I tried hard to concentrate on Bob's tall, compact, beautiful body. It didn't work. Nor, as he tried to pry my legs apart, would my Lamaze breathing techniques; he'd taken the course with me and would spot it at my first deep cleansing breath. My knees remained sandwiched together like a recalcitrant Oreo. "Not yet," I whispered.

"Now. Please."

"Just one second," I pleaded, concentrating on finding someone on whom to focus, some wonderful, sensual man who would put a swing in my step and a zing in my labia. No one, just a series of faces, men I had known, men I would like to know, but all whizzing by as if on a too-fast film strip, with a voice-over by Bob saying, "Mmmmm."

"Bob."

"Don't stop. Oh, God, don't stop."

In ten minutes, he was sound asleep. It took me another hour.

So, on Tuesday morning, I decided to face the issue boldly. "I'm going to the city today."

"That's nice," he responded.

Enough boldness for one day. After he left, and before Mrs. Foster, the baby sitter, was due to arrive and eavesdrop, I called Mary Alice and told her about my appointment with Claymore.

"How can I possibly thank you, Judith? You know I'm an agnostic, but believe me, if there is a God, then He will bless you. Or should I say, She will bless you."

"I haven't even bought my train ticket yet, Mary Alice. I'll call you tomorrow and tell you what happened."

"Can't you tell me tonight? I feel so terribly impotent, just sitting here. Impotent. What a strange word to choose. Impotent . . ."

"I don't want Bob to hear our conversation. I think it's better to keep him out of this, so I'm doing it on my own."

"I thought the two of you had a very honest, open relationship."

I assured her that it was as open as I could handle and made a date to see her the next morning at ten, this time at my house. I really didn't like her, I thought. Then why was I spending the day as her agent? Not for Mary Alice, I realized. For me. To satisfy my own intense curiosity. To be somehow a part of the Fleckstein case, to position myself in the center of all those currents of passion and emotion and intrigue. And less than an hour later, I found myself in front of Orsini's, ready to insert myself even deeper into the situation. But it was only twelve-fifteen, and nothing could happen until Clay arrived at one.

I strolled along Fifth Avenue. The snow that still frosted Shorehaven was gone in Manhattan, melted away by the intensity of city life. I peered into Valentino's window. They had some gray silk blouses that one must possess to match one's gray wool slacks and one's peach and gray knit sweater. Soft and cool and rich and secure. Gucci, in a direct rebuke, had forsaken the calm, understated colors and was pushing red. Red silk, red wool, red suede. Red to go with one's bright, multi-textured life.

"Hi," said a voice next to me. I glanced away from the window, half expecting to see Claymore grinning at me. Instead, it was a stranger, a man about my age, a pleasant, ordinary-looking, brown-eyed stranger who wore a navy blue overcoat exactly like Bob's. "Are you buying anything?" he asked. His smile was friendly.

"Are you selling anything?" I responded. His expression changed almost microscopically, only his eyes glazing over, the curtain descending to hide the human being; my four words had transmogrified me from a person to a piece of ass.

"What are you in the market for?" His voice thickened.

"Actually, I'm just window shopping," I said, smiling at him. He looked a little confused. "I was just being facetious when I asked you what you were selling."

"Oh, facetious. Do you work around here?"

"No."

"Oh. By the way, my name's Jonathan."

"Hi. Judith. You know, we sound like refugees from a first-grade reader. 'See Judith and Jonathan. See them jump.' "

He grinned, the curtain lifting from his eyes for the second act. "Can I buy you a drink?"

"No thanks. I have a lunch date."

"Can I have your number?"

"No."

"Why not?"

"I'm married." He looked skeptical, so I raised my left hand and passed it before his eyes. "I'm very married."

"Why are all the nice ones married?" he asked, talking to a red suede jacket in the window.

"Nice meeting you, Jonathan. I have to go. Bye."

95

"Judith. Hey, wait. Would you like my number? I mean, in case it doesn't work out."

I felt startled that I was tempted by his offer, surprised that it didn't really sound so terribly absurd. In case it doesn't work out.

"No," I answered, somewhat hesitantly, my timing barely within the limits of propriety. I should have snapped out a brusque "No thanks." Still, I managed a small, regretful smile and added: "But I appreciate the offer." I headed back into the tide of Fifth Avenue pedestrians, savoring a feeling of wistfulness and elation as I moved toward Claymore—and his safe connection with Bob. But how extraordinarily pleasurable it had been, that ordinary pick-up attempt by an ordinary man, the sort of thing that must happen to other women all the time. Just Jonathan and me. For the first time since my wedding, I had spoken with a man who knew nothing about my background, nothing of my marital status. Jonathan had seen me naked and unformed; I could create myself.

I had been married for ten years, nearly all my adult life, and for the first three or four I had viewed even a serious discussion with another man as an implicit act of faithlessness. Men became asexual beings who happened to wear their vaginas inside out. And soon after that, after leaving graduate school with its occasional tempter in Harris tweeds or washed-out jeans, I had only Bob. I met other women's husbands at parties, at community events, but amidst the laughter, the gossip, I remained Bob's wife. I chatted and chuckled with shopkeepers, doctors, dentists, and insurance agents, and paid them with Bob's money. Thus he was, even by default, the only man in my life. Even my friend Claymore was a friend I saw only in Bob's presence; this was the first time I was going to be alone with him.

I paused at the corner of Fifth Avenue, waiting obediently for the light to change. My left hand, with its heavy gold wedding band, was stuffed deep into my coat pocket. Somehow, I thought, I had floated through a revolution in women's rights; I had embraced its rhetoric, been deeply touched by its insights, and yet remained curiously unaffected by it in terms of my own life. Even Fleckstein's women had managed to cut the umbilical cord between themselves and their husbands. They were able to sustain life and breath outside marriage. But I wasn't completely certain of this. Weren't they still nourished by a Shorehaven husband—albeit not their own? Wasn't their adultery still within the normal range of response for middle-class, middle-American, nearly middle-aged wives?

I ruminated on this, my eyes fixed firmly on the sidewalk, until I reached Fifty-Sixth Street. I spotted Claymore standing in front of Orsini's, enveloped in a seal coat. From a distance, with his giant walrus mustache, he looked like an immense, squat Arctic animal that had hopped on an ice floe shuttle to Manhattan to satisfy some obscure mammalian curiosity. But instead of clapping his flippers together in glee at seeing me, he sauntered over and gave me a light kiss on the lips. Very Manhattan. Shorehaven men offer large, smacking cheek kisses, kisses loud enough to draw attention to their innocence.

"Why is a magnificent creature like you kept like a caged animal in Scarsdale?" he demanded.

"Scarsdale is in Westchester, Clay. I live in Shorehaven."

"Shorehaven, Scarsdale, Greenwich. They're interchangeable. Terrible places. They stifle the soul."

He took my arm and led me into the restaurant, where we checked our coats with a rather irresponsible-looking young woman and walked upstairs. The maître d' smiled at us and said "Good afternoon, Counselor" to Claymore. Claymore nodded at him with restrained dignity that would have impressed everyone in his old neighborhood in Flatbush. We followed the maître d' to a small table in a corner. A delicate crystal vase of red and purple anemones stood on the white linen cloth.

"I thought we'd sit out of the way," said Claymore. "It's more private." I nodded, glancing around the room. Jackie Onassis and Lee Radziwill apparently were lunching elsewhere. The captain came to take our orders for drinks and I ordered a Lillet.

"Judith, love, that's a charming aperitif, but let's order a bottle of Orvieto, shall we?" I nodded and peered around the room again. A few women were scattered about, all fairly chic, all bearing a faint resemblance to the fuzzy photos in Eugenia Shepard's column. Most of the diners were men though, businessmen, talking intently to justify their expense accounts. "Is there anyone here you know?" asked Clay, interrupting my reverie. I shook my head. "Then you can relax and enjoy yourself."

I smiled at him a little vaguely. "This is so lovely, Clay. I know how busy you are and I really appreciate it."

"Judith, I hardly view this as a sacrifice. I see it as a rare pleasure." A waiter brought the wine, and after the tasting ceremony, Claymore leaned back in his chair. "To us," he toasted, lifting his glass and smiling. He really likes me, I mused. I'm not just one of his friend's wives whom he has to humor. He really sees me as a person, a friend.

"To us," I echoed, and took a too-large swallow of wine. I coughed and sputtered for a few seconds.

"Relax, Judith," he murmured, slowly moving his index finger down the side of his mustache. "I'm on your side, you know."

I reached for his hand and squeezed it. Such a lovely man, I thought. "I guess I'd better tell you why I called this meeting."

"I can guess, Judith. And to say I'm flattered would be a gross understatement."

"You can't guess. This is a biggie."

"Yes, I can. Don't forget, I'm paid to be perceptive. And we've known each other a long time." He raised his eyebrows slightly, just like Oskar Werner did to Simone Signoret in *Ship of Fools*, very caring and tolerant and loving. But they *were* lovers, I thought, suddenly. And we're friends. Claymore and I have the warmest, closest superficial relationship I know of. We're two people who have a great deal in common and who like each other a hell of a lot. He can't think I want to start something with him, can he? I looked at him, with his eyelids lowered, his lips moist and opened seductively to display the even edges of his capped teeth. Can he? It seemed that he could.

"Clay," I began, speaking rapidly to avert mutual embarrassment, "this is a very sticky legal problem and you're going to have to be extremely perceptive. I need a friend. Or actually, a friend of mine needs a friend. Can I lay it on you?" I wanted to add an "old pal" or a "good buddy" but felt it would be too jarring.

"A very sticky legal problem," he repeated, sitting straight up and resting his arms on the table. He smiled, a reflexive lawyer's smile, but it took him a moment to speak. "When you said it was important, I knew it had to be some terribly knotty problem that only I could unravel." He had made a quick recovery. But why had he instinctively assumed that my "important" meant sex?

"Judith, my precious," he continued, "talk to me."

As precisely as I could, I told him the story of Mary Alice's affair, the photography sessions, and the murder. He concentrated, chewing the knuckle on his index finger, until we were interrupted by a waiter. We ordered lunch, and I gave him a quick sketch of Fleckstein's reputation. "Wasn't one of your partners representing him?" I asked.

"Yes, but I didn't know much about the details—just the usual office gossip. But, holy shit, Judith, this is terrific. Much better than an SEC fraud. I love it."

"Clay, be serious."

"Judith, I have a Nikon. Do you think she'd let me take some pictures of her feet? I'm partial to feet, you know."

"Clay, please."

"I'd waive my fee. Just for a few shots. I could get an interesting angle from her arch and . . ."

"Look, this poor woman's life is about to go down the tubes. You're the only one who can help her."

"You're appealing to my ego."

"Of course."

"All right, I'll be serious." The waiter came with our order, veal francese for me, osso buco for Claymore. "Judith," he said, his fork poised for the kill, "she has to go straight to the police."

"Come on! How can she? What if her husband found out? And what if they don't have the pictures? Wouldn't that only implicate her unnecessarily?"

"Judith, my angel, my life's delight, shut up and listen. She should go to the police, but with an attorney. But, first, she has to take a lie detector test."

"What do you mean? I thought they weren't admissible. What good would a lie detector test do?"

"Judith, are you going to second-guess me or listen? Did you come here for fun and games or for professional advice?"

"Sorry."

"All right. As I was saying, she should have a test. Now, you are correct in saying that lie detectors are not generally admissible in court, although there are exceptions that I won't bother going into. How's your veal?"

"Delicious. Your osso buco?"

"Adequate. But anyway, we're not dealing here with a court proceeding. She should take the test with one of the better firms I can recommend. They're up to about seven or eight hundred dollars now, but if you go to a less reputable place, the police will be far less likely to accept the results. Understand?"

"Yes." If he brought the same intensity to bed that he brought to the law, he'd be superb. The thought briefly flitted through my mind that maybe I had been too eager to avoid a misunderstanding.

"Now, she has the test taken secretly, and if she passes, and note that I said if, we bring the results to the police. To the D.A., actually. I have a good working relationship with a couple of assistant D.A.s in Nassau County, and I'm sure they'd be courteous. The important thing here is to nip it in the bud. If they've found his pictures, and I'd say it's quite likely that he held on to them, then it's only a matter of time before they confront your friend Mary Alice."

"Can I ask you something now?"

"You already have."

"You're cute, Clay, cute. Now, look, are lie detector tests infallible?"

"No, of course not. A person might be very emotional and that could give a misleading reading. Or a pathological liar might be able to get by entirely. I don't know. Some lawyers swear by them, but I've seen a couple of cases that make me very leery. Anyway, your friend wouldn't have to make a public announcement that she was taking the test. If she passes, then we take the results to the authorities. They know it's not infallible too, but they'll give it a lot of weight."

"Do you think it can be done without her husband finding out?"

"Maybe. If she does it fast. You have to realize, Judith, that the cops aren't children. All they want to do is solve the case, and they recognize the value of discretion."

At least, I thought, pushing a few grains of risotto around my plate, there's hope for Mary Alice. I peered up at Claymore and realized he had been staring at me. "Judith," he sighed.

"Yes?" I responded, feeling a tremendous sense of foreboding.

"Are you planning on finishing your veal?" I lifted the slice of veal onto his plate, and he ate it in two large bites. "Very nice," he pronounced, and he passed the next half hour recalling the good times he and Bob had had at Columbia—rushing fraternities, getting drunk, double-dating. "You know," he told me over espresso, "Bob always dated very bright, competent women. But you're the only one who had a sense of humor. I wonder if he realizes it."

"Sure. Our marriage has been one long gale of laughter."

"Is everything okay, Judith?"

"Everything's fine, Clay. Really."

Then, as we stood up to go, he said: "Your husband is a lucky man."

"Clay, that's right out of a grade C movie."

"I know. But being clever is so exhausting. I try to be trite at least once a day. It's relaxing."

We walked downstairs, retrieved our coats, and strolled back to Fifth Avenue. The air was still and cold and heavy clouds of snow descended onto the sidewalk.

"Thanks for lunch. And for your help."

"My pleasure."

"Clay." He looked deep into my eyes. "I'm glad you're my friend."

"Thanks," he said. "You know, they didn't predict snow this morning."

We kissed and said goodbye, vowing to get together soon so Bob and I could meet his newest girlfriend, a textile designer who was six feet tall. Then, slightly woozy after two glasses of wine, I managed to propel myself onto the two-fifty train. In less than three hours in Manhattan, I considered, there had been more action for me than in all the years in Shorehaven. Jonathan. Clay. But so what? If I had married a Jonathan, he might still be loitering in front of Gucci's, saying hi to strange women, while I wiped the kiddies' noses or taught a seminar on New Deal agencies. And with Clay,

I'd have a duplex on Central Park West and an over-stuffed ass rubbing mine every night in an antique brass bed. Or a charter membership in the Former Mrs. Katz Club. Claymore had been married three times and would doubtless try and try again.

So I had Bob. Fine-looking. Intelligent. Sexually competent. Pleasant to our children. I could have married a Bruce Fleckstein.

Chapter Eight

"The wages of sin," Mary Alice intoned, as she trudged into my living room the next morning. She looked objectively rotten, her freckled face blotchy with no makeup, her small body lost in a pair of baggy black slacks and a loose gray sweater.

"What are the wages of sin?" I inquired.

"I forget the rest of the quote," she sighed. "Judith, answer this question if you can. Why do we have this drive to destroy ourselves? Why can't we be content to live a simple, peaceful existence, cultivating one or two really meaningful relationships?"

"Damned if I know. Do you want to hear what the lawyer said?"

"Yes, of course. Here I am, babbling on and on, when you've gone out of your way to help me. To be a friend. And you know what they say about a friend in need, don't you?"

"Right. Okay, Mary Alice, let me tell you about Claymore Katz."

"Is Claymore Katz really his name?"

"No. It's really J. Winthrop Aldrich IV, but he felt it wasn't ethnic enough."

"Really? I've never heard of that. The other way around . . ."

"I'm just kidding, Mary Alice. Now, let me tell you what he had to say." Trying to sound as cool and rational as possible, as if we were discussing a minor legal problem involving a contractual dispute or a real estate transaction, I related my conversation with Claymore, including his suggestion about taking a lie detector test. She looked almost lost in the wing chair, a child with crow's feet, staring at me intently. A fine imitation of intelligent concentration. Possibly the real thing. When I finished, she breathed deeply and said: "I have to think about it."

"Is there anything particular that's bothering you?" I asked.

"No, nothing special."

"Is it the money?"

"No."

"Are you worried about Keith finding out?"

"Not really. Not if the lawyer says they can keep it quiet."

"Then what's the matter?" She shrugged her shoulders. "Look, Mary Alice, you're the one who has to make the decision, but Claymore did say time was an important factor. The longer you wait, the more chance you have of the police finding the photographs and tracing them to you."

"I know. I know." She tilted her head in the other direction. "Judith, would I have to tell the lawyer the whole story?"

"Well, you wouldn't have to count the hairs on Fleckstein's chest for him, but you would have to go into some detail."

"How did you know that Bruce had hair on his chest?"

"I didn't. I made an assumption to illustrate a point."

"Well, he did have hair on his chest. Lots. Very curly."

"That's nice," I breathed. She had a gene·programmed for digressions, a mind born to meander.

"And would I have to tell the lie detector man everything? Or the lie detector woman. It's interesting, isn't it, that we insist on sexually stereotyping every profession."

"Yes, you'd have to tell him." I sighed. "Or her. But look, Claymore Katz is a very urbane human being. He's not going to sit in judgment over you. He's been divorced three times. I think he's immune to shock."

"Is he good-looking?"

"No, Mary Alice. He's not good-looking."

"Then how come he was able to attract three different women?"

Maybe Fleckstein took the pictures to blackmail her into silence, I mused. If you say one more word, he threatened, I'll send these pictures to the *Shorehaven Sentinel*. Now shut up and fuck. "I'll give you Claymore's office number, Mary Alice. If you want to call him, you can. Now, would you like a cup of coffee?"

"No. I'm off stimulants."

"Well, keep me company." In the kitchen, I reached up into the cabinet and withdrew my mug with the big "J" on it. "Can I get you anything?" I asked.

"Some water at room temperature with the juice of half a lemon."

"With or without pits?" I inquired.

"Oh, Judith. I know when you're teasing me. Without pits."

I began making small talk. Of course, with Mary Alice, anything but small talk was a waste of words, but I managed to make her feel more at ease. I was at an uncomfortable advantage. I knew her life, her fantasies. All she knew about me was what I chose to tell her. But, then, she had chosen to confide in me.

"Did Bruce ever talk personally to you?" I asked suddenly.

"Well, of course," she answered, casting her eyes down in an attempt at modesty.

"No, I mean about himself, his life, his family, his friends."

"Not really. A little, maybe."

"Did he ever say anything about Norma, his wife?"

"I know her name," she snapped. "Not much. Well, he did say they had grown apart and that she was cold in bed but that he couldn't leave her because one of their children was hyperkinetic."

"Oh." I'm generally confused by statements that are supposed to be self-explanatory but really aren't. I decided to let it pass. "Do you think she knew about you and Bruce? Or that Bruce was having an affair with someone?"

Mary Alice smoothed her fine blond hair with her tiny, babylike hands. "No," she asserted. "I'm sure she didn't know, because he said he could always account for every minute of his time."

"What did he mean by that?" I've had weeks of frenetic activity and couldn't account for more than a half hour.

"Well, he'd call her. From the motel." I must have stared at her, because she sat straight up and began to explain. "You see, he'd tell her he was at the dental clinic at North Shore Hospital, about to start working there, and that he missed her. That way she couldn't call his office and find he was taking too long for lunch."

"I see. Well, then, did he ever mention anything about his business affairs? Was he making enough money?"

"He once said there's more to life than just being a periodontist. He wanted to experience everything and have style."

"What did he mean by style?" The cool, long-fingered elegance of characters in a Noel Coward play came to mind. But Bruce Fleckstein's hairy chest sticking out of a flowered Qiana shirt?

"Style? I don't know," she admitted. "But he wore black underwear."

"Black underwear." If I found a man pleasing enough to join in a motel room, what would I do if he unzipped his fly to display black underwear? Would I laugh? Would I politely excuse myself? "Mary Alice, did he ever mention anything about pornography?"

"He showed me some pictures a couple of times." She wiped the moisture from her glass off the table, folded her napkin neatly, and placed it in the garbage can. "Do you have any tissues?" she asked.

"Upstairs in the bathroom. What kind of pictures?"

"Pictures. You know, Judith." She was beginning to sound exasperated. She gazed angrily into the garbage.

"I don't know, Mary Alice. Tell me."

"Pictures. Of women doing things. Like playing with themselves. Or using a big thing."

"Thing," as I had known since about age eight, was a cutesy synonym for penis. "Using a big thing? Do you mean a dildo?"

"Yes. I need a tissue." She walked out of the kitchen, the heavy, lumbering walk of someone hugely obese or terribly tired. A moment later she returned, clutching a wad of green tissues.

"What kind of pictures were they, Mary Alice?" She gazed at me blankly. "I mean, were they in color? Professional-looking?"

"I don't remember. I think they were in color."

"Were they taken with a Polaroid? Were they square? Sort of stiff?"

"Yes," she whispered, staring at the white tile floor. "I have to go home now."

"Okay. I'll speak to you in a couple of days. Do you have Claymore's number?"

"Yes." I followed her into the living room, where she retrieved her jacket from the couch. "I'll speak to you," she said.

"Fine. Don't forget that if you're going to take that lie detector test, time is a factor."

"I won't. Bye." I watched as she strode rapidly down the path toward her white Mercedes. Keith had its neg-

109

ative, in black. Then, drawing a deep breath to insulate myself from the cold, I chased after her.

"One more question," I called over the purr of the car's ignition. She peered straight ahead, as though I hadn't spoken. "Did he show you those pictures before or after he took pictures of you?"

"After." She gunned her engine and roared out of the driveway.

I stood watching her car's exhaust trail waft over the snowy lawns until I realized that my ankles and feet were painfully cold. I dashed inside, taking a deep breath of the dry, heated air. Mary Alice had seemed so startled when I suggested that the photographs had been taken with a Polaroid, just as hers were. Or had it been an act? Could she really have repressed the unavoidable conclusion that M. Bruce liked to show his work around? Had she been that stupid, that pathetically passive, that she had not confronted him immediately?

And, I wondered, climbing upstairs, why hadn't she called Claymore immediately? She had asked for legal advice and gotten it. Was she afraid she'd be too emotional and flunk the lie detector test? Could she really believe that by gritting her teeth and letting time pass, the whole thing would go away?

I had vague answers to these questions, but the unfathomable one remained: Why had she let this happen to her? I could comprehend part of it, certainly. But it was as if I were holding a diamond in my hand. I could count the facets, ascertain the carat weight, probe for carbon flaws. And yet, despite exhaustive examination, the damned thing wouldn't sparkle for me.

For example, I realized I had as much prurient interest as the next person. At a fraternity party at Wisconsin, I had been barely able to contain my delight in viewing *Three Sailors and a Girl,* complete with false noses and a cast of four abysmally unattractive people, all with bad skin. It wasn't *Wild Strawberries,* but I reveled in it, roaring when the ejaculate rushed back into the penis when the film was rewound. But it did not in the least tempt me to take off my plaid skirt and blue tights and pose.

I had no trouble at all understanding Mary Alice's need for a passionate sexual encounter. After all, what more is demanded from any of us besides a clean kitchen floor, two or three or four reasonably amiable children, and a steak and salad at seven o'clock? No one even cares any more if we can type. But a lover would. A lover would notice that we shave under our arms twice a week. Or that we reread *King Lear* once a year.

But Mary Alice and Scotty and several other women had gone beyond a little extramarital clitoral stimulation, beyond sharing their bodies and their thoughts. They had given Fleckstein their core of privacy, their soul. Or had he taken possession of them? Had he been an evil to be exorcised? Thinking it over, I knew that Lucifer as periodontist was too banal, even for Shorehaven. And isn't a contract with the devil a two-party agreement?

And how open should we be? I could not imagine telling Bob everything, even in those days in graduate school when I loved him without qualification. I kept back my sexual fantasies as I kept back my other fantasies—my Pulitzer prize in history, the friends of his I'd date after he died at forty of a heart attack.

Perhaps, if he insisted, I would own up to wanting a Pulitzer prize, but I wouldn't give him even an outline of my acceptance speech.

I truly could not comprehend Mary Alice's letting herself be persuaded by a stranger, albeit a slick one, to tell all—and then allow it to be recorded for posterity. What did she hold back, keep for herself? Or was I wrong? Was it better to let everything go, to divest oneself of all those quirky little vestiges that adhere to the psyche, to say to the world, "So what?"

I mulled this over all day but came up with no answers. When Kate came home from school, I asked her what she had done. "Nothing much. We talked about Japan." She too had her world. Would she grow out of it and lie in bed with a boy her first week at Radcliffe or Brown and tell him everything? Or would she be a chip off the aging block, a throwback to the outmoded Era of Privacy, her mother's daughter?

By eight forty-five the next morning, Thursday, I grew weary of thinking alone. I called Nancy, my last iron in the fire, and invited myself over.

"All right. I'll just call Little Cupcake and tell him not to bother dropping by. Maybe he'll write up a report on the Fleckstein murder and mail it to me. These days, it doesn't pay to be subtle."

"Can I come over early tomorrow morning? Before you start working?"

"I guess so. I should have something to tell you. I just happened to mention the murder, and he said he's been hearing about it for the last couple of weeks till it's coming out of his ears. Of course, that does make sense because the poor sweet thing doesn't have anything like a brain to absorb what other people do."

"Doesn't it bother you," I asked, tapping my fingers against the phone, "that Cupcake is so, so unendowed mentally? I mean, if you're going to have an affair, it seems to me you'd want someone you could talk to, even for just a few minutes afterwards."

"Doesn't bother me a bit. He's a darling. I like him."

"But wouldn't you rather have someone with more of an intellect?"

"No. Would you?"

"We're not talking about me."

"Yes, we are," she said. "I'll see you tomorrow."

Be honest, I commanded myself. If I were going to indulge in a little fun between the breakfast dishes and the school bus, I wouldn't select a partner on the basis of IQ either. Bob had enough intelligence. He also had enough sexual expertise to satisfy me, at least in the purely mechanical sense. For what, then, would I trade in the security, the reflexive closeness, the familiarity, the occasional interesting conversation, the tolerable sex? Not for a roll in the hay with a semiliterate Cupcake. And not for a couple of throwaway remarks about my substance as a hairy, braceleted arm slid under my sweater. Then for what? Maybe for fun. Not for laughs, but for fun. Thinking about it, I hadn't had any real fun with Bob in about six or seven years. But can you abrogate your marriage vows on the basis of Lack of Fun, a Dearth of Enjoyment?

By the time I drove to Nancy's the next morning, I was quite cranky, annoyed at everything from Bob's unvarying "Good morning to you" to having to stop at the gas station to see why the station wagon was making an ominous gagging sound. The real reason for my pique, I knew, was that at some point I would have to make several changes in my life. Or not make them.

"Shit," I muttered, as I pulled into the long driveway of Nancy's house. Although it really wasn't Nancy's house as much as it was her husband's. Larry, ten years out of Yale's School of Architecture and fourteen years into his trust fund from his family's paper business, had bought a twenty-room Victorian monster overlooking Long Island Sound and then had completely gutted the inside. The result was a sweep of glistening white ceramic floors, white furniture, white walls, relieved only by the chrome frames of the white-on-white embossments made by a friend of his, a graphic artist. Everywhere there were built-in drawers, bins, closets, and cabinets to preclude the possibility of clutter. Even the children's rooms, up the transparent spiral staircase made of some exotic form of plastic, were a glaring shiny white, although Larry conceded that they could have two stuffed animals each on their beds—providing he approved of their choice of color.

So, once in the door, we scurried into Nancy's office, the only room in the house that had escaped Larry's pristine vision. Her desk, strewn with copies of *Foreign Affairs* and *Economist* and *Cosmopolitan,* was a giant affair of tortuously carved oak. On the wall opposite the door was a large, wood-framed Victorian couch, covered in a dull-looking fabric that had probably once been a shiny red, white, and green chintz, but now had the dry, faded appearance of flowers long forgotten in a vase. The only other furniture was a pair of ladderback chairs, with needlepoint cushions sewn by Nancy's cousin Betty—with the invitation "Set right down" in a sturdy continental stitch. Nancy kept the room as a reminder of her roots, a once-gracious way of life now grown musty and obsolete. Also, she knew its existence within the house disturbed Larry. When he took clients on the grand tour, he'd whisk them by her office door, mumbling that it led to the air conditioning equipment. He couldn't laugh at it; it was worse than having a lunatic old aunt hidden away in the attic.

"Could you open a window in here?" I asked Nancy.

"Why? Does it smell?"

"It's a little stuffy."

"Are you here to criticize or to hear about the murder?"

"I'm here to criticize," I said and opened a window. The air was damp and icy cold, but preferable to the stale atmosphere of the office. Nancy embraced the spectrum of old southern bugaboos: handling frogs will give you warts, drafts are immediately followed by influenza, eating capon makes men lose their potency. "Don't panic," I reassured her, "I'll close it in a minute."

"In a minute I could catch a chill and die."

"So talk fast." I closed the window and sat on the couch.

"Well, all Cupcake is hearing is the gossip. The precinct isn't directly involved in the case. I gather that whenever there's a murder, there's a special homicide unit that does all the investigating. But they rely on the precinct to fill them in on local color. Of which there is an abundance in this case. Anyhow, he says that everyone in the entire world is a suspect. The Mafia, Brucieboy's entire family, every woman he ever laid a hand on. And your neighbor, the Great American Mother. That redheaded little flower, who's always cheerful."

"You mean Marilyn Tuccio?" I asked, trying to sound astonished.

"Yes. Seems that she made some kind of a threat against Brucie to his nurse. They think she might be some kind of religious fanatic who wants to cleanse the world."

"That is the most asinine thing I have ever heard in my entire life. She's not a religious fanatic. She's a practicing Catholic."

"Same thing."

"It's not the same thing," I insisted. "And she didn't threaten him, for God's sake. She just made some offhand remark to his nurse that he'd get into trouble if he kept coming on to every creature he met who had a vagina. Well, you know, Marilyn didn't say it quite that way, but that's what she meant."

Nancy lit a Chesterfield and picked a shred of tobacco off her tongue with long white fingers. Of all the people I know, only she still smokes unfiltered cigarettes. If you're going to kill yourself, she announced, at least do it with taste and dignity. "You spoke to Marilyn Tuccio about the murder?" she asked.

"Yes. Just briefly. A detective came around asking questions, so I mentioned it to her."

"I see. Well, getting back to the list of suspects, the nurse is also in the top ten. It seems Bruce was filling one of her cavities and she was pressuring him to get a divorce."

"Okay. Now let me get this straight. There's no one particular person who's a suspect?"

"Well, as I said, Cupcake is not exactly at the center of the investigation. But apparently the boys at the precinct are just tickled about this case. I mean, what do they have around here? A couple of robberies, a few kids getting high and smashing up their daddies' cars? This is the juiciest thing that's happened in years. And they just love the idea that Bruce was sticking it to all the local ladies. But Cupcake says that the case is wide open. Bruce made so many enemies that almost anything is a possibility."

"What do you mean by enemies? Real enemies?"

"Well, he didn't do anything blatantly terrible. But Jim—Cupcake—spoke to one of the homicide men who was interviewing people at Bruce's club, and this fellow said that old Bruce made everyone nervous. I mean, each of the members knew a few of the ladies Bruce was sleeping with, and they were all awed by his success. Also, the homicide man said they were all afraid of Bruce's fatal charm, that he could have been zapping *anyone*, even their own wives. Also, he was involved in some strange business deals."

"Like the pornography thing?"

"That, yes, and some franchise operation that wasn't on the up and up and a deal with buying and selling gold that was beyond Cupcake's ability to comprehend."

"So, in other words, what they have is that Fleckstein was a runaround and a wheeler-dealer and he made a lot of people uncomfortable. Right?" Nancy nodded. "What else did you get?" She lifted her hands, ran them over her auburn hair, and smiled. "Come on," I urged, "be serious."

"Okay, but it will take great effort. There were no fingerprints in Fleckstein's office, no fingerprints that didn't belong. But Jim says any self-respecting killer has enough sense to wear gloves, But they did find something interesting. You'll love this."

"What? What?"

116

"Pictures. Some of Brucie's pretty pictures. Cupcake says the boys at the precinct are almost delirious with joy. The captain finally got disgusted and put them in his safe, but then the homicide guys told him they wanted everyone to have a look—that maybe they'd recognize one of the subjects."

"God!"

"Now here's the interesting part. They only found about seven or eight pictures, and they were sort of stuck behind one of his drawers. You know, those skinny little drawers dentists use to keep their tools in. Jesus, Brucie should have kept his tool in a drawer. Maybe he wouldn't be dead now."

"Is it really so strange that they found only a few pictures?"

"Sure was. Because the drawer itself was completely empty. The pictures they found were kind of wedged in back. And they found a piece of paper, like the corner of a picture, stuck to the back part of the drawer. They think the murderer might have gone through the office, found the pictures, and taken them."

I eased off my shoes and put my feet up on the couch, trying to find a way to let my back muscles relax. "But Bruce could have decided to take the pictures. I mean, he might have wanted to get rid of them."

"Listen, Sherlock, I'm a step ahead of you. Jim says that a few of the drawers weren't completely closed, including the one with the pictures. And they were broken into."

"So they think the murderer was after the pictures?"

"Well, they're leaning toward that, but they're not really certain. Listen, it could have been a completely casual killing and the murderer just happened to find them. Maybe he took them home to get his rocks off. Or maybe your neighbor took them away to burn them so they couldn't corrupt any more souls."

"Nancy, she's not a religious nut. Look, I go to temple sometimes. Does that make me a religious fanatic?"

"No, but it certainly detracts from your claim that you're a rational human being. I mean, the chopped liver and the Yiddish expressions are charming, but you don't have to drag God into it."

I sighed, knowing how futile an argument would be. "All right. You're wrong, but I'm not going to pursue it. What else did Little Cupcake have to say?"

"That was it," she said. I believed her. Nancy's memory is excellent. She can interview a celebrity for an article and recall the entire conversation without referring to her notes. Slowly, stretching, talking casually, we left the office and walked downstairs, the sparkling white rooms more glaring than bright sunlight after a movie matinee.

"I wish," I said, as I sat in a plexiglass kitchen chair, "that I could have asked Cupcake a few questions."

"Why not? Give him a call, a little sweet talk. He likes tits." She stood at the refrigerator, holding a bottle of Chablis. Expertly, she extracted the cork.

"Before noon?" I asked, eyeing the wine.

She put the cork on the white formica counter and turned to me. "When are you going to stop trying to reform me?"

"It's just that it bothers me to see you drinking so much. It can't be doing you any good."

"How do you know? Do I seem miserable? Sick? Deranged?"

"No. But have you ever wondered why you drink so much?"

"No. I know why. I enjoy it. And I enjoy writing and fucking and nice clothes. Just accept it. Accept me. As I am. As I accept you. Do I ask you why you're in such a twit over this murder?"

"No, but I'll be glad to talk about it. I mean, if you really want to hear . . ."

"But I don't. I accept the fact that you find this murder very interesting. Now, what are you going to do about it?"

"I don't know," I answered.

"Why don't you just pay a call on some of the people involved. Ask questions. If you want to be a detective, be a detective."

"Come on, Nancy. How could I? What excuse could I give?"

"Are you smart, Judith?"

"Yes. Very."

"Then you'll think of something."

Chapter Nine

I needed time. I had to concentrate on the murder, determine how to reach the principals in the Fleckstein case. There had to be a way for me, me, who had spent the four weeks preceding my qualifying exams in French and German reading a bookcase full of whodunits. Me, who devoured mounds of Dorothy Sayers and John Dickson Carrs, piles of Christies, mountains of Stouts. But the weekend was too hectic. Saturday morning, Joey climbed into our bed at six-thirty, cuddled in the crook of my arm, and threw up on the quilt. He said: "I don't think I feel so good." A mere stomach virus, but I spent the day trailing after him with a glass of ginger ale and peering closely to look for blotches or pustules or rashes. By evening, he was well. I was enervated. But at Bob's insistence, we kept a date with his newest client.

We met them at a local seafood restaurant. Walking from the parking lot, I noticed Bob's head lowered, as if to protect his face from the wind—but there wasn't even a breeze.

"I know how you feel," I said warmly. "It's no fun giving up a perfectly good Saturday night for strangers."

Bob stopped between a Seville and a BMW. "He's not a stranger. He's a client and a damned good one too." He sniffed and strode toward the entrance, with me two lengths behind, teetering on too-high heels that

Bob claimed made my legs look better. I hadn't asked better than what. Or whose.

The latest superstar in the Singer Associates firmament was a buck-toothed toy manufacturer. His wife was a large-boned, matronly child psychologist. Bob had told me she worked with disturbed children. She looked as if she could cure autism by merely clutching a child to her shelf of a bosom. She and I smiled over drinks, beamed over menus, proclaiming that we had heard wonderful things about the other. The men discussed a survey on consumer trust and faith in the toy industry, shaking their heads at the cynicism of the American consumer. As we reached the end of our clam bisque, I excused myself to call and check on Joey.

"He's okay, darling," Bob hissed. "Stop worrying."

"That's all right," Sylvia the psychologist said. "I think her concern is very touching."

"Listen to my Sylvia, Bob," ordered Lou the Toy Tycoon. "She's a real pro when it comes to mamas and kiddies."

Bob obeyed. Lou was good for a fifty thousand dollar a year retainer; he needed all the favorable publicity Bob could get him. His overadvertised leading line, a doll called Saucy Suzette and her black soul sister Lovely Laverne, was in frantic demand. But their limbs tended to break easily when youngsters took off their Naughty-Nighty Negligee to change them into their Peachy-Beachy Bikini, leaving the kids with ten-inch, ten-dollar amputee dolls. The Federal Trade Commission was not amused.

"He's fine," I said, returning from the telephone booth. At my place was a two-pound lobster and a small mountain of French fries.

"I told you he was all right," Bob said. I smiled sweetly at Lou and Sylvia. They smiled back. We plunged into our seafood with an intensity bred from the realization that all small talk had been exhausted.

"Mmmm," we said. "Delicious." "Would you like to try one of my mussels?" "No thanks, but how about a clam?"

Sylvia looked up. "What a nice community this is. I mean, to support such a good restaurant." I began to feel a real empathy for her; she was finding the evening as painful as I was.

"Shorehaven is a nice town," I agreed.

"Didn't you have a murder here recently?" Lou chimed in. He had refused a bib and had two blotches of butter on his tie.

"Yes," I enthused. "It's caused quite a stir around here."

"Judith, dear, let's skip the gory details," Bob said, his mouth finding its way into a pleasant smile.

"You're a psychologist," I said to Sylvia, looking past him. "Let me ask you a question. It seems that the murdered man was a real Don Juan type, spreading joy to quite a few of the local ladies. What makes a man do that?"

"I'll tell you what makes a man do that, little girl," Lou chuckled, his heavy lips shiny from the butter.

"Well," Sylvia said slowly, "that's not really my field. I deal with children, and I'm not a Freudian, but . . ."

"Judith . . ." Bob began.

"But," Sylvia continued, and Bob snapped shut his mouth, "from what I recall, a Don Juan type would have an unresolved Oedipus complex. He'd be seeking his mother in all women, but of course he'd never find her."

"What do you mean by that?" I asked.

"You know what an Oedipus complex means, Judith," Bob said.

"I mean," I continued, looking at Sylvia, "how does that manifest itself?"

"I see what you're getting at. Well, even though a Don Juan seem to be hypersexual, he's not really look-

123

ing for genital sex. He's looking for self-esteem, which no one can really give him. So he's doomed to disappointment with every woman he has relations with."

"All right," I said. "I'm with you so far. But this particular guy seemed to be toying with the women. I mean, initially he was charming, very pleasant, but later he became terribly manipulative. Why not just love 'em and leave 'em? Why the need to humiliate?"

"Because they disappointed him. They didn't give him what he wanted. In a sense, he felt they let him down because they complied with his demands for sex."

"What kind of woman would a man like this attract? Would he seek out any special type?"

"I really don't know," she said thoughtfully, rubbing her chin with her left hand. She was wearing probably the largest diamond I had ever seen, a stunner, a real sparkler. "But a Don Juan is very eager to have his needs fulfilled, so he's going to do his best to enchant women. He could be very sensitive, saying just what he thinks the woman wants to hear. And because he's essentially a blank, a cipher, they can read anything into him they want. So he'd probably be able to attract a fairly wide range of women, assuming he's reasonably attractive."

"You know, you're right," I said, full of admiration for her. "He seemed to have very catholic tastes and . . ." Bob kicked my ankle under the table.

"But you've got to understand," Sylvia continued, "that this man would be terribly narcissistic. He has to continually prove his ability to excite women. He couldn't settle down to a deep, mutual relationship."

"Well," I said, "he was married. Could he have a good marriage?"

"I don't see how. People like this are generally quite troubled."

"Does that mean his wife would have to be a sickie too?"

"No. Not necessarily. Unassertive, perhaps, or maybe . . ."

"Judith's really interested in this case. We don't have much excitement around here," Bob explained. He waved his fork with apparent indifference and several strands of coleslaw fell on the table.

"Well," pronounced Lou, "it's not every day that a fella gets bumped off for trying to spread around a little sunshine and light. I mean, what kind of thanks is that for all his trouble?" Sylvia eyed her crab and exhaled softly. She knew she had married a buffoon, I realized. And she wasn't going to do anything about it. A nice, bright lady, maybe a little too sweet, but very decent. And she would stick it out, a poor third after Saucy Suzette and Lovely Laverne, as long as Lou would have her. I ordered ice cream cake with hot fudge sauce for dessert.

"Why did you bring up the murder?" Bob asked the next morning.

"I didn't bring it up. Your client did."

"But you didn't have to go on and on about it."

"I didn't. I just asked Sylvia a couple of questions." My hands were cold, so I put them in my bathrobe pockets. I felt a chewed piece of gum wrapped in a bit of cellophane and a piece of Kate's tinker-toy set. "Why do you think she stays with him?" I asked Bob. "I mean, once you get past her sweetie-pie facade, she's very nice. And he's such a boob."

"He's not a boob. He's a goddamn dynamic guy who built a twenty million dollar a year business from nothing."

"Bob." I reached for his hand. We were having a second cup of coffee after breakfast. "I can understand that he's your client and you have to do a good job for him. But you don't have to love him. I mean, he's the antithesis of everything you've ever cared about."

"You don't just dismiss someone because he isn't sitting in an ivory tower studying Mesopotamian art."

"I'm not. But he's so crass, so simplistic, and she's so . . ."

"She's what? A psychologist? Big deal. You don't have to romanticize every woman who works. And did you see that rock on her finger? Could she have gotten that on a psychologist's salary?"

"Do you think that's why she stays married to him?"

"Judith, is it necessary to analyze every goddamned relationship you come across? In public?"

"I'm interested in people. What's wrong with that? What should I have talked about? Saucy Suzette? I wouldn't let Kate have one if it were the only toy in the world."

"And why did you have to order ice cream cake for dessert?"

"Because I wanted it."

"I ordered a fruit cup. And I'm not getting a double chin."

"Are you trying to tell me I'm getting fat? I'm not."

"But you're going to get there if you don't watch out."

"I haven't gained any weight," I lied.

"Whatever you say, Judith. But, remember, obesity turns me off."

"And charm turns me on." I stood, put the milk back in the refrigerator, and walked out of the kitchen, not looking back.

But the next morning I did penance at the health club—two hours of exercise and swimming. I hate the place. Trim 'n' Slim is a haven for local women who say things like "I want to feel good about my body," and "I'm getting fat," while they search their torsos for an imaginary roll of flab to squeeze. Each morning they arrive there in sleek droves to exercise, lie in the sun-

126

room, relax in the sauna. Then they spend another hour reapplying their makeup and blow-drying their hair.

That morning I tried to make my peace with them, stretching and twisting in the midst of twenty bodies leaner and firmer than mine. "This one is for the inside of the thighs, girls," the instructor said. After the final, agonizing, waist-slimming stretch, I lay in the sunroom for about a minute. It occurred to me there that by the time my skin was a glowing bronze I'd have terminal skin cancer from the ultraviolet light, so I stood up, wrapped my towel around me, and walked into the sauna. The intense pine wood smell was masked by the aroma of sweat, which in turn was disguised by the even stronger smell of perfume. Four women lounged on the three tiers of benches, all, I realized, older than I, and all with tenderly tended bodies. They stopped exercising only on Sundays and once every two or three years to check into the hospital for a little cosmetic surgery.

One of them, a woman in her forties who looked a little like Marlene Dietrich in *Destry Rides Again* had two thin, pale curved lines under her breasts, faint souvenirs of the plastic surgeon's hands. They were ordinary-sized breasts, like two average MacIntosh apples, and I wonder if she had had them made larger or smaller. Another had a huge, fluffy tuft of brown pubic hair, as if she was wearing a wiglet. ("Order one of our special hairpieces," the ad would say, "and get a snatch to match.") A third had an elegant figure with a tiny waist, her absolute perfection marred only by two parallel incisions on her stomach, one straight up and down the middle, a smaller one on her right side. I peeked at her face to see if she was eighteen or forty and swallowed a gasp. It was Brenda Dunck, Bruce Fleckstein's sister-in-law.

She was lying on her side on the top level of benches, her hair wrapped in a turquoise towel, staring at a knothole in the wood near the ceiling. I wanted urgently to do something, say something to her, but although my heart was racing and my lower bowel began signaling for relief, I couldn't think of any way to approach her and dissipate the tension. What could I ask? Did your brother-in-law have a pleasant interment?

She sat up and stretched, her long, perfectly filed dark red nails pointing in ten different directions. What could I say? A mild, curious "Aren't you Brenda Dunck?" sounded far too coy. She stood and daintily made her way down to my level, delicately weaving between the stretched-out bodies of the other women. Suddenly, she glanced in my direction and gave me a sweet, sad smile.

"Hello. Aren't you Scotty's friend? I'm Brenda Dunck."

"Yes, of course," I smiled back. "How are you?" I rose and put my towel around me.

"Well, as well as can be expected." Her toenails were polished in the same deep red as her fingernails. She held the heavy sauna door open for me, and we stepped out into the chilly tiled hallway.

"Shall we have a cup of bouillon?" I suggested. I said "Shall" instead of "Would you like," because it sounded more sophisticated, British almost, and I realized, having seen Brenda with Scotty, that she was trying very hard to be a lady.

"Fine," she concurred, and we walked toward the lockers, me grasping my towel around me and she taking long, slow strides, like a nude bride walking down the aisle. Even her chin was raised, as though she were posing for the photographer who would be making her wedding album. Near the locker room, she took a bathrobe from a row of hooks. It was a white and turquoise terrycloth that perfectly matched the towel on her head. We walked silently into the lounge.

"How do you know Scotty?" she asked as we lay down on the leatherette chaises. The chaises were alternating colors of orange, turquoise, and yellow, and I noted she chose the turquoise one. Had she coordinated her robe with the health club decor?

"Scotty's husband, Drew, prepped with my husband's roommate in graduate school." This was technically true, although we discovered it long after Joey and North had become friends. But I had gotten the word "prepped" in. It was one of those key words that would set Brenda's heart aflutter. I considered working in a reference to my mother as "Mumsy," but I couldn't do it gracefully. "How are all of you doing?" I inquired instead.

"Pretty well. Norma, my sister-in-law, was fairly controlled during the *shiva*—I mean the mourning period."

"I know what *shiva* means," I said. "I'm Jewish."

"Oh. I thought you were. I mean, you look it. Not that there's anything wrong with that; you're just dark."

I smiled. "It comes from centuries under the hot Spanish sun." More bullshit. The closest my family came to being Sephardic was the three days my parents spent in Madrid on their guided United Federation of Teachers' tour. My father took eight rolls of slides and my mother caught dysentery.

The tough, skinny lesbian who ran the locker room, Cookie, came and took our order for two cups of bouillon. Within a minute, she brought two steaming styrofoam cups back to us. Brenda took a delicate sip of the hot liquid and then glanced at me. "I'm terribly embarrassed," she murmured, "but I forgot your name."

"Please, don't be embarrassed," I soothed. "Our meeting was hardly under auspicious circumstances." If I had clipped my consonants just a little more, I would have sounded like Judith Anderson. "My name is Judith Singer."

"Now I remember. Of course." There was an awkward quiet moment. I worried that she would ask me why I went to the funeral.

"I must tell you," I declared, plunging in, "that I am absolutely appalled by the publicity this case has received. Heavens, it must be so terribly trying for the family." *Newsday* had run a series of three enthralling articles on the case.

"It's been awful," she agreed. She drew her feet up close to her body and began to massage her ankles. "I never believed in censorship, but now I do. I mean, freedom of the press can go too far."

I nodded, wondering if Brenda's ankle massage was just a nervous habit, or did she think it kept them thin? "I agree with you. Utterly," I lied. I'm one of those who believes that even to consider tampering with the First Amendment is a cardinal sin. Why am I wasting my time with this bubblehead, I thought, when I could be home working on my dissertation? And then I got an idea. "You know, Brenda, I'm writing my doctoral dissertation on that very subject, First Amendment rights. Maybe that's why your family's case made such a profound impression on me."

"You mean your Ph.D.?" she asked, in such tones of awe that I knew I had said precisely the right thing.

"Yes. The uses and abuses of freedom of the press." I watched that sink in. She nodded and looked serious. "Actually, it would be an absolute boon to my work if I could interview some of the members of your family, some of your brother-in-law's friends, to get their attitudes, their reactions to all the newspaper publicity. Anonymously, of course. But," I allowed graciously, "that might be too much of an interference." She didn't agree, so I kept on talking. "Of course, selfishly, it would make a brilliant illustrative chapter, seeing how an egomaniacal press has the power to destroy a decent, moral American family."

"Well, I don't know," said Brenda. "I guess you could interview me. And I could ask Norma. But I don't know how Dicky, my husband, would feel. I mean, there's been so much attention, and he's very upset about it."

"That's totally understandable. But you might want

to tell him that I could present the proper credentials and give him a signed statement guaranteeing anonymity."

"Well, I could talk to him."

"Wonderful. Just a second." I ran to Cookie's desk in the locker room and grabbed a pencil and gym schedule before she had time to intimidate me. I scurried back to the lounge. "Here," I said to Brenda, scribbling on the paper, "my phone number. Call me any time. And just let me add one thing. I certainly don't want to pressure you, but do you know what your cooperation would do?" She looked at me questioningly. I decided she was just bright enough to realize that she was somehow inferior to other people, but not clever enough to remedy the situation. "Your cooperation, your views, would become part of the historical record, a vivid example that scholars and journalists could study in decades to come."

"I see," she replied. Actually, one of the reasons I hadn't written my dissertation was the feeling that two years of work on a book that, if I was extraordinarily lucky, about twenty people would read, was just not worth it. "I'll speak to Dicky tonight and call you tomorrow or Wednesday. Is that okay?"

"Fine," I said. I wanted to leave then and call Dr. Ramsey, my advisor, and ask for a letter saying that yes, indeed, Judith Singer was a doctoral candidate at New York University. "I would appreciate anything you can do. And," I added, standing up, "I really enjoyed chatting with you."

Brenda smiled and reclined on the chaise. Her eyes closed, and I guessed either the meeting had been trying for her or else it was her usual nap time. Back in the locker room, I mused on how deliciously clever I was. Now I could ask all the questions I wanted to. Beautiful! However, by the time I dressed, I decided that I was incredibly foolish, impossibly dense. Norma and/or Dicky would see through my fiction, laugh at my request. And if they didn't, if they agreed to talk to me, what could I gain? And what if word of this venture got back to Bob? And what about Ramsey? Would he write a letter for me? Would he then expect, in twenty-five days or less, a completed dissertation on the banking community's influence on monetary policy in 1932-1933?

In my car I peered into the rear-view mirror. The sauna notwithstanding, my face was no longer young and dewy fresh. What did I have to lose? My virginity, my independence, my career were gone. Bob wouldn't move out over this. Who else would make his breakfast and iron his shirts? The skin around my eyes was thinning, preparing a fertile field for a crop of wrinkles. I readjusted the mirror and drove home.

With a half hour to spare before Joey's bus arrived, I called Dr. Ramsey. He sounded pleased to hear from me and asked pointedly if I had at last realized the error of my ways.

"I never said I was abandoning my dissertation forever," I reminded him. "I just needed a little time off to raise a couple of children."

"My dear Mrs. Singer, I have seen more fine minds apply for a leave of absence to raise a couple of tykes or to work for a year or two in their family's business. They never return. They go limp under the burden of materialism, and in Academe, a bell tolls for another lost soul."

"Well, I may yet be saved. With your help, of course. Could you possibly send me a letter saying I'm a doctoral candidate? Once the weather gets warm, I may drive up to Hyde Park, and I need some credentials before I can examine any of the papers."

"Why wait for spring, Mrs. Singer? Put on a warm sweater and a pair of galoshes and go now."

"Well, I'll need your letter first."

"It will be posted within the hour."

I replaced the receiver and hugged myself, but not

132

from joy. I felt terribly cold. How rotten, deceiving Dr. Ramsey to further my little game. Now I'd have to finish my dissertation just to prove my sincerity. And, I thought, rubbing my icy hands together, I really didn't want to. Not at all. If I could spend the rest of my life in seminars, reading, talking about American history, I would be deeply satisfied. But I had no desire to teach, no taste at all for intradepartmental warfare. Yet I had to do something. In four or five years Kate and Joey would no longer suffice as an excuse for housewifery. Then what could I tell people who asked me what I did? "Oh, I read a lot and polish silver."

Ah, but clothed in a doctorate, I could simply say, "I teach." And when they asked me what grade, I'd just smile and say, "At the university level." Bob would introduce me as his wife, Dr. Singer. Kate would finally have a good role model, and Joey would view women as professionals and marry a doctor or a lawyer and share the housework with her. And with my own salary, I could pay a housekeeper, order my groceries on the phone, trade in the station wagon for a pale yellow MG.

In keeping with my new image as a competent human being in control of her life, I made a slenderizing lunch of cottage cheese and grapefruit sections. Naturally, when Joey came home, he refused even to consider it. I gave him a peanut butter and jelly sandwich. We shared half a box of Mallomars for dessert.

By evening, I had diagnosed myself as a manic-depressive. I would turn myself in to a quiet sanitarium in upstate New York for four or five years of lithium treatment.

Bob asked: "Is anything wrong? You're so quiet."

"No. Just tired, I guess." Feeling came in great waves. I grew giddy at the prospect of really talking to the Fleckstein family, depressed at the thought of having to write my dissertation, and inconsolable at the idea of not writing it, of continuing my life as it was.

Fortunately, the phone rang at nine o'clock and a soft voice asked: "Is this Judith Singer?"

Brenda Dunck! I assured her that it was and, trying to sound casual, asked how she was.

"Fine, thank you. The reason I'm calling is what we talked about today. You know? Well, I spoke with my husband, and he said I could talk to you if he could listen in and if he could look at what you write to make sure everything's okay. Is that okay?"

"Terrific," I boomed, and then slipping back into my cultured voice, added: "Would your husband be willing to sit for an interview?"

If Dicky refused, then my chances of talking to Norma and the family's friends would be nil.

"He said sure, but he doesn't have much to say. I mean, he said he wasn't surprised at what the newspapers printed because they're in business to sell papers."

"Well, that's an intriguing perspective in itself," I commented. "I'd like to go into that. What causes a person to become cynical? Or to be so realistic, if you look at it from another angle?" I knew that I was trying to make chicken salad out of chicken shit, but at this point, I needed all the alchemy I could get.

"By the way, what school are you going to for your Ph.D.?"

"NYU."

"Oh." Brenda sounded disappointed.

I remembered with whom I was dealing. "It's known for its history department. I was tempted to go to Harvard, but then everyone would have assumed all I could get was second best."

"Oh, you were right," she assured me. We agreed to meet the next evening at eight, at their house. I trotted downstairs and rapped on the door of Bob's darkroom.

"Are you going to come home for dinner tomorrow night?"

"Judith, what do you want from me?" he called from behind the closed door. "I'm up to my ass in work, the goddamn phone never stops ringing. Look, I made it home tonight. Do you think I like working twelve hours a day? Do you think that's my idea of fun?"

"I know, darling," I cooed through the door, trying to sound loving. "But I have to get away from the kids for a couple of hours. Maybe do some shopping or go to the movies with someone if her husband is working late. Would you mind if I got a sitter?"

"No. Go ahead." My Christlike sweetness, my gracious refusal to throw down the gauntlet and call him a neurotic, work-addicted bastard who richly deserved the massive coronary he was striving for, paid off. It generally did.

"Maybe I'll take myself out to dinner," I called.

"Wonderful, Judith. It will do you good." He sounded so relieved. "Is there anything else?"

"No. I'm going up to do the dishes, and I'll probably go right to bed after that."

"Good. Fine. I'll see you in the morning."

When the dishes were finished, I locked myself in the bathroom for an hour of hydrotherapy. The bathroom was the best room in the house, having been built by the previous owner, Sol Slutsky, the Sultan of Plumbing Supplies. Sol may have liked red flocked wallpaper in the dining room, gold-flecked mirrored walls in the living room, but, bless him, he had taste in bathrooms. We gutted every room in the house except the baths. Ours was huge, a shimmering marvel of sea green tile with what Sol had called "all the options." A toilet with a flush more silent than a January dawn, a sunken bathtub big enough for two, a glassed-in shower that converted to a steam room at the twist of a knob, and a bidet; Mrs. Sol—I think her name was Henrietta—had warned me against the bidet, whispering as we toured the house that it would dry up my insides like a prune.

Now, sitting on it, feeling the fountain of lukewarm water rising inside me, I contemplated waiting up for Bob and telling him the truth. "I need a baby sitter because I have to go out and investigate a murder," I would tell him.

"Are you crazy?" he would yell. Or if he were in a more relaxed mood: "Why are we paying taxes, Judith? Don't you think the police have a right to their job?" He would not understand.

In the shower, the steaming water from six spigots spraying my body, I began to relax, to grow mellow, to feel even a bit of compassion for Bob. I knew he hadn't been happy in years, hadn't been happy, in fact, from the day he joined his family's business. He alone had been the holdout, the sensitive Singer too fine, too pure, to join the P.R. game. For years he had held high his well-molded chin and staunchly refused to hear his parents' pleas. And then one night, coming home late after a Dostoevski seminar, he told me he would join Singer Associates. "But only for a year. Just to show them it wouldn't work out."

"But you know it won't work. Why do you have to prove it to them? Let them learn to accept you. It's their problem, not yours."

"Look. It's just for a year, and I'll make a small fortune and then we'll take six months and go to Europe. It'll be okay."

It was okay. Okay for Singer Associates. Bob was gifted. His press releases were gems. He was the most talented flack since Aaron fronted for Moses. So he stayed. We never went to Europe, because his clients would be lost if he were away for more than a week. We bought our house. He joined the City Athletic Club, and began referring to his former doctoral advisor as an "intellectual masturbator." For three years I urged him to quit. He would say, "Soon, soon." And then, finally, he said, "No. I like it. And Judith . . ." I looked at him. "I haven't heard you complaining about having to live on eighty thousand a year." Away from clients, he rarely laughed aloud. He hardly ever read a book. On weekends, he'd take his camera and photograph leaves and flowers, then spend hours in a darkroom enlarging the petals until they ceased to be petals of flowers and became giant membranes. And in all the years, I had never had the courage to ask him if he was unhappy with what he had become. Maybe he was happy, in his own way. Maybe it was me, feeling uncomfortable because the man I was living with was not the man I married.

I turned off the shower and wrapped my hair in a large, soft towel. Perhaps Bob's implicit message was right: I never had it so good. Surely, all the women who flocked to Fleckstein must have been unhappier than I. Why else would they thumb their noses at their husbands and put out for old Bruce? Or was I the truly unhappy one, so dispirited that I lacked the juice to find an alternative to the hollow man who was my husband?

I opened the door and saw Bob lying in bed. He peered at me, large-breasted, long-legged, not perfect, but not bad.

"Hi," I said.

His eyes ranged all over my body. "Judith, don't tell me you haven't gained weight. I can see it in your waist."

"Good night."

"Good night."

Chapter Ten

The Duncks' house was in an area called Shorecrest, an enclave about a quarter of a mile square, featuring three types of houses: a split-level, something called a splanch—an unfortunate marriage of a ranch and a split-level—and a colonial model. Dicky and Brenda had opted for tradition and selected the colonial model. Their mailbox was embossed with a vicious-looking eagle clenching arrows in one talon and their address, a gilt number 14, in the other.

"Hi, hon," said Dicky as he opened the door, his thin goatee jerking upward as he smiled. "Good to see you." He was dressed for breakfast at a Dartmouth reunion: khaki slacks, a properly bled madras shirt, penny loafers without socks. He had captured the elusive essence of WASPdom, I thought. Almost. On his left hand, he wore the optional but acceptable plain gold wedding band, but on his right ring finger was a large gold ring with his initials, R.D., in a sort of Chinese scrollwork design, a tiny diamond twinkling between the two letters. His Bar Mitzvah ring.

"Hi. I'm Judith Singer."

"Sure. I remember you from the funeral. Come in. Make yourself at home." That was difficult. He led me into a living room stuffed with reproductions of colonial American furniture. Five or six chairs, a hutch with lots of tiny drawers, a large couch with spindle legs, a spinning wheel, all in the same gleaming maple finish. The walls and chairs were covered in a red and blue fabric that, at a glance, seemed to be embossed with a minuscule print of apothecary jars and randomly scattered scenes of Mount Vernon.

"Sorry," I said, tripping over a small footstool.

"That's all right." It was Brenda, dressed in a red lounging robe, sitting in a New England rocking chair. I hadn't seen her. A stellar beginning to my detective career. "Would you like coffee?"

"Yes, please." When she had disappeared into the kitchen, I opened an old attaché case of Bob's and took out a notebook and a pen. I was sitting on a ladderback chair, about a foot away from Dicky. I handed him Ramsey's letter, which had arrived in that day's mail. "Here are my credentials."

"Thanks." He read it slowly, his lips moving with each word. I noticed he was rubbing the NYU crest between his fingers. Was he checking out the paper because he was in the printing business, or was he, by a laying on of hands, trying to feel if I were for real?

"Gee. Pretty as a picture and a brain besides," he said, smiling. I smiled back. Words were not coming.

"Are you going to take notes?" he asked, glancing at the notebook. "Because if you are, just write that ole Dicky Dunck thinks newspapers are full of bull doody, and you can quote me. Oh," he hesitated, "pardon my French."

"That's all right. I'd love to quote you, but I won't." He peered at me curiously. "You see," I explained, "I want you to feel free to express yourself as openly as possible, and I think that's best done anonymously. Of course, if you want your name to be used . . ."

"To tell you the truth, darling," and he said "darling" in an easy, unaffectionate Garment Center way, "dolling," and he lowered his voice a little, "I'd just as soon not see the Dunck family name in print again. Except on a stock certificate. Right?" He chuckled twice, in triads, his laughter going up a half note with each new chuckle.

I smiled again, a very self-conscious smile, feeling my upper lip curling under with numbness. "Right," I agreed.

"I mean, a lot of local folks know that Norma is my sister, but ever since all this newspaper publicity, everyone in the whole world knows that a Dunck is involved in this mess. Really, sweetheart, was it necessary to call Norma 'the former Norma Dunck'? Geez, everybody knows her as Norma Fleckstein. I mean, she's not one of those women's libbers who use two names all the time."

I slowly wrote "hostile abt use of Dunck name" in my notebook just to kill thirty seconds.

"Here's coffee," announced Brenda suddenly. The thick blue carpet that stretched from wall to wall had muffled her entrance. She set a tray down on the oversize seat of the spinning wheel; it was their coffee table. We stood, bending low, to put sugar and cream in our coffee.

"Well," I said a moment later, picking up my notebook, "whom shall I interview first?" No takers. "How about you, Brenda?"

"All right." The light from a pair of pewter sconces gleamed on her black hair. It was pulled back into a bun, like a pioneer woman, except that a pioneer woman could not have achieved the intense ebony of Number 46, Clairol Midnight Black.

"As I explained, I'm trying to explore First Amendment privileges vis-à-vis the individual's right to privacy inherent in Anglo-Saxon common law." That sentence, if it could be captured and recycled, could fertilize every front lawn in Shorehaven for the next ten years. Dicky and Brenda looked at me and nodded seriously. "But I want more than a dry recital of legal doctrine and constitutional history. I want humanity: human feelings, human emotions."

"Oh, yes," said Brenda.

"Good. Now, what were your first reactions when you saw the initial accounts in the *Times* and *Newsday*?"

"You mean the first things that were written?"

"Yes. Before the articles dealing with your brother-in-law's legal difficulties."

"Well, I think I just saw that little thing in the *Times,* because it was on the page next to the obituary, and I wanted to see that the obituary had gotten in, because none of us thought to call the *Times* until late the night it happened."

"And how did you feel about seeing the article?"

"Well, I don't know. I mean, it was straightforward and I was very upset, so I don't think I reacted at all." She shrugged her shoulders apologetically.

"Sure you did, sweetie," boomed Dicky, talking to her for the first time since I had arrived. "Remember, you got really p.o.'d when you saw they gave Norma's maiden name, because you said everyone would know we're related to them. Remember?"

Brenda took a deep breath and let it out slowly through pursed lips. "Yes. Now I remember," she said softly, not looking at him. "I was concerned about the children," she said to me. "I was thinking that it was bad enough that their uncle was murdered, and that if our name was somehow dragged into it and associated with the Flecksteins, it might be very difficult for them in school." And for the Duncks in their role as house Jews at their country club.

"I see." I wrote "B embarrassed abt Fleckstein assn."

"You see, we weren't actually all that close," she explained. "I mean, there was some tension, and the only time we all got together was on holidays. We hadn't socialized with them for years."

"And Brenda thought he was a little flashy. Right, sugar? Remember, you said he was crude?"

142

"I may have," she said softly. "But in any case, we weren't terribly friendly with them."

"Because of the tension over your father-in-law's estate?" I asked Brenda. It was not an inquiry destined to be well received. Brenda sat back, stiffly erect in her chair. Dicky's face turned pink, then red, then almost purple. I could see a faint stubble above his ears where he shaved his head. "I see I've shocked you," I said, trying to recover the ground I'd lost. "I meant to."

They stared at me, allowing confusion to mingle with their distaste at my ill breeding. "Look," I continued, "that's the whole point of my dissertation. Newspapers aren't just a series of isolated articles. Once they begin to abuse their power, nothing is sacred. Frankly, I never met either of you before the day of the funeral, and yet I heard about your family dispute from two or three people."

"Well, did you happen to know that we patched up that little quarrel?" Dicky demanded. "Did you happen to hear that?"

"No. And that's just my point. The gossips aren't interested in the fact that you reconciled. All they're interested in is turning a normal family dispute into a *casus belli*, a veritable pitched battle." If I couldn't make them relax, I could at least exhaust them with my verbosity.

"I understand," said Brenda, who obviously didn't. Her eyebrows were pulled together, making two furrows over her small hooked nose. "Anyhow," she continued, "things were patched up. I mean, we weren't close friends, but at least things were more pleasant. I mean, Bruce even got Dicky some business."

"Let bygones be bygones," Dicky muttered.

"What kind of business?" I asked.

"Just some printing," he answered. "For a friend of his. No big deal." We all relaxed a little.

"All right," I said, "let's get to that infamous article about your brother-in-law's association with organized

143

crime figures. How did you feel about that, Brenda?"

"Well, let me think." She took her thumb and index finger and delicately removed a loose eyelash from the outer corner of her eye; she placed it on the edge of an ashtray as though she couldn't bear to flick it away. "I was stunned. Absolutely stunned. I mean, Bruce always seemed to be a nice, decent family man. A professional. The mere thought that he could be mixed up in some shady business was crazy. I mean, beyond my comprehension. Frankly, I still don't believe it. There must be some mistake."

They probably confused your brother-in-law with another Dr. Marvin Bruce Fleckstein, I thought. Dicky leaned forward.

"Those newspaper guys are a bunch of Grade A Number One creepos," he said. "Look, sweetie, I'm not saying he didn't have a few magazines or something in his office. He's a consenting adult, right? But let's not be simps. I mean, didn't your husband ever buy a copy of *Playboy*?"

Yes. He had said he liked the interviews. "Of course. And to be perfectly honest, I've even peeked at them myself."

"See what I mean?" declared Dicky. He slipped his loafers off his sockless feet and stretched out his legs. I glanced down and noticed he bit his toenails. "That kind of stuff may be a little off color, but it's all over the place. It's not pornography." Brenda saw me peering at his toenails and looked upset. I pretended to be concentrating on one of the maple legs of the spinning wheel, about six inches from Dicky's feet.

"In other words," I said, forcing myself to look him straight in the eye, "you believe the article was a total fabrication?"

"Fabrication? You mean a lot of horse manure? Damn straight. Right, angel pie?"

"Yes," answered Brenda, still focusing on his feet, as if her glare could force his toenails to regenerate instantly. She turned to me. "You see, Bruce and I were just friendly. We weren't all that close. But as far as I know, he wouldn't have gone in for those kinds of books or dirty movies or anything like that."

"And as far as you know, he had no contact with anyone involved in organized crime? That was one of the allegations made in the paper," I explained.

"Absolutely, one hundred percent no way," Dicky asserted. "Listen, he may have had a couple of friends with Italian last names, but does that make them Mafia? Holy Moly, if your last name ends in a vowel, the goddamn U.S. Attorney's office starts an investigation."

"Unless your name is Shapiro," I murmured.

"Who's Shapiro?" Brenda asked.

"I get you," Dicky said. "Very cute. Huh, huh, huh. You are one real sharp cookie."

"Seriously, I know what you mean," I added. "My neighbor was your brother-in-law's last patient, and the police have been bothering her like crazy. She's willing to bet it's because her last name's Italian."

"Who is that?" asked Dicky, rather sharply.

"I know," answered Brenda. "Marilyn Tuccio. Am I right?" She looked to me for confirmation. I nodded, feeling uncomfortable; I had violated Marilyn's confidence. Brenda turned to Dicky. "I heard Norma telling someone that the police had asked her about Marilyn, whether Marilyn and Bruce were friendly. The police said that Marilyn was probably the last one to see him alive."

"Oh," said Dicky. "I hadn't heard that. What does her husband do?" Brenda shrugged her shoulders.

"He's a pediatric surgeon," I responded.

"Oh. Not a godfather, if you know what I mean?"

"No," I said. I glanced down at Dicky's toenails again and at the blue veins running through his feet. They matched the rug. "Well, you people have been wonderfully cooperative and I truly appreciate it. One

145

more thing. Could one of you possibly call Norma Fleckstein and see if she'd be willing to talk to me?"

"All right," said Brenda.

"Fine. I'll call you in a couple of days. And thank you so much. Both of you." They smiled at me and stood up. Dicky manipulated his feet back into his shoes. "And, of course, when my dissertation is written, you'll get a copy."

We walked to the door, and Brenda handed me my coat, a large yellow plaid, like a good-quality horse blanket, that I had bought during my second year of college.

"I love your coat," Brenda said, fingering it. "So English."

"Thanks. And thanks again for your help. I'll call you."

"Bye," said Dicky.

"Bye-bye," said Brenda.

As I drove through the dark streets, illuminated in patches by reconverted barn lamps and plaster, white-faced jockeys clutching flickering lanterns, I tried to make some sense of my interview with the Duncks. I couldn't. My mind was crammed full of a hundred different thoughts, packed so tight that it was impossible for a single idea to surface. Dicky. Brenda. How could she sleep with a man who munched on his toenails? Why hadn't I pressed for the names of Bruce's Italian friends? Why hadn't I asked where they were on the evening of the murder? Why hadn't I asked Mary Alice where she had been that same evening? Why did Fay believe Bruce was evil? It was a strong word. Why not fatuous? Absurd? Why not call him a cad, a bounder, a disturbed human being who used women to stifle his own personal pain?

As I pulled into the driveway, I saw Bob's car parked in front of the garage door. He had beaten me home. I stowed the attaché case under the front seat of the sta-

146

tion wagon and strolled inside, trying to look casual. "Hi," I called out. Bob was sitting in the living room, jacket off, but tie still on; he was only half relaxed.

"Hi," he answered, his long, slender legs stretched out in front of him. "Where were you?"

"No place special." I leaned down and kissed him lightly on the cheek. "I mean, no one was free and I didn't want to go to a movie by myself, so I just drove around and did a little shopping."

"Shopping? That's nice. Where?" He was the casual cop, coolly manipulating the interrogation so the suspect would get a false sense of security.

"At A&S." A local department store. "They're open every night." Damn, I thought. I just should have said "A&S" so he could have checked and discovered it was open. This way, I was volunteering too much information. It looked suspicious.

"Buy anything?"

Why not simply tell him where I had been? What could he do to me? Disapprove? Yell? Throw a temper tantrum on the living room floor? "No. You were right. I did gain a few pounds. Nothing I tried on looked right." Not bad for a spontaneous lie. But how do adulterers handle it? Do they have a prearranged alibi with a friend? Do they make up a detailed scenario so intrinsically boring that their spouses tune out after the first sentence?

"Well, let's go upstairs," he said.

"Okay." I tried to sound casual. "Did you pay Mrs. Foster?"

"Yeah. You owe me four fifty."

We walked into the bedroom and he closed the door quietly. "How was your day?" I asked.

"Fine." He watched me as I undressed, his finger crooked over the knot of his tie. He watched as I took off my bra. Intently. I wondered if he were really anxious for sex or just examining his territory to make sure there was no scarlet "A" on either breast. I took off my

147

slacks, and then my underpants. If he were any sort of detective, he'd notice that half the elastic was hanging out of the waistband and realize that I'd never wear a pair of torn pants if I had a rendezvous to fuck another man.

"Come here," he said. Maybe I was wrong. He had just been standing there, waiting for me because he wanted me. He knew I wouldn't do anything. Just as I knew that he wouldn't. He was too regular in his sexual habits, too involved with his clients to risk being away from his desk in a hotel with a woman and missing a phone call. "Judith." I walked to him and put my arms around his neck.

He didn't respond. Instead, he stuck his finger into my vagina.

"Bob. What are you doing?"

"Nothing." He took his finger out. I pulled away.

"What do you mean, 'nothing'?"

"Nothing. What's the matter? Can't I touch you?"

Of course, he could touch me. But in all the years we'd been together, he'd always started out with at least two long kisses, to show me he wasn't out just to get laid. "What do you mean, 'Can't I touch you?' You know you can, but you never just stick your finger into me, like I'm a pot of chocolate pudding." Thank God, I mused, I was as dry as an eighty-year-old Victorian maiden aunt. Tension seems to draw my juices to other parts of my body, joints that grow stiff with fear and need fast lubrication.

"Do we have to do things the same way all the time?" he demanded. "You're the one who always wants to try new things, Judith. So I try and what happens? You pull away."

I went to my closet and put on my nightgown. "I'm not pulling away."

"Good," he said, and took off his clothes and sat on the edge of the bed. Outside the wind began to blow. A branch scraped against the window. "Come here."

"No."

"No? What does that mean?" He looked up at the ceiling, as if imploring the gods to help him understand. "Don't you love me?"

"Yes, I love you. I just don't feel like doing anything tonight."

"Are you tired?"

No. "Yes."

"Christ. I thought a night out would do you some good." He stomped over to his pajama drawer, as best he could with bare feet, and put on a pair of blue ski pajamas his mother had given him for Chanukah. Then he marched to his side of the bed and climbed in. I got into my side and leaned back against the headboard. "I know why you did it," I said to him.

"Look, Judith, can't we talk tomorrow? I'm exhausted."

"Sure. Tomorrow you'll be home by ten and you'll only be tired. Then we can have a real friendly, peppy talk."

"Is sarcasm necessary?"

"Would you prefer blatant hostility?"

He puffed up his mouth and cheeks with air and slowly, squeezing his lips together like a tire valve, breathed out. It was a signal that despite his staggering fatigue, he was willing to be tolerant. "All right," he sighed, "what's bothering you?"

"Nothing." We faced moments like these about once a month, and the instigator, usually me, invariably backed off. Was it that we realized it was ridiculous to fight over silly little irritants that would fade away before the next morning's orange juice? Or did we tacitly recognize the fragility of our union, that despite its calm center, it was surrounded by a wall full of weak chinks; poke any one of them too hard and the whole structure would come crashing down, suffocating us, destroying our children.

"Nothing? Are you sure?" he persisted. Bob was a

149

naturally cautious businessman. If we were entering into a truce, he wanted me to understand that I was abandoning all hostile intent, all hope for further appeal, of my own free will.

"Okay. You want it; you'll have it," I announced, pulling the quilt up to my chin to make sure no distracting flesh was showing. "I know damn well what you were doing with your finger. You were checking me out." I clenched my teeth and my fists, probably so I wouldn't bite him or scratch him. "You didn't believe I went to A&S. You really thought I was out having a flaming affair with someone. I absolutely cannot believe it. With whom? The goddamn mailman? The Good Humor man? The teen-age studs at the gas station? Who? Just answer me."

"Are you crazy?"

"Don't try to put me on the defensive. I come home, you stick your finger up me, and then you ask me if I'm crazy."

He slammed his fist down on the mattress. It made a soft thud. "Jesus Christ, I don't believe you. I really don't. What the hell is wrong if a husband touches his wife?"

"I'll tell you what's wrong," forcing my teeth apart so I could talk louder. "In all the years we've known each other you've never done anything like that. All of a sudden you come on to me like a crazed gynecologist. You didn't want sex. You didn't even have a hard-on, and don't deny it, because I looked. My God, in all the years you've been coming home at insane hours I never once suspected that you were working on anything except public relations. And all I do is spend a few hours away from the house and you think I'm carrying on some sort of torrid affair."

"God," he said. I had a brief flutter of pity for him; although he was suspicious enough not to even consider accepting my fidelity as given, I was indeed lying to him. I could have told him where I'd been. I could have

150

trusted him. And he could have trusted me. "You've gone completely off the deep end," he continued. "You need a psychiatrist. You really do."

"Look, when you begin to even approach fifty percent on the scale of normal human response, I'll go to a psychiatrist."

He squeezed his eyes until they were just a slit of cold blue light, his best dirty look. He used it sparingly to maximize the effect. Then, sliding down further onto the bed, he turned his back and yanked the yellow quilt over his head.

Chapter Eleven

I pulled into Nancy's driveway at nine-fifteen the next morning, drove around the side of the house, where Larry had pulled out a graceful old grape arbor, replacing it with a flat slab of metal, a sculpture called *Sacre Coeur,* and parked the car in the back. Nancy's office faced the back of the house, and if she was working, I could get her attention by calling her name in my best Delancey Street voice. But I glimpsed her through the kitchen window, wearing a faded Disneyland T-shirt, and before I could ring the bell, she noticed me and walked barefoot to the door.

"What's wrong?" she asked.

"Aren't you cold like that?" It was a glaringly bright day, but painfully cold, the ground hard, unyielding, frozen. "You'll wind up with pneumonia."

"Why, Judith, thank you. To think, you got up this early just to come over and nag me. I do appreciate it. I mean, you could have just called and read me an article on cirrhosis of the liver."

"Sorry." I threw my coat and gloves on a chair and walked over to her cabinets. By pressing the side, a white door sprung open to reveal a set of gleaming white dishes. I took a mug and poured myself some coffee. "I had a fight."

"Good. It clears the sinuses." She watched me as I

stared into the depths of the coffee. "All right. Tell me about it."

"It wasn't just a minor quibble. It was a real fight."

"Well, that happens here on the average of three nights a week. Larry usually winds up calling me a bohemian. He thinks that's the cruelest thing you can say to anyone."

"But we don't fight. You know that."

"I know that, Judith. But you have to understand that that's almost beyond my comprehension. I mean, I cannot begin to imagine being in the same room with Larry for more than an hour without discovering at least five major flaws in his character. So we fight a lot. But then it's over, finished. We can screw or go out for a pizza."

"But our relationship is different. I mean, I don't . . ."

"You mean you don't have any lovers to take up the slack? Judith, I'm not saying my way is right and yours is wrong. Look, I average a new man about every eight months, and while it does add a certain degree of enjoyment, it surely doesn't make my life any more meaningful. But I have them, and when I periodically get my act together and do an article, I have my work. I'm not saying I'm in any way measurably happier than you, but at least my energies are diffused. And I'm not putting all my eggs in Larry's basket. He's sweet and he's interesting and I love him, but he's in no way equipped to take responsibility for my happiness." She sighed and scratched the slightly upturned tip of her perfect nose. "Look, tell me what happened. I want to be able to understand."

So I told her, giving her a word by word, gesture by gesture account of Judith and Bob in Their Bedroom. She concentrated intently, nodding and saying "Mmm" at several strategic junctures. "See why I'm upset?" I asked finally.

"I see why you had the fight," she said. "But I don't

see why you're still so miserable. He didn't pack his bags, did he?"

"No. He even gave me a peck on the cheek before he left for the office. But it wasn't sincere."

"It wasn't sincere," she repeated to the ceiling, a WASP Tevye talking to a blond God who might possibly comprehend why people behave with such gross excesses of emotion. Then, peering at me again, she added: "You want nooky and sincerity too?"

"Yes. And a flat stomach."

"Done," she proclaimed. "Now, would you care to tell me where you were last evening? I'd be pleased to listen." She took her hands and pushed her long auburn hair behind her ears. "Unless you really were shopping at A&S, in which case you can skip it."

"No. I was at the Duncks' house, interviewing them about Fleckstein."

"Well, I'll be," she breathed. "You really did something."

"You didn't think I would?" I asked lightly, trying to sound indifferent.

"Judith, I don't have the energy to make assumptions and then deal with the consequences. But let's say I find it interesting that you actually whipped it up to visit the Duncks. Now, I have to go upstairs and take a shower because the exterminator is coming." She gazed at me seriously. "Larry was lying in bed last night and thought he heard termites breathing. That shows the level at which we concentrate on each other. Look, walk me upstairs and talk while I'm getting ready."

We climbed the plastic staircase and ambled down the long hall to the master bedroom. I flopped on the bed, the room's only piece of furniture, a huge square covered in a white furry throw that rested on a white lacquered platform, about a foot off the floor.

"You made your bed already?" I shouted to Nancy, who already had the water running in the bathroom.

"No," she yelled back. "Larry makes it each morning

155

before he goes to work. He's afraid someone will come in and see I use pastel sheets. God, the shame of it. Now, what happened at the Duncks'?"

"Do I have to shout?"

"Yes."

In my loudest voice, I gave a synopsis of the interview, as well as a finely drawn description of Dicky's toenails.

"That has to be one of the most nauseating things I've ever heard," Nancy remarked. She walked to the wall opposite her bed and kicked it gently. A door swung open, revealing a large walk-in closet with built-in alcoves for shoes, handbags, and sweaters. "I'd take two nose-pickers and an ass-scratcher to that any day. Oh, speaking of the Family Fleckstein, I saw Little Cupcake yesterday."

"I don't believe you. I really don't believe you," I said. "I've been here for at least twenty minutes and you haven't said a word about him. You know how interested I am in the murder, Nancy."

She pulled on a pair of burgundy corduroy jeans and, zipping up the fly, gazed at me with an expression midway between mild pain and resigned tolerance. "It was you, not I, my dear friend, who dashed to my doorstep in a veritable snit because you had a fight with Bob. Therefore," she cleared her throat, "I merely sat and listened to your plaint, virtually brimming with sympathy and warmth, while you spewed out all the venom in your system."

"Eat it," I suggested. She ignored me, turning her back and pulling a cream-colored turtleneck over her head. "Anyhow," I continued, "what did Cupcake have to say?"

"He said 'Hey, Nancy, baby, how's it going?' " she replied, forcing her voice to its lowest register and putting on a thick Brooklyn accent.

"Is that how he talks?"

"No. But that's how he thinks," she said, her voice reverting to its flower of southern womanhood tone. "In any case, our beloved friend has managed to keep her bony ass out of a sling."

"Who? What?"

"Mary Alice. It seems that our crackerjack police department, through unstinting devotion and tireless investigation, has come up with the names of four of Brucie's fuckees."

"Who? Who?" I realized as I said it that I sounded like an overwrought owl.

"Well, there was his nurse," she said, holding up a thumb as she began her count.

"That's Lorna Lewis."

"Right. I hate alliterative names. They suck."

"Okay," I said, not daring to interrupt her flow to examine this latest addition to Nancy's long list of strange opinions.

"Well, according to the precinct gossip, which, I gather, comes straight from the geniuses on the homicide squad, Brucie was humping her two, three days a week. Now, it seems she had the bad judgment to confide in one of the nurses who works in the office next door, and that broad told the cops that Lorna believed he was going to dump Norma and make her an honest woman. Lord, have you ever heard of such incredible self-deception?"

"All the time," I said. "What else did Cupcake say about Lorna?"

Nancy disappeared into her closet and returned with a pair of brown leather boots. She placed them on the floor and sat next to them. Then she pointed her toes and aimed for the inside of the boot. "Well, not much else. He did say she didn't seem so insanely in love that she wasn't protecting her own ass. Apparently, she's on her second marriage, and she was in no way going to say goodbye to number two until number three made the break with Norma. Lorna is not one to burn bridges, it seems. But according to this other nurse, she had given Brucie a deadline. If he wasn't out of his

157

house by Easter, she would stop playing with him and quit."

"What was so significant about Easter?"

"How should I know? Judith, by now it should be screechingly obvious that all these people are totally off the wall, and that any statement they make is by definition fraught with irrationality. Who knows? Maybe he had plans to stick a cottontail up her ass and photograph it. I don't know and I don't care."

"All right. Anything more on Lorna Lewis?"

"No. Let's go downstairs. I want a piece of halvah."

"Feh," I remarked. "How can you eat halvah in the morning?"

"By opening my mouth, inserting a piece, and chewing slowly and carefully." We returned to the kitchen, Nancy sprinting delicately down the plastic stairs, me clutching the handrail as I went gingerly from one slick step to another. "Want a bite? This is the marbleized kind. The best," she declared, her mouth full of the rich, crumbly candy.

"No. Nancy, why don't you eat something nourishing in the morning? Grits. You could eat grits."

"Grits taste like ground-up horse shit. Want to hear more?"

"Yes. This instant. Chew fast."

"Relax. Well, two of the other women I never heard of. One of them belongs to Brucie's club. Her husband's said to be *the* king of preteen fashions."

"What's her name?"

"I forget. Some Jewish name."

"Great. That's really terrific. I marvel at your powers of recollection. If it was Belinda Jo Slattery, Jr., you'd remember it."

"Women can't be juniors. Anyway, it was Naomi Goldberg."

"Really?"

"No. But if you think I'm going to sit here and take shit from you, you're whistling Dixie."

158

"I would never whistle Dixie," I vowed.

"I know that." Nancy smiled. "Do you actually think I could sustain a fifteen-year friendship with someone who even knew the words? Anyhow, do you want to know how they came to recognize this petunia? It seems she'd been over to the Sixth Precinct a few times having fits because she said her neighbors had trained their dogs to crap on her lawn. She wanted them arrested and executed."

"Oh my God," I interrupted.

"What?"

"I know who that is. Linda Berman. Fay Jacobs' husband's sister. You know Fay, the history teacher at Shorehaven High."

"So?"

"So, Fay told me about her. She's supposed to be very attractive and very crazy. And very rich. She's had all types of plastic surgery, and just because she doesn't look like Catherine Deneuve, she has about four malpractice suits going. None of the plastic surgeons around here will operate on her any more. The last I heard, she was going to Argentina or some place to get dimples put in."

"On her face or her ass?"

"I didn't ask. But Fay told me she's really bananas. She actually hired a private detective to spy on her neighbors when they walked their dogs."

Nancy stretched her legs and lifted her feet onto a kitchen chair. "Did Fay say anything about her and Brucie?"

I sat quietly for a moment. Fay had told me about Fleckstein's overtures to her, about his affair with Jean Burns, and had alluded to others. But nothing about crazy Linda. Perhaps she didn't have a confidential relationship with her sister-in-law. Or she felt constrained by family loyalties. Or her abhorrence of what Bruce Fleckstein stood for was so great that she simply didn't

159

want to discuss the subject further. "How did the police get on to her?"

"Well, the homicide people had given them copies of the pictures they found in Brucie's drawer. They figured someone in the precinct might recognize one of the ladies, since we're all one big, happy community. So after about forty-eight hours of salivating over the photographs, a sergeant, in a rare moment of lucidity, decided to have a look at the faces and recognized her—the Dog Shit Lady."

"Did they interview her?" I asked. Nancy had left a small piece of halvah on the table. I ate it. It was delicious.

"Sure. It turns out the pictures were taken in her kitchen. The minute the homicide cop saw the clock over her stove, he realized it was the same one as in the pictures. It seems that she and Brucie were into produce."

"Produce?" I echoed. "What do you mean, 'produce'?"

"Produce. Fruits and vegetables. Maybe under all that silicone beats the heart of Mother Earth. There were some great shots of her with carrots and bananas dangling out of her assorted orifices."

I shrugged my shoulders. "You know, whips are understandable. Leather, chains, all that stuff. But I can't comprehend bananas. Anyhow, what did she say?"

"She denied the whole thing, even knowing Bruce. Naturally. Then they offered to show her the pictures, but she refused to look. But after a minute or two, she broke down and 'fessed up. She said she hadn't seen Brucie in six months. She showed up one day at the motel—probably with a suitcase full of kumquats—and he wasn't there. Then she called his office and he wouldn't come to the phone. She called the next day, and his nurse told her he had a very busy schedule and he'd call her in a week or two. He never did."

"Nice guy."

"The greatest. Anyhow, that was it for Miss Fruit of the Month. The third one was someone named Ginger Wick. Now, come on, don't ask me how I can remember her name. Did you ever hear of her?"

"No."

"Neither did I. It seems she owns the lab where Brucie sent all his work. And her husband is some sort of hotshot specialist who only does very esoteric types of dental surgery. Anyway, the cops got her name from some dentist who saw them carrying on in a hotel in Las Vegas. It turns out that she and Brucie had done business over the phone for a couple of years, and one night they met at a convention in Las Vegas. It was love at first sight, according to her, and they broke up about a year ago."

. "How long had they been carrying on?"

"A few months. Brucie finally ended it by telling her that he couldn't handle the guilt. But he continued to use her lab."

"Any pictures?"

"She says no."

"What does Cupcake think?"

"He doesn't."

"What about the fourth? You're obviously saving the best for last."

"Meg Brill." A grin spread over Nancy's face. Her green eyes sparkled.

"Oh, no!" Meg Brill was the class mother of Kate's first grade. She was short, pudgy woman with fat red cheeks and curly mouse-brown hair, which she wore pulled back into a pony tail—tied with a large colored ribbon to match her outfit. Sweet and friendly, like an energetic beagle puppy, she talked ceaselessly and was always aflutter organizing PTA bake sales and car-wash days. "She's so sexless," I exclaimed, and then added, "but that's not fair."

"Christ, would you stop being so guilt-ridden, Judith. She *is* sexless. By normal standards, anyway. And she's

161

a royal pain. Lord, she's always calling me, asking me if I can make southern fried chicken for some damned bazaar."

"How did the police find out about her?"

"She volunteered the information."

"You're kidding."

"No. The cops came calling because she was in his file. A patient. Anyhow, they asked her if she knew anything about Brucie, and she began weeping copiously. Well, they calmed her down, and she told them she had had an affair with him about two years ago. According to her, it was your average, run-of-the-mill adulterous liaison. No chains. No clever little torture devices. No pictures."

"Did the police believe her?"

"Sure. Why not? According to this old detective on the homicide squad who's taken a fatherly interest in Little Cupcake, they were embarrassed by the whole thing and wished she hadn't decided that confession was good for the soul. Anyhow, that's it, at least in terms of what the cops already know. But there are still a few beauties in the pictures that they haven't identified." Nancy explained that the police had not yet discovered the identities of either three or four of Fleckstein's subjects. The reason they were unsure about the precise number was that two of them had their faces covered: one by a mask and another by her hands, placed peek-a-boo style over her eyes. Although Miss Peek-a-boo's body was startlingly similar to one of the unmasked lovelies, the police maintained a reasonable doubt as to whether the two were indeed one.

"So what have they done?" I asked Nancy. "It seems that all they've accomplished is to widen the scope of the investigation. They keep on discovering more and more suspects. Any one of them could have slipped it to Fleckstein. They all had a motive, God knows."

"I know. But look at it this way. All your information is coming from Little Cupcake." She stressed the

162

"your," disassociating herself from the investigation, stressing her role as a conduit.

"You don't think he's reliable?"

Nancy put her feet down and shifted back in her chair so she was sitting upright, her posture elegant, regal. "Shit, I don't doubt that he's reliable. He's just limited. Seriously, besides his intelligence, or lack thereof, he's just another cop. All he's getting is the station house gossip and a few tidbits from this homicide fellow who's become his big-ass buddy. And the only reason he's keeping his ears open is that he thinks I find it amusing, and he does want to keep me amused. Now, if you're serious, the guy who's heading the investigation is the one to talk to. For all we know, he might have the case practically wrapped up."

"What's his name?"

"I don't know," she answered. "And what difference would it make if I did?"

"None, I suppose," I answered thoughtfully, "although I think it was in one of the newspaper accounts." I picked up the halvah wrapper and began to shred it into an ashtray. "So, in other words, everyone is still a suspect."

"Yes. I did ask him if anyone had an airtight alibi."

"So? What did he say?"

"Well, he said that no one could prove that they were in one place with a flock of reliable witnesses between five and seven that evening. See, that's the problem. Brucie's office is no more than five or ten minutes from most of the suspects' houses. An irate husband could tell his wife he's going up to the can and sneak out and commit murder and then tippy-toe back and flush the toilet. Nobody would ever know."

"Right. And if some woman's children are sitting around and watching television, they'd swear she was home, while actually she could have slipped out without anyone knowing. God, I could take on ten men on the kitchen floor while Kate is watching *The Flintstones*."

163

"Why don't you?"

"That's when I give Joey his bath."

"I see. Well, at least you're growing up. It's better than your old tune about adultery being ethically repugnant."

It was getting late, nearly time to meet Joey's school bus. I resented the intrusion of obligations on my relationships; I wanted to live in a purer world. One of the reasons I adored Bette Davis movies was that she had time, time for Celeste Holm or Miriam Hopkins. I would watch her, cigarette smoking, those glorious protruding eyes focusing on her companion. She would sit back in a restaurant or put her feet up in the living room, and she and her friends could indulge in hours of conversation, uninterrupted by strangers telephoning to inquire if she would collect for the Heart Fund, or by children demanding to be fed or bathed or soothed or tucked in. She could enfold herself in the luxury of friendship undiffused by pediatricians' appointments, uncomplicated by trips to the dry cleaners and Sunday school car pools.

"Speak to you soon," I said.

Ultimately, I was responsible, I thought, as I backed my car out of her driveway. The pebbles made brisk crunching noises under the tires. I had chosen to have children—whom I truly loved—and had agreed to the migration from Manhattan to Long Island. But, in fairness to myself, no one had ever made the connection for me. No one had ever even hinted that if one has children, one has almost no time to pursue adult relationships. True, I had heard that motherhood is demanding, that one must spend nights in a rocking chair with one's breast in an infant's eager mouth. And I had heard that one must give up a tennis game to cuddle a sick child and be willing to confront diarrhea and neighborhood bullies. But no one had ever said explicitly that children would impinge on every aspect of one's life. And no one had said that the need for real grown-up talk would lock one further into marriage; the only time for long, wide-ranging, probing conversations was late at night, with one's husband, who would tell you again and again and again how, despite all his hopes, all his planning, he had somehow allowed the presidency of his college fraternity to slip through his hands.

I pulled my car into the garage with a quarter hour to spare until Joey's bus was due. I could do a crossword puzzle, put on a facial mask to tighten my pores. Or, to honor the memory of M. Bruce Fleckstein, sit down with a yard of dental floss and make the spaces between my teeth the cleanest in town. Ruminating on my options, I opened the door which led from the garage to a small alcove beyond the kitchen. Something was very wrong.

Interestingly, before my intellect made the connection that something was amiss, my body sensed danger and reacted. It felt the cold air as I put one of my feet into the kitchen, it tensed all the muscles within its jurisdiction and ordered a general alert of the blood vessels in preparation for fight or flight. My body knew, independent of my mind, that when it walked into a warm kitchen from the icy outdoors that it should feel good. It didn't because—and here my intellect reestablished its primacy—the kitchen was as bitterly cold as the unheated garage.

The freezing air came as a persistent, cold blast, which meant that the forty-year-old oil burner hadn't simply given up the ghost. Indeed, as I took three tentative steps forward, I knew the cold rush of air must be coming from an open door or window. But when I had left for Nancy's, all doors and windows had been locked.

I stood absolutely still, forcing myself to breathe through my nose so that if there was an intruder, he wouldn't hear me panting with panic and have time to take out his switchblade. There was silence. No chirping

165

birds, no heavy-breathing rapist. No sounds of scurrying footsteps upstairs as burglars ran from room to room searching for negotiable securities. I climbed out of my shoes and took another silent, stockinged step into the kitchen.

Whoever it was had gone. The kitchen door that led to the back yard was flung open, its handle, either unscrewed or knocked out, lying on the floor right by the stove. I glared at it, annoyed, as if it were part of a very expensive toy one of the children had wrecked after five minutes of use. Then the fear returned, and then anger. Some miserable, rotten, slimy bastard had broken into my house, defiled my property. As I spun around to head for the phone, I saw it. The message. In red spray paint on my refrigerator door, four foot-high letters: M.Y.O.B. The period after the "Y" was larger than the others, and the paint had trickled down the door and dripped on the floor. like drops of blood.

I grabbed the telephone decisively and then held it, debating, should I call 911, the police emergency number? Well, someone had broken into my house. But it wasn't an emergency, was it? My life wasn't in imminent peril. Maybe I should call the local precinct. But they wouldn't think it was an emergency and the desk sergeant would put me on hold and the intruder would return. I had all the makings of a Talmudic scholar, I thought, as I dialed 911

"Police emergency."

"Someone broke into my house."

"Your address, please."

"They've gone."

"Lady, just give me your address."

I decided 911 was not interested in a dialogue, so I gave the man the address, slipped back into my shoes, and trotted outside to wait for Joey. His school bus came just as I walked out the door, and I grabbed his hand. "Mrs. Tuccio asked you to come for lunch."

"I don't want to go."

"Come on, Joey."

"I hate her peanut butter. It's the smooth kind."

I banged on Marilyn's door and she opened it. "Parlez-vous français?" I asked her rapidly.

"Un peu."

"Il ya un criminal qui broke into chez moi. Compris?"

"Oui. Is there anything . . . ?"

"Les gendarmes sont coming," I continued. "Gee, Marilyn, Joey's so glad you asked him for lunch."

"I love having Joey for lunch. And Tommy is so excited that you're coming, Joey." Tommy was her youngest, a three-year-old mechanical genius who had once fixed my toaster. Marilyn took Joey's hand, pulled him gently inside and said, "See you later."

I tore across the street and paced my lawn, from the now-barren tulip bed to the white birch tree and back again. Within a minute, two police cars screeched up. Four men leapt out of the cars.

"You the lady who called about a break-in?" asked a heavy, gray-haired cop with three chins.

"Yes. This way."

I took them in the front door, through the hall past the living room and dining room and into the kitchen.

"Geez," said the gray-haired cop to a tall, good-looking blond one. "He took the fucking handle off the goddamn door. Hardly ever see that. They usually just kick the whole door in."

I waited for him to turn to me and say, "Pardon my language." Instead, he demanded in a harsh voice: "Did you touch anything?"

I was about to say no, that I had been very careful, but at that moment he and the three others noticed my refrigerator. Then they glanced at each other. One of them, a short pale man with gold-rimmed glasses, sighed and shrugged his shoulders. He looked like an accountant whose books wouldn't balance.

"Lady, was this here before?" asked the gray-haired one, pointing to the scarlet M.Y.O.B.

Did I look like the type who would go in for that kind of decorating scheme? "No. Whoever broke in did it."

"You and you," he said to the accountant and a black cop with a very sad face, "check out the house and outside." He turned to the beautiful blond whose name tag said "Hogan." "Okay, Jimbo, what the fuck does M.Y.O.B. mean?"

"It means mind your own business," Jimbo said.

Jimbo. Jim. Jim Hogan. My God, Jimbo is Nancy's Cupcake. Tall and Troy Donahue handsome, with a firm, square chin and soft blue-gray eyes, he looked like he should have a cheerleader tucked under each arm.

"Who would want someone here to mind their own business?" the gray-haired one asked. His name tag said "Brown."

"Did you hear anyone enter the premises?" asked Cupcake.

"Did you touch anything?" demanded Brown.

"Is your husband home?" Cupcake asked.

"What does my husband have to do with this?" I inquired. They gazed at me blankly. I sat down in a chair, my elbows resting on the table, my forehead in my hands. Then, glancing up at them, I said: "Now, first of all, I didn't touch anything except for the door from the garage and the telephone. I had to call you. I didn't hear anyone leave, and I was out all morning at a friend's house. Nancy Miller over on Blackthorne Lane." I gazed at Brown as I said this, not wanting Cupcake to know that I knew. But it wouldn't hurt if he knew I was Nancy's friend. Maybe he'd look harder for the intruder. "And," I said, "as far as minding my own business, I'm not sure."

"What do you mean, you're not sure?" Brown snapped.

"Easy, Roy," murmured Cupcake.

The phone rang. I knew it would be Bob, making his prelunch checkup.

"Hello," he said, still distant after the previous night's fight. "How are you?"

"Fine, thank you. The police are here."

"The police?" he demanded, not sounding anywhere near as startled as I imagined he should. "What are the police doing?"

"Someone broke in, so I called the police," I answered.

"Is everyone okay?"

"Yes."

"Did they take my cameras?"

"I don't know. I haven't been downstairs yet."

"I'll hold on. Go check."

"Bob, I'm sure everything's all right. Whoever it was just sprayed some graffiti on the refrigerator door."

"What?"

I knew an explanation was in order, but with the police milling about the kitchen, I decided to be as literal as possible. Also, I had a faint, nearly futile hope that Bob would not demand an immediate accounting. "Whoever it was just wrote M.Y.O.B. in red spray paint."

"What?"

"M.Y.O.B."

"I heard you. I heard you. I'm coming home."

"You don't have to come home, dear. I'll manage."

"What the hell's wrong with you, Judith? Some goddamn crazy breaks into my house and defaces my property, and you tell me not to come home. Now, listen, just sit tight and I'll grab a taxi. I should be home in about forty minutes."

I hung up the phone and turned to face Brown. "You didn't answer my question, lady."

"The phone rang."

"All right. I was asking you who would tell you to mind your own business." He took his index finger, placed it in his ear, and twirled it around several times. Then he peered at me, ready to listen to my response. I glanced at his ear, with its generous tuft of gray hair sticking out. "Well, lady?"

"I don't know," I mumbled, shrugging my shoulders, trying to appear as befuddled as the police. "Maybe it means something else."

"Like what?"

"Maybe it's the initials of some radical political group."

"You in politics, lady?"

"Well, I'm a registered Democrat."

"That's not politics. I mean, are you in any extremist group?"

"No."

"Then what makes you think M.Y.O.B. is some group's initials? Why couldn't it be for 'mind your own business'? Huh? Why not?"

The sad-looking black cop returned to the kitchen. "Nothing upstairs," he said sorrowfully. He had a round, babyish, unhappy face, like a very dark Dean Rusk. As he finished speaking, the bland, forgettable accountant/cop reappeared.

"Outside's okay," he reported to Brown. He peered at me. "Did you know you have a crack in your foundation, near the azalea bushes?"

"No, I didn't."

"Well, you do, and you should take care of it. Otherwise, you'll start getting water."

Brown glanced at him with mild distaste. "Why don't you two guys get going? We can take it from here. Actually, I can take it from here. Why don't the three of you leave? I'll see you later." They shuffled out obediently, Cupcake flashing a dazzling, whiter-than-white toothy smile at me.

"All right, let's get back to my question," Brown urged gruffly.

"Would you like to sit down?"

"No. Now, look, I want to get down to business. I'll say it again, lady. Who would want you to mind your own business?"

"I don't know." I concentrated on a thread hanging from the hem of the tablecloth, rather than on Brown and his bullet-laden gun belt. I had no doubt about what the right thing to do was: tell the police that I had spoken to some of the people involved in the Fleckstein case. But Brown seemed extraordinarily unsympathetic, incapable of registering any really human feeling beyond annoyance. And if I mentioned speaking to some of the principals in the case, I might have to tell them about Mary Alice, who, so far, was safely out of the running. I glanced at Brown, at the solid roll of fat resting on top of his belt, and realized how ridiculous it would seem to such a man that I had become enmeshed in a police matter. More than ridiculous—unnatural. I was an object, a minor pain, an itch in his hairy ear. "I really don't know," I reiterated.

"Well, lady, you'd better think about it. I mean, this isn't your average burglary, where I can just go back and make a report and you call up your friendly insurance man. This is what I call a weird thing. Now, can you think of anyone. . . ?"

"Not really."

"Not really. All right then, I'll tell you what. I've got to get back to do a few things, but I'll be back later. Now, listen, don't let anyone in this kitchen. Get me? The guys from forensics may want to look this over. And while I'm gone, why don't you just sit down and do some real serious thinking?"

I promised I would, and he left after writing down my name and phone number. "Don't forget, lady," he called as he walked down the path toward the driveway, "try to do some serious remembering."

I trudged up the stairs and walked into my bedroom. It looked curiously peaceful, the yellow walls and yellow bedspread and curtains gave off a warm, pleasant glow, the comfortable, hazy feeling you get lying on a quiet beach with your eyes closed. I called Marilyn Tuccio, telling her that the police would be back and asking if she could hold on to Joey for the rest of the afternoon. Yes, she said, no problem at all and sorry about my trouble.

I kicked my shoes under my dresser and lay down on the bed. For a minute or two, I managed a serious internal debate over how to handle the grand pickle I was in—the hang-out route or stonewalling it. A weepy, sniveling, embarrassed confession versus a cool, remote denial of any involvement in murderous doings. But my mind, weary, began to meander, back to college, back to old boyfriends, old pleasures, into its favorite idle pastime—recalling old sexual encounters. I was back in the summer of fifty-nine, relishing Danny Simon's perfect seventeen-year-old body when I heard Bob's familiar two short rings on the doorbell. Retrieving my shoes, I shuffled downstairs, knowing that when I opened the door I would be facing a thirty-seven-year-old man who had never given me as much joy as Danny had that July and August before college.

"All right. What happened? For God's sake," Bob blurted, pushing past me to get into the house. "Where's Joey?"

"He's over at Marilyn Tuccio's. I sent him there because I didn't want him to get upset." I spoke in a slow, calm, deliberate voice. My soothing tone was contagious. Bob stopped his angry stomping toward the kitchen, returned, and put his arm around me. Turning, I hugged him hard, knowing that within five minutes an embrace would be out of the question, even the lightest kiss would not be considered. So I hugged his slim, tight, pampered waist and then let go, taking him by the hand, leading him into the kitchen. We stood before the refrigerator like two aborigines examining an artifact of a culture vastly more civilized and complex.

"What does it mean?" he asked.

172

"It means mind your own business," I explained softly.

"Oh," he said, and took two steps to the left, as if to view the painting from another angle. "How do you know that?"

"I know it. That's all." My volume control was going awry; my voice was becoming loud, strident. "Didn't anyone in high school ever say M.Y.O.B. to you?"

"Never."

"Well, maybe you just never got involved enough with people." It was a mean, hurtful remark, and I began regretting it as I uttered the last syllable. I began to apologize, but Bob cut me off.

"Listen, Judith, let's get out of high school and into the present, if you will. Now, what is this all about?" Again I opened my mouth, hoping a few soothing words would spill out, but he persisted before I could find anything nice to say. "Come on. Why would someone come in and do something like this? Do you have any idea?"

"Yes. Maybe."

"Good. Perhaps you would like to share it with me." He brought his lips together. His mouth was tight, hard, ungenerous. His face was about a foot from mine, and I could smell his aftershave lotion, sweet, citrusy. I've never liked perfumed men, moving in on me like ambulatory limes.

"I think it's all because of the Fleckstein murder." I waited for his eyes to widen with amazement, for him to speak, to press me for details. But he just stood in place, staring at me. "The Fleckstein murder, you know." I briefly considered extricating myself gracefully. I knew just how to do it; the script was an old one. I could stand just where I was, eyes cast down, and slowly, slowly lift my head so Bob could see two shimmering tears, one on each pale cheek. He would be moved, but only slightly, so then I would collapse softly into his arms, give a gentle sob, and sniff, "Darling, I've been such a fool." And he would put his powerful arms around me and say: "Don't worry, baby. I'll take care of everything." He might even stroke my hair. "The Fleckstein murder," I repeated. "I told you about the whole goddamn thing. Don't you ever listen?"

"What does the murder have to do with us? Who the hell broke into my house?"

"Might I point out to you, Robert, that we own the house jointly? Don't you think you could whip it up enough to call it 'our house'?"

He slammed his fist against the refrigerator door. "All right," he bellowed, "would you please tell me what that cocksucking murder has to do with our motherfucking house? Is that better?"

"You're so cute when you're mad," I said lightly, and instantly saw I had gone too far. Both hands clenched into white-knuckled fists, Bob took a step toward me. "All right. Calm down. I was doing a little investigating. Nothing serious."

"What?" he croaked.

"I asked a few people a couple of questions about the murder," I explained, and shrugged my shoulders to show him how utterly casual I felt about the whole incident: a mere petty intrigue in a life filled with exquisitely fascinating moments.

"Judith, are you crazy?"

"You seem to be asking me that question a lot lately."

"Well, you've certainly given me reason." He had lowered his voice a little, but his fists were still clenched. When he saw me looking at them, he jammed his hands into his pockets.

"No, I haven't. Look, you get excited by dirty public images that need laundering; I get excited by a good murder. It's really just a matter of taste. Different strokes for different folks. You do your thing, I do mine."

"My thing, as you call it, happens to be my profession. Now, look, Judith, your thing happens to be being a wife and mother." He paused and seemed to remember something. "And, of course, being a historian. All of which preclude detective work. Now, please," he began to shout, "would you tell me what the fuck you've been doing?" His moods were alternating with the regularity of a machine: a ting of cool rationality followed by a thump of fury, and then another ting, another thump.

"I just spoke to a few people involved in the case. I was curious, that's all."

"That's all?"

"Yes."

"You have nothing more to say on the subject?"

"No. I mean, if you were interested in the murder, I'd be glad to discuss it with you, but it's obvious you aren't."

"All right. I'm interested."

"No, you're not."

He turned on his heels and marched out of the kitchen, very neatly, just as he had been taught in ROTC, the year before he became a liberal. I heard him stomping up the stairs. The bedroom door crashed shut.

He's probably looking for the master list of his camera equipment, I mused. Just to check. Just to make sure that the crazed murderer/housebreaker wasn't also a photography buff, panting to make off with his telephoto lens. I had to admit to a certain grudging admiration for M. Bruce. All he needed was a Polaroid and a few props. No massive leather bags of equipment to lug around, no malfunctioning electronic flashes to impinge on his creativity.

The bedroom door creaked open, and I listened to Bob's funereal march down the stairs. I walked into the living room and sat on the couch in a gesture of rapprochement; I'd meet him halfway.

"He's coming," Bob announced from the hallway.

"Who?" I demanded anxiously.

"The guy who's in charge of the Fleckstein investigation," he responded casually, sauntering into the living room. He leaned against the fireplace mantel.

"Are you nuts?" I demanded. "How could you just call up someone like that without talking to me about it?"

"Judith, don't you realize I've just been saying the same thing to you?"

"You're so mature!" I screamed at him. "Thanks. Thanks a lot. I'll always remember your kindness. A husband turning his wife in. Thanks." I stood and turned my back toward him.

"If you're planning on going anywhere, don't. The lieutenant's coming in fifteen minutes. He wants to talk to you."

Chapter Twelve

When the doorbell rang, I casually kicked off my shoes and drew my feet up onto the couch. Bob glared at me and took several deep breaths, overtures to a gloriously orchestrated aria of snide remarks. But he couldn't find anything to say. I looked away from him and concentrated on the prismatic effect of early afternoon light passing through a crystal ashtray on the coffee table.

"The doorbell," he hissed. "Aren't you going to get it?"

"Do I look like a butler?"

He shrugged his shoulders, appropriating my favorite gesture of studied casualness, and began sauntering toward the door. "It's all right, Judith, I'll get it. Just do me one favor," he said as he turned the corner to the entrance hall. "Please put your shoes on. You're not a teen-ager." I glanced down at my shoes, two scuffed loafers, Gucci derivatives, with stretched-out tongues sticking out at me, and kicked them under the couch.

I listened to the door open and to the muffled voices. Mumble, mumble, Bob Singer. Mumble, mumble, Lieutenant Mumble. She's inside. Fine, mumble, mumble. They came into the room. Bob's voice said: "This is Lieutenant Sharpe." I sensed they were standing about two feet away, observing me, as if I were a witch who had drawn a charmed circle that they were unable to cross.

"Judith," Bob said, barely suppressing a whine.

I raised my head and glanced at Sharpe. Then I swallowed hard, to mask my surprise. Instead of the fascistic, gross hulk I had anticipated, complete with a chewed-up cigar and yellowed, mottled skin, I was looking into a pair of big, soft, liquid brown eyes. And although his hair was gray, he was no more than thirty-eight or thirty-nine. There was no coarseness, no brutality. His bland-looking, snub-nosed face was toughened only by its obvious intelligence—and fatigue. He had bags under his eyes, blue-gray smudges, really, and a pale gray stubble of a beard.

Bob cleared his throat, preparing to repeat the introduction. But Sharpe crossed the invisible magic line I had drawn and held out his hand. "I'm Nelson Sharpe." Having no other choice, I stood to shake hands with him. He was fairly short, about two or three inches taller than I, but he had the advantage of shoes.

"Judith Singer." His handshake was firm, not the limp clasp many men use with women, nor the over-compensating, knuckle-crushing grip. Bob cleared his throat again. Sharpe's hands, I noticed, were quite large, with long, heavy fingers. Fair compensation, I thought, for his lack of height. I've always subscribed to the myth—or perhaps the fact—that you can look at some part of a man's body and determine the size and shape of his penis. I remember sitting up late one night in the dorm before an exam, discussing this. Someone said all you had to do was check the size of the toes. No, chimed in someone else, it's the shoe size. Wrong, declared another, it's the fingers; small, thin fingers mean you may be very disappointed. Nancy then presented a corollary to this digital theory, which was thumbs only. If you know the thumbs, you know the man.

"I think we should talk about the Fleckstein case, Mrs. Singer," he said. His big hands hung at his sides. "Your husband said you had done some investigating."

178

Sharpe spoke in such a calm, neutral manner that I drew up stiff and straight, alert. Knowing he couldn't possibly feel neutral about the case, I realized he was either trying to put me at ease or treating me like a crazy lady, keeping his voice subdued so as not to overstimulate my shattered nerves.

"Tell him, Judith," Bob ordered. "Go ahead."

"Tell him what?" I sat back on the couch. Sharpe chose a gold club chair on the opposite side of the coffee table. I gazed at Bob, trying to look confused, quizzical. He remained standing, uncertain whether to align himself with me on the couch or to take the matching club chair next to Sharpe, on the side of law and order.

"For God's sake, Judith, stop playing games. Tell Lieutenant Sharpe how you've been poking your nose into the Fleckstein business. Get it over with." Turning from me, he looked at Sharpe, raising his eyebrows and twisting up a corner of his mouth in a regulation gesture of helplessness. Women aren't easy, his expression said. Sharpe gave him a brief blink and continued to look bland.

"What would you like to know, Lieutenant?" I asked.

"Everything, Judith. Everything. Just start talking, and if he has any questions, he'll ask." Bob smiled modestly at Sharpe, pleased that he had made the policeman's lot a happier one.

"Mr. Singer," said Sharpe, taking a pen and a small notebook from his breast pocket, "would you please leave the room?"

There followed a moment of absolute silence, a moment where animation was suspended, where all thoughts froze in the journey from brain to mouth and stood in the petrified stillness of shock. Perfect, profound quiet, until Bob managed a squeaky, "What?"

"Could you please leave the room? I'd like to speak with Mrs. Singer alone." He massaged the tip of his small nose with the back of his hand, ordinarily a tough gesture, but Sharpe's nose was so pert, so cute, that it belonged on a face in an ad for baby food. "I'd like to get down to work, Mr. Singer," he added.

His three sentences had given Bob time to recuperate somewhat. "Look, Sharpe, in case you happened to forget, my wife is entitled to have someone with her. If not me, then I'll call my attorney. My wife is certainly entitled to have counsel present during her interrogation."

"What are you talking about, 'interrogation'?" I demanded. "He hasn't even brought out his rubber hose yet."

"Be quiet, Judith, for once in your life. Now listen, Sharpe . . ."

"Mr. Singer, all I want to do is ask Mrs. Singer a few questions. She is not a suspect. If at any time the situation warrants it, I will inform her of her rights."

"Yeah, sure," Bob grumbled. I would not have been surprised if he had stuck out his tongue at Sharpe and sneered: "So's your old man."

"Look, Mr. Singer," Sharpe began pleasantly.

I cut him off. "Bob, could you please leave the room? If I need anything, I'll call you." If he had refused, if he had stamped his foot or raised his voice, I would have folded immediately. But all Bob did was stare at me, his lower jaw drooping. "Look, Bob, why don't you pick up Joey at Marilyn Tuccio's and take him for a walk or something?"

He stood, giving me one of those bottomless, chilling looks that only blue-eyed people can manage. He tightened the knot on his tie. "Okay, Judith. If you don't want help, do without it. Just don't come crying to me later." He grabbed his coat and jacket, which he had thrown over the piano bench, and marched toward the door.

"Will you come to see me on visiting day?" I called after him. "Maybe they'll let us hold hands through the bars." The door slammed noisily. I must have stood to run after him and apologize, because Sharpe said: "Could you please sit down, Mrs. Singer?"

"Oh. Sorry. Sure." I felt very weak and very ill, and prayed that if I threw up, I would miss his blue polyester slacks.

"You know Marilyn Tuccio?" he inquired, opening his notebook.

"Yes. I know her fairly well. And the fact that even for a moment you considered her a suspect is patently absurd. Good God, instead of making a deliberate effort to discover a rational—or even an irrational—motive for the murder, you people have been following all sorts of half-crocked innuendos. And from people like Lorna Lewis, no less. Really, how could you give credence to a person like Lorna Lewis? She was sleeping with Fleckstein, for God's sake. I would hardly call that a disinterested party."

"You talk," said Sharpe, a hint of a smile crossing his face.

"Yes. And I think too."

"Yes. Now, how do you know about Lorna Lewis?"

"I listen."

His right hand reached for his cheek and he rubbed his face, back and forth, back and forth. "Mrs. Singer, let me tell you something. For the last few weeks, I've been working eighteen hours a day trying to make some sense out of this case. I'm very, very tired. So if you can be of any help, I would greatly appreciate it."

"You're trying to humor me."

"Yes," he said hesitantly. "Only because it seems necessary. Believe me, it's taking my last ounce of energy, and if you don't cooperate soon, I'll probably fall asleep in this chair."

He did look tired, his lips almost ash white. His entire body, abandoning the struggle against gravity, drooped down, earthward. "Would you like some coffee?" I asked, wanting to help him.

"No. No thanks."

"Juice? A Coke? A piece of fruit?"

"A piece of fruit would be fine."

181

"An apple? An orange?"

"An apple, please."

I rose and walked into the kitchen. "The apples are in the refrigerator," I called to him. "Can I touch it?"

"Wait." He came into the kitchen, over to the refrigerator, and stuck his fingers into the rubber seal around the door. He held it open while I bent down to the fruit bin and took out an apple.

"Want to check it for fingerprints?" I asked, holding it up by the stem.

"I'll pass."

I washed the apple in cold water and then, with two sheets of paper towels, rubbed it to a high gloss. "Here," I said.

"Thanks," he said, gazing at me. His eyes were very large and round, like Paul McCartney's, but with the softness of a kindly old dog—and very alert. Tired as he was, his eyes were vibrant, wide awake, taking in everything, every detail in the room, especially me. "Looks like a nice apple," he muttered.

"Hope so," I replied encouragingly.

He took a small bite and, for less than a second, let his eyes run down my body to about knee level, then quickly raised them again and looked at me, brown eyes to brown eyes. "Very good."

"Well, it's all I have. Can't afford bananas."

"Bananas?"

"Bananas. Like Lady Bountiful in Fleckstein's picture, the fruit and vegetable queen."

He roared with laughter, a loud, rich sound from such a quiet, tired man. Then, suddenly sobering, he said: "Let's sit down."

He followed me into the living room, where we resumed our previously staked out positions on the chair and couch.

"So you've seen the pictures," he commented, crossing his legs, his left ankle resting above his right knee, making a large triangle with his groin at the apex.

"No. Where would I see the pictures?"

"Where would you get all the information you have? I don't know." Sharpe held the apple in his right hand. His left rested motionlessly on his crossed left leg. His thighs were thick, muscular, a contrast to the rest of his body, which was of average build.

"Okay," I breathed tiredly, as if his weariness were contagious. "Where do you want to start?"

"You pick the place."

"Okay. My refrigerator. When I came home this morning . . ."

He stood suddenly. "Can I use your phone?"

"In the kitchen."

He walked inside, a gray tweedy jacket covering what I sensed was a firm, flat behind. He returned within a minute. "I just wanted someone from forensics to come down to check out the refrigerator. They're on their way." Crossing in front of me, he sat on the other end of the couch. "All right, about your refrigerator."

"Nothing. I mean, I walked in this morning—I had been out from a little after nine to about eleven-thirty— and there it was. 'M.Y.O.B.' "

"Where had you been?" I gave him Nancy's name and address, and he jotted it down. "Now," he continued, "have you any idea who might have wanted to deliver a message like that to you?"

"I suppose."

"Who?" He shifted a few inches closer to me.

"Someone who evidently doesn't want me poking into the Fleckstein case."

"And do you have any idea who that person might be?"

"No. Not really. Well, a vague idea."

"Who?"

"I'd rather not say."

Sharpe gnawed on his upper lip for a few seconds before exploding. "For Christ's sake! Now, listen, I'm investigating a murder, and all I have to show is a slew of suspects and not one damn solitary lead." He swallowed, rather slowly and ostentatiously, and seemed to calm down. "Look, if you could possibly help me, even with a vague supposition, I would be grateful."

"Well, I'm not really positive. Actually," I said, moving as close to the arm of the couch as I could, "it's just a hypothesis."

"Why don't you try it out on me?" he suggested.

"I'd rather not."

For a moment, he studied the half-eaten apple and then, looking straight ahead, said: "You know I can have you arrested and held as a material witness."

"What?"

"You heard me," he replied softly and turned to meet my eyes in a fixed, unblinking stare.

"Bullshit," I announced. His stare widened. "That's a cheap trick, trying to scare me. I'm really surprised at you. How can you hold me as a material witness? What have I witnessed? What concrete information am I holding back? Just what are you going to say to the judge? 'Book her on a withheld theory charge, Your Honor.' Look, if you want to talk, I'll talk, but I don't appreciate your trying to browbeat me into submission."

"You're not easy," he remarked.

"You are?"

"Okay. Let's talk."

I realized that without Sharpe's approval, I could do no more investigating. So I decided to cooperate. I began with Mary Alice, without mentioning her name, telling Sharpe that although Fleckstein had never attempted to blackmail her, the threat was implicit; he had the pictures, he might someday use them. Another friend, I reported, recalling my discussion with Fay Jacobs, had been propositioned by him. A mother of one of my son's friends had been involved with him. I ran my hand across my forehead, a gesture of disbelief; the combination of Fleckstein and Scotty Hughes still seemed so incredible. And he had come on strong to

Marilyn Tuccio. In fact, everywhere I turned, I seemed to encounter women who had some connection with Fleckstein.

"And what about you?" Sharpe asked.

"No."

"Never met him? Never saw him in your life?"

I explained that I had seen him once, as a patient. "But he never looked south of my gums."

"He didn't?" Sharpe sounded surprised, which pleased me.

"I was six months pregnant and gargantuan."

He rubbed his cheek and sideburn. "How do you explain Fleckstein's success with women and yet maintain that your neighbor, Mrs. Tuccio, was immune?"

"Well, he didn't score all the time. That other friend I told you about, the older one, refused his advances. And Marilyn is just not the type. To begin with, she's very religious. Sincerely religious; it's an integral part of her personality. And she's very busy. And," I added, watching his big fingers move up and down his cheek, "she's happily married."

"Then why has she been complaining that her husband is never home?" His point, but he played the game modestly, scoring with a quiet dignity rather than with a smug "aha!"

"She has? To whom?"

"I really can't tell you. But she did tell someone that her husband sees more of his operating room nurses than he sees of her. Doesn't that sound like a dissatisfied wife to you?"

"No. She's just mildly pissed at Mike, that's all. She's not going to run out and have a wild affair with the first creep that flashes a pinky ring in front of her eyes. Can't you see that?"

"Maybe."

"Maybe. And you take the word of a person like Lorna Lewis, an interested party if ever there was one, over Marilyn Tuccio's."

"All right, now that we're on the subject of Lorna Lewis, would you mind telling me how you know about what she told the police?"

"Yes."

"Well?"

"Yes. I would mind. I can't tell you."

He reached across the back of the couch, gripped my upper arm and held it tightly. "You can tell me."

With my left hand, I loosened his fingers and pushed his hand away. "I don't appreciate police brutality. I'm not going to tell you and that's that."

"You have to tell me. If there's a leak in this investigation, I have to know about it."

"All I'll tell you is that I didn't get my information from the police." That was technically true. I got it from Nancy, who had gotten it from the police.

"Don't think," he said, "that just because you're very bright and very pretty I won't arrest you. I have a job to do and that comes first."

"Arrest me on what charges? Felonious intelligence?" Why had he said I was pretty? It made me even more nervous. From the moment I had first glanced at him, I had been aware of his physical presence; it seemed to fill the room, obliterating everything else, even Bob. He had a silent sexual tension in his body that few men have. It was as if behind his intense quality of observing every detail, every movement, behind another almost tangible aura of contemplativeness and calm, there lay a great network of acutely sensitive nerves, needing to be touched and—ultimately—soothed.

"Please," he began, and the doorbell rang. "I'll get it."

"Hi, Lieutenant," said the woman at the door, a small fluffy blond, a bad mixture of Jean Harlow and Sandra Dee. She wore a blue ski jacket and carried a large brown suitcase.

"Hi," he responded and, turning to me, explained: "She's from the forensics lab, to check out your refrig-

186

erator." Sharpe pointed to the kitchen, and she strolled there slowly, the two rounded cheeks of her behind gently rolling under her rust-colored slacks. I hated her. "All right, let's go back inside," he said, putting his warm hand on my back to guide me into the living room.

"Is she a police officer?" I asked.

"Yes."

"What's her name?"

"I don't know. Marsha something-or-other."

"Does she just do this sort of thing, or does she go to the scenes of murders and things like that?"

"Would you mind sitting down? We were discussing the Fleckstein case."

"Do you want to hear about the Duncks?" I asked. He sat about three feet away from me on the couch. "Do you know who they are?"

"Yes, thank you. But we have another matter to finish first."

"You mean about your putting me in jail with a lot of junkies and prostitutes and letting me be subjected to vicious physical attacks by prison-hardened, sadistic lesbians?"

"All right. Tell me about the Duncks." He was tolerating me out of amusement and curiosity, not because I had manipulated him.

Giving him as much detail as possible, I recounted my interview with Brenda and Dicky.

"How did you get them to talk to you?" he asked. "Just walk up and flash a smile?"

"Well, this is kind of embarrassing."

"Tell me anyway. I'll ignore your blushing."

I explained how I had arranged for a letter from my doctoral advisor, Ramsey, and the subterfuge I had used with the Duncks.

"A history student," he said softly. "So was I."

"American?"

"No. European."

"Where?"

"Fordham."

"You're Catholic?"

"No."

"What?"

"Nominally a Methodist. May I ask the questions?"

"Okay."

"Are you planning any more investigative work?"

I told him I had the possibility of an interview with Norma Fleckstein and, if that got me anywhere, with some of Bruce's nearest and dearest friends.

"You can't," he declared.

"Not if you throw me in jail so I can get my face cut up with razor blades."

"I mean," he said patiently, "that somebody wants you to mind your own business. That was the point of that little note on your refrigerator, remember? So, please, let me handle it."

"We'll see," I responded, as noncommittally as possible. Just then, the woman from the lab walked in from the kitchen.

"No prints," she announced. "A few smudges on the door handle. I'll take her prints, but I doubt if it'll mean anything." Without looking at me, as though I were a murder victim she found at the scene of a crime, she inked my fingers and pressed them on a card.

"Do you enjoy your work?" I asked her.

"Yeah," she answered. "You can go wash your hands off now." I waited. She looked at Sharpe and smiled. I couldn't determine whether she was flirting with him or trying to ingratiate herself with a superior officer. I had it in for her; it didn't occur to me that she was simply being friendly. "I got pictures and a sample of the paint, Lieutenant, but I don't think we'll find anything. It looks like ordinary red aerosol."

"What about the kitchen door?" he asked, standing to talk.

"Handle knocked out with a screwdriver and a hammer. Piece of junk. No problem to break in."

"No prints?" he demanded.

"Would I keep it a secret from you, Lieutenant?" she asked, and they smiled at each other.

"Can I clean off my refrigerator now?" I chimed in.

"Have fun, sweetie," she said. "You're going to have to repaint it." She performed her slow, ass-rolling glide back into the kitchen and came back zipping her ski jacket. "See you," she said to Sharpe, and picked up her suitcase. Buttocks undulating, she left.

I waited for him to sit again, but he stood still, hands in his pants pockets. "Anything else?" he inquired.

"About what?"

"Anything else you want to share with me about your investigation?"

"I can't think of anything else that's germane," I told him.

"Okay." Reaching down to the coffee table, he picked up his notebook and jammed it into his jacket pocket. "Just remember you received a message. I'm sure I don't have to tell you that the person who left it didn't break into your house just so you would be titillated. If you happen to think of anything you'd like to add, I'll leave you my number. You can call me." He extracted his notebook, ripped off a corner of a page, and wrote on it. He was left-handed.

"Do you have a coat?"

"It's in the car." He turned and strode to the door. I followed.

"Bye," I said, as he opened the door. He walked across the lawn, to a blue compact car parked in front of the house. I closed the door and dashed up the stairs to Kate's room, which faces the front of the house. I pulled back the shade about an inch and peered outside. Sharpe was sitting in his car, hands and forearms resting on the wheel, gazing straight ahead. After two or three minutes, he gunned the motor and drove off.

I curled up on Kate's bed, rubbed the crisp gingham bedspread between my fingers, and began to cry. Perhaps it was from relief, that an ordeal had ended. Or from fear, knowing a killer had my number. Or from a more familiar fear, recognizing that soon either Bob or I would have to make some concessions, renegotiate the terms of our contract. In some ways, confronting a killer seemed an easier prospect. Or maybe it was Sharpe. I wiped my eyes with the backs of my hands. Maybe I was crying because I hadn't been touched so deeply by a man's presence since . . . it had been so long, I couldn't really remember since when.

For another ten minutes I wallowed in my misery, feeling terribly shaky, very alone. Then the door opened and a little voice called: "Mommy, I'm here with Daddy." I wiped my eyes one last time and trudged downstairs.

Joey stood leaning against Bob, who was carrying two paper bags: one with a Baskin-Robbins logo and the other, much larger, of ordinary brown paper. This, he announced, hefting it, is white appliance paint. For the refrigerator. Joey and I will fix things up, he said to the closet behind me, won't we, Joey? They hung up their coats and headed for the kitchen. Joey dashed out for newspaper, masking tape, and more newspaper. Kate arrived soon after, and the three of them worked and giggled together, while the odor of paint wafted into the living room, where I was sitting, excluded by tacit fiat from the camaraderie of the kitchen.

"I'll make dinner," I announced at four o'clock, standing at the threshold of the kitchen, looking in.

"You can't," Bob hissed.

"What do you mean, I can't?"

"He means, Mommy," Kate broke in gently, "that no one can touch the refrigerator until tomorrow morning. It has to dry."

"It has to dry," Joey parroted. "So Daddy's taking us out for Chinese food."

"Right after the locksmith comes," added Bob, to whoever might be listening.

The locksmith came an hour later, and when he had finished banging and grinding, we left for the restaurant. Bob paid no more attention to me than he would to a shadow, but Kate took up the slack, seeing that we were all properly seated and that our teacups were clean. The waiter came, and Bob said: "Wonton soup."

"I'd rather have hot and sour soup," I countered.

"A separate bowl of hot and sour soup for the lady," Bob told the waiter, clearly believing that by this small concession he had effectively cut me off from the rest of the family. We ate in silence, dish after dish, occasionally asking one of the children about their day in an ostentatiously concerned manner.

"Aren't you going to read your fortune cookie?" asked Joey.

"No. I'd rather be surprised."

"Surprised?" he repeated, his four-year-old blue eyes wide and curious, not yet iced over, out-of-business like his father's.

"Okay," I said and opened the cookie to extract the thin strip of paper. I read: "A wise man takes no tea before noon." That, actually, was a relief. I had feared something like "A good wife is more precious than jade." Or "Women beware of short, gray-haired cops." With big, powerful hands.

When we pulled the car into the garage, I felt frightened; maybe the house had been broken into again. Maybe someone was lurking in the dining room. "Let me go in first," I said.

"I'll do it," Bob declared, still avoiding my glance. He marched into the house while I held the children back in the garage. "Come on in," he called impatiently. "Everything's fine." As we walked inside, past him, he lowered his voice and whispered to me: "Stop being so paranoid." Everything was fine. The new lock on the kitchen door twinkled its brass welcome, and the smell of paint was undiffused by fresh air. No broken windows. All doors secure.

"Hey, kids," Bob said, giving them his extra-wide grin, "how about my giving you a special shower in my bathroom?"

"Oh, Daddy," breathed Kate.

"Me and Kate together?" asked Joey.

"Sure. Why not? Now go upstairs and get undressed, you two," he said, chuckling a little, like a warm, cuddly daddy in a fifties situation comedy. Until that moment, he had bathed the children once each, as infants, and then declined to do it again. "They make me nervous. I'm afraid I'll drop them," he explained. And in my soul of souls, I was afraid he would, if only to prove a point. Upstairs, the children squeaked and giggled in their bedrooms, nearly euphoric that they had captured Bob's interest.

I remained in the living room while they showered, their squeals of pleasure muted only slightly by distance. When they finally trooped downstairs, faces gleaming and hair wet and lined with comb marks, I felt like a desiccated maiden aunt kissing her fruitful sister's children good night.

"Night, Mommy," they chimed.

"Come on, kids. I'll tuck you both in." Bob's sleeves were rolled up, the hair on his arms wet and darkened and matted.

"Could you read me a story, Daddy?" Kate asked.

"It's a little late for that, honey," he responded. She accepted it without a trace of a whimper. Then, hand in hand in hand, the Three Happy Singers dashed up the stairs. I waited. And waited some more. A half hour must have passed before I realized that Bob would not be coming down. Slowly, I mounted the stairs.

He was lying in bed in green and white striped pajamas, the quilt pulled taut and folded neatly around his chest. His hands were clutching a copy of *Business Week,* and he was studying its pages with seeming fascination. On its cover was a man in a beige suit with a string tie, his elbow resting on a large globe.

"Can we talk?" I began.

"I'm reading."

"I see that. Could you put your magazine aside for a minute?"

He rested the magazine on top of his chest and looked at me.

"Would you like me to explain why I got involved in this case?" *Business Week* rose an inch as he took a deep breath. Otherwise he remained motionless, his gaze steady. "Well? Shall I explain?"

"I really don't care," he said softly.

I squirmed a little. I swallowed. I ran my fingers over my eyebrows. "What do you mean, you don't care?"

"I simply mean that if you are going to continue this insane quest of yours, if you are going to continue to subject the family to jeopardy, then I will simply do my best to protect my children and leave you to your own devices. You can do what you want."

"Bob." I walked to his side of the bed and touched his shoulder.

"Don't touch me, Judith. Don't touch me until you get your head screwed on straight again. Do I make myself understood?"

He turned over and reached for the light. I undressed in the dark and climbed under the cold cover to lie on even colder sheets. "Bob," I whispered, easing over to his side of the bed. "Bob." He shook his body, as though ridding himself of a pesty mosquito. I inched away, fluffed my pillow into a high, soft mound, pulled the quilt over my ears and, eventually, fell asleep.

Chapter Thirteen

All I saw of Bob the next morning was a gold paisley tie stretched across his pillow with a note on top: "Took early train. Please have stain (prob fr coffee) removed. R.M.S." I stood, stretched, and made the bed, making certain the spread neatly covered the tie. Then, prancing downstairs, I made the children a more than usually elaborate breakfast and sent them off to school with a showy display of hugs and kisses.

As I poured myself a second cup of coffee, I contemplated washing a pile of wool sweaters or making a call to Hyde Park to make arrangements for examining the Roosevelt-Morgenthau correspondence. Before I could decide, the phone rang.

"Hello," I said hopefully.

"This is Brenda Dunck."

"Hi. How are you?" I inquired, as effusively as I could manage.

"Fine, thank you. You know my sister-in-law, Norma? Well, Dicky, my husband, spoke to her and she said it would be okay if you wanted to talk to her."

"Oh."

"You see, we're leaving today for a couple of days' vacation, and I thought if you wanted to see her, I should let you know before we left. I can give you her number, or if you want, I could call her."

"That's really very nice of you," I said slowly. "Very

nice." I took a sip of coffee. "Brenda, could you manage to hold off for a while? I have an awful lot of notes I have to transcribe."

"Yes, of course. The only reason I called is that you seemed so interested and you asked me to do it."

"I know, Brenda, and I truly appreciate your help. But I'll take a raincheck for a while. Thanks so much."

"Okay."

"I'll be in touch with you."

"Okay. Bye."

That was that. Anyone else who spoke to me about the case would get the same message, that I was no longer interested. There would be no more anonymous warnings. No more stiff, rejecting backs late in the night. I breathed what should have been a sigh of relief but wasn't. Another sigh, and I picked up the phone and called information. "In Shorehaven, please. The number of Marvin Bruce Fleckstein, a residence." I made the call.

"Hello," said a voice, hoarse and dull-sounding.

"Is this Norma Fleckstein?"

"Yes," the voice said, hesitantly.

"Hello. I'm Judith Singer. Your sister-in-law, Brenda, told me it was all right to call you. I'm doing my doctoral dissertation on the problems posed by freedom of the press and . . ."

"Yes. Why do you want to speak to me?"

"Because you've been hurt by scurrilous news stories," I said, trying to sound comforting and outraged at the same time.

"Well, I guess it would be all right. When do you want to come?"

"This morning?" I suggested.

"No. This morning's not good. The accountant is coming. Is tomorrow all right?" Only the dentalized *t*s of her slight New York accent prevented her from sounding like a robot. Her pitch didn't alter, her voice didn't rise at the end of a question, her timbre was flat, lifeless.

"Fine. Thank you. Would ten o'clock be too early?"

"No, that's all right."

"Fine. I'll see you then." She hung up without saying goodbye.

Upstairs in the bedroom, I took off my nightgown and sat on the edge of the bed, letting a wave of guilt flood over me. What kind of a person am I who would use this exhausted, grief stricken widow to satisfy my own perverse curiosity? I lumbered into the bathroom and turned on the shower. That poor, frightened creature. It wasn't right. Well, I'd make certain to be very gentle.

The water was hot, biting, and I let it pelt me, listening to it smash against my shower cap, feeling my skin turn rosy under its sharp attack. Ping, ping, ping, it went, smacking the small of my back. Ping, ping, ding. The ding, I realized, was not part of the score. It was the doorbell. I turned off the shower, grabbed a towel, and half dried myself, feeling, as I pulled on my jeans, clammy, wet patches in the backs of my legs. Ding. Again. Who the hell was it? And then I realized: Jehovah's Witnesses. Only they would ring my doorbell so early. I was the only one on the block who hadn't slammed the door in their faces, the only one who told them thank you, but no thank you. They took this very minor courtesy as a sign of my salvageable soul, so every month or two they would drop by, first thing in the morning, a wan, blond girl in her late teens and an older Japanese man, to see if I was ripe for conversion.

Ding. "Just a minute," I yelled and then regretted it. Had I remained silent, they would have gone away. Now I'd have to go down and reject them again. I put on a bra and quickly grabbed an old red sweater and pulled it over my head. Ding. Ding. Persistent little devils, I thought, and ran a brush through my hair. Ding. I ran down the stairs to the door, and with a force born of pique, yanked it open.

"Don't you even ask who it is?" It was Sharpe, leaning against the door frame, looking quite spiffy in a yellow turtleneck and a tweedy sport jacket. "I could have been the murderer."

"I was expecting Jehovah's Witnesses," I explained. My voice sounded feeble. I thought of my face, without makeup, and took a step back, out of the bright sunlight.

"You had an appointment?"

"No. But who else would be willing to come out and freeze their asses off at nine o'clock in the morning?" I looked at him and asked: "Don't you ever wear a coat?"

"No. It's just another thing to worry about. I keep it in the car." His eyes were fixed on mine, but he let them run down, all the way to my feet. "Don't you ever wear shoes?"

"I just got out of the shower."

"I was wondering why you took so long to answer the door. I figured you were out."

"Or lying in a pool of blood because I didn't cooperate with you."

"No," he said in his soft, slow way, "the murderer seems to lean toward thin, pointed weapons. The medical examiner thinks it was something like an ice pick. It makes a very narrow wound that doesn't bleed too much." He paused for a second, waiting for a reaction, but I remained impassive, a look I had cultivated before a mirror when I was eighteen and wanted very much to appear blasé. "Are you going to ask me to come in?" he finally said.

"Yes, of course," I answered, opening the door wider for him to pass through. He walked in, missing a golden opportunity to brush up against me. "Would you like some coffee?"

"Please," he replied, and walked right into the kitchen. I scurried after him. "Aren't you going to ask me why I'm here?"

The kitchen still smelled of paint, and I saw him looking at the refrigerator door. "I assume you came to browbeat me into talking. Milk? Cream? Sugar?"

"Cream. One sugar. No, if a killer can't terrorize you by breaking into your house, what can I do?"

"Well, the bloodless fatal wound was pretty effective."

"Obviously not effective enough," he said, sipping his coffee and looking at me. "No, I came to save you some time. I figured when you saw the police cars parked across the street, you'd have to spend at least a half hour investigating. So I'll tell you why we're here."

"What police cars?" I demanded, knowing as I said it how stupid I must sound. I walked to the front door, opened it, and, sure enough, two police cars were parked across the street. Sharpe's blue car was in my driveway. Silently, I closed the door and came back to the kitchen. "You're right. Police cars."

"And you're going to tell me you hadn't noticed them."

"I hadn't. I was in the shower."

"And when you were talking to me at your front door?"

"I guess it didn't register. I probably associated them with you."

"Do I look like I rate a full escort? And you did open the door without asking who was there." He contemplated me. "Do you have any more coffee?"

I poured him another cup. "It's perfectly obvious," I said firmly, "that you're getting nowhere fast with the investigation, so you decided to come here and make baseless accusations just to keep your deductive processes in order."

He laughed. "Okay. So I just called out two squad

cars so I could impress you with the power of the Nassau County P.D."

"All right," I said, leaning against the sink, "why are two police cars parked across the street?"

"Because we found what appears to be the murder weapon."

The motor on the electric clock whirred, the odor of paint permeated the kitchen, and I noticed that Sharpe wore black loafers, not the brown shoes cops wear in police procedurals.

"Can we go inside?" I asked. He stood, still holding his coffee mug, and led the way into the living room. He sat on the couch and looked at me, his expression bland, blank, unreadable. I set my mug on the coffee table and sat on the floor, about three feet away from him. "You found the weapon? Here?"

"At your neighbor's, Mrs. Tuccio's."

"Impossible."

"We found it."

"Where?"

"In front of her house, in the grating of a storm sewer."

"How did you find it?"

"What do you mean?" he asked. "We drove over first thing this morning and poked around a little. It was there."

I took a long, slow breath and stood. "A little elf came to you in your dreams last night and whispered in your ear that if you looked in Marilyn Tuccio's sewer you would find a nice surprise, better than a pot of gold? Or did a brilliant application of investigative logic lead you straight to that particular section of gutter?"

"Jesus, you're a pisser," he said softly.

"What was it? An anonymous letter?"

"Phone call," he muttered, gazing at his shiny black loafers. "Man or woman?"

"Couldn't tell. They called into the precinct and whispered to the desk officer." He drew his fingers

200

through his hair. "It happened about eleven last night. From about eleven-twenty on, we had someone watching the house, but we had to wait until it was light to search. We've been here since early this morning."

"Hello, police," I croaked, holding an imaginary telephone receiver to my ear. "Check out Marilyn Tuccio's storm sewer. We murderers always bury our weapons in our own front yards." Replacing the invisible receiver, I peered at him and cleared my throat. "What did Marilyn say when you showed her the search warrant?"

"We didn't need one. The storm sewer is public property. The caller was very specific. Told us to look in the grating in the storm sewer at the right front of the house. It was there."

"What was it"

"An awl. Wrapped in a plastic bag."

"Any chance of identifying it for sure?"

"I don't know. We sent it to the lab. Can I use your bathroom?"

"Upstairs. First door on the left." He moved quickly, taking the steps two at a time. The door closed. I moved to the corner of the couch where Sharpe had been sitting. The cushions were warm. I heard the toilet flush. In a moment, he walked down.

"Did you notice anything unusual last night, about nine or ten o'clock?" he asked, sitting right next to me.

"No. I went to sleep early."

"Yeah. I saw your husband leave about six-thirty this morning."

"Oh."

"You know why I asked you about last night?"

"Yes. If someone called you around eleven, it might have been planted right before. Unless you're assuming that Marilyn put it right into the sewer after she perpetrated the dastardly deed."

"Well, it seems to have been placed there fairly recently. The plastic bag showed no signs of wear."

"And if it had been there since the murder, it would be encrusted with gook."

"Right," he said. He was leaning back on the couch, his arm casually draped over the back of both his cushion and mine. His face was about a foot away from mine. Sharpe had shaved close that morning; there was a raw, red patch along his left cheek.

I looked away, down to the gold carpet, studying its flat weave. "And so you think that after she committed the murder, Marilyn hid the awl behind her unbleached flour and then, yesterday, decided to wedge it into the sewer and give you a call, just so you wouldn't be bored." I felt him looking at me and glanced at him to check. He was. "That's a pretty sorry hypothesis." I paused. "Look, I'm sorry. I didn't mean to sound so sarcastic." He stared at the fireplace, not even acknowledging that he had heard me. "I apologize," I said softly, putting my hand on top of his. It felt so warm that I pulled my hand away.

"It's okay," Sharpe said. "Don't feel bad. It's just that this is one of the toughest cases I've ever worked on. Nothing seems to be going right. Every time I think we have a good lead, it turns out not to be a lead."

"So you don't really suspect Marilyn Tuccio?"

"I don't know. See, on every case that comes in—other than the really obvious ones—we spend the first twenty-four hours convinced we have it almost wrapped up. We know who did it and all we have to do is tie up a couple of loose ends. And this time we knew it was your neighbor. She had a motive . . ."

"What?"

"Well, it seemed like a motive. She made that announcement to Fleckstein's nurse that he'd better watch out. And she certainly had the opportunity, being alone with him."

"And she always carries an awl in her handbag," I observed.

202

"I know, I know. Anyhow, by the morning after he was murdered, we knew that dozens of people in this town had a motive. Anyway, we're thinking about quite a few other people now, but she was told to get a lawyer."

"She has one," I said. "Helen Fields, the Assemblywoman."

"So I heard."

"Marilyn's beyond subtlety. One of your people thought she might be linked up with Fleckstein's Mafia connections because her last name is Italian." I paused for an instant. "Was that you?"

"Are you kidding?" he asked incredulously. "Do you think I would do something like that?"

"No, of course not," I responded, feeling horribly guilty for hurting his feelings again. "Well," I said lamely, "where are you going to go from here?"

"Back to my office."

"No, I mean in terms of the investigation."

"Oh, well," he said carefully, "that depends largely on you."

"Me?"

"I'm going to ask a favor of you."

"Look, would you stop patronizing me?"

"What should I do? Lose my temper? Alienate you?" he asked testily. "You're useful. You know this community. You're observant."

"All right. What do you want me to do?"

"Relax," he said, noticing I was sitting, tense and rigid, at the edge of the couch. "It won't be too painful. I just want you to look at the photographs. See if you can recognize anybody. Unless you were bullshitting me about not having seen them."

"I was not bullshitting you. I don't know. How would I recognize anybody?"

"Why don't you give it a try?"

"I don't know."

"I'll bring them over tomorrow. You won't even have to come down to headquarters."

"No. I mean, I'm busy tomorrow. There's no way I could make it," I said, remembering my date with Norma Fleckstein.

"Okay," he said, standing up, "I'll see you the day after tomorrow then. About nine-thirty?"

"I don't know," I repeated. What would happen if I saw Mary Alice in one of the pictures? Could I deny flatly that I knew her? Even if I did, Sharpe would be astute enough to realize I was reacting to something, and then there would be no stopping him. He was intelligent and tenacious. He'd keep after me until I told him everything I knew.

"Well, don't worry about it now," he said. "See you day after tomorrow."

"All right."

"Bye." He turned and walked briskly out the front door.

At times I am capable of tremendous self-control, so I restrained myself from peeping through the living room curtains to watch Sharpe walk to his car. Instead, I remained on the couch and concentrated on his image, on his yellow turtleneck, how it covered him so neatly; he had no paunch, no limp, flaccid pectoral muscles. He was lean and firm and exquisitely compact. The insides of his thighs would never ripple when he sat, his waist and hips would form one taut, fluid line. Suddenly, with no conscious realization of the leap from lust to guilt, I walked to the telephone and called Bob.

"Hi," I said to his secretary, Candi, a tall, thin woman about my age who still wore miniskirts and short white boots. "Is he in?"

"I'm sorry, Mrs. Singer. He's in conference at the moment. But he told me to tell you if you called that he'll be working very late tonight. Is there any message?"

Was there any message? But all I said was: "No. No message. Have a nice day."

I didn't feel hurt or even angry. Bob was far more resolute than I. When we first began dating, we would have staring contests, gazing unblinkingly into each other's eyes until one of us laughed or averted our glance; it was always me. But this time I couldn't win because I wasn't going to join the game. He could fix his eyes on mine forever, but I would have neither a giggle nor a tearful apology to offer him. Or even a plea to please, Bob, let's call a halt. You win by default.

The receiver was still in my hand, so I called Mary Alice.

"Let me get it upstairs," she said, after I had identified myself. She put me on hold, and I waited for two or three minutes until she picked up the phone again. "My sister's here," she informed me, which I assumed was an explanation for the delay.

"That's nice," I said.

"Actually, Judith, it's not so nice."

"I'm sorry to hear it."

"Her husband moved out on her. It's been an unbelievable shock, as I'm sure you can well imagine."

"Which sister is this?" I asked reflexively.

"Mary Jeanne."

"The one from Larchmont?"

"No. That's Mary Elizabeth. Mary Jeanne lives in Darien. I should say lived. She says a house without a husband is not a home, and she's bereft, absolutely bereft. Do you know why he left her?"

"No."

"Because he's forty-two years old and wants to find himself. Can you imagine that? Forty-two years old, in line for a major vice-presidency at IBM, and he wants to find himself. Never mind about Mary Jeanne. It's a good thing that all the rest of us married men who work in New York, so at least she had her sisters to rely on. She's feeling terribly rejected. She was on the phone with her psychiatrist for over a half an hour just to keep from having a complete nervous breakdown, and do you know what he said?"

"Listen, Mary Alice . . ."

"He said her husband was a cad. A cad. And when a psychiatrist says that . . ."

"Mary Alice, I have to talk to you about the Fleckstein case."

"Judith, please. What more can I say? Here I am wrapped up in my sister's problem. What does she have left to live for? 'Abandon all hope, all ye who enter here.' Right? How can I concentrate on my own problems right now?"

"The police want me to look at some pictures they found in Fleckstein's office," I said.

"Judith, no!" she breathed, her voice suddenly thick and heavy. "You can't. I told you what I did in private. Like the way you talk to a priest or a doctor. Does our relationship mean nothing to you? Does the confidentiality of all the things I said come down to a big fat zero? Judith, I can't believe . . ."

"Mary Alice, shut up." There was silence. "Now listen to me. Why don't you call Claymore Katz? If your picture is there, sooner or later someone is going to recognize it. If the cops can't get anywhere, they're going to be showing the photographs around to more and more people. Just by the law of averages . . ."

"I don't know. I just don't want to get involved in all this."

"But you are involved," I said. Again there was silence.

Finally she spoke. "Do what you have to do, Judith."

"Look, Mary Alice, I'll tell you what. I'll look at the pictures, but I'm sure I won't recognize yours if it's there."

"What do you mean? Why won't you recognize it?"

"I mean, I realize you were talking to me as a conduit to a lawyer and that makes the conversation privileged."

"Really?"

"I don't know. But I don't think I'll recognize your picture if I see it."

"But what if you do?" Actually, she was even stupider than Nancy or I had surmised.

"I'll make it a point not to. Do you understand me, Mary Alice?"

"Yes. Now I do. But still . . ."

"What?" I asked, trying to sound patient.

"How would you like it if I saw pictures of you?"

She was right, of course. If someone had taken a snapshot of me, even lying supine with my own husband blanketing me, missionary style, I would want no one—not even Bob—to see it. "You're right, Mary Alice." I couldn't think of anything else to say.

"And it's not as if I'm the only one, Judith. Believe me. He told me some of the people he did things with, and you'd be shocked. I mean, I really didn't do anything so unusual. Not really."

"Like who?" I asked. "What names did he mention?"

"Lots of people," she insisted.

Realizing I was back in the game-playing business, I bantered: "Oh, come on. Lots of people? He really mentioned names to you?"

"He most certainly did. Would you believe Ginger Wick?" I could; Nancy had already told me. "Everyone thinks Ginger is such a genius career lady, but Bruce told me about some of the things she liked to do. And let me tell you something, Judith," she sputtered, the words pouring out too quickly for her to scrutinize their import, "what Ginger Wick liked would make you realize that she isn't so liberated. And Ms. Gordon-Jaffee." She spit out the "Ms." Laura Gordon-Jaffee was a local feminist who had become involved in a national group that raised money to finance litigation in sex discrimination cases. By all reports she was intelligent, effective, and violently energetic. Her name had been mentioned in a magazine article on the new leaders of the liberation movement.

I was stunned. "Laura Gordon-Jaffee? How did someone like that get hooked up with Bruce Fleckstein?"

"What do you mean, 'someone like that'?"

I had been something less than diplomatic. "I mean, she's so busy. Traveling around. Making speeches. Organizing."

"I don't know. But Bruce told me all about her."

"What did he say?"

"Well, that for a women's libber, she sure liked it a lot."

"Liked what?"

"You know. Sex."

"Oh." I felt relieved. If Laura Gordon-Jaffee had been fixated on handcuffs or baby-doll pajamas, I would have hung up the phone, baked a pile of brownies, and waited patiently for my grandchildren to be born. "Did he mention anyone else?"

"No one that I can remember."

"Are you positive?"

"Yes. Those were the only names I recognized."

I said goodbye, again promising that her face would remain foggy in my memory when I looked at the photos. But I pleaded with her to call a lawyer; if Bruce had told her about his other paramours, maybe he had told them about her. But Mary Alice denied it, assuring me that he had promised to keep their liaison secret.

"Pea brain," I muttered as I got off the phone. My stomach began making plaintive grumbling noises, so I poured myself a glass of milk. I took two big swallows, when the phone rang. It was Nancy.

"Busy, busy," she commented. "You were chatting away for quite a while. Someone fascinating? Arthur Schlesinger? The Pope?"

"Even better," I answered wearily. "Mary Alice."

"Sorry to hear it."

"Nancy, are you free tonight?"

"Free?" she asked blankly.

"Could you have dinner with me? Or is Larry coming home?"

"I'll tell him to work late," she said. "Anything wrong?"

"Yes. No. I don't know. I just feel like getting out for a while. Let's go some place really nice. I'll break out a new pair of pantyhose, okay?"

"Fine. Do you want me to pick you up?"

"Would you? About seven?"

"See you then," she said. "I'll make a reservation some place nice. You sound as though you could use it."

I gulped down the rest of my milk and called Mrs. Foster, who said yes, she'd love to baby-sit for her little lambs. Mrs. Foster calls all the children she sits for her little lambs.

Later, in my bedroom, I opened my closet and reached into the back pocket of an old pair of white jeans that hadn't fit since Joey was conceived. My worldly goods, I thought, and counted out forty-five dollars. More than enough for dinner and a baby sitter. But not nearly sufficient for even a down payment on a really nasty divorce lawyer.

Chapter Fourteen

"A bottle of Chablis," Nancy informed the waiter. "We'll order later." We sat in the back room of Hermann Lomm's, a local restaurant that had risen to fame on the basis of its magnificent T-bone steaks and crisp, salty German-fried potatoes. I settled back into an uncomfortable large Papa Bear chair upholstered with red vinyl and nail studs. Not the atmosphere for a quiet, cathartic cry with a good friend. This was a tough meat and potatoes place. I leaned over the table and arranged the packets of sugar and artificial sweetener into neat little piles.

"How lovely and precise," observed Nancy. "Do you think you could stop your housekeeping chores and talk to me?"

"Sure," I said, giving her a weak smile. "I think my life may be in ruins." I waited for a quip, but she said nothing. "Bob has withdrawn from me completely. Someone—probably the murderer—broke into my house. And the cop who's in charge of the investigation keeps threatening to arrest me, and I want to have an affair with him."

"Judith," she breathed, "you have been busy."

"It's better than cleaning out closets," I retorted.

"For heaven's sakes, stop trying to be cool. Tell me what happened."

For the next half hour, over a bottle of icy wine and a

Caesar salad, I recounted everything that had happened; from the moment I walked into my house and saw the M.Y.O.B. on my refrigerator to my planned meeting with Norma Fleckstein to my last glimpse of Sharpe walking out of my living room on his lovely, powerful legs.

"I assume you want my reaction to all this," Nancy finally said. I nodded. "Well, let's start with the break-in. It's fairly clear . . ." The waiter came and took our order for dinner: steak for two, medium rare, fried potatoes, sautéed onions. "And a carafe of red wine," she called as he trotted toward the kitchen.

"I don't think I should have any more to drink," I said.

"Hush, Judith. Now, as to the break-in. Nice people generally do not force someone's door in unless they are deeply perturbed about something." She lifted her long hair from under the collar of her yellow silk shirt and let it fall casually onto her shoulders. Three businessmen at the next table watched her. "Therefore, I think you ought to take the message seriously."

"I do. It is serious."

"All right. Now, it's clear that it's someone involved in this nasty murder. Most likely it's not the Mafia. I really can't imagine some hood pulling up to your house in a shiny blue Cadillac and spray-painting your refrigerator. Right? I mean, they tend to be more forthright in their requests."

I agreed. "Whoever it is," I said, "is an amateur. And not terribly subtle, either."

Nancy looked up. The waiter came and placed a large platter of thickly sliced steak in the middle of the table. We sat silently as he served us.

"All right," Nancy said after he left, "so we can exclude the pros. Now, of all the people in Shorehaven who might have wanted to see Fleckstein laid out with a lily in his hand, do you have any idea who might be the one?"

"Yes."

"Who?"

"Well, it's just a feeling, you know. Nothing based on fact."

"I see," she said, spearing a piece of potato with her fork. "And that's what you told this stud Sharpe and that's why he threatened to arrest you."

"Right."

"Well, if he can't get it out of you, I certainly can't." She stared down at her plate, contemplating her steak. "Since when," she asked, looking up, "do you go for WASPs? You've always seemed to be drawn to those glowering, intense, cerebral Jewish types."

"Oh, Nancy, I've never met anyone like Sharpe. You should see him."

"Oh, Nancy," she mimicked. "My God, you sound positively pubescent. Do you dream about walking hand in hand with him through a field of clover?"

"No. I dream of finding some nice, seedy motel room and screwing until we both expire from exhaustion."

"Oh, boy," she said. "Can you handle that, Judith?"

"I doubt it. Anyway, I don't know if he's interested."

"What do you think?"

"I think he is. But it's just a feeling. I mean, I have nothing concrete . . ."

"Eat your dinner," she ordered.

I did, along with a glass of resiny red wine. And then another. Oddly, I didn't feel at all tipsy, just extremely alert. Nancy sat back in her chair, half her steak left over, while I again went over all the details of the case, all the reactions of the people I had spoken with: Fay, Mary Alice, Scotty Hughes, the Duncks, Marilyn.

"Do you have any plans to speak with his nurse, Lorna Lewis?" she inquired.

"Yes. She's next on my list, after Norma."

"Do you think it could have been her?"

"Nancy. Come on."

"I just asked. Don't get so touchy."

"Look, all I'll say is that the police believe she left Fleckstein's office first, before he finished up with Marilyn Tuccio."

"And did she? Or do you think she came back later?"

I filled my mouth with air and exhaled slowly. "I don't know anything for sure."

"Boy," Nancy commented, "you want to keep everything to yourself. What do you want to do, wrap it all up in a neat little package and present it to your cop as a token of your love?"

"I don't know," I said thoughtfully.

"All right, I won't push you. Now, what about the Duncks?"

"Well, I told you everything I know about them. He belongs to your club, doesn't he?"

"Yes. And everyone agrees that the admissions committee made a truly tragic error. I mean, Lord, he is so adolescent. Now let me get something straight. I was right, he did have a fight with Bruce over money?"

"Yes. But according to Brenda, they had kissed and made up. Apparently, Fleckstein even steered some business his way."

"I see. And what about Mary Alice?"

"Well, she had a motive. And so did all the women he photographed."

"Was he actually involved in blackmail?"

"I don't have any more information on that than I had the day we spoke to Mary Alice. Of course, he did have the pictures, so the threat was implicit. And he seemed to have a knack for selecting women with successful husbands, women who could pay."

"You see," said Nancy, "that's why I pick nice, sweet young guys who have no imagination beyond their own cocks. They like me, I like them, we have a good time, and that's all. Lord, these convoluted relationships. I don't understand them at all."

"Well, these women needed something. Don't you?"

214

"Yes. I need lots of good, straight sex."

"Don't you need love? Attention?"

"Judith, they're not exactly ignoring me. And I get love from Larry. Attention too. Sometimes he's painfully boring and he has the soul of a Calvinist, but he really loves me. And I love him."

"I know you do. But why do you need other men too?"

"Because they give me things that Larry can't." I peered at her curiously. "Passion. Spontaneity. Novelty. And excitement."

"Can't you get that from Larry?"

"Can you get that from Bob?"

"That's unfair."

"No, it isn't."

We sat for a while, silent, and then I switched the subject to her article on the fleeing suburbanite. It was going well, she said, and would probably be finished in another two weeks. The waiter came with the check. Nancy picked it up, saying it was her treat.

"Why?" I demanded.

"Why not?" she responded.

She drove me home, and as I reached for the door to get out, she took my hand and squeezed it. "You'll be okay," she said.

I strode into the house, somewhat belligerently, propelled by the wine, but Bob hadn't come home yet. I paid Mrs. Foster, marched upstairs and, swaying a little, undressed and got into bed. Bob's gold tie was still lying limp on his pillow. Within five minutes I was asleep.

He came home that night, I knew, because his side of the bed had been slept in. But by the time I awoke, at seven, he was gone—and so was his tie. I found it a moment later, in the bathroom waste basket, curled up beside a foil packet of Alka-Seltzer and a wad of crumpled tissues. He's been drinking to forget me, I thought. But he's such a lousy drinker; his stomach gets upset

215

after a half of a martini. And the tissues. He's been crying. Or he used them to wipe some whore's lipstick off his mouth and God knows where else. I picked them up and examined them: normal, used, mucousy tissues. I threw them back with disgust.

With a loud sigh, I showered and dressed, then went downstairs to make breakfast for the children. Feeling heavy with guilt, I called a mother of one of Joey's friends and arranged to have the bus leave him at her house after nursery school. That way, I could stay as long as I had to with Norma Fleckstein, without worrying that my son was standing before a locked, empty house, bleating with fear and hunger.

At nine-fifty, I checked Fleckstein's address in the telephone book. At nine fifty-five, I got in the car and drove there. And at ten on the dot, Norma Fleckstein answered the door in a coral cashmere sweater set with matching slacks, a black mourner's ribbon pinned over her left breast like fourth prize in some terribly depressing contest.

"Hello," I said.

"Hello," she answered. "Easy, Prince," she commanded, as a mammoth German shepherd pushed its way past her and growled at me. "He's really very gentle," she explained, as the dog stuck his snout between my legs. "Stop that, Prince. Bad dog. Bad dog." Prince took a long sniff and, clearly uninterested in what I had to offer, turned and skulked away into the house. "Come in," Norma said.

I did, but gingerly. I love dogs in general, but German shepherds make me extremely nervous. Somehow, I feel they're still in cahoots with the Nazis, and at a command from some place deep in the bowels of Argentina or the Schwarzwald, they'll leap up and devour every Jew within a ten-mile radius.

She led me into her living room which was surprisingly pleasant: grass green carpet, green and white upholstered couch and chairs, and light, sleek white wood furniture. The room was like a garden, with plants all about, hanging from the ceiling, growing up walls, covering tables, giving off the moist, earthy smell of spring.

"A lovely room," I said, smiling. She didn't acknowledge my compliment, so I launched into my spiel about doctoral dissertations, and abusive press, the rights of the individual, and the agony of unwanted notoriety. Norma nodded several times, not so much committing herself to my thesis as indicating that she understood what I was saying. She lit a cigarette, took a deep drag, and asked in a hushed, flat voice: "What do you want from me?"

"Well, before I ask for your personal reactions, I'd like to know what happened when the articles first appeared. Did anyone call you to give you moral support? Any friends react adversely?"

"Would you like a cigarette?" she asked, offering me a Parliament, as neat with its recessed filter as she was.

"No. No thank you."

She clutched the cigarettes and a gold lighter in her left hand. "I'm sorry. What was your question?"

"I was asking about how your friends reacted."

"Well, several friends called. Some came over."

"What did they say? Were they shocked? Did they dismiss it? Did they make any comments about the press?" The last question, I knew, was completely asinine, but I wanted to seem full of my topic.

"I told them it was all a bunch of lies and they believed me. What did Bruce need to do anything like that for? He made a very nice living in his practice, and he made some very fine investments. We didn't need any more than we had." She talked without inflection or passion, as though she had carefully memorized a speech in a language she didn't understand.

"Well," I asked, "who do you think was responsible for his legal problems and all this negative publicity?"

"Someone was out to get him. To destroy him." This, too, was said in a dead voice.

217

"Who?" I asked, displaying as little curiosity as I could.

"I don't know. I'd rather not say."

"Someone close?"

"Please," she began, stabbing out her cigarette in a large white ceramic ashtray and reaching into the pack for another.

"Your brother?"

Her finger had just flicked the lighter. She let it burn, leaving her cigarette unlit. "How did you hear that?"

"Frankly," I said, "I knew that your husband and Dicky were on the outs over your father's will. Is that right?"

She lit her cigarette and flicked the lighter shut. "Yes, but it's not like it sounds. My father had given Dicky a lot of money when he was alive. Dicky was always starting some new business and then failing, and my father must have poured in over fifty thousand dollars before he died. He had a massive coronary. So he left his estate to me because Dicky had already gotten his share."

"And you mean Dicky still wanted more?"

"Yes," she answered, leaning forward slightly. "Dicky said that he was a businessman and the oldest and I was already provided for because I had made a good marriage."

"And your husband," I commented, casting my eyes down in a ritual gesture of sadness, "your husband felt that you were entitled to your share?"

"That's right. I mean, I wasn't going to make a big deal about it, but Bruce said it was a matter of principle."

"Of course," I agreed.

"But how did you know about Dicky?"

"Oh. That. Well, in researching this chapter of my dissertation, I heard that there was some tension between you and the Duncks." She sat stiffly, waiting for me to elaborate. I did. "But then I heard that your husband had sent some business his way." I didn't mention that I heard it slip from Brenda Dunck. "Then all of a sudden, your husband is under investigation. So, I thought to myself, who might have something against him? Who might still be holding a grudge, especially if the business didn't pan out? Your brother, right?"

"Yes," she breathed. "But the terrible thing is that Bruce didn't know anything about pornography or anything like that. I think he had heard about some people who needed a printer, and just to be decent, he told them about Dicky. The next thing, he's involved in this awful investigation. He got a subpoena."

"Really?"

"Yes. They came here looking for things."

"Who came?"

"I don't know. Police. They were wearing regular clothes. They had a search warrant and they came late one morning."

"What did you do?"

"I called Bruce, but he was out, so I left a message with his service to hurry home."

"His nurse wasn't in?"

"No. They generally take the same lunch hour. Anyway, these men, there must have been three or four of them, were all over the house. Do you know what they found?"

"What?"

"Nothing."

"Of course. Was that the first you knew about your husband being investigated?"

"Yes. Bruce told me that he hadn't wanted to upset me. But he said everything would be all right, not to worry. He had a lawyer."

"And was everything all right?" She hung her head. "I'm sorry. I meant, was the investigation pursued?"

"Well, nothing else happened until after Bruce was, was killed. Then all those news stories were printed."

"And then what happened?"

"Nothing. Some reporters called, but I just hung up on them."

"And what about these so-called Mafia connections?"

"That's ridiculous. Bruce was a professional man, a well-known periodontist. He had even been called in to consult on one of the Kennedys' in-law's gum problems."

"Oh," I said, and nodded respectfully. "One more thing. How did your husband know that it was Dicky who was causing all the trouble? I admit it's a natural guess, because that's what I came up with, but did he know it for certain?"

Norma ran her hand over her neat, short, frosted hair. She wore earrings of coral surrounded by a small semicircle of diamonds; they looked real. "He told me that the day he went down to court to talk to the Grand Jury, he ran into this man he hardly knew, the man he sent to Dicky just to be nice and throw a little business his way. I mean, Dicky needs all the money he can get. My sister-in-law should have married a rich man. She buys antiques."

"Oh," I commented. "And about the man your husband met when he went to the Grand Jury?"

"Well, this man told him that he had heard from someone he knew who worked with the government investigators that Dicky had been the one."

"Did your husband ever confront Dicky?"

"No."

"Why not?"

"He said that he was sure Dicky would come to his senses and realize how important family loyalties were. And he didn't want to be mean because Dicky was my brother and he didn't want to hurt me."

"Did you and he discuss the case often?"

"No. Bruce said he wanted his home to be a haven in the storm."

"You were very close?" She didn't answer. "Were you close?" I asked again, more softly this time.

"Yes," she responded, her eyes filling with tears.

"I'm really sorry. This must be so painful for you. The horror of your loss, then the newspaper articles, and then this thing with your brother."

"It's all right," she said. "And I'm not angry at Dicky. I know him too well. He's always been kind of weak, childish." She glanced at me. "Do you have any more questions?"

For another ten minutes, I asked her about her reaction to the newspaper coverage. She was, understandably, outraged. Her children had been protected, she said, but she lived in fear that one of their schoolmates would taunt them about Fleckstein's legal troubles.

I stood to leave. I had been there less than a half hour. "I want to thank you," I said.

"That's all right," she responded. As she rose, her slacks fell perfectly into place. "I hope I helped you."

"You did." As we walked to the door, Prince, who must have been roused by our footsteps, came barreling in.

"Easy, Prince," she snapped, and held his chain collar.

"Bye," I said, slipping out the door as quickly as possible. "Thanks again."

Well, I thought, at least I confirmed a wild guess. But it's Dicky who should have been killed, if the murder had anything to do with the porno ring. Not Bruce. So, I mused, as I drove past the glistening white colonials and low-slung ranch houses on the Flecksteins' street, who did it? I felt I knew, but I wasn't sure. Lots of people, lots of motives. And a seemingly grieving widow, numbed with grief over the loss of her loyal and loving husband.

Chapter Fifteen

By the time I reached home, I felt more sanguine. It's really getting clearer, I said to myself. Soon it will all fall into place. I almost skipped into the house. It's coming! I've almost got it! Then who did it? I sank into a kitchen chair, with an almost palpable sense of a thick, black cloud descending upon my head. It wasn't getting clearer at all. It was as murky as ever.

Just to prove to myself that I was still alive, I called Shorehaven High School. Could Mrs. Jacobs call me during her lunch hour? Thank you. Maybe all I needed was a little more information.

I dashed about puffing up cushions, jamming toys onto shelves, dropping the children's mud-encrusted clothes into the washing machine. Responding to a massive surge of adrenalin, I grabbed a stray crayon and made an extensive shopping list, with neat categories for paper goods, detergents, pasta, and condiments, plus Swiss cheese, eggs, yogurt, milk, spinach, cucumbers . . . and the doorbell rang.

"Who's there?" I demanded, grinning a little. I pictured my two second-string saviors from Jehovah's Witnesses.

"Nelson Sharpe." I ran my fingers down the sides of my nose to erase the oily sheen and opened the door.

"Hi. I thought you were coming tomorrow."

"Well, I took the day off, but I happened to be in the

neighborhood." He was wearing a pair of faded jeans and a gray sweat shirt and looked very unofficial. "Can I come in?"

"Sure."

"You look nice," he said. In anticipation of Norma Fleckstein's breathtaking good grooming, I had put on a pair of good red slacks, a red and white sweater, and enough bronzing gel to grease a Mack truck.

I closed the door behind him. "Thank you." I stifled the urge to add: "You don't really mean it." Then, glancing at him, I wanted to say, "So do you." His sweat shirt was stretched at the neck and a little patch of curly brown and gray hair peeked out at me. Was he really being casual, sloppy even, on his day off, or had he dressed with care, sensing that jeans and a jock's sweat shirt were dynamite? "Do you have the pictures?" I asked.

"No. I'll bring them tomorrow. Is anything new? Make any startling discoveries in the last twenty-four hours?" I opened my mouth to speak but then decided not to. "All right. Something happened," he said. "What? Tell me."

"Dicky Dunck was the informer in the Fleckstein case."

"Jesus H. Christ, Judith," he bellowed, "would you please tell me where in the hell you're getting your information? I'm not kidding now." His face was quite flushed, and I knew he was really angry, but he had called me Judith, so I didn't mind at all.

"I'd be delighted, Nelson," I replied. "Now, just so you won't get apoplexy in the middle of my living room, I heard it from Norma Fleckstein. Aren't I being cooperative?"

"Norma Fleckstein!" he yelled.

"I thought you'd say that," I observed. "Calm down for a second and let me explain. Norma said that Bruce just happened to run into a casual acquaintance whom he had referred to Dicky Dunck for some printing business. Now this individual—whom he told Norma he barely knew—told Bruce that he had heard through a police source that Dicky was the informant." As precisely as I could, I repeated the conversation I had had with Norma. "Is it true about Dicky?" I asked. He said nothing. "Come on. I told you everything I know."

He chewed his lower lip. "Okay, but, Judith, if this goes any further, you're in big trouble." I sat motionless next to him on the living room couch, which had become our base of operations, and said nothing. "Yes," he said, "Dunck was an informer."

"Wow!"

"But Fleckstein couldn't have heard it from the police, even secondhand. We weren't in the case until Fleckstein was killed. It was the U.S. Attorney's office, and they were dealing with the IRS and the FBI. I can't understand why he told her it was the police."

"It was probably a misinterpretation on Norma's part; anybody in law enforcement is ipso facto a cop. Now, getting back to Dicky. I thought it was a porno film distributorship. Why would they need a printer?"

"They had books too. Not many. But real raunchy stuff."

"Like what?"

"I'd rather not say."

"Good God, Nelson. I'm not a sixteen-year-old virgin. Tell me."

"Something to appeal to the average white-collar child molester. And some homosexual S & M stuff."

"Literature or pictures?"

"If you stretch the definition, you could call it literature."

"So tell me. What happened?" I kicked off my shoes and put my feet on the coffee table.

"Well, to make it short, Fleckstein had a patient who had a friend who needed some capital for a little investment in the arts. The cinema. Fleckstein went in for about twenty thou and later put in some more, we don't know exactly how much. Anyhow, at some point his partners suggested they had some promising manuscripts and needed a printer, so he suggested his brother-in-law."

"So why did Dicky become an informer?"

"He said he was repulsed by the content."

"Come on," I said.

"Their payments weren't as generous as Dicky had anticipated."

"So he spilled the beans?"

"You've been reading too much Dashiell Hammett."

"I'm trying to communicate with you on your level."

"Don't be such a wise ass," he said, grinning.

"Anyhow, what happened? Dicky ran to squeal?"

"Sort of."

I put my feet flat on the floor. "Sort of?"

"Judith, this is confidential."

"I know. I know."

"The IRS had another informant, but they needed someone else for corroboration. One of their agents went to talk to Dicky, and he caved in within a few minutes."

"Did he make a deal with them?"

"Yes. He would be an unindicted co-conspirator."

"Who was the other informant?"

"I'm not going to tell you. Anyhow, his connection with Fleckstein was tenuous. Now, tell me your impression of Norma Fleckstein."

"She's a complete cipher," I said slowly. "There's a heaviness about her, a dullness, but it's definitely not stupidity. I think she's fairly bright. It may be that she's still reeling because of shock. She described Fleckstein as a good husband, a good breadwinner. If you take her at her word, she had absolutely no idea that he was involved in any murky business deals—and definitely no extramarital relationships." I almost choked on "extramarital" but kept talking. "But she should have sensed something was going on."

226

"Maybe she didn't want to know," Sharpe said.

"Maybe."

We were silent.

"I think I'm hungry," he finally said.

"Can I make you some lunch?"

"Okay."

"Only if you give me a rundown on everybody's alibi."

"All right. But it's not very gracious of you to put preconditions on lunch after you've offered it."

"I know. But no alibis, no tuna fish."

"Oh. Tuna fish."

"You don't like tuna fish?"

"Not particularly."

"How about a Wonder Bread and Miracle Whip sandwich?"

"Do you really want to get into ethnic jokes, Judith?" I smiled. "How about some eggs? Do you have any eggs?" he asked.

"A few. How do you want them?"

"Come into the kitchen. I'll make you an omelet you'll remember for the rest of your life."

It was a memorable omelet, more moist and fluffy than any I had ever made. "Great," I pronounced. "Magnificent. Where did you learn to cook like this?"

"I was a cook in the Air Force."

"And from that you became a cop?"

"No. My father was a cop. Actually, he was chief of police of a six-man force in Bay Harbor. That's a little incorporated village about fifteen miles from . . ." The phone rang. It was Fay Jacobs.

"Judith," she asked, "is anything wrong?"

"No. Sorry if I worried you. Hold on and I'll take the phone upstairs." I handed the receiver to Sharpe and whispered: "Business call. Will you hang up when I pick up the phone?"

"Sure," he said.

I dashed up the stairs to the bedroom and lifted the

227

phone. There was a definite click and I knew he'd hung up.

"Fay. Sorry to bother you, but I figured you'd have a free minute during your lunch hour. Hope I didn't disturb you."

"That's all right, Judith. How are you? I really enjoyed our lunch. It made me regret working; I have so little free time to visit with friends."

"Well, we'll have a gala lunch during Easter vacation. Fay, I was wondering. Are you going to any more of those Women in History seminars? I'd love to go with you."

"Well, I really haven't heard of any coming up," she said. "But I know they were planning a few more."

"Good. Will you let me know?"

"Yes, of course."

"By the way, do you know Laura Gordon-Jaffee, the feminist?"

"I've met her a few times. She's quite a dynamo."

"A nice person?"

"Yes. She seems pleasant."

"Is she married?"

"Yes. Apparently successfully, although I don't know how she finds the time."

"Is her husband involved in the movement?"

"Not in any active way. He's part of the family that owns Jaffee's, the bookstores. I hear he's a financial whiz of some sort and really built the company up from a small Mom and Pop operation."

"And they get along well?"

"I think so. I saw them about a year ago at a school budget hearing. He was wearing a button that said 'I am a feminist.' "

"Wonderful," I said. "Fay, do you have a few minutes? Tell me what's new and exciting in your life." She told me that she was going to spend July in Colorado, in a workshop for high school history teachers to attempt

228

to synthesize the other social sciences into the eleventh- and twelfth-grade history curricula.

"Fay, I'm jealous. It sounds absolutely lovely. Will your husband be going along?"

"I don't think so," she said, almost too quickly. "Things are very busy at the bank."

"I see," I said, sensing that I should tread softly. "Bob's been working insane hours also. Oh, by the way, remember we were discussing Bruce Fleckstein?"

"Yes," she said slowly. "Certainly."

"Something you mentioned intrigued me. You said that he always seemed to pick women whose husbands were successful."

"And that's why you asked me about Laura Gordon-Jaffee's husband."

"Fay . . ."

"That's all right, Judith. Frankly, I'd heard rumors, but I couldn't believe them. What could she possibly see in him?"

"I'll draw you a picture," I said.

"Oh, that. Well, at least he showed some taste. Now I feel flattered. I thought he was limited to bubble-brains and neurotics."

Like Fay's sister-in-law, Linda Berman, I wondered? But I decided not to ask. Instead, I said: "When you said the husbands were successful, did you mean financially?"

"Yes. Financially and well thought of in their respective fields. Why do you ask, Judith?"

"Curiosity, Fay. I wonder if it was just coincidence." I glanced up. Sharpe was standing in the doorway. Scowling, I waved my hand at him to leave. He remained, his left shoulder resting on the frame of the door. "Look, it was wonderful talking to you," I said into the phone, still glaring at Sharpe.

"Thanks so much for calling, Judith. I'll let you know as soon as I hear anything about the next history seminar."

"Thanks. I'll look forward to hearing from you. Bye." I put the receiver down gently and swung around to confront Sharpe. "You had no right to listen in on my conversation."

"I wasn't listening in."

"If you had any subtlety, you'd have my phone tapped."

"I wasn't eavesdropping. I just came up because you were taking so long."

"I told you it was business."

"M.Y.O.B.," he said.

"That's not even remotely funny. I think you're very rude."

"Who's Fay?" he inquired.

"You bastard! You said you weren't listening."

"I wasn't. I just heard the name Fay."

"Would you please leave this house this instant!" He smiled. "I mean it, Lieutenant. Now. Out."

"Don't you want to hear everybody's alibi?" he asked. He hadn't stopped smiling. "You can take notes."

"All right," I said, coldly, correctly. "Let's go downstairs."

"Judith?"

"What is it?"

"Does it make you nervous having me in your bedroom?" He took a step into the room to demonstrate that he was willfully violating my territorial integrity.

"Yes, it makes me nervous." I marched to the door, turning slightly so I could pass him. Sharpe did what I hoped he would do, what I lacked the decisiveness, the courage, to try. He grabbed me, held me, and kissed me, a long, deep, probing kiss.

Pulling my head back a few inches, I made a pro forma protest. "Please." Then, allowing him no time to respond, I brought my lips back to his. We tried strong kisses, tender kisses, lips, teeth, and tongue. Sharpe seemed to enjoy kissing for kissing's sake, not merely as

230

a prelude to copping a feel, not as an automatic accompaniment to lovemaking, something to keep the mouth busy when the rest of the body is flailing about. He was a naturally gifted kisser.

"Judith," he whispered. There was something large and wonderful under his jeans, pressing against me, and I sensed my fingers moving almost reflexively, itching to reach for his zipper.

But instead I broke away. "Nelson, I can't handle this. Please."

"Please."

"No. Please." I stepped back so we stood apart, plenty of space for our chests to rise and fall with our heavy breathing.

"Should I apologize?" he asked. "I'm sorry, but you're a great woman. I've never met anyone like you."

I reached for his hand and squeezed it. "Let's talk alibis," I suggested, feeling positively radiant.

"I don't want to talk alibis," he said as he followed me down to the living room. "Please, Judith, let's just sit down and discuss," he hesitated, "other things."

"I don't want to discuss other things," I murmured, lowering myself into the wing chair and crossing my legs tightly. "Not now."

Sharpe took his usual seat on the couch and peered at me across the coffee table. "Why are you sitting all the way over there?"

"Because this whole situation makes me nervous."

"Oh." He drew his hands together as if he were preparing to pray and rested his chin on top of his two middle fingers. "Are you," he demanded, quietly and precisely, "interested in me?"

"No. I'm just stringing you along because I'm a hard, mean bitch who loves toying with men's emotions." I sighed and continued, my tone softer. "Of course, I'm interested. But I don't want to talk about it now. Could we please change the subject?"

"Okay."

231

"Are you married?"

"I thought I heard you say you wanted to change the subject?"

"I have."

"No, you haven't."

"You're being evasive," I said accusingly.

"I'm married."

"What's her name?"

"June." Blond, slender, carrying armfuls of fresh daisies.

"Does she work?"

"Yes."

"Well?"

"She teaches deaf children."

"Do you have kids?" I inquired.

"Three," he answered. "Do you want me to tell you about them?"

"No," I said. Then I sighed. "How old are they?"

"Karen, the oldest, is eighteen. John is sixteen and Emily's twelve. Can we talk things over now?"

"No."

"Why not?"

"Because I'd rather not." He had been a father when I was a high school senior. "Okay, what is Norma Fleckstein's alibi?"

"You really want to get back to business?" he asked. I nodded. "Well, in the time span we're dealing with, she was driving her children somewhere and then she came home. Two of her children were with her; the other was at a friend's house for dinner."

"Could Norma have slipped out of the house?"

"Doubtful," he said thoughtfully, "but it's possible. This is the thing, Judith. All the alibis are fairly reasonable, but none are really airtight."

"What's your definition of airtight?"

"I don't know. Being on a scheduled airline flying over Ohio and talking with three nuns who've never seen you before but remember you distinctly."

232

"I see. Now, what about his various and assorted women?"

"Which one?"

"Lorna Lewis."

"Home, making dinner. Kids in the kitchen."

"Any others?"

"Sure there were others. The guy couldn't keep his pants on. But everyone we can tie up to Fleckstein swears their affairs with him were over with months ago."

"Do you believe them?"

"I can't prove anything one way or the other. We interviewed the manager of a motel he liked to use. All this guy could give us was that Fleckstein was a very steady customer, but that he always paid for the room while the woman waited outside in the car."

I brushed some hair off my forehead. So that's how they do it. "He never noticed them walking to the room?" I asked.

"No. Fleckstein always used a room in the back. He'd just pull the car around and park it in front of the room."

"Did you speak to any chambermaids? Waiters? Did they ever have room service?"

"Judith, the Tudor Rose is not exactly the Plaza, and they weren't there for a leisurely champagne dinner." He grinned at me. "Would you consider coming over here now? It's safe."

I shook my head no, but managed to relax the claw-like grip I had on the arms of the chair. "The Duncks?"

"He was in his printing shop. She was at her health club."

"The health club. Isn't that a good alibi?"

"As good as any of them. She had a massage at five, but after that we don't know. No one can say for sure when she left. She claims she was resting in the lounge and fell asleep until seven."

"Do you believe her?"

233

"As much as I believe any of them."

"But Marilyn Tuccio was at the A&P. That you do know. She has her supermarket check."

"Yes, but it doesn't have the time on it. And doesn't it strike you as odd that someone would keep a supermarket check?"

"Sure, but not Marilyn if you really think about it. She keeps track of everything. Nothing escapes her."

"Maybe," he said, sounding noncommittal. "Judith, sit next to me. I won't lay a hand on you unless I have your written consent."

I shrugged my shoulders as though this was the sort of thing I encountered twice a day: virile, magnetic men pleading with me to sit beside them. I walked to the couch and sat down.

"What about the Mafia connection?" I asked. "Is that worth pursuing? Could they have done it?"

Sharpe didn't answer. I doubted if he even heard my question. Staring at my sweater, he said, "Your nipples are hard," and brushed his fingertips lightly over my breast.

"Jesus!" I yelled at him. "What's wrong with you?"

"Nothing's wrong. You know that. We're going to be good together. You're very sensitive," he said in a low husky voice.

"And you're goddamn insensitive," I replied harshly, trying not to cry and feeling my throat tighten with the effort. "Can't you understand that when I say no I mean no? I'm not being coy with you. If and when I decide I want to sleep with you, I'll drop you a line. Okay? If you're still interested, fine. If not, you're under no obligation. But right now I can't get involved. I have a husband . . ."

"And you talk about *me* being insensitive. Christ, why don't you take a look at him?"

"My husband is none of your business," I said.

234

"No, but you are."

"Look, I don't bring up your wife, do I? Or doesn't she care if you screw around?"

"Is that what you think I want? A quick hump?"

"How should I know what you want? I hardly know you."

"All right. I'm sorry if I put too much pressure on you. It won't happen again." I must have looked somewhat incredulous, because he added: "I promise. But I really resent the implication that all I want from you is a fast fuck; you're putting both of us down. Jesus, I'm not a Bruce Fleckstein. I don't go around trying to make it with every woman I meet." He paused for a second. "I know I have no way of proving that to you, but you can either believe me or not."

"I believe you," I said, although I was still uncertain. "Shall we change the subject now?"

"Sure. Where were we? Organized crime?"

"You really were paying attention."

"I told you I was interested in more than your body." He grinned as I stiffened. "Judith, for God's sake, relax. I'm just teasing. Okay. As far as we know, this was no hit. The U.S. Attorney offered Fleckstein immunity and he didn't take it. Either he was in too tight with his business friends or he was scared to testify against them. We don't know. But the murder, well, it looks like an amateur's work. Clever, maybe, but not a professional job."

"Couldn't you check with Fleckstein's lawyer to see if he was involved with the Mafia?"

"No. It's still a privileged communication."

"Do you really think the murderer was smart?" I asked.

"Smart or lucky. I don't know which."

"Tell me about the murder itself. What did the coroner say?"

"Medical examiner, Judith, medical examiner.

You've got to get the right jargon if you're going to stay in business. No big deal. Thin, pointed instrument in the base of the skull. Death probably within ten minutes if not instantaneously."

"And the mirror? I remember reading they found one of those little mirrors near the body."

"Well, I can only guess, but most likely it was used to see if he was dead. The murderer probably held it in front of Fleckstein's mouth to see if it would fog over."

"Yuch," I said, picturing the murderer kneeling beside the inert shell of the once-great Long Island Lover. "Okay. One final question. What about the husbands of all the women? Anything on them?"

"Nothing so far," he said. "Unless one of them knew about the affair, and we have no indication, one way or the other, that that's what happened."

"Okay," I said, and stood.

"Okay? That's all, folks? Don't you want to tell me who did it? Save me a lot of work? Show the world what bunglers the police are?"

"You're not a bungler. But I'm not sure. Something's missing."

"You're telling me!"

"We'll get it," I said. "It'll come."

"Judith, I hate to say it, but I've been at this long enough to know that your confidence is almost wholly unjustified."

"Trust me," I reassured him and glanced at my watch. "Oh, God, I have to pick up my son at his friend's and I'm a half hour late."

"All right. I'll see you tomorrow about nine-thirty."

"Tomorrow? Look, I just finished explaining . . ."

"You agreed to look at the pictures. Remember?"

"Okay," I conceded, and walked to the closet to get my coat.

"Aren't you going to say goodbye, Judith?"

"Bye."

"See you tomorrow," he said.

All that afternoon and evening, making paper air-planes with the children, licking the oozing sauce of a Burger King Whopper off my lips, I kissed Sharpe again and again, but this time allowing myself to lift his sweat shirt and rub his chest, permitting my fingers to slowly lower the zipper on his jeans and reach inside. But my fantasies were plagued by coitus interruptus; I was, after all, a Married Woman.

So on the equal time principle, I tried to conjure up a scene with Bob. In his graduate school apartment, the first time we had slept together, unable to spare the time to pull down the bedspread. In a hotel room in Florida, the children safely ensconced in my in-laws' condominium, making love in a large marble bathtub with only the gold cherubs on the faucets watching us. But time had dulled my nerve endings. Too many twenty-minute preprogrammed rolls around the marital bed had burned into my consciousness a diagram of Bob's body, his odor, his voice, his style.

But he did have loyalty, habit, and, perhaps, a resi-due of love in his favor, so I waited, propped up on two pillows, for him to return. He did—at eleven-fifteen. I heard a key in the door and then a loud clearing of his throat and heavy footsteps coming up the stairs.

"Hello, Judith," he said.

"Hello, Robert," I responded with a smile, trying to show how unnecessary all this formality was between old friends.

"How was your day?" he asked.

"Fine. And yours?"

"Fine, thank you."

"Good," I replied. "Now can we cut the shit and talk?"

"What do you want to talk about?" he asked.

How Roosevelt tried to pack the Supreme Court. The spreading crack in the toilet in the green bathroom. "About us."

"I told you there's nothing to say," he responded. He

pulled off his tie, blue and presumably unstained, and hung it neatly in his closet. "You've gotten yourself involved in something that's way over your head, and until you realize that, I can't deal with you." He began unbuttoning his shirt and turned away from me slightly, as if depriving me of a view of his chest.

"What makes you think I'm in over my head?"

He faced me, displaying a large white expanse of undershirt. "Come on, Judith. What the hell do you know about crime?"

"If you're willing to listen, I'll be glad to tell you."

"Judith, what are you doing?" he demanded. "Trying to set yourself up as Sam Spade or something? Listen, I know you better than maybe you know yourself." He raised his hand like a traffic cop as I tried to interrupt. "And I have great respect for your intelligence and ability. But this is out of your league. You're endangering yourself and maybe even the kids, and I won't have it."

"Bob, just let me get a word in. Really, I'm not out of my league. I know exactly what I'm doing, and I think I have a few ideas that might lead to a solution. The police lieutenant, Sharpe, doesn't think I'm being silly. He's been listening to what I have to say, so I think you could give me the same courtesy."

"That short, gray-haired guy? He's just humoring you."

"He is not."

"Believe me, he is. Look, what does he need you for? Now, Judith, I care for you very much. You know I do. But I can't sit back and watch you become embroiled in a dangerous game that you can't begin to cope with. Judith, I'm not being condescending," he added. "I know how hard it is for you staying at home, how bored you are. So I've been thinking. If you want to finish up your dissertation, I'll arrange for a housekeeper. Is that fair?"

"I don't want to finish my dissertation. Not now, anyway.'"

"Then what do you want?"

"I want to find the murderer."

His body became rigid as I spoke, but he forced himself to relax. As I sat watching him, he strolled over and sat beside me on the edge of the bed. He took my hand between his. "You know that's unreasonable," he cooed. "Let me ask you this. Would you like to talk with a psychiatrist? Judith, I'm not being cruel. I'm not saying you're crazy or anything. People sometimes go to a psychiatrist just to get their priorities in order. David is going." David was his certifiably crazy brother. "Here you are, a brilliant, educated woman stuck with two children with no outlet for your intelligence. I understand how frustrating that must be. Really, I do."

"Bob, I don't need a psychiatrist."

"I didn't say *need*."

"All right, I don't want a psychiatrist. I'm very happy doing what I'm doing, looking into this murder. If I thought for a second that something would happen to the children because of my involvement, I would stop immediately." That was the absolute truth. "But nothing will happen to them. And, frankly, if I wanted to complete my dissertation, I would have managed to do it, with or without a housekeeper. I just don't know if I want to spend the rest of my life in a classroom talking to hundreds of glassy-eyed sophomores."

"So do something else. Go to law school. Clay said you have a good, analytical mind. Remember? Lots of women are becoming lawyers."

"I don't want to be a lawyer."

"What do you want to be? A detective?" he asked, his voice laden with irony.

"I don't know. I just want to be left alone to decide for myself. God, it's my future."

"Judith, it's our future."

"Our future? When it's me, it's our future; when it's you, it's your life." He let my hand drop. "You know how I felt about your working for your family. And I

239

really resent your plugging away twelve hours a day and never seeing the children, never really seeing me. So if you're that sincere about our future, why don't you leave the firm and get a nice nine-to-five job so we can be together?"

"Don't you like living the way you do? How could we live in this style," and his hand made a grand sweep around the room, "on a nine-to-five job?"

"Who says we have to live this way?"

"You're being ridiculous."

"I'm only talking about our future."

He stomped over to his dresser, grabbed his pajamas, and marched into the bathroom to change. He wouldn't talk to me for the remainder of the night. And I heard the door slam at six-thirty as he left.

Chapter Sixteen

At nine twenty-five the next morning, I opened the door to greet Sharpe. He nodded and walked into the house, not actually avoiding my glance, but not establishing intimate eye contact either.

"Would you like some coffee?" I asked, after my "hi" got no response.

"No." He rubbed the back of his hand across his lips. "No, thank you." This was it, I figured, the end of a brief but golden era. No screwing, no personal visits. If you have something to tell the police, please call your local precinct. They will relay the message. Thank you and goodbye.

"Okay," I breathed. "Let's have it."

"You haven't told me everything." He had thick, straight eyebrows, and they were drawn together, creating two deep, grim furrows. I tried a smile, but it didn't work. "I think it's time we had it out, Judith. Apparently, there's a lot you know about Fleckstein that you haven't told me. Correct?"

"Yes."

"You could at least attempt to deny it," he said.

"Why should I? I told you I have a vague idea about who sprayed my refrigerator. But that's it—just an idea, based on speculation. I think whoever did it was the murderer, but I'm not even certain about that. But that's old news to you. I told you I don't want to point a finger at someone who might be a blessed innocent."

"Is that all you kept from me?" he asked. "Or is there more?"

"You're playing games with me and I don't like it," I said, my voice rising. "If something's bothering you, tell me."

"I'm playing games?" he shouted, taking a step toward me. "What about you? I trusted you. I discussed the case with you. Christ, I came right out and let you know how I feel about you, goddamn it, and you're telling me I'm playing games! Come on, Judith. I'm investigating a murder. I have to know everything. I can't play games, not even with you. Now come on."

I walked up to him, put my arms around him, and gently bit his lower lip. "Don't be angry. Please." I kissed him, lightly at first, delicate little kisses, and then harder. "Please, Nelson."

Putting his hands on the small of my back, he pulled me toward him. He began rubbing himself against me rhythmically, up and down, up and down. "Judith." This is what is called committing oneself, I thought, and allowed myself a small moan of pleasure. "Judith." His tongue was all over my mouth. And suddenly he pulled back. "No."

I stared at him. "No?"

"No. Not now." We swallowed simultaneously. "We have to talk."

"We're doomed," I told him. "You know that, don't you? We're characters in some terrible Greek myth, assigned to a double bed in a dark corner of Hades, destined to be eternally frustrated. Whenever you're ready, I won't be able to handle it, and whenever I want you, you'll want to talk." I trudged over to the couch and sat down.

"We'll get there," he smiled, sitting next to me and kissing me gently on the forehead.

"No, we won't," I answered hopelessly. Here I was,

ready to abrogate my nuptial vows, tear up my marriage contract, toss caution and guilt to the winds, and all I got was a raincheck. "All right, Sharpe. You want to talk business, let's talk. What terribly vital snippet of information did I withhold from you? Come on. You're angry with me, remember? I'm Judith, the immature one who likes to play games."

"Not as much as your friend, Mrs. Mahoney."

"Mary Alice!" I emitted a whoop of laughter, then clapped my hand over my mouth. "Oh, Nelson, she came to you. Fantastic!"

"Sure. Fantastic. Only you forgot to mention to me that she existed. And so, late yesterday afternoon, I dropped into my office, and there's a message for me to call an assistant D.A. I called and guess what? He has in his office a fine, public-spirited citizen with her lawyer whom *you* just happened to recommend to her."

"Claymore Katz!"

"The same."

"But I didn't tell them to go to you," I said lamely.

"I know that, Judith. I appreciate the care you've taken to protect me from some of the more sordid aspects of the investigation."

"Nelson!" I tried to sound indignant but, knowing I had no justification for that, managed to sound only mildly petulant.

"Did you think I wouldn't find out? Who do you think is in charge of this investigation?"

"I know, I know. But she told me what she did in confidence. And if she came to you, it means that she passed a lie detector test. And that means she didn't murder Fleckstein, so I wasn't shielding a murderer or screwing up your investigation."

"Lie detectors aren't foolproof," he said. "I don't care what you've heard. I'm convinced a pathological liar could pass a polygraph test with flying colors. Christ, I've seen it happen."

"Do you really think Mary Alice might have done it? Truthfully, Nelson, do you suspect her?"

"No, not really. For what it's worth, she did pass the test, and she was pretty convincing about not having seen him for a while. But, listen, I want you to tell me everything she told you about her affair with Fleckstein. It's his technique I'm interested in."

"Yours is better."

"Judith, cut the crap." But he smiled.

"Okay. Well, he seems to have started with a telephone call, letting a woman he had just met know how devastatingly attractive she was—and could she have lunch?"

"You heard this from your friend?"

"Mary Alice. Yes. And another friend, too." The moment I said it, I regretted it.

"What other friend?"

"Oh, just some woman I know."

"The name."

"What will you do if I don't tell you?" He didn't answer. "All right. It was Fay Jacobs. She teaches at Shorehaven High. But, listen, she never met with him at all. She felt that he was pure, undiluted slime. Evil, she said."

"Evil? That's interesting."

"Nelson, come on. She's a terrific lady." And I was a louse.

"I'll check her out."

"Please! She hasn't told anybody else about this, and if you start questioning her, she'll know you got to her through me."

"All right. I'll do it quietly. Now tell me more about Fleckstein." I said nothing. "Don't worry, Judith. Unless there's a reason, she'll never know a thing. Now talk."

For about twenty minutes, we dissected Fleckstein's methods. How long he usually took to score. How he was able to convince some of the women to let him take photographs. Why he apparently couldn't convince others. Or didn't he bother with all of his women? Was it a periodic kink rather than a compulsion? And the prospect of blackmail: Mary Alice seemed to have sensed the possibility, but had he actually attempted to force any of his women into a corner? Could the murderer have been some bland, anonymous woman who came into his office on tiptoes, stabbed him, and disappeared with the photographs? A Madame X who . . . And the doorbell rang. Ding.

"Who could that be?" I demanded.

"Why don't you find out?"

"It could be the murderer."

"Why would the murderer ring your front doorbell?"

"Why not?"

"Just answer it," he said.

"I could be stabbed through the forehead with an awl. Awls are cheap." Ding. "Just a minute," I called to the door.

"I'm right here. I have a gun. Don't worry."

"You have a gun?"

"Yes. Of course."

"But I don't like guns."

"Judith, I carry a gun because I have to. I'm a cop. I believe in gun control laws, okay? Look, should I answer the door?"

"No." The bell rang again just as I tugged open the door. And there was Nancy, dressed all in white—slacks, sweater, fur jacket—a frosty, remote Episcopalian princess.

"You certainly took your own sweet time, Judith," she declared loudly. "Taking a test flight on a new vibrator?"

"Shhh."

"Listen, I have marvelous goodies for you. They found the murder weapon right in your sweet little neighbor's storm sewer. Cupcake was just over, and he told me it's in the police lab right now."

245

"Why didn't you call first?" I whispered.

"What's wrong with you? You're acting like a constipated chicken. I just decided to pop over. I've done that before, you know."

"Nothing's wrong with me," I hissed at her, making a jerking movement with my head in the direction of the living room. "He's in there," I mouthed.

"Who?" she asked, lowering her voice.

"I'm Nelson Sharpe," he said, as he turned the corner into the entrance hallway.

"Lieutenant Sharpe," I amended. "Homicide." Nancy was trying to appear only mildly interested in the proceedings. "He's investigating the Fleckstein murder. Remember, the dentist who was killed?"

"Yes, I recall reading about it," Nancy said thoughtfully.

"You recall reading about it," Sharpe echoed and glanced at me sourly. "Look, I want to know what's going on." He turned to Nancy. "How did you know about the awl?"

"I'm a journalist," she said, flashing one of her down-home friendly smiles. "Nancy MacLaren, Lieutenant." She stuck out her hand and he shook it. "Nice to meet you." Until that moment, she had never used her maiden name professionally.

"And where did you hear about the awl?"

"Now, Lieutenant, you don't really expect me to tell you that. I have to protect my sources." She turned away from and gave me a huge grin. "Sorry to have bothered you, Judith. I just wanted some historical background for an article I'm working on. I'll get back to you later." She turned and strode to the driveway.

"Judith," Sharpe began.

"Nelson, it's true. She is a journalist."

"And she's covering the Fleckstein case, right? Come on. I know every reporter assigned to this investigation. Who is she?"

"She told you. Nancy MacLaren." A very smart person. She knew Sharpe couldn't trace her without her last name and she assumed—correctly—that I wouldn't tell him.

Sharpe grasped my wrist and led me into the living room. "Judith, this is serious. I'm supposed to be in charge of this case, and suddenly everyone is an expert. You. Your friends. The investigation is leaking like a goddamn sieve and I'm getting nowhere. Now, please, will you tell me everything you know from beginning to end— I'm willing to let you go along for the ride, but only if you help."

"Okay. But before I waste too much time talking, don't you want me to look at the pictures?"

"All right. But this is only a temporary stay of execution. As soon as you're finished, we'll talk." He reached into his inside jacket pocket and extracted a small manila envelope. "Here they are." He handed the envelope to me across the coffee table. Squeezing the two metal tabs together, I opened the envelope and peeked in. Outstretched legs and pubic hair. I closed it.

"Feel awkward?" he asked. I nodded. "They're kind of raw. Have you ever seen any pornography?"

"Sure. That's the strange thing," I tried to explain. "I'm positive there's nothing here I haven't seen before, but I feel like I'm unlocking Pandora's box."

"I don't think he ever photographed Pandora," he said.

"Nelson, please be serious." He walked over to me, and for a moment I thought he was going to grab me, inflamed by the recollection of the contents of the envelope. But he just put his arms around me and hugged me, gently, asexually. But I pulled back and demanded: "Are you trying to protect me? Because if you are . . ."

"I'm just trying to hug you."

"I don't have to be sheltered, you know."

"I know," he said. "Did you think I was being condescending?"

"No," I answered. "But I am a little edgy. It's odd,

I've seen movies of all sorts of things, of women getting it in every imaginable orifice, of lesbians, animals, you name it. And it never bothered me. I've even been excited by some of it. But this is different. It's in context, if you know what I mean. These are women who might be my friends—even me. They have kids, they squeeze cantaloupes in the supermarket. And suddenly I'm looking in on their inner life, which they never thought would go public. Aren't there aspects of your life, your imagination, that you wouldn't want anyone to know about?"

"I guess so."

"So?" I gave him the envelope.

"Judith, you talk about the photographs being in context, right? Well, consider the context. Someone murdered Fleckstein. I have to find the killer. That's my context. Look, I could sit back and say he was a vile human being, a rotten, manipulative scum—and he was. But that wouldn't stop me from doing my job, even if it means wading in the muck he created. Now, you've involved yourself in this investigation. Somehow, something about it hit a nerve and you responded. So you're faced with a choice. You can follow it through to its logical conclusion—assuming there is one—or you can say goodbye, this isn't amusing any more. It's up to you. But I can't do that. It's my job."

"Let me see them." He handed me the envelope I had returned to him. I reached in and pulled out the photographs. There were a number of them, probably ten or twelve. "Let's go into the dining room. It may be easier if I spread them out on a table." I sorted the pictures out quickly, all over the table, as if I were dealing a fast hand of solitaire. "These three are the same person," I said to him.

"Yes," he agreed. The woman had long, straight brown hair that reached the middle of her back, like a Bennington freshman. Except this woman was in her mid-thirties. You could see from the deeply etched

248

laugh lines that ran from the edge of her nostrils to the middle of her chin. And she was laughing. In all three pictures, she sat naked on a red plastic chair with wooden arms, chuckling away at something terribly amusing. In one of the pictures, her arms were crossed under tiny, almost nonexistent breasts; in the second, her hands were held, peek-a-boo fashion, over her eyes; in the third, she had folded her hands daintily in her lap.

"Well," I said, "at least she doesn't look exploited."

"Maybe not," he concurred. "But look at this." He pointed to a shadowy corner of the picture that took in the edge of the bed. On the red carpeted floor lay a huge dildo.

"God," I breathed, "I've never seen anything like it."

"Wait till we get together."

"Is that what they call the hard sell?"

"Absolutely," he said. And then he was back to business. "Do you know her? Have you ever seen her?"

"Never. Even if she wore her hair differently and she was dressed. She has a very long, stretched-out face; I would have recognized her if I'd seen her before."

"And her?" He pointed to a picture of a slightly pudgy woman. She was dressed in the best Forty-Second Street style—black bikini panties, a black bra with holes cut out in the center so her nipples peered at the camera, brownish pink unseeing eyes. And she wore a black rhinestone-studded mask; she looked like a racy guest panelist on *I've Got a Secret*. In her hand was a riding crop.

"I can't tell with the mask. But the whip doesn't go. I mean, she should be tall and lean and tough-looking." I picked up the photograph. "No, I don't recognize her. But he certainly had eclectic tastes."

"And a passion for props," Sharpe added. "We tried to trace some of them down. Checked with one of those sex-shop owners. But the guy said they were very common, the kind everybody uses."

249

"Sure," I said. "A dime a dozen. They're on special at Pathmark this week. Two for ninety-nine cents, with a coupon." I stopped suddenly. "Oh, God."

"What? What is it?"

I was staring at a photograph of a woman and a large dog. "Nelson, this was taken in Fleckstein's house." Right on his living room floor, to be exact. The same green rug, the same profusion of lush, leafy plants, the same upholstery fabric. "And that's Prince!"

"Who's Prince?"

"The dog. The Nazi dog. I saw it at Norma Fleckstein's."

"It wasn't around when I was there," he said.

"Well, it was when I was. I mean, it's not one of those nasty toy poodles or Yorkshires that you could step on and never see."

"It certainly isn't. Now, what about the Princess?"

"Who?"

"The woman with Prince."

"Let me see." I leaned over the table and studied the picture. The woman, lying next to the Flecksteins' glass mask; I had seen one before in *Gent* or *Oui* or *Penthouse* or *Stud*, serious reading in the drugstore while waiting for a prescription to be filled.

"Does she seem at all familiar?" Sharpe demanded.

"Wait." Her eyes were visible, but I couldn't determine the color. The mask cast a shadow over them. "It's almost impossible to see her," I said. "Isn't it strange," I turned to Sharpe, "that all these women's fantasies seem so predictable to me? There's no real novelty. Maybe it's the suburbs, maybe in Manhattan . . . " I glanced at the picture again, at the woman's body. Small, slender, tiny-waisted, almost perfect except for two small scars on her stomach, one long one down the middle and a smaller one running parallel on the right side. "Nelson!"

"What? What is it?"

250

"Just a question. In the medical examiner's report, did . . ."

"Judith!"

"Wait. Did the report indicate how tall the murderer was? You know, from the angle of the wound?"

"Shorter than Fleckstein. Now, come on, Judith."

"How much shorter?"

"A few inches, probably."

"Not very short, like five foot three?"

"No. The angle was less than twenty-five degrees. And from the position of Fleckstein's body, we know the murderer was standing, not sitting in the dentist's chair."

"Could it have been done by a woman?"

"Yes."

"But not a very petite one?"

"Goddamn it, Judith!"

"Nelson."

"What?"

"This is Brenda Dunck."

Chapter Seventeen

Sharpe stood utterly still, not breathing. Finally, he turned toward me and said: "I hope this isn't your idea of a joke."

"Nelson," I breathed. "Are you crazy?"

"Not until now. But if you're kidding . . . Look, I've been drowning in this case for weeks. I'm about five days beyond humor."

"Nelson. It's Brenda."

"How do you know?" he snapped. "Her face is covered."

I yanked out one of the dining room chairs and plopped down on it. "Sit," I ordered. He pulled up a chair, placed it beside mine, and sat. "All right. I can recognize her because I know her body."

"Would you care to explain?"

"We belong to the same health club. I was sitting in the sauna one day and saw her. She has this fantastic body with a teeny Scarlett O'Hara waist and those two incisions going down her stomach."

"Probably a caesarean and an appendectomy. Very common. I checked with the medical examiner."

"Not that common," I insisted. "Nelson, there are millions of women walking around out there without two scars on their stomachs. And who else has a waist like that?"

"I don't know," he mumbled.

"And her pubic hair. She only has that little stripe."

"Are you sure?"

"Why don't you want to believe me?" I picked up the photograph and examined it again. "Look, she even has the same long, polished toenails." Her right foot, resting on Prince's haunches, was turned toward the camera; her first two toenails were visible.

Sharpe leaned over and gazed at the picture. "You're positive?"

"Yes," I said wearily.

"Okay. Then where does that get us? You said she's short?"

"Yes. No more than five three."

"Well, unless she took a flying leap at Fleckstein, she couldn't have done it."

"She's not the flying-leap type. She's very studied, trying to be graceful, stately. She wants to be a WASP."

"Then she should have fucked an English sheepdog," he remarked. "Okay, where does all this leave us?"

"I don't know." I slumped in the chair, head in my hands.

"Maybe it gets us nowhere," Sharpe mused. "Maybe she was just another one of his broads."

"No."

"Why not?"

"I don't know. Just be quiet for a minute." He sat, an inch from me, watching me think, which of course made thinking impossible. "Nelson, maybe you should leave now. I can't concentrate. I'll call you if I come up with anything."

"I don't want to leave."

"Don't you have any police work to do?"

"I'm doing it," he insisted. "Look, let's get out for a while. I'll buy you lunch."

"I can't. My son's coming home from school."

"Can't he make his own lunch?"

"Nelson, he's four years old."

"No kidding. I didn't realize you had such a little one. What's his name?"

"Joseph. Joey."

"Do you have any others?"

"Katherine. She's six. Do you know what's really odd?"

"What?"

"The fact that we're calmly considering sleeping together and we don't even know the most basic details of each other's lives. Doesn't that strike you as strange?"

"No. Judith, we're in tune with each other. Does that happen with every guy you meet?"

"No. Only with about sixty percent of them. And out of sixty percent, I only have time to sleep with half of them."

"Look," he said, "we're adults. We've been around long enough to develop a sense of what other people are all about. Does it make any substantive difference if you know what my middle name is?"

"No, but it would make you more real. What is it anyway?"

"Lawrence. Does that make me more of a person to you?"

"Mine's Eve."

"Great. Now I know all I need to know about you. All right, Judith Eve, can I take you out to lunch?"

"No. I told you, my son's coming home any minute."

"Can't he go somewhere? Play with a friend?"

"I should abandon my child so you can seduce me?"

"Judith. I have a key to a friend's apartment. Ten minutes from here. I'll tell you my mother's maiden name on the way over."

"I thought you were so angry with me when you came in. How come you have the key?"

"I was hoping we could work it out."

"But we're working on a case. What about Brenda Dunck?"

"She doesn't do a thing for me. You do."

"Please. Let's finish the business at hand," I said. "I need time to go over all the information we have."

"You can think at the apartment. It's very peaceful there. I'll try not to disturb you."

"Nelson," I said, and the doorbell rang. It was Joey.

"Mommy, you weren't at the bus stop, so I came here by myself. Remember you told me if you weren't there to come and ring the bell? So I did."

"Good boy," I said, taking his hand. "This is Lieutenant Sharpe, Joey. A policeman."

"Hi, Joey," said Sharpe.

"You got a gun?" Joey asked.

"Here," Sharpe indicated, opening his jacket to show his holster, clipped on his belt. He also had an erection.

"Can I see it?" Joey demanded.

"No. Look at it where it is. Guns are dangerous."

"Lieutenant Sharpe is just going, Joey. What would you like for lunch?"

"Peanut butter and jelly. Cut in squares."

"What would you like for lunch?" Sharpe asked me softly.

"Goodbye, Lieutenant," I said forcefully.

"Goodbye, Joey," he said. "Nice meeting you." Joey ignored him. Sharpe looked at me and murmured: "I'll pick you up in half an hour."

"No."

"Forty-five minutes." He waved to Joey and left.

"So," I said to Joey, struggling to open a new jar of grape jelly and calm down at the same time, "what did you do in school today?"

"Why do we have so many cops?"

"Police. They're just checking things out to make sure everybody's nice and safe and obeying the law. That's their job."

I prepared the sandwich, meticulously cutting it into precise, clean-edged squares. "Here," I presented it to him. He ate slowly, taking minuscule bites and rolling them around his mouth. "You're eating very slowly," I observed tartly.

"You said I shouldn't eat fast. You want me to get a tummy ache and throw up?"

"No." I replaced the lid on the peanut butter jar. "What do you want to do this afternoon?" I asked. "Want to play with North?"

"No. He farts."

"Joey, come on. That's so silly. Let me call Mrs. Hughes."

"No."

I stood by the sink, waiting for my maternal instincts to overpower my desire for Sharpe. "How about Jenny? Can I call her mother?"

"No."

"I heard she has some wonderful new toy."

"What?"

"I'm not sure. Want to go over and see?"

"Oh, okay." Before he could change his mind, I called boring little Jenny's tedious mother.

Forty minutes later I was sitting in Sharpe's Dodge Dart, waiting for a traffic light to change. No one can force me to go through with this, I thought. I can just tell him that I find adultery morally abhorrent. Or simply say that I need time to resolve things—one way or another—with Bob. I twisted the fastener on my shoulder bag open and shut, open and shut. Look, Nelson, I could say, can't we just be good friends?

"What if," I began, my voice hoarse and distant, "I decided to change my mind?"

The light changed. He pulled over to the curb. "Do you want to change your mind?" he asked quietly.

"I don't know. What would happen if I did?"

"I'd make a U-turn and take you home."

"Just like that? No recriminations? I can't believe that."

"What would you expect me to do? Beat you over the head and zap it to you while you're unconscious?"

"Would you still talk to me?" I demanded.

"Yes. I don't know. I guess I'd be upset or hurt or something, but I'd still talk to you. Although I'd probably want to sulk for a couple of days." He paused and lifted my hands between his; his palms were damp. "Judith, I like you. And I want to go to bed with you. But if it's more than you can handle, I'm not going to push. I don't want that on my record. It has to be your decision."

"It's all up to me?"

"I've already made up my mind. I have no problems with it."

I ran my hand along the dashboard. "What if I'm lousy? What if you think I'm the most boring lay in the world?"

"I'll roll over and fall asleep. Just give me a poke when you want to go home. Judith, calm down. What if you think I'm lousy? What would you do?"

"Oh," I responded, feeling enormously relieved. I would pat him on the head and tell him these things happen, especially if a man is nervous. And I would smile, not mockingly, but with great compassion. But if that was the case, why was I going?

"Well?"

"Drive," I said. "I have to be home in two hours."

His friend's apartment house was in a town about five miles due south of Shorehaven, a red brick six-story building flanked on the left by a butcher shop and on the right by a beauty salon. The address, a large Two Twenty-Five, was written in gilt script on the building's glass door; under it was the apartment's name.

"The Versailles?" I asked. "It's actually called The Versailles?"

"Well, it has mirrors in the lobby."

We parked the car in a space in the back of the building and walked in through the back entrance.

"You've been here before?" I inquired.

"Sure. This friend of mine took the apartment right after his divorce, so he could be near his kids."

"And you've visited him here?"

"No. He just gave me the key so that every day when he's at work I can take a new woman to the apartment and get laid. Judith, he's my friend, a guy I went to high school with. Of course, I've visited him here. He's been pretty broken up since his divorce."

"Why did he get a divorce?"

"His wife was screwing around." He pushed the elevator button and the door opened immediately. "After you," he said. We rode in silence to the fourth floor. I thought: his friend's wife still has custody of the kids.

Still not speaking, we walked down the blue-carpeted hall to apartment 4E. Under the bell, his friend's name was printed in neat white capital letters on a black plastic tab: Greenberg. At least, I pondered, peering at Sharpe's small nose, he's probably not a latent anti-Semite. He unlocked the door and held it open for me.

"Oh, I forgot to tell you," he said, "when I called the office after I left you this morning, they had gotten the lab report on the awl."

"Tell me." I sat in a small green chair that exactly matched the green couch in Greenberg's living room, a muddy, brown-tinged green common to motels and budget-decorated offices, the kind of green used for a furnished apartment that will not show dirt, that will survive from tenant to tenant.

"It's almost definitely the murder weapon," said Sharpe, still standing. "There wasn't enough blood for a test, but the length of the bloodstain exactly matched the depth of the wound."

"That's interesting." We smiled at each other. Then I cleared my throat; we became very sober. We remembered why we were in Greenberg's apartment. Sharpe took my hand and helped me from the chair. For a moment we stood in uncomfortable silence.

259

"Judith," he finally whispered, as he began to kiss me, "who did it?"

"I'm not sure. Is that why you brought me here? To sweet-talk me and get me to tell you everything?"

"No. Because," he said slowly, "you're lovely."

"You're lovely too," I whispered later, lying beside him in Greenberg's bed and running my hand over his stomach. The hair on his head was completely gray, but the hair on his chest merely brown and gray, and traveling still lower, brown and dark and curly, as though his mind had matured and mellowed years ahead of his genitals. "I can't begin to tell you," I began.

"I know," he answered softly, and kissed the tips of my fingers.

"But I want to tell you. I thought it was going to be terrible."

"You did? Why?"

"I'm not really sure. I thought I'd panic and become completely stiff or something."

"Or something?"

"I thought that under that charming facade, you were a quivering, insecure wreck of a human being and that you wouldn't be able to get it up." He laughed loudly, the sound echoing off Greenberg's dresser, with its bottle of Brut and plexiglassed snapshots of his two daughters. "I was going to tell you how it didn't matter."

"That's very kind of you."

"And I thought you wouldn't be circumcised and I might not like it. Or I'd like it too much."

"Well, they snipped it off before I was old enough to file a complaint. I'm not very exotic, am I?"

"Everything about you is exactly the way it should be."

"You know something?" he asked, pulling me tight against him. "You're the best thing that's happened to me in years. Do you know that?" I rested my head on his shoulder, hoping that that would suffice as an acknowledgment. "Judith, talk to me."

"You were wonderful," I responded.

"So were you. Jesus, you've got some great moves. But talk to me. Tell me what you're thinking."

"What I'm thinking?"

"Yes."

"I'm thinking," I said, "that I'm too overwhelmed to think. I mean, it was so different from what I'd expected."

"Tell me what you thought it would be like," he urged, cupping my behind in his hands and rubbing it gently.

"I assumed it would be fast and neat and that it would clear my sinuses."

"At the beginning, you seemed to be in a rush."

"I know. And then, when I slowed down, I was surprised that we were so aware of each other as it was happening. In a way, I guess I hoped the sex would be divorced from everything I was feeling, so it would be easier to cope with. Sex, pure and simple." I pulled away slightly so I could look at his face. "Nelson, in a way I was doing exactly what I kept accusing you of wanting to do—just grabbing a quick lay. But it didn't happen that way and I'm glad it didn't. But I don't want to talk about it any more, okay?"

"Okay. We'll talk about it tomorrow."

"Tomorrow's Saturday," I said.

"Shit."

We dressed slowly, watching each other, helping each other with zippers and buttons, squirreling away our visions of each other for the long, cold weekend.

"Are you working tomorrow?" I asked as we drove home.

"Probably in the morning. I promised my kids I'd take them ice-skating in the afternoon."

"You ice-skate?"

"Sure. Do you?"

"I used to," I said.

He dropped me off with about five minutes to spare

before Kate's school bus pulled up to the corner. As she and I drove to pick up Joey, she interrogated me. Why was Daddy mad? Was I mad at Daddy? I coughed and some of Nelson's semen dripped onto my underpants. Would Daddy and I get a divorce? She was frightened, her voice quavering despite her attempt to sound casual. I reassured her; people can get very angry with each other even though they're in love.

"Don't you ever get angry at me, Kate? I mean, really angry?"

"I guess so. But this is different. Daddy wouldn't even talk to you. The other night when we went to the restaurant, he hardly even looked at you. I know, Mommy. I saw it."

"I know you did, Kate. But try to understand that when two grown-ups live together for years and years, they sometimes get on each other's nerves. And if I want to do something, something I'm really interested in, and if Daddy doesn't want me to do it, who wins? Who's the boss?"

"You're both the boss," she responded. I had trained her well.

"That's right. So there can be problems if we disagree."

"I know that. But it was weird. Daddy didn't yell at you."

"I know. But everything will be all right. Don't worry, honey."

Kate stared out the car window. "Do you still love each other?"

"Of course, we love each other. If we didn't, we wouldn't care about each other and then we couldn't get mad. Could we?"

"I don't know," she said softly.

The beginning of the evening must have been a relief for her. Bob came home and talked.

"Hello, Judith." He gave me a light kiss that didn't quite touch my cheek. "How was your day today?" Not

262

bad, I told him, managing to speak and hold the salad bowl at the same time. "Guess who died yesterday?" he asked cheerfully. "Sam Brown." His accountant had taken his last deduction. "The funeral was at eleven, but I had a meeting. I'll send a donation."

"I'm sorry to hear that. I mean, that he died." I served dinner.

"A penny for your thoughts," he said later, sipping coffee.

I contemplated a kissy-kissy response, going over, sitting on his lap and kittenishly rubbing his nose with mine. "There's a new wrinkle in the Fleckstein case. I'm trying to figure it out."

He slammed both fists down on the table. "Kids," he said, his voice tight with control, "why don't you run outside and play."

"It's dark, Daddy," Kate informed him.

"And cold," added Joey.

"Oh. Then go downstairs and watch some TV. Now. Hurry up." They trod out of the dining room sullenly, casting suspicious glances at us as they turned the corner into the hallway.

"Now what's this?" Bob demanded. "I thought all that was over."

"All what was over?" I asked. "The Fleckstein case? How could it be over?"

"I thought it was clear that you had severed your connection with it."

"Are you serious? Where did you get that idea?"

"Well, you hadn't said anything for a couple of days, so I assumed . . ."

"Let me tell you something," I said carefully. "For the last couple of days, if you can stretch your mind back that far, you have not been home. Excuse me, you have been home for short spurts of time, but all you've been is a physical presence. You don't talk. You won't listen to what I have to say. And then you drift away to your office where the only contact I have with you is through your half-assed secretary who gives me messages and tells me you're in meetings while you're probably hovering over her with your ear smack against the receiver listening to how I take the news of your vital, successful business career. So don't tell me . . ." My voice faded. My anger at Bob became a pale mist and blew away. I had it! The Fleckstein case. It made sense.

"If you think I have nothing better to do than listen in on your conversations with my secretary, who, by the way, happens to be a very nice person, you're crazy."

I stood and looked into the kitchen. "Excuse me. I have to make a phone call." I walked inside and found my bag on top of the dishwasher. Ferreting through it, I discovered the small piece of paper on which Nelson had written his telephone number.

"Homicide, Detective Dugan," said a horrible, nasal voice.

"Lieutenant Sharpe, please."

"He's not here. What is this in reference to?" Bob remained at the dining room table, sticking his index finger into his cup and making little polka dots of coffee around his saucer.

"It's about the Fleckstein case. Could you have him call me?" I gave him my name and number.

"Is it something I could help you with, miss?" Maybe this guy was just kidding around, trying out new voices for a course in undercover disguises; this was number eight—the irritatingly adenoidal.

"No thanks. I prefer to speak with the Lieutenant." We said our goodbyes, and I returned to the dining room. "Bob, please listen. I've just come up with a terrific idea about the case. Please. I'm sorry I was so bitchy before. Just listen."

He stood, resting his palms on the table, and cleared his throat, as if he were about to introduce a distinguished roster of after-dinner speakers. "Judith, I'm not interested. I'm tired. I've worked very hard this week. I'm going to bed."

I glanced at the clock. "But it's not even eight o'clock."

"I said I was tired." His exit was fairly impressive, with chin held high and long-legged, graceful strides. He may have left his substance in graduate school, but his form was still superb.

"Good night," I called after him. It would be far better, I then thought, to be alone with the dishes when Sharpe calls than up to my elbows in graying bath water trying to wash Joey's ears. So I called the children, bathed them so rapidly that they barely had time to shriek about soap in their eyes, and tucked them into bed. Back downstairs at eight-fifteen, I scraped wilted lettuce, bits of roasted potatoes and challah, crusty ends of apple pie into the garbage. The Sabbath candles flickered in the dining room, giving the room an inappropriate romantic glow. Eight-seventeen. Maybe Sharpe had sent his children to the movies and was socking it to June. After this afternoon? Why not? He does have a strong sex drive. What did I expect? His undying adoration? A vow of perpetual fidelity?

The phone remained silent until nine-thirty, during which time I lay on the floor in the den listening to Sinatra sing "You Go to My Head" many, many times.

"Judith," he said.

"Oh, hi," I responded, my voice tortured into a lazy, casual register. "I've gotten a brainstorm."

"About the case?"

"Yes, of course."

"Talk to me first," he urged softly. "Tell me what you're thinking about."

"I'm thinking," I whispered, "about a periodontist with a puncture wound in the base of his skull. Please, Nelson, listen to me."

"I will if you say something nice first."

I cupped my hand around the mouthpiece to block the path of my whisper. "I think you're the nicest, most beautiful man I've ever met and I wish I were with you right now, touching you."

"Touching me where?"

"On the base of your skull. Can we talk now?"

"Okay. But did you really mean what you just said, about me being the most beautiful man you've ever met?"

"Yes. But don't you want to hear my brilliant theory?"

"Shoot," he said, in normal conversational tones.

"Well, I was talking to my husband about . . ."

"You mean you're discussing the case with your husband now?"

"Would you please listen?"

"Sorry."

"Now, as I was saying, I was talking to my husband about some of the drawbacks of his having a successful career, and all of a sudden the words got stuck in my throat."

"What words?"

"Nelson, I'll tell you if you give me just a half a second to breathe and begin my next sentence."

"Well, breathe faster."

"All right. Anyhow, I got caught on the word 'successful.' Now think for a moment. What does that have to do with the case?" Silence. "Well, does it ring any bells?"

"Quiet," he snapped. I took the phone for a walk around the den while he concentrated, picking up a gum wrapper, sending Joey's Mighty Mo bulldozer rumbling across the floor. "Judith," he said briskly. I froze in front of the television set. "I think I know what you're trying to say. Hot shit, you're absolutely brilliant." He gave a delighted laugh. "But tell me everything, in your own words, slowly."

I sat on a cracked leather recliner, put my feet up, and took a deep breath. "Okay. What did all of Fleckstein's women have in common? No special physical type. No common ethnic background. No one definite personality trait. Right? The common bond was that they were all married to successful men. Every single one of them had a dynamo for a husband; all except one. Are you following me?"

"Brenda Dunck," Sharpe said. "Judith, I love your ass."

"Would you please be serious."

"I'm talking in a professional sense. I love your ass in other ways, but I'll save that for another time. Come on. Keep talking."

"All right. Dicky Dunck was considered a loser by his peers. I got it from Norma that he had run through a couple of businesses before he started this printing thing. Their father kept lending him money, and that's why Norma got the bulk of the old man's estate. Remember? I told you about that. Now, I got the word from someone else—which I forgot to mention to you—that Dicky's business had been in trouble and he had to get a bank loan to meet his payroll."

"You forgot to tell me? Jesus H. Christ, Judith, I've had two men checking the local banks for a week. Why didn't you tell me?"

"Okay. I'm sorry. Just calm down."

"Okay," he said, more evenly. "Go on."

"Now, the fact that he needed this bank loan would seem to indicate that he hadn't broken out of his old pattern; he was probably failing again, although he claimed it was just a cash flow problem. Now that has other ramifications, but I'll get to those later. Anyway, let's take it as a given that he was a business failure."

"Right."

"Okay. So why would Bruce break *his* pattern and start making it with the wife of someone who was a loser in his eyes?"

267

"Maybe he was just hot for Brenda."

"No. Fleckstein was much too calculating."

"What do you mean?" Sharpe asked. "Maybe she had been waving it in front of him for years and he decided to take her up on it."

"No, I don't think so. Look, despite all his activity, he just wasn't an impulsive, horny guy. All his seductions were really very cold and methodical, if you think about them. He used the same technique over and over: a little phone call, a little flattery, a little lunch. It was all a power play, a game."

"A game," he repeated. "You may be right. For him, all the fun was probably in getting there, not being there."

"Yes," I said, curling the telephone cord around my ring finger. "And that's precisely the reason he wouldn't allow himself to be swept off his feet by anyone. It just wasn't his nature. Now another thing. If you can believe Norma—and my friend Mary Alice backs her up—he was very protective of his family life. It's not inconsistent with his playing around; there was no real emotional involvement there. He'd call Norma right before one of his assignations, to tell her that he was off to the dental clinic. He always covered himself; he didn't want anything to jeopardize their relationship. He had built up this image as a loving husband, devoted father. Right?

"So why would he risk this whole image by having an affair with his sister-in-law? It would be too dangerous. Too close to home."

Sharpe breathed deeply. "Okay. What you're saying then is that Fleckstein had a definite motive for sleeping with Brenda. That it was somehow manipulative. Not a sex thing. So let's take that a step further. What did he want from her? Did he try to blackmail her? Why?" He inhaled again. "And if he wanted to blackmail her, why was she wearing that goddamn weirdo mask in all the photographs?"

"First of all, we don't know what pictures the murderer took; there may have been some without the mask. Also, for Fleckstein's purposes, he didn't need a face. Think about it, Nelson. Her body was distinctive enough. The incisions, the waist. My God, what I wouldn't give for that waist."

"I love your waist," he said. "It's perfect."

"You are an adorable man," I whispered. "Okay now, enough of this. Back to the business at hand. Bruce didn't care about her face showing, for a couple of reasons. One, he didn't want to make her suspicious, although she's so dim, so gullible, that he probably could have gotten her to autograph the pictures. And, two, the face wasn't necessary because he knew that the person who saw the photographs would instantly recognize her body."

"I knew you'd say that," he said.

"If you knew, then why am I going through all this?"

"Because I want to make sure I'm following your reasoning. And so we can bounce ideas off each other."

"All right," I conceded. "But this is where I'm not too sure of my ground. He apparently told Brenda that if she didn't help him in some way, he'd show the pictures to Dicky. But what did he want her to do? Work on Dicky to stop cooperating with the government?"

"I don't think so," Sharpe said. "Look, Judith, at the time Fleckstein was killed, the case was before the Grand Jury. That means the investigatory work was just about complete. The boom was about to be lowered. Now, all of a sudden, Fleckstein hears from one of his mob friends that his brother-in-law was cooperating."

"Right. That's what Norma told me. He ran into this guy he supposedly barely knew who told him that Dicky was the informer."

"All right, time was running out for Fleckstein. He had to stop Dunck from testifying at a trial. Now, he could try to appeal to family loyalty, but Dunck hated

269

him. And if there was any family loyalty to begin with, Dunck wouldn't be talking, right?"

"That's putting it mildly," I agreed. "Dicky hated Bruce because Bruce wouldn't give up a dime of his father-in-law's estate. From the way Norma spoke, I think she would have been willing to part with some of it, but Bruce wouldn't let her. Oh, I just remembered. When Dicky needed that loan, he asked Bruce to co-sign it. Bruce refused."

"How did you know that, Judith?" he asked, reasonably, calmly.

"From the bank officer."

"What?"

"Fay Jacobs, that lovely woman you were so paranoid about—she's married to an officer of Shorehaven National."

"You're right. I had her checked out. Jesus, you're incredible."

"So are you," I said softly and then shook my head, as if to clear away the fuzziness. "God, this double-edged relationship is making me schizzy. Let's get back to business."

"It's all right with me."

"I know, but I keep fluctuating between deductive rationality and unbridled lust. Anyhow, yes, Dicky hated Bruce Fleckstein. He wouldn't even consider backing off because he wanted Bruce to suffer. I'm sure of it."

"So am I. Now, Fleckstein had two choices. He could let his brother-in-law keep talking and go straight to the can, or he could find a way to silence Dunck. He could quickly pull a power play—and for him there was only one power play, sex—go through his usual photography number and then show the results to Dunck. That would destroy Dunck emotionally. Or Fleckstein could threaten that he had lots and lots of pictures and that if Dunck didn't shut up, he'd see that they were spread all over town. And if you're right about the Duncks, about them being big social climbers, that would also be a disaster."

"So you think Dicky killed him, too?" I said slowly.

"Yes. But there are a lot of holes I want filled in. And I want you to help me. Will you?"

"Sure," I agreed.

"Okay. I want to meet with you tomorrow. Strictly business, Judith. I want you to talk to Brenda. See what she knows. Get a better feel as to what she's like. Make sure she's not conniving to clear herself and get rid of her husband at the same time. She may be smarter than you give her credit for. It's an irregular procedure, but if she'll talk to you, it will save us a lot of time."

Just then a vision appeared, of me and Bob and Sharpe sitting around our kitchen table on a freezing Saturday morning, sipping steaming mugs of coffee and passing photographs to each other. "Not tomorrow. My husband will be home."

"What do you mean?" he demanded. "Judith, I'm not interested in playing perverse games. What do you think? That I want to put myself between you and your husband and see which one of us squirms the most? Look, why don't you just meet me at my office? Okay?"

"How can I just pick myself up and go to your office?"

"What do you mean?" he asked. He really didn't understand.

"I mean, what can I tell my husband?"

"I can't believe I'm hearing you right. What do you need, a written note from your husband saying he gives permission for Judith Singer to visit police headquarters?"

I immediately put up another obstacle. "What happens if he has to work tomorrow? Who will stay with the kids?"

"How about a baby sitter?"

"Well," I said uncertainly.

"I'll pay for it."

"I can afford a baby sitter," I said tersely.

"Then what's your problem?"

"I'll see you tomorrow. About ten o'clock?"

"Fine," he said, and gave me the address.

"All right," I said. "I'll see you around ten."

"Make it eleven. That way I can take my kids skating in the morning."

After we said goodbye, I tiptoed slowly up the stairs, walking near the railing to minimize the squeaks of the floorboards. I half expected to find Bob lurking in the hall outside our bedroom, paralyzed with fury after having eavesdropped on my conversation. "You bitch, you whore," he would croak, his face twisted with anger. Or maybe he'd be urbanely unconcerned, lounging about in his maroon bathrobe and saying: "Well, darling, glad you've found a little extracurricular activity. I was beginning to think that I was the only one who needed broader horizons."

Of course, he was fast asleep, his feet sticking out of the end of the quilt, pigeon-toed, despite the orthopedic shoes his mother had forced him to wear until he went off to college. I undressed in the dark and eased into bed. He didn't stir.

Nor did he react visibly the next morning when I told him I had to meet with Sharpe. He simply shrugged his shoulders and said: "Do whatever you want."

"Well, he seems to think I might be on to something," I explained.

"Sure," he said, pouring himself another glass of orange juice.

I left my Grape-Nuts to get soggy and went upstairs to dress. What does one wear to police headquarters? What does one wear to meet one's lover? Jeans were too casual. A dress might be appropriate, but Bob might reasonably wonder why I was getting so gussied up to discuss murder. I settled on my reliable gray slacks and a yellow cashmere sweater I had bought between concerts at the Edinburgh Festival in 1965. Waving goodbye to Bob and jangling my car keys, I thought I looked very sophisticated, extremely efficient, and lovely in a simple, understated way.

"Hey, you look terrific," Sharpe whispered as he stood to greet me. "Hello, Mrs. Singer," he said aloud, shaking my hand. He closed the door behind me. His office was almost exactly what I'd expected: cream-colored walls instead of institutional green, and furnished with a large, heavy wood desk and several straight-backed wooden chairs with green plastic cushions. A gray filing cabinet was crowned with two styrofoam coffee cups.

"It's lovely," I said, looking around. "So gracious, but without that decorator look."

"Thank you, Mrs. Singer," he replied.

"You're ever so welcome, Lieutenant. Okay, what can I do?"

"I want you to get as much out of Brenda Dunck as you can. Make damn sure you haven't underestimated her." He was sitting on his desk, resting most of his weight on the palms of his hands, his legs spread apart. "We'll follow you over there and wait out of sight. You'll be wired, so we can hear what's going on. I don't want any trouble. It took me an hour to convince the captain to let a civilian help out. It's not our usual procedure. If anything happens to you, it's my ass, Judith, so be damned careful."

"Isn't the wiring a little extreme?"

"Judith, this is a murder investigation. I can't send you in there cold. I'm still not certain about her, and I'm not going to take any risks. You're not armed and you could scream your bloody head off and I might not hear you. Okay?"

I shifted in the wooden chair. Its straight back forced you to sit erect, like a society doyenne. "Okay, but it can't be today; I just realized it."

"Why not?" he demanded irritably. "Why put it off?"

"Two reasons. She called me early in the week, about having cleared the way for me to talk to Norma and told me she and Dicky were going away for a few days. She might not even be home yet."

"I'll check it out."

"Also, don't you think I should speak to her alone? Dicky's probably home today. Wouldn't it be better to wait until Monday when he'll be at his printing plant?"

"I guess so," Sharpe conceded. "But I want you wired, Judith. No arguments, okay? Just take it on faith."

"All right. But I don't think she's dangerous. Nelson, this isn't some mystery where the murderer is the least likely person. It was Dicky. It follows from everything we know about him."

Sharpe pushed himself off his desk and began pacing around it. "I know. I follow you. But we can't be one hundred percent certain."

"I am."

"Judith, with all due respect, you haven't been in the homicide business very long. It's dangerous to make blanket assumptions."

"I'm not assuming anything. I'm just examining the natural consequences of his character." I stood, stiff from the chair, and faced him. "Think about the kind of person he is. Ineffectual. Immature. A cuckold. Right?" Sharpe nodded. "And then think of my refrigerator."

"Your refrigerator," he repeated slowly.

"Yes. Remember the first day you came to my house?" We smiled at each other. "Seriously, I told you I had an idea of who did it. I knew then and I know now that it was Dicky Dunck. All you have to do is listen to him, hear the way he talks, like an adolescent who got stuck in a time warp in the mid-fifties. Anyone else would have written 'Watch out' or 'Be careful' or some such thing. But 'M.Y.O.B.' It's absolutely consistent with his use of language. And he calls himself 'Dicky,' for God's sake. You know and I know that almost any other adult would call himself Richard or Rich or Rick or even Dick. But Dicky? He's still a kid, Nelson. He says things like 'bull doody.' Can you think of anyone else involved in the case who would talk like that?"

He reached for my hand, but caught himself. His office was separated from the rest of his unit by a glass partition. "I think you're right, Judith. Really I do. But I can't make an arrest on the basis of diction. So first thing Monday morning I'll have you wired and we'll go over there. Okay?"

"Okay," I agreed.

"Good," he said. "Now, since it's only eleven-fifteen, and since the morning is shot, why don't we go somewhere?"

"What do you have in mind?"

"Well, we could have a cup of coffee or something."

"I think I'd prefer something. I really don't want coffee."

He smiled. "We'll have to go to a motel. Can you hack that?"

"Yes."

"Good. Can I drive your car? I lent mine to one of the men."

"I'll drive."

"I know the way."

"You can direct me." I drove to the motel, about ten miles east, making sure not to exceed the speed limit. Sharpe made the arrangements and we walked to our room.

"Judith."

"Yes?"

"Promise you won't do anything crazy. You won't go

to see Brenda Dunck before Monday, before I'm with you. Please?"

"Why would I do something like that?"

"Because you want to be independent. But promise you'll wait for me."

"I promise."

"We're in this together."

"I know," I said, as he lifted my sweater over my head.

Chapter Eighteen

"The adhesive tape itches," I complained to Sharpe.

"You're just nervous."

"Of course, I'm nervous," I hissed. "I'm a middle-class Jewish suburbanite, not some crazed guerrilla with a grenade between my teeth. You come over here with a policewoman who wires me up and then says, 'You're being very, very brave.' And then you give me a fifteen-minute lecture on how I shouldn't sit in any soft, upholstered chairs because you want to be sure the transmitter will pick up my screams and God forbid a single, solitary sound should be muffled. What do you want, Nelson? You want me to be calm?"

"Shhh," he said, hugging me. "Now, listen, if she makes any threatening gestures, or if you feel even the least bit suspicious about anything, just say 'Mrs. Dunck.' You call her Brenda normally, right?" I nodded. "Good, then if I hear 'Mrs. Dunck' I'll know that you need me and I'll be in within thirty seconds."

We sat in the kitchen, waiting for a call from the surveillance team that Dicky had gone. I reached into the pocket of my denim skirt, the only thing I owned with pockets large enough and loose enough to conceal the transmitter, and felt for the switch; I was to turn it on the moment I rang her doorbell.

"Stop playing with it. Leave it alone, for Christ's sake."

"And you're telling me I'm nervous? Nelson, you have a terminal case of projection; you're a wreck. Relax. I'll be all right."

"I know. I know. Sorry." He blew an absent-minded kiss across the table and stared out of the window at our bird-feeding station. "Listen," he said, turning to me, "let's go through this one more time. The transmitter's working fine. So if for some reason something goes wrong and we don't hear anything after one minute, we'll be in. That means you've *got* to start talking the second she opens the door. I don't give a damn what kind of inane conversation—recite poetry or say, 'Hi, Brenda. How's tricks?' or something. But talk."

"I'll tell her I'm from the ASPCA and I'm investigating a report about cruelty to animals."

"Listen, she's built like a brick shit-house. Old Prince is a lucky dog."

"That was a sexist remark."

"That was a sexist picture I saw."

"If you think she's so wonderful," I said caustically, "why don't you go in and try your luck? She might be receptive."

"Judith, would you please try to relax?"

"Up yours." I glared at him and he reached over and held my hand. We sat that way for about five minutes, until the phone rang. "That's probably the surveillance team. You answer it."

"Look, it's your house, you get it. It could even be Brenda."

It was Sergeant Fuller from headquarters. The team had radioed in that Dicky had left five minutes earlier.

"Do they know I'm sleeping with you?" I asked, putting on my coat.

"Who?"

"All your homicide people."

"Are you nuts? Of course not."

"Then who do they think I am?"

278

"A very smart broad who's helping me with the case."

"Why do you have to say 'broad'?"

"Come on, Judith. Let's get moving."

I arrived at the Duncks' at nine forty-five. Reaching into my skirt pocket, I turned on the transmitter and rang the bell. No answer. I wanted to say "Nobody's home" loud enough for Sharpe to hear, but decided that if Brenda opened the door, it might seem somewhat odd. I rang again and hummed "Yankee Doodle." This time there were footsteps. The door opened.

"Hi, Brenda. Sorry to disturb you, but I'd like to talk."

"That's all right," she responded. "Come in. I've been working around the house and didn't have time to get dressed." That was patently false; her eyes were still puffy from sleep, and she shuffled slowly back into the house, clutching a navy blue quilted robe around her that she hadn't had time to fasten. When we reached the entrance to the living room, she turned and stared at me blankly. "What is this all about?" she asked.

I gazed at her, not really wanting to begin. She had no makeup on, only a glaze of the night's facial cream, and she seemed worn and fragile. Minuscule red veins ran through her cheeks, and the residue of eyeliner, two black dots in the inside corners of her eyes, gave her a slightly cockeyed appearance.

"It's about Bruce," I said.

"Bruce," she echoed, pulling her bathrobe tighter around her.

"Please, let's sit down," I urged, walking into the living room. I selected the rocking chair, removing my coat and arranging my skirt so as not to stifle the transmitter. "You know I've been speaking to a lot of people," I said.

"Yes, I guess so."

"Well, I've come up with some information that I

think is important for you to know about. Shall I begin?" She nodded. "You know that your husband was informing against Bruce. He was telling the government about Bruce's involvement in that pornography business."

Her eyes opened wide in amazement—or a brilliant imitation of it. She let go of her bathrobe and it opened slightly, displaying not the diaphanous blue nightgown I had expected but a chaste, white flannel one, with pink rosebuds and red trimming.

"What do you mean?" she said. "What did Dicky know about anything?"

"Remember you mentioned that Bruce had given him some business? Well, do you know what it was?"

"Something about dental hygiene. For the schools."

"No," I said. "It was pornography."

"No."

"Yes. And when Bruce's cohorts didn't pay what your husband thought they had promised, he agreed to inform against them."

"Oh, God." Brenda clasped her hands together until the knuckles gleamed white. "Oh, my God."

"Did Bruce say anything to you about it?"

"Bruce? What do you mean?"

She studied her blue carpeting, clearly uncertain as to how to deal with me.

"Come on, Brenda," I persisted, not wanting to give her time to analyze the situation.

"He said, I mean, Bruce said . . ." She stopped. I fixed my eyes on her. "Bruce said once, when I happened to run into him, that Dicky didn't appreciate all he'd done for him. So I said, 'What do you mean?' And he said Dicky was being a little bit greedy."

"And then what?"

"Nothing. He changed the subject. He said it wasn't important and he didn't want to drag me into it."

"And did you speak to Dicky about it?"

"No."

"Why not?"

"Because," she said slowly, "because he doesn't like me to poke my nose into his business."

"Dicky told you that?" She nodded. "When did you and Bruce have this conversation?"

"I forget. No, really. I can never remember when things happened."

"Was it after you and he began sleeping together?"

Her entire body shook as if she had been taken with a sudden high fever. "Who told you that?" she whispered.

"What?" I asked, afraid the transmitter wouldn't pick up her voice. She repeated the question. "Brenda," I said, "I can't tell you the source of my information. But let me reassure you. It's still a deep secret. No one wants to hurt you or ruin your reputation. All they want is to find out who killed Bruce. Okay? Now, I'm here to help you, to give you whatever information I have and to listen to whatever you have to say. Look, I'm not going to give you a lot of bull and say I'm your friend and that you should trust me implicitly." I knew Sharpe would be annoyed by this, but I wanted to be as straight with her as possible. If I took the warm, loving friend line, she would probably recoil. "But I know what's going on," I continued, "and I sincerely want to help you. So I'd like you to tell me about it." Pausing for a minute, I swallowed and took a deep breath. "Brenda, I saw the pictures Bruce took of you."

She began crying. Not a loud wail, but a silent rush of tears that poured over the oily coating of her facial cream. She wept and wept. I handed her a tissue from my handbag. "Brenda," I said, more for the transmitter than for her sake, "tell me about it."

"I can't," she sobbed.

"Brenda, I'm not here to make judgments. If it's any comfort to you, there are a lot of other women in the same boat." She looked at me, her small, dark eyes ringed with red. "That's right. Bruce had lots of affairs,

281

and he took lots of photographs. Really, he seemed to have a great need to do this, and I guess the need gave him the persuasive power to convince a lot of women. So you're not alone. Now, please, tell me exactly what happened."

She sat still, only her hands moving, the right hand kneading and squeezing the left. "You swear you won't tell anyone?" she pleaded. This put me in a bind. Of course, I literally wouldn't have to tell anyone; it was all being recorded and my recollection would be redundant.

"Brenda, I'm not going to spread it around. God, it could have been anyone—even me." She looked dubious. "It's true. And I won't spread it all over Shorehaven. I swear to that. I'll only give information that has a bearing on the murder, and then I know someone on the police force who is very, very discreet." I could envision Sharpe pounding his fist against his dashboard and cursing me. "Now tell me," I insisted.

"Well," she said softly, "it all began a couple of weeks before, before he was killed."

"Could you speak a little louder? I have a slight hearing loss."

"Sorry. I said it began about two weeks before Bruce was murdered. It was like this. He called me up one morning and just started talking. You know, just friendly. Asked how I was doing and all that. Then he asked me to meet him for lunch."

"Exactly what did he say on the phone?"

Brenda shifted slightly into a good little girl position, back straight and hands clasped. "I forget."

"No you don't. Come on," I insisted, keeping up the pressure.

"Well, he started by saying things like he was thinking about how I looked in a bathing suit last summer and how . . . I'd rather not."

"Brenda, you're not going to shock me."

282

"All right. He said my body drove him crazy and he wanted me."

"And what did you say?"

"I said, I said nothing. I mean, I was surprised. And then he said he knew I'd felt the same way about him for years and it was time we stopped playing games with each other. So I said I'd meet him that afternoon. Just to talk."

"So you had been attracted to him?" I asked.

"A little," she said, so offhandedly that I knew it had been a lot. "So I met him and we had lunch and we went to a motel."

"And?"

"And I slept with him."

"No photographs?"

"No, not until the third or fourth time. The fourth, I think. I mean, I met him every day, and the fourth day he called and said that Norma was going to be away all day at a tennis clinic so why didn't I meet him at his house."

Fleckstein must have felt in a terrible bind, I thought. With an indictment looming over his head, pressure from his Mafia pals, he was willing to defile his cozy little nest. "What was the state of your relationship at the time?" I asked.

"Well, he said he loved me. The first day we were together, in the restaurant, he told me that he had worshipped me from afar for years and that the only reason he had stayed married to Norma was because she was Dicky's sister and it was the best way he knew to keep seeing me." She spoke quickly, as if to glide over the blatant dishonesty of his words. "It meant a lot to him to see me, he said. Even if he couldn't have me. You see, he said he had always loved me but didn't think I could ever care for him."

"What made him change his mind?"

"He said he finally decided that it couldn't go on like

283

that. He had to have me or know for sure that I would never care."

"And the pictures?"

"Please," she pleaded, "I don't want to talk any more."

"Come on, Brenda. I know it's difficult but it's important."

"Well, the third time we saw each other, at the motel, he started telling me about his sex fantasies."

"What were they?"

"Raping women he saved."

"Saved?"

"Yes. From fires and things. And then being a shepherd in the Alps and doing it with the shepherdess and the sheep. And then he asked me mine. So I told him a couple of things." Sharpe, I knew, would take this in stride, but I had a painful image of the men on the surveillance team snickering.

"And so the next day you went to his house," I said slowly. "And there was Prince."

"Yes, but it wasn't the way it looked. Not really, I mean, he, the dog, wouldn't do anything. We were just kidding around and all that. You know. The dog couldn't, he didn't have a, an," she lowered her voice, "an erection."

What an incredible let-down, I thought. "And what did he say about taking the pictures?"

"He? Oh, Bruce. Well, he just wanted to remember this moment always. That it was a symbol of our mutual trust. He said he'd put them in a safe where no one would ever see them."

"Did he talk to you at all about Dicky?"

"No. Just what I told you, about Dicky being greedy."

I shifted my position in the rocking chair. The transmitter rested lightly against my right thigh. "Didn't he ask you anything about Dicky? Anything at all?"

"Well, naturally we talked about Norma and Dicky. He said they were sexually repressed because their parents were prudes."

"How did he know Dicky was repressed? Did he ask you about your sex life?"

"Well, we talked about it a little." I waited. "I mean, I told him a few things. He had told me about Norma." She examined her wedding band. "So I told him about Dicky. That sometimes he didn't get aroused too easily. That's not unusual, you know."

"Is he impotent, Brenda?"

She sighed. "Yes. Not when we were first married, though. But the last two or three years."

"You don't have sex with him at all?" My voice sounded subdued, as though I were discussing a common medical problem, chronic postnasal drip, nagging backache.

"No. Maybe it's my fault, I don't know. He says I'm too demanding and that turns guys off."

"All right. Now, when was the last time you saw Bruce?"

"The day he was killed."

"And you didn't tell the police that?"

"How could I? They'd tell Dicky."

"I doubt if they would," I said. "But tell me what happened. Was anything different?"

"Well, Bruce was very sweet and loving. He said he wanted to make up his mind about our future. That we should stop seeing each other for a little while, and both of us should decide whether we should break up or if we should get divorced and marry each other. He said it would cause talk all over town, but our love would protect us from the world. He said he'd call me in a couple of weeks." She gazed at me. "That's what he said."

"Anything else? Think."

"Well, he said because of me his problems were over."

285

"What did he mean by that?" I inquired.

"I asked him. He told me I had brought meaning to his life."

"Anything else, Brenda? Think."

"No. That was all. But you have to tell me something. Where did you see the pictures? Please. You have to tell me."

"The police found them in his office."

"In a safe?" she asked.

"I'm not sure," I lied. "But only a few upper-echelon police have seen them."

"And you."

"Yes."

"Were you working with the police when you came over that night?"

"No. But I'm cooperating with them now. I think that's important, don't you?" She didn't respond. "Now, what has Dicky said about Bruce?"

"Nothing."

"Nothing?"

"I mean, he always disliked him. Says he was a pushy guy and he could never understand Norma's falling for him. I could see what he meant in a way. Bruce seemed a little flashy, with his shirt opened a lot and the chains. But deep down he had a lot of breeding. I think he dressed that way to please Norma and her friends."

"I see. Now what about Dicky and Norma?"

"Well, they were very close when they were kids. Their mother was sick a lot, and Norma practically raised him. But they drifted apart."

"I see. Now, about the day of the murder. Did Dicky say anything at all about Bruce? Did he act differently in any way?"

"No." She stared at me. "You don't think Dicky had anything to do with it, do you?"

"I'm not sure about anything," I said lightly. "But tell me about the day of the murder."

She hesitated a few seconds and then began. "Well,

Dicky was at the plant until seven or eight. He came home in a good mood. Said our problems were over."

"What did he mean by that?"

"Oh, not what you're thinking. I think he got a new account. But he wasn't upset or anything."

"And when did you hear about the murder?"

"A few minutes after Dicky came home. Norma's next door neighbor called to tell us. We drove right over."

"And how did Dicky react?"

"He was upset. We were both upset." Her voice grew softer. "Please, I can't talk anymore."

I stood stiffly. The chair, copied from one designed for an eighteenth-century body, was very uncomfortable. "I'll keep in touch, Brenda. And call me if you want to talk. But one thing. Let's keep this private. If you tell your husband I was here, he might start asking a lot of questions neither one of us wants to answer. All right?" She nodded. We walked to the front door. On a small maple shelf under a mirror was a picture of Brenda and Dicky sitting at a banquet table, holding hands across a dish of celery and olives. "Do you have a picture of Dicky that I could have?" I asked. "It could eliminate him as even a potential suspect."

"I can't give you that one. He'd miss it. It's from an Israel Bond dinner where his cousin Murray was honored."

"Oh, of course. Could you possibly find another?" She excused herself and walked to the back of the house.

"Here," she said, extending a newspaper clipping. It was a picture of Dicky standing in front of his plant, a large sign, "Power Printing," appearing to rise from his shaved head. "This was in the *Shorehaven Sentinel* when the plant opened. We've got lots of copies."

"Thank you." I walked out slowly and went to my car. The street was deserted.

Driving past the corner nearest the Duncks' house, I

287

spotted Sharpe's car, its engine running. A lighting company repair truck was parked behind it. Sharpe put his car into gear and began following me home. For about two blocks I resisted peering into the rear-view mirror to check his expression, but finally allowed myself a glimpse. I could see nothing; the sun reflected off his windshield, and all the mirror reflected was a bright patch of light. Would he be beaming with pride, his big, round eyes crinkled at the corners, sparkling with pleasure? Or would he be wearing his bland, snub-nosed cop face, like the first time we met, showing nothing, giving nothing, taking everything in? Maybe he'd be in the midst of one of his mini temper tantrums, those quick, cold flashes of anger when he sensed that some facet of the case was no longer under his control. "Judith," he would spit as he exited from his car, "I told you, goddamn it, not to . . ."

He had told me to keep an emotional distance from Brenda, to constantly consider the possibility that she could be the murderer. But she wasn't; I knew it. Long ago Brenda had given up control of her life, long ago resigned herself to not making waves. When her ass of a husband—and she knew he was an utter ass—told her not to poke her nose into his business, she obeyed. She probably wasn't even interested any more. The limits of her life were her own lovely, aging body: the careful application of makeup to hide the flaws, the painstaking exercises, the perfect, precise application of nail polish. Even if she had been aroused enough, frightened enough to have killed Fleckstein, she would have folded immediately after. Brenda no more had the ability to sustain a cool facade than Fleckstein had to lead an open, uncalculating life.

I pulled my car into the driveway, got out, and leaned against the front fender, watching Sharpe drive up the street. He parked and walked to me silently, wearing a face without expression.

"I did a good job," I said quietly.

288

His lips parted slightly and he began to smile. "I wouldn't have done it exactly that way," he began.

"Which is precisely the reason you sent me in there."

"Did you turn off the transmitter?" he asked. I told him I had. "You know something, Judith? When I think about it, you were great. Really great. And asking her for his picture! Brilliant. Just pray she doesn't decide to tell him. What made you think of it?" He took my face in his hands and leaned over to kiss me.

"Not in front of my house," I hissed. "Let's go inside."

"The only thing I don't understand is why you had to tell her you had police contacts." Sharpe sat on the living room couch, loosening a hideous black tie with large green splotches that I'd been too nervous to notice earlier.

"What was wrong with saying that?"

"What was wrong? Your value is as a neighbor, a friend. She's obviously scared shitless of the police."

"But I'm not her friend and she knows it. And if I began a whole buddy-buddy routine, she'd sense it was totally out of character for me and be suspicious as hell. What should I have done, give her the 'we women' number, told her sisterhood is powerful?"

He put his arms around me and pulled me close. "Did anyone ever tell you," he whispered, "that you're a very smart woman?"

"Yes, all the time. How about telling me that I'm your ideal sex object, that it's painful to keep your hands off me?"

"You know that's true," he said. "But if I told you that without your prompting me, you'd get sore as hell. Now, tell me about the photograph. How did you think to ask for it?"

"Well, I thought that since we've settled on Dicky, it would be a good idea to start showing his picture around. Maybe, just maybe, there was someone in Fleckstein's building who saw him come in. I mean,

289

Dicky is distinctive-looking. What about the guy who discovered the corpse?"

"Judith, no one says corpse any more."

"I say corpse and I'm a good detective."

"All right, corpse. We can show it to Dr. Goldberg, the chiropractor, who found him. In fact, we can trot it around the whole building. It shouldn't be too hard. Most of the tenants are doctors and dentists, and they'll have a record of their appointments for that afternoon. That way, we can contact any patients who might have been in the building at the time of the murder."

"Sure. But won't that take a long time?"

"Judith, it has to be done. It's slow, but nine-tenths of detective work is like that: pure tedium. You speak to people, try to jog their memories, ring doorbells until your fingers get numb."

"All right, you take that part, I'll take the glamor." I sat with Sharpe's hand in mine, pressing flat the long veins in his hand, watching them fill again.

"What are you thinking about?" he asked.

"About Marilyn Tuccio. Wouldn't she be a natural person to interview?"

"Sure. We can talk to her again. But as I remember, she said something about seeing a doctor—a guy in a white coat. That was it. Unless maybe Dunck had the foresight to do that. It's certainly worth asking."

"Nelson, she didn't just see a doctor."

"What?"

"I'm almost positive. I remember her saying something about how she felt uncomfortable being alone with Fleckstein in his office, and that when she left, she felt relieved that there had been a couple of people in the hall. One of them was a doctor, but she didn't say anything about the other. Or others."

"Call her," he said.

"And say what?"

"Ask her to come over here."

"Not yet."

"Jesus, Judith."

"Would you please listen to me, Nelson?" He nodded. "Good. Before she comes over—have you figured out how you're going to deal with her? Don't forget, she's been a suspect all along. She's retained a lawyer, and I'm sure she's not terribly enamored of the police. What are you going to say to her? Can you give her blanket assurance that she's not a suspect?"

"All right. Why don't you call her and say you have me over here and that I'd like to talk with her? You can mention something about her not being a suspect any more."

"In other words, she's in the clear."

"Correct."

Hearing Marilyn's usual cheery hello made me hesitate for a moment. I knew how intelligent she was, how resourceful. Could she actually have done it? "Hi," I said, "It's me, Judith." Marilyn Tuccio, the avenging angel, wiping out the schmutz of Shorehaven with one mighty blow. As quickly as I had conjured it, the image faded. I knew Marilyn, knew her character. She might occasionally get a bit overemotional about fiscal integrity, but she was not a killer. "Marilyn, can you come over here now? The man from homicide in charge of the Fleckstein case is here—Lieutenant Sharpe. He's decided you're not a suspect."

"He's at your house?" she asked blankly.

"Yes. I'll explain in detail later. Why don't you just come over?"

"Fine," she said, somewhat hesitantly. "Be right there. But Judith . . ."

"Trust me, Marilyn."

"That goes without saying." She arrived within three minutes, looking fresh and crisp in black wool slacks and a long-sleeved T-shirt that said "Adoption—Not Abortion" in pink letters.

"Marilyn," I said, gazing at her shirt and shaking my head.

"You always said that even though we don't agree on a lot of things you still respect my opinion. And as you know, Judith, this is one of my strongest."

"I know. But must it be emblazoned on your chest?"

"Judith, I can show you pictures of fetuses, little tiny babies . . ."

"Mrs. Tuccio?" asked Sharpe, walking over. "I'm Nelson Sharpe." He extended his hand and she shook it. "I know you spoke with a couple of the detectives working on the case, but if you have a few minutes, I'd like to ask you a couple of questions."

Marilyn favored him with a mildly hostile glance, as if uncertain whether he was just another rotten cop or real vermin. "I have a question or two first," she said coldly. "Am I still a suspect?"

"No," Sharpe said.

"And am I supposed to believe you? What if I call my lawyer? Would you tell her the same thing?"

"Yes."

"May I use your phone, Judith?" I nodded. She strode into the kitchen, and Sharpe and I listened to her. "Miss Fields, please. Helen? Marilyn Tuccio. Fine. Fine. And you? Oh, I'm sorry. Yes. I'm here with a Lieutenant Sharpe. Yes. He says I'm not a suspect. Would you talk with him?"

Sharpe walked into the kitchen, and Marilyn returned. I could hear him saying, "Hello, Miss Fields. How are you?"

Marilyn cut short my eavesdropping. "Judith, what's happening?"

"Well, I just started asking a few questions about the case and one thing led to another and then someone broke into my house, remember? The day I brought Joey over? Well, whoever did it was probably the murderer. That's when I met Lieutenant Sharpe, and we've come up with a few things."

"I see," she said. "Is he competent?"

"Very."

292

"Not like that buffoon who came to interview me. That nasty, ill-bred bigot."

"No," I assured her. "He seems to be a decent sort."

Sharpe called Marilyn into the kitchen and came back to me. "What did you say to her?" he asked.

"I told her you were a nice person. She was terribly offended by that goon of yours who visited her, the one who insinuated that her family must have Mafia connections because their last name is Tuccio."

"My men are not goons, Judith."

Marilyn returned, and the three of us sat in the living room, Sharpe and I on matching club chairs and Marilyn on our usual section of the couch.

"Well," she said, "my lawyer says you're okay, so I guess you are. What can I do for you?"

"First," he said, "I'd like to offer an apology. I understand one of the men in my squad was something less than polite to you. I'll make it a point to speak to him about it." He spoke with great softness and sincerity and smiled at Marilyn. She beamed back at him. "Now, Mrs. Singer reminded me—and I'm sure it's in the notes of your interview—that as you left Dr. Fleckstein's office you noticed a couple of people in the hall. Could you recall that, Mrs. Tuccio?"

"Let me think. One was a doctor or a dentist. He had on a white coat."

"Young? Old? Middle-aged?" I interjected.

"Midle-aged, I think. Kind of hefty. Gray hair. Oh, yes, he had on wire-rimmed glasses."

"Sounds like Goldberg," Sharpe said to me. "Now," he said to Marilyn, "try to think back to the moment you left the office. You had felt uncomfortable being alone with Dr. Fleckstein. It was late. You were in a hurry to get to the supermarket and get home. You opened the door and what did you see? Picture it in your mind." His voice was tender, monotonous—almost hypnotic.

"I see," Marilyn answered hesitantly, "I see a woman at the end of the hall and . . ."

"What does she look like?" I demanded.

"Shh," said Sharpe.

"I also see a man down the hall the other way, to the left, taking a drink from the water fountain."

"Good," said Sharpe. "Excellent. Now, describe the woman for me."

"Let's see. Older. Sixty or sixty-five. Carrying a shopping bag, I think. I really can't remember. It's kind of vague."

"That's understandable," he said. "It's just an ordinary scene, an event that's totally unremarkable. Actually, you've got an exceptional memory. Very visual. Now, the man. He's leaning over the water fountain. Is it a high fountain or a low one?"

"High. One of those where you press a pedal with your foot to get the water."

"Good. How high would you say the fountain is?"

"Oh, about four feet."

"Fine. Now, is this man really stooping over the fountain? Or is he bending his head to get a drink? Let's try to figure out how tall he is."

"He was bending over, but not too much. I think he must have been of medium height."

"All right. Now, this thirsty man, was he wearing a coat?"

"Yes. An overcoat."

"Do you remember the color?"

"No."

"Okay. So if he was wearing an overcoat, it would indicate he was either coming in or going out. Was he carrying anything?"

"No. I mean, I don't think so. I'm sorry."

"You're doing beautifully, Mrs. Tuccio. Now, could you get a feeling about his age?"

"Not really. His back was toward me. But it wasn't a

294

kid. I mean, teen-agers don't wear overcoats these days."

"Right. Now, was there anything distinctive about this man? What struck you when you saw him?"

Marilyn rubbed her forehead. "This may sound strange," she began.

"Tell me," Sharpe said.

"I remember seeing him and thinking about St. Paul."

"St. Paul?" I repeated.

"Why did I think that?" Marilyn asked herself. "Oh, I've got it! There was a light reflecting off his head, like a halo."

"You mean he was bald?" Sharpe asked gently.

"Yes, that's it! He had no hair. He was completely bald. I remember now. His head was very, very shiny, and the light gave him a kind of saintly aura."

"Sounds like our friend," I said to Sharpe.

"Sounds like you're right," he grinned at me. "Good work, Mrs. Tuccio."

Marilyn inched forward on the couch. "Is there anything else?" she asked Sharpe.

"No, I think that about does it for now," he responded. "I appreciate your help—especially since you must be soured on the police." He said this in a sad, restrained tone, as though the mere thought of her distress was deeply disheartening to him.

She smiled at him, tacitly assuring him that she bore no grudges. "I'm just glad it's over," she said. "Would you mind if I dashed out? Today's my bread day, and I have some dough I have to punch down."

"Of course not," Sharpe said. "Good meeting you."

"Nice meeting you," she answered. I walked her to the door. "Judith," she whispered in the hallway, "I can't tell you how much I appreciate what you've done."

"Really, Marilyn . . ."

"Now don't be modest," she said. "I don't know how I can ever repay you."

295

"How about a loaf of bread?"

"I'll send one over later," she said. I handed her her coat and she sped out the door.

Sharpe and I collided as I ran back into the living room. "Congratulations," he said solemnly, and shook my hand.

"But it's not over yet," I protested. "We don't know for sure. What if it isn't him? What if we can't tie it to him?"

"Don't worry."

"What do you mean 'don't worry'?" I spoke with my teeth nearly clenched together, my hands curled into tight fists by my sides.

"Judith, what's wrong with you? I said not to worry. I'll get a search warrant and check things out. We'll get him. Relax."

"But what if you don't?"

"Come upstairs with me," he said, taking my hand. "First I'll help you to relax and then I'll explain things."

"No."

"Come on."

"No," I said. "My son's due home from school in a half hour."

"So I'll work fast. I can relax you in a half hour."

"No, Nelson. Not here."

"You're being ridiculous."

"I am not being ridiculous. I'm not going to fool around in my own house and that's that."

"You're tense."

"Of course, I'm tense," I said angrily. "Here we are, about to catch a murderer, and you want to screw."

"We don't have to screw, you know. We can . . ."

"Nelson, can't we just sit and talk? I've had one hell of a morning. What do you expect me to do, get all cute and snuggly?"

"Fine. I'll be glad to talk," he said slowly.

"And don't treat me like some goddamn loony, with that soft, sweetie-pie voice of yours."

He grabbed my arms. "Look, will you lay off? This morning hasn't been a goddamn motherfucking bed of roses for me either. You're upset. I'm upset. Okay, let's just sit down and talk."

"Good," I snapped. "Fine."

We sat next to each other on the couch, neither touching nor exchanging glances. Finally I turned to him. "Okay. Let's be friends," I said and kissed his ear.

"Okay," he said quietly, taking care not to break the spirit of the truce. "Would you like to know what I'm going to do?"

"Yes."

"All right. I'm going to leave here in a little while and apply for a search warrant. I'll get a night warrant so I can go to his printing plant when he's at home."

"Can you do that?"

"Of course, I can do it. Look, you can justify a night warrant on several grounds, but I'm going to say that he might become violent. I don't want to set him off. He's dangerous."

"How will you get in when he's not there?" I asked.

"If necessary, we can break in. Then I'll have a look around. I especially want to check his safe—if he has one—and file cabinets."

I leaned toward him so that our shoulders touched. "You think you'll find anything there?"

"I hope so," he said, taking my hand and rubbing it between his. "Dunck's a squirrel, a saver. Remember, he held on to that awl until he decided to dump it at Marilyn Tuccio's house. And if he saved the awl, he may very well have saved the photographs."

"I think you're right," I agreed. "He knew the power those pictures gave Bruce. He probably thought it would pass to him. And if you can believe Brenda, and he hasn't said anything to her, he may want to hold them, to use them against *her* someday." Sharpe nodded. "But how can you get into a safe?" I asked.

"Break in."

"Really?"

"Sure. As long as we have the right warrant."

"When will you be going there?"

"I don't know. Probably about nine or ten. Maybe later."

"Can I go? Please?"

"No." I pulled my hand from his and glared at him. "I'm sorry, Judith. I know how much this means to you, but there's no way."

"Of course, there's a way. You're in charge of the investigation."

"Yes, but that means I have to do things the right way, and there could be all sorts of complications if you came along. Look, I'll call you as soon as it's over."

"When will that be?"

"I don't know. It depends on whether we find enough evidence to arrest him."

"So it might not be for a while, maybe not even until tomorrow."

"That's right."

'Okay," I said, shrugging my shoulders

Sharpe glanced at me suspiciously. "What do you mean, 'okay'?"

"Okay," I said, shrugging my shoulders.

"You're planning something, Judith. What is it?"

"Would it be so terrible if I just parked my car across from the plant and waited?"

"Yes, it would. Look, do you want to put the entire investigation in jeopardy?"

"If it weren't for me, you know damn well you wouldn't have come near Dunck or his lousy, rotten printing plant."

"I know, Judith," he said quietly. "But you're not a cop. You can't be there. No way."

It was Sharpe's "no way" that incensed me. "Get out of this house," I hissed. "Get out and don't ever come back."

He rose and turned to me. "I'll call you the second I can."

"Don't bother," I said, marching to the door and holding it open for him. "It's your ballgame now. You're the cop. And I've served my purpose." Sharpe sighed wearily and walked off.

A gray, icy rain began falling, coating the street with slush. Every now and then a car would drive by leaving its tread marks, which were soon obscured by another layer of freezing rain. Later, the children, home from school, tailed me, whining for snacks, whimpering that they had nothing to do. I banished them to their rooms, with two fig newtons each for sustenance, warning them not to come down until four-thirty, when *Sesame Street* would begin.

"But that's a baby program," Kate protested.

"You're mean, Mommy," said Joey.

This was it, I mused, planting myself on Sharpe's seat on the couch. Goodbye homicide, hello New Deal. Nice knowing you, Nelson; Bob, can you ever forgive me? The telephone rang. Maybe it was Nancy. I could get a baby sitter for Wednesday; if she was finished with her article, we could go to the city and take in a matinee. Something light. A musical maybe. Or a frothy comedy about adultery.

"Hello," I said, my voice leaden.

"Hi," replied a man's voice. "How're ya doing?"

"Fine," I said, feeling perkier. I prayed it wasn't a salesman hawking perpetual light bulbs to benefit the blind or offering home delivery on Sunday's *Newsday* at a shockingly reduced rate. "Who is this, please?"

"Dicky Dunck."

All the clichés about panic—heart palpitations, perspiration, violent intestinal contractions—proved valid. "Oh, hi," I said, my tongue heavy with an invisible coating of fear. "How are you?"

"Fine. Superbimento, in fact. Listen, I was wondering, sweetheart. Could I drop by? I came up with a couple of ideas about your doctorate and I'd like to tell you them."

"Gosh," I answered, and that was probably the first time in my life I had said gosh, "I have a houseful of kids and I'm entertaining their mommies." That sounded warm and homey. "I'm sorry."

"Oh, because I just passed by, and I didn't see any cars in your driveway."

"It's a few of the women on the block."

"Oh. Well, how about later?" he asked, sounding quite casual.

Several options tore through my mind. I could tell him sorry, but I had plans for the next few months. I could arrange to meet him and find out what he wanted. Surely, if Brenda had told him about our meeting, she would have mentioned that I had a contact on the police force; he wouldn't dare to hurt me. Or . . . "Look," I began, "why don't I meet you tonight? After dinner, okay?"

"Sure. How does eight o'clock hit you?"

"Well, that's a bit early. What time do you get home from work?"

"Five-thirty. Six."

"I see. Well, my husband doesn't get home until about seven-thirty or eight, and I won't be finished with the dishes until nine. Would that be all right? Should I come to your house?"

"No," he said, without hesitation. "My wife's going to be doing something to her hair, so she doesn't want company, if you get me. How about a drinkie-poo somewhere?"

"Fine." Could he really think I was so dumb? Didn't he care? Could he be that dumb? Could he be that smart?

"Good. You know that French place? La Crevette?"

"Yes."

"I'll meet you at nine in their parking lot. The one on a hill in the back, okay?"

"Great," I replied. "See you at nine."

I finally decided; he was dumb. But he was also desperate, and like a worm that tries to burrow underground when it senses the earth about it moving, Dicky had an instinct to survive. Primitive, but very real. But what would he do? Take out another awl and kill me in the parking lot? He'd certainly realize that that would finish him. I could meet him, talk to him, kid him along, and then report everything to Sharpe. But if I met Dicky and he rammed the awl into the base of my skull before we had a chance to chat, how could I manipulate him into a confession? I picked up the phone and dialed.

"Lieutenant Sharpe, please."

"He's out. Can I help?"

"Look," I said, "this is important. Would you tell him that Judith Singer called and that I just spoke with Dicky Dunck and he wants to meet me. It's about the Fleckstein case," I explained.

"I know, I know," the detective said excitedly. "You're the lady who recognized the picture of his wife. He called you?"

"Yes."

"Okay, now listen to me. You sit right where you are. Keep all your doors locked and don't open them for anyone."

"I'm not meeting him until nine tonight."

"You're meeting him?" he asked incredulously. "Look, lady, just sit tight. I'm going to run over to the courthouse to get Sharpe. He's over there getting a warrant. Now don't do anything. I'll get him to call you."

"Okay."

"Now give me your address and phone number."

"He already has them."

"Lady, please."

I gave him the information and we said goodbye. I

walked through the house, checking the front door, back door, and garage entrance. Everything was securely locked.

Moments later, as if by a signal, the children emerged from their rooms. I walked to the den with them, and we sat on the floor, singing.

"I've been working on the railroad," crooned Joey. I started biting my nails, beginning with my right index finger. In the background, I vaguely heard Kate's "Free to be, you and me" crescendo. Still no call from Sharpe.

"How about 'Old MacDonald'?" I suggested.

"Too babyish," sighed Kate.

"Too dumb," Joey said.

We launched into a series of folk songs and began a *Sesame Street* medley. In the middle of "Rubber Duckie," the doorbell rang.

"I'll get it, I'll get it," the children shouted, stumbling over each other.

"I will get it," I announced. "Stay down here. Or else."

Or else, I thought, you might be hit by a stray bullet. I edged along the hall and, nearing the door, flattened my body against the wall. "Who's there?" I said, louder than I expected.

"It's me. Nelson Sharpe." Why would he give his last name?

"What's your middle name?" I demanded.

"For Christ's sake," said the muffled voice. "Would you open up?" It had to be Dicky, I thought. But how would he know about Sharpe? Had Sharpe originally interviewed him? Had he been following us? Or had I been wrong all along? Could it be someone else? Someone I hadn't seriously suspected. "Okay. My middle name is Lawrence. I have a B.A. in European history and . . ." I opened the door, Sharpe was standing there looking serious. Behind him was a policewoman, a few inches taller than he, with broad shoulders and a massive, perfectly coiffed Afro. A gun rested on her slim right hip. If I were planning anything illegal and spotted her, I would instantaneously change my plans and spend the rest of my life in a cloistered order, doing only good works. She looked tough.

"Mrs. Singer, this is Officer Jackson." That's why he had used his last name. "Can we come in?"

"Yes, of course," I said, opening the door. The squad car was pulling away. "Hi," I said to Officer Jackson.

"Hi," she said, in a surprisingly small voice for such a formidable-looking woman. "They asked me to keep you company for a while." She sounded like Jacqueline Kennedy. We smiled. "Can I look around?"

"Sure," I said. Her head swiveled right and left, as though she was tuning her radar to the air currents of my house. "Oh, I didn't have time to make my bed this morning," I added.

"Neither did I," she replied, although I'm sure that was simply politeness; an unmade bed in Jackson's house would have sense enough to make itself. "Now, you have two children, right? Where are they?"

I walked to the stairs and peered into the den. Kate and Joey were hovering at the foot of the steps, staring back at me. I motioned them to come up and introduced them to Sharpe and Jackson. Kate gaped at Jackson, alternating her glance between the badge and the black holster. Joey looked at Sharpe and asked: "You again?"

"Yes. Your mother is helping the police."

"Big deal," Joey responded. Before I could cringe, Jackson asked the children to take her around the house. Kate led her, gazing back occasionally with awe and adoration. Joey tagged behind, making loud, flatulent noises between pursed lips. He was not immune, I knew, to preschool obnoxiousness, but something about Sharpe seemed to bring out the worst in him. Did he have some sort of Oedipal sixth sense, some finely at-

303

tuned perspicacity, that told him that Sharpe was a threat? Or was it merely four-year-old bravado before a cop?

"I can't leave you alone for a minute," Sharpe said as soon as they were up the stairs.

"Nelson, please hold me," I whispered. He led me into the kitchen, away from the staircase, and he put his arms around me. We stood, pressed tightly together, swaying slightly from side to side. "I'm okay now," I said finally, and sat down at the table. He sat opposite me. "All right, let me tell you about the arrangements," I said, sounding quite matter-of-fact.

He knew where La Crevette was, and said it would be no problem securing the area. "I can have a couple of men in parked cars, maybe one in a taxi, in the lot, and I'll check out the building for a back entrance. Don't worry, we'll be right there." He looked at me earnestly. "You want to go, don't you?" I said nothing. "Okay, if you don't, don't worry about it. It's no problem."

"I want to go."

"You're sure?"

"Yes." I paused. "Oh, he's leaving his plant about five-thirty or six. I asked him when he was going home for dinner."

"Judith, you're great," he said, managing a small smile. We were nervous. I played with the saltshaker while he shoved the napkin holder back and forth between his hands. "I'm leaving Jackson to watch the house. She's good. And she's on the rape squad, so she's used to dealing with kids."

"With kids? On the rape squad?"

"Come on. Don't get yourself upset."

"I'm not upset."

"Yes, you are. Anyway, we'll wire you again. But this time you're going to wear a bulletproof vest, so wear a coat with pockets for the transmitter."

304

"If you're going to be so close, won't he hear the transmission?"

"No, the equipment will be inside a car with the windows closed. Now, you stay in your car until he gets out. We want to see that he's not carrying a weapon. If he is, although I doubt it, just fall to the floor of your car. We'll take care of him." He stopped his napkin holder game. "Are you listening to me, Judith?"

"Of course," I shot back. "Now, look, how should I steer the conversation? I think . . ." We spoke for another half hour and then he stood to leave, squeezing my hand.

"You'll do fine," he murmured. "You always do."

When I opened the front door for Sharpe, I saw that the sleet had changed to snow. Not the big, puffy wet flakes that melt upon impact with concrete, but a deluge of stiff, granular snow that clung to the driveway. Sharpe stood on the front step, turning his head slowly, like a hunting dog trying to pick up a fading scent.

"It looks bad," he observed, his eyes darting up to the luminous, low-hanging clouds. "Get your car into the garage."

"What?" I asked, although I had heard him.

"Your car. Get it into the garage. You don't want the windows iced up so badly that it will take a half hour to scrape them off, do you?" I sensed him looking at me and returned his glance. "Judith, are you sure. . . . ?"

"I'm sure. I was just thinking. I have to call my husband so he'll be home in time to stay with the children. What if he's working late? Nelson, wouldn't it be awful if the whole investigation fell through because I couldn't get a baby sitter?"

His hair and eyebrows were coated with snow. He looked like a kid who had applied cotton bunting for the Santa Claus role in the school's Christmas pageant. His smooth, unlined skin and great brown eyes were those of an enchanting ten-year-old. "Fuck the baby sitter," he said out of the corner of his mouth. "Jackson will be here. Don't get so hung up on logistics. Okay?"

"Okay," I snapped, and took a deep breath of cold air. I stood at the doorway, feeling the warmth of the house on my back and the frigid, damp March air on my face. "Okay," I said again, more calmly. "Now, what's the schedule?"

"We have a man surveilling his plant and another at his house. As soon as he leaves, I'll be notified, and once he's home for a few minutes, we'll get into the plant. Hopefully, we should finish there in an hour, an hour and a half at most. If there's still time, I'll call you or come over. Otherwise, I'll be in the parking lot. But for Christ's sake, don't look around for me."

"I know, I know," I said absently, thinking how much I disliked driving in the snow.

"The only thing is," he began, and took his index finger and wiped the snow off his eyebrows.

"The only thing is what?" I demanded.

"Nothing really."

"Nelson," I said forcefully, "I am about to confront a homicidal maniac, not some cute sociopath who specializes in misdemeanors. He kills, he breaks into people's houses. He has no decency, no honor. He bites his toenails, for God's sake."

"Really? You never told me that."

I shivered and held myself tight. "Does that make a difference?" I asked.

"Well, it's not grounds for arrest in New York. Look, Judith, all I was going to say is that if it's snowing very hard, we may have to change our plans about securing our people in parked cars."

"You're worried about them getting frostbite? What about me?"

"All I'm saying is that if it's bad out, their car windows will get frosted or covered with snow and they won't be able to see a goddamn thing. Don't worry, we'll find some place else for them."

306

"You know what worries me," I said, lowering my voice. Jackson and the children were a few feet away from me in the living room. "What really makes me nervous is all those old detective novels." Sharpe looked at me blandly, listening. "Do you know what happens in them? The detective has a fantastic affair with some wonderful woman and guess what happens to her?" He shook his head. "She gets killed in the end," I explained. "You know why?" Again he shook his head. "So that in the next case the detective can have another fantastic affair with another wonderful woman, who will ultimately die so that in the next case . . ." A small, quavering sigh escaped me.

"Judith, this is life. Reality. And nothing can happen to you because there can't possibly be another woman in the next case who even remotely resembles you. Okay?"

"That's what you say now." For a moment we said nothing. Then we looked at each other and laughed. "All right. You'd better be going. It's getting late."

"Are you okay?"

"Yes, I'm fine. I'll see you later." I stepped back into the house. "Be careful," I called after him. He didn't look back.

For several minutes, I sat on the living room floor with the children, the three of us looking up in awe at Officer Jackson, who held court on the piano bench, her back erect, her head lifted slightly. Kate informed me that she had dropped all her other career plans and was going to become a policewoman. Joey told me that Jackson had never killed anyone but had once punched a guy out.

"I just want to give my husband a call, see what his plans are," I said to Jackson. She nodded. I called Bob's office from the bedroom, fully expecting his secretary to proclaim that he was in conference and couldn't be disturbed for the next twenty-four hours. Instead, she said he had just left.

307

Maybe, I pondered, clambering downstairs, his train will be stuck in a snowdrift. Nothing perilous, and they'd have sandwiches and coffee in the bar car, just enough to keep him tied up till about ten-thirty or eleven. But glancing out the living room window, I saw only about a half inch of snow on the ground. "I guess I'll make dinner," I said to the three of them. They blinked at me with great disinterest. Jackson said she'd watch television with them, but to call her if I heard any strange sounds. Like Dicky cackling in my back yard, I mused, his awl gleaming in the moonlight.

I stuck my hand into the freezer and fished out a large aluminum container of meatballs and plunked it into a pot to thaw. There was, fortunately, a whole packet of spaghetti, and I managed to throw together a salad. In less than three hours, I would be encased in a bulletproof vest, and here I was slicing radishes. I felt I should be overwhelmed by a sense of absurdity, but somehow the whole situation seemed rather cozy. What harm could befall a woman who at the very next moment was going to make her own salad dressing? With parsley and tarragon and dill. I set the table in the dining room and was just measuring the coffee when the doorbell rang.

Jackson got there first, her silver badge reflecting the hallway light, her hand about five inches away from her gun. "Did you hear anyone drive up?" she asked, in her silvery voice.

"It's probably my husband," I answered softly. "Who's there?"

"Me," said Bob, his voice muffled by the thick oak door.

"It's him," I assured Jackson and opened the door. "Hi."

But he was staring at Jackson, his mouth open slightly. "Hi," she said to him. "I'm Officer Sandra Jackson."

"Come in," I urged Bob, as I would a shy guest, taking his hand and guiding him over the threshold. "Everything's fine."

He found his voice. "How can everything be fine if there's a policewoman in the house? Would you please explain that to me, Judith?" He began to unbutton his coat. "I'll need a wooden hanger," he informed me. Being in no mood to argue, I walked the two feet to the hall closet and handed him a hanger. He put his coat on it, then shook it a couple of times so the snow that had accumulated on his walk from the driveway fell onto the floor. He removed his brown plaid cashmere scarf and placed it around the wire part of the hanger, the silk lining facing down. "Now, would someone like to explain what's going on here?" he demanded, handing me his coat.

I handed it back to him. "I'll tell you as soon as you put your coat away," I said. He glared at me. Jackson shot me her first real smile of the day.

"Daddy, Daddy." The children exploded up from the den, hugging Bob's waist and standing on tiptoe to be kissed.

"You're home for dinner," observed Kate with a satisfied smile.

"Isn't it nice," I observed, "having Daddy home? Let's eat."

For the first time in weeks, the conversation at the dinner table was animated. Bob, of course, sat isolated in his bleak silence, but the rest of us had a grand discussion about fingerprints. As I stood to serve the spaghetti, I whispered to Bob: "Sorry we didn't get a chance to talk. I'll explain after dinner." He lifted his fork and stabbed a meatball.

We finished eating a few minutes before seven. Jackson told the children to go downstairs and watch television; they obeyed without protest. She glanced from Bob to me. "I'll wait downstairs with the kids." I nodded. "But we'll have to get started in about fifteen minutes." She stood. "Nice talking to you, Mr. Singer." He had not acknowledged her presence throughout the entire meal.

"All right," I began, "let me fill you in." He bit into a cold Sara Lee brownie. "It's really very difficult," I said, "because you haven't been listening to me, so you don't know what's going on. But I'll try to give you a rundown to bring you up to date."

"Why is that woman in my house?" he asked. "Who is she?"

"She's with the rape squad," and he stared at me. "No, no, this has nothing to do with rape. They just wanted a woman because they're going to wire me up and I have to take off my sweater for that and they don't want a man to have to do that because God forbid he should see my bra."

"Wire you up?" he asked. "What do you mean?"

"Oh. It's an electronic gadget . . ."

"Don't treat me like an ass, Judith. Would you please explain to me why the police think they have to wire you up?"

I poured myself another cup of coffee. "All right. You know I've been working with the police on the Fleckstein case. Well, they're convinced that the murderer is the same person who wrote M.Y.O.B. on the refrigerator. Well, he called me and asked to meet me, and the police want to hear our conversation. That's all."

"That's not all," he said coldly.

"Of course, it isn't," I agreed. "They've got a search warrant, and they're going to go through his office as soon as he's out. Hopefully, they'll find something there to link him to the murder. You see, Fleckstein had a habit of taking pictures of the women he was having affairs with." He looked at me blankly. "I mean, photographs of them undressed, in various get-ups. Nothing really imaginative, but potentially terribly embarrassing. Anyway, they think Dicky Dunck—he's the man they

310

suspect—took the pictures from Fleckstein's office when he killed him. Now Dicky has a feeling I'm involved, but what we want to find out is whether he realizes he's the prime suspect. Hopefully, I can get him to talk and incriminate himself."

"This is insane," Bob bellowed, standing up. "This is crazy. You're going to risk your life meeting some killer. Are you sick?"

"Don't worry," I said sweetly. "I'll have on a bulletproof vest and there will be cops all around. They'll be able to see everything and hear every word that's said." Bob's face was flushed, his eyes wide open with shock. "Bob, sit down. Please hear me out." He stiffened for a moment, but finally sat. "Look, I know things haven't been going well with us," I began, and my eyes filled with tears. "But I've been enjoying this case more than anything I can remember in a long time. Look at me, please.

"I know you see this as some demented obsession of mine, some psychotic episode that's totally out of character. But, look, we've been living out here for years, and I haven't been happy for a second. I know that's not fair, but ultimately it's true. I've been bored silly, floundering between the supermarket and car pools, and all of a sudden, I found something. A murder. A puzzle. It fell into my lap, and all of a sudden it was something I could latch on to. Not just out of boredom. It's fascinating, trying to put the pieces together, working with the police." I paused for a second. Bob didn't find the phrase "working with the police" any more absurd than the rest of my explanation, so I continued. "And I'm good at it. I mean, at detective work. Can't you understand that?"

"I can understand it," he said slowly. "And I told you that I sympathize with you. Maybe we should have stayed in the city. I don't know. But you can't continue with this. I won't let you. You're a married woman, a mother, a person with responsibilities. You can't just go

311

off on something wild like this because it's fun. It's not fun. It's serious business." He reached for another brownie and held it aloft in his left hand. It seemed to be a very conscious gesture: his wedding ring gleamed at me. "There are millions of things you can do," he said. "All sorts of community work, with pollution or kids taking drugs. You can get a job if you want to, go back to school. Whatever. But I draw the line with this, Judith. I'm not going to let you do it."

He nibbled his brownie and put it down on his plate. His thumb and index finger were covered with chocolate, and I handed him another napkin. "I can't accept that, Bob," I said.

"I'm sorry. You'll have to."

"No. I don't need your permission. This is something I want to do and I'm going to do it."

"Even though I don't want you to?"

"Yes."

"I might not be here when you get back. I mean that, Judith."

"I hope you will."

"And if I'm not? You're willing to let ten years of marriage go down the drain? You're willing to risk our relationship?"

"Our relationship hasn't been doing very well for the last few years, has it? I mean, it's been running on its own momentum, but it's not really moving, just coasting. Maybe if I can come to terms with myself, focus in on who I am—and who you are—we can come up with something better."

"You never said you weren't happy."

"I never said I was. You never asked."

"I'm going upstairs," he said. "You still have time to change your mind."

A moment later, gripping the edge of the table, I made a conscious decision; I would not go to pieces. There was simply no time for that sort of indulgence. Instead, I quickly cleared the table and rushed the children off to bed. I kissed them in an offhand fashion, rejecting the notion of clutching them to my breast and whispering, "Goodbye, my darlings." Jackson was pacing downstairs, waiting to deck me out in a transmitter that had been delivered a few minutes before.

She was just finishing taping the wire around my midriff when the doorbell rang. We had a brief debate over who should answer it, which she finally won. It was Sharpe.

"You're early," I said.

"We got in a little after five-thirty."

"And?"

"And we found shit."

"Shit?" I asked.

"Nothing," he said, his eyes cast down. "Not one goddamn thing. Except . . ." he began.

"Except what?" Jackson demanded. Until that time, she had refrained from asking questions. Being on the rape squad, she informed me, she had had some contact with the cops in homicide, but they were distinct domains. She hadn't wanted to tread on their turf. But now, her investigatory appetite was whetted; she wanted in.

"The safe was completely empty," Sharpe muttered.

"Oh," she said, raising her eyebrows.

"What does that mean?" I asked. "That he cleaned it out?"

"That's only conjecture," he said.

"It seems likely, doesn't it," Lieutenant?" asked Jackson.

"Well, I guess so." He leaned against the door, looking tired and defeated. His large hands, red and raw from the cold, dangled from the sleeves of his green sweater. "It's not a new safe. Looked like it had plenty of use. Who the hell knows?"

"Let's go into the living room," I suggested. Jackson and I walked in and sat down, and Sharpe followed, shuffling his feet along the carpet, staring down at the floor.

"Shit," he said. Jackson and I glanced at each other. She shrugged her shoulders. I tried to think of something to say, something to comfort him. But he spoke first. "You know what really gets me? I didn't think, from everything I know about him, that he had the brains to clear out the safe. Who knows? Maybe he never had anything. Maybe he didn't . . ."

"Um," I said. I had almost slipped and called him "Nelson" in front of Jackson. "Look, Lieutenant, he did call to set up a date with me. And you know and I know that he couldn't care less about my dissertation. That means he has something to say. So let's just relax and see what happens at nine o'clock."

"She's right, Lieutenant," said Jackson. "And that makes this meeting even more important." He shot her a quick, angry look, and she sank back into her chair a little. Apparently, it wasn't department protocol to inform a superior officer that his intuition was less than keen.

We sat silently for several miserable minutes until Jackson suggested I try on the bulletproof vest. I had imagined a nifty neon-orange chest protector, but it was a tunic of dull gray-green.

"It's not as heavy as I thought it would be."

"They're making them lighter now," Jackson said. She sent me to the closet to get my coat, but it wouldn't close over the vest. We finally settled on Bob's down-filled ski jacket.

"I look like a polar bear in drag."

"Worse," said Sharpe. We all chuckled and then fell silent.

"Can I take it off for a few minutes?" I asked.

"Please don't," said Jackson. "Otherwise, I'll have to readjust the microphone."

The two of them sat quietly, occasionally exchanging a remark about surveillance techniques. I paced back and forth, unable to position my bulk in a chair. A sour sweat began to rise from my body, soaking my forehead and trickling between my breasts. Finally, Sharpe announced that it was eight o'clock. "That means we're in place," he said. I looked at him, not comprehending. "It means that all my men are in position in the parking lot. We don't want any undue movement in case he checks the place out early."

"Oh," I said and paced some more. "I'm going outside."

"Don't," snapped Sharpe. "He may drive by."

"I'll go into the back yard," I said, and walked toward the kitchen door. Jackson followed a few seconds later, pulling on her coat. The snow emitted its own eerie light, brightening now and then when the moon appeared from behind a cloud. I walked to the children's swing set, cleared the edge of the slide of snow, and managed to sit down. Jackson stood about a foot away, a giant looming black presence in the white snows of Shorehaven.

"Feeling scared?" she asked.

"I'm not sure. Mainly just sick to my stomach."

"That's scared," she said. "We all get it, in one way or another. With me, every time I'm a decoy, I go to the bathroom for an hour straight before I go out."

"But once you're working, are you scared?"

"Yes." She fell silent. "But when things start happening, the minute a suspect approaches me, I'm okay. It's all business from that point on."

"But you're a pro," I said softly. "You've been trained. You know what to do."

She gazed at me. "From what I've heard about you, you're no slouch. You've got all the right instincts."

I grinned at her. She grinned back. Then we turned as Sharpe appeared at the kitchen door, motioning us to come in. We trudged back to the house.

"I just got a call," he announced. "Dunck just left."

"It's not even eight-thirty," I protested.

"I know," he said. "Maybe he'll go somewhere first. You just get there at nine, okay? Just like you planned." I nodded. "Hey," he said suddenly, "where's your husband?"

"Upstairs in the bedroom." He looked at me quizzically.

"Mr. Singer doesn't seem to approve," said Jackson, her little girl's voice transforming her irony into an innocent observation.

We remained in the kitchen, silent for the most part, sharing a quart of orange juice. Suddenly I looked at Sharpe.

"You said all your people are in position?" He nodded. "That means you won't be there."

"I will," he said. "I'll be on the floor of your car, under a blanket. Let me tell you, if you think your bulletproof vest is uncomfortable, you should try that sometime."

At ten minutes to nine, we began to move. Jackson would stay at the house until I got home. Sharpe went to the trunk of his car and took out a large brown blanket. He lay down on the floor of my car, in front of the back seat, and covered himself.

"Couldn't you wait to do that until we get there?" I asked.

"No," he said. "Come on. Let's go."

I started the engine and turned on the windshield wipers. It was snowing again. At the stop sign on the corner nearest my house, I braked too hard and went into a slight skid.

"Easy," he said, his voice muffled.

I drove on slowly. "Nelson," I said, "if anything happens . . ."

"Stop it. Nothing's going to happen, Judith."

"But if anything does . . ."

"I'll see that you get a police honor guard at your funeral."

"Nelson, please."

316

"Judith, relax. I'll see that your kids are well taken care of, and I'll even find someone nice for your husband."

"That's not funny."

"Yes, it is. You're great and everything will be all right."

"Nelson," I began.

"Drive," he told me. "We should be there soon."

"The entrance to the parking lot is right up the street. I can see it from here."

Chapter Nineteen

The last thing Sharpe said to me before I pulled into the parking lot was, "Keep a window open." I rolled it down. He shifted under the blanket, making a soft, shuffling noise, and then was silent. I couldn't even hear him breathing.

In low gear, I eased the car up the driveway and into the lot, past two Cadillacs, a BMW, a Volkswagen, and an empty suburban taxi. The last, I thought, must belong to the cops. At least I hoped so; I would not feel secure with an Eldorado-owning homicide detective. Swallowing hard, I peered about the lot. It was empty. "No one here," I said, not moving my lips. Just then, my headlights picked up a black Mercedes at the far end of the lot. Slowly, wary of the slippery asphalt, terrified of my own audacity, I drove toward it. And there was Dicky, leaning against the driver's door.

"Hi," I said. He gave me a wide smile, showing a wide stretch of uneven teeth. Then he ambled over, unlocked my door, and said: "How're you doing, sweetheart? Listen, get out. It's a gorgeous night. We can talk here and then later go for a drink." As I turned the engine off, I noticed it had begun snowing hard. The air was bitter and damp. Short, powerful gusts of wind whipped by, rearranging the snow into small white mountains, plateaus, and valleys.

He opened the door of my car and offered me his

hand. I took it, trying to exit with a degree of grace despite the bulk of the bulletproof vest. Would he notice that I looked at least twenty pounds heavier? The sleeves of Bob's ski jacket hung to my knuckles. My finger tips were numb.

"I really appreciate your wanting to help with my dissertation." He didn't respond. "It's so thoughtful of you," I continued.

"Okay, cunt," he hissed, "what did you tell my wife?"

"I beg your pardon?"

"I said, you'd better cut out your smart-ass business and tell me what you told my wife, goddamn it." His eyes were squeezed into narrow slits, but his hands, in blue gloves that matched his cap, were out of his pockets, weaponless. He flexed his fingers. If he tried to strangle me, Sharpe could probably stop him in time.

"If you insist on using such foul language," I announced, "I won't talk to you. I'm not accustomed to hearing such filth." He opened his eyes slightly and looked around, uncertain of what to do. "You owe me an apology," I added.

He hesitated a moment and, without looking at me, muttered, "Sorry." He then fell silent, clearly because he had no alternative to fall back on after Plan A—Intimidation—had failed.

"Now, do you want to know what I told your wife?" He nodded. "Well, what did she say to you?"

"Listen, I'm the one who's asking the questions. Get it, baby?" He had retreated to Plan A. "She called me as soon as you left the house, and you want to know what she said? She said, 'You were the one testifying against Bruce.' That's what she said."

"Well, it's true, isn't it? You were testifying against him. And I know why. Because you hated him."

"Bull doody. He was my brother-in-law."

"You hated him because he had everything you didn't. Money. Women. Success." I sounded like a syn-

320

opsis of yesterday's soap opera. Dicky glared at me angrily and was about to reply, when I heard a soft sneeze. "A-choo." Short, brief, but distinct. Dicky froze for a second, but it didn't seem to register. I took my hand, wiped it under my nose, and sniffled. Then, I stared at him accusingly. "Bruce Fleckstein was hanging over your head for years and years. That's why you wanted to destroy him."

"What do you mean 'destroy'?" he said. "That's the dumbest thing I ever heard. All I was doing was being a good citizen. What was I supposed to do, lie to the government? Huh? Is that what I should have done? Concealed a federal crime? Now come on. What else did you tell my wife? Huh?"

"Why don't you ask me what she told me, Dicky?" I asked calmly. Perhaps I was being a sophist, but I reasoned that since Brenda had broken our vow of confidentiality, I could plunge right in.

He stepped back, mouth slightly open, and leaned against his car door again. "Okay," he whispered. "What did she tell you?"

"She told me the two of you had been having some problems."

"What do you mean, problems? That's nuts."

"Bedroom problems, Dicky. And when you found . out that she and Bruce were having an affair, you killed him."

In the snowy evening light, I thought I saw his skin turn a greenish color. But all he said was: "Boy, are you ever off your rocker, honey-bunny."

What had I expected? A confession? Sharpe had told me to save a direct accusation as the final weapon. I had used it too soon. I tried to recoup. "I'm not off my rocker. It's the truth."

"No, it's not."

"Yes, it is. Bruce made certain you didn't inherit anything from your father. He refused to co-sign a bank loan for you. And when he finally threw you a bone, when he threw some business your way, his friends didn't pay you what you had expected. That's the truth, Dicky," I said softly. "And then you thought you had him. You were going to get even with him once and for all. So you talked to the government. You were going to see Bruce go to jail."

"Fuck you," he sneered.

"But then he got you again. He slept with Brenda. And he took all those pretty pictures of Brenda—and Prince. I know. I saw them, Dicky." He was crying now, not aloud, but tears were rolling down his cheeks. "And she told Bruce that you were impotent, and he teased you about it, didn't he? And so you killed him."

"No," he said weakly. "No."

"Dicky, there's an eyewitness. Someone who saw you in front of his office right before the murder."

"No. You're trying to scare me." He was trembling now, a cocky little kid who had mixed in with the big guys only to discover he wasn't tough enough.

"No, I'm not trying to scare you. I'm telling you the truth. Someone saw you. At the water fountain. Remember you took a drink, Dicky? Was your mouth dry before you went in to kill him?"

He ran his tongue over his lips. He tried to flex his fingers again. But he had no fight left in him. "He was going to show the pictures all around," he said, nearly whimpering. "First those, and then he told me he had more with her face showing."

"So you killed him. He was going to blackmail you."

He nodded, but I wanted him to say it for the transmitter. "So you killed him, right, Dicky?"

I was concentrating on him, so I only dimly heard the sound of a car door opening in the background. Asses, I thought. Couldn't they wait? And suddenly there was a woman's voice.

"Shut up, Dicky." I looked beyond him, and there was Norma Fleckstein, dashing around the side of the Mercedes. She had been hiding there the whole time.

322

"Norma?" I said. Strangely, the first thing I noticed was her quilted orange jumpsuit. The second was the small paring knife in her right hand. "Were you there too?" I asked, so stunned at her presence that I couldn't even begin to appear nonchalant.

"No. She had nothing to do with it," cried Dicky.

"Shut up," she barked at him and began moving toward me, the knife pointed down, toward the snow. "You'd better tell me everything you know," she said. I considered it for a split second and then ran—half trot, half skid—toward the center of the parking lot. She dashed after me, her long, skinny legs taking greater strides than mine, her body, quick and responsive after her hours and years of tennis clinics, more capable of speed. She caught up with me by a large trash bin near the restaurant's back door.

"Talk," she said, grabbing my sleeve and aiming the knife at my heart. Where were the police, I thought, looking about hysterically. Ah, they know the vest will absorb the knife wound.

"I admire your family loyalty, Norma."

"What?"

"I said, I admire your family loyalty, coming here to protect your brother . . ."

"Don't think *I'm* that stupid," she growled. Suddenly, before I could respond, she ran behind me and put her left arm around my neck. Her right hand held the knife to my throat.

"Norma," said Dicky, lumbering through the snow toward us, "Norma, sweetie, don't . . ."

"Shut up, dummy. You screwed up again," she said. "Now," she hissed into my ear," "tell me what you know."

"So you killed him," I said, very loudly.

"No. She wasn't even there. Honest," whined Dicky.

"Shut up, shut up," Norma yelled.

"Norma, don't worry. I'll protect you. Look, I killed him. Norma had nothing to do with it. I just told her about the pictures, and she told me to do what I had to do. That's all."

I tried to swallow, but the knife was too near my throat. Finally, I rasped: "So you set your brother up to kill your husband."

"She didn't set me up," Dicky protested, staring from the knife to Norma's face and back again.

"Both of you," Norma shrieked, "just keep quiet. And you, you damn nosy bitch, you're in trouble." And then her voice grew mellow, silky with unaccustomed power. "What am I going to do with you, Judith Singer? You know too much."

Suddenly the parking lot was suffused with light. I turned my head a fraction of an inch and saw four or five plainclothes police running from different parts of the lot. And then Sharpe, his gun drawn, looking white and terrified.

"Put the knife down, Mrs. Fleckstein," Sharpe said, his voice amazingly calm. The revolver, clutched in his left hand, remained steady.

"Drop dead," she responded.

Off to the left, a policeman was searching Dicky. Another covered him with a gun.

"Come on, Mrs. Fleckstein," Sharpe said, "you have everything to gain by cooperating with us."

"Norma, let her go. Please, Norma. I'll cover for you," Dicky pleaded. He spoke over the head of a detective who was patting his legs, searching for a weapon. A tall, thin cop was putting handcuffs on his wrists. She ignored them.

"Please, Norma."

"You're a jerk, Dicky. You always were," she said, drawing her arm tighter around my neck. "Now just keep quiet."

"Mrs. Fleckstein," Sharpe began again.

"I want a plane," she declared.

"What?" asked Sharpe.

324

"A plane. I want to get out of here, and if you don't get me one, I'll kill her."

"Mrs. Fleckstein, we might be able to arrange for a plane," Sharpe said. "But first we have a few things to talk about." I felt Norma's grip ease slightly. But then Sharpe's attention was drawn from us, to the left and behind us. He stood and aimed his gun at that area. "Mrs. Dunck! Brenda! Don't do it!" Sharp yelled, his voice hoarse with horror.

"Where?" Dicky croaked.

"What?" squeaked Norma, who swiveled around. In that instant, I wrenched myself out of her grasp and dropped to the ground. Within seconds, about five pairs of feet were gathered about me. One of the officers, not Sharpe, twisted Norma's wrist and caught the knife just as it fell from her hand.

"You have the right to remain silent," a voice began to drone.

"Norma, the policeman said 'Brenda.' Where is she, Norma?" Dicky called to her.

"Dummy. He tricked us."

"You have the right to an attorney and if you can't afford . . ."

I lay in the snow, sobbing. Sharpe knelt down and hugged me. I felt nothing, insulated by the vest, except when his hand moved upward and began stroking my hair. Another cop in a leather jacket walked over to us and held my hand.

"I have to throw up," I said.

The other policeman helped me up. Sharpe stood at my side. "Okay. It's okay."

I dragged myself over to a pink Cadillac and leaned against it. Sharpe followed me. "Would you please just leave me alone for a minute? I'm going to be sick."

"Go ahead," he said softly. "I'm right here with you."

"Can't I even throw up by myself? For God's sake . . ."

"It's all right, Judith."

"No, it's not, I have to puke. Why didn't you come sooner?"

"I don't know. It happened so fast."

"But you're policemen. You should have . . ."

"I know, I know. Oh, Jesus." He looked ready to cry.

"I'm all right now, Nelson." I wiped my tears with my icy hands.

"Wait for me," he said. He walked toward Norma and Dicky. "Why don't we have a talk?" he asked them. I followed him but remained about three feet back. From somewhere, still another cop materialized and handed me a handkerchief.

"It really wasn't her fault," said Dicky.

"Shut up," said Norma. She eyed Sharpe with disdain. "I want my lawyer. Ed Mollin. State Senator Ed Mollin."

A few minutes later they were driven to headquarters. Sharpe and I remained in the parking lot. "Are you sure you're okay, Judith?" he asked, as I stood there crying and shivering.

"I think so," I sniffed. "Just the aftermath of terror." I stood before him, motionless, as he took Bob's jacket off me and removed the bulletproof vest.

"Put this back on," he said, handing me the jacket. "I'll take the transmitter off in the car."

"Now."

Gently, he lifted my sweater and gingerly peeled off the surgical tape. He stuffed the microphone and wire into his pants pocket. Then, silently, we walked back to the car.

"Nelson, was it you who sneezed? God, I thought it was all over then."

"No, it was Norma, although I couldn't see anything when it happened. I figured it was you or Dunck. Christ, that must have thrown him for a loop."

"He must have been terrified."

"Yes," he muttered, "I guess so." Then he held me

326

and said: "Judith, that was the worst minute of my life. Seeing you there. And her with that knife."

"I know. I know. But you got me out." We kissed, several times, not from desire but to reassure each other that I was still alive, still sound. I rubbed my cheek against his, feeling the prickles of his beard. "Nelson?" I said.

"Yes, Judith."

"Nelson, what was her role? Do you think Norma was really involved? Or did she just egg Dicky on?"

"We'll see. I'll drive you home and then get over to headquarters for the interrogation." I gazed at him. "Judith," he said, "you can't be there. I'm sorry, because if it wasn't for you we'd still be playing guessing games. But it wouldn't be right. Anyway, I think you should get home and have a good, stiff drink." Bob would have suggested a cup of hot chocolate and a Valium.

I kissed the tip of his nose. "You know, half of me wants to kick you in the nuts for being such a rotten bastard, but the other half just wants to go home and enjoy a peaceful nervous breakdown."

"Anyway, Judith, in all fairness, your husband is probably scared out of his mind. I guess you should be home with him."

"Where I belong," I said sourly.

"I didn't say that."

"He's probably sound asleep."

"Doubtful. Anyway, I'll have someone pick you up tomorrow morning. We'll have to take a statement from you, and then I'll fill you in on the interrogation. All right?" I nodded. "I don't have to tell you that you performed magnificently."

"Yes, you do."

"You performed magnificently."

"Thank you. You're not upset that I hit him with the accusation too soon? I thought you'd be furious."

"I don't argue with results. You handled it like a pro."

He drove me home in silence. His mind was obviously on the interrogation, now that he was sure I would not go to pieces. In the garage, I gave him a light brush on the lips and went in to fetch Jackson. She was sitting at the kitchen table, and I heard her leap up as I opened the door.

"You're okay," she breathed, half query, half statement.

"Yes. We got them."

"Them?"

"Could you do me a favor?" I requested. "Could you let Lieutenant Sharpe fill you in? I'm just so tired . . ."

"Sure."

I followed her to the closet while she put on her coat. "I enjoyed meeting you," I said.

"Same here. By the way, your husband came down a few times to ask if I had heard anything. He's a wreck. You could wipe the floor with him."

"I'll go up now." I opened the front door, and she walked out to the driveway and got in Sharpe's car. He was brushing the snow from his windshield with an ungloved hand.

"Judith." Bob stood at the top of the stairs, still dressed, only his tie and jacket removed. "Is everything . . ." He began crying and walking downstairs at the same time; I reached for his hand so he wouldn't trip. "Judith," he sobbed, and turned his head so I wouldn't see him cry.

"Come on," I said, turning his face toward mine. "Look at me. I'm fine." He tried to avert his head again: so I drew him close and hugged him. Two hugs, two men—within ten minutes, I thought. "Let's have a drink," I suggested. "Something strong."

"I'll get some brandy," he sniffled. Then he took a clumsy step and held me in his arms. I felt no comfort,

328

no warmth, only a great deal of sorrow that I had frightened him so.

"We have brandy?" I asked, giving him a final squeeze.

"Yes. From St. Thomas, three or four years ago. Remember?"

"That's right." He returned carrying a bottle of cognac and two juice glasses emblazoned with football helmets, from Welch's Grape Jelly. I led the way to the bedroom and, without talking, we sat on the bed and began sipping the cognac.

"I'll never develop a taste for it," I mused. He shrugged his shoulders. "Bob?" He looked at me, the whites of his eyes stained a vivid red: "Would you like to hear what happened?"

"I guess so."

It took about ten minutes to give him a synopsis of the case. By that time, I was on my second glass of cognac and employing expansive sweeps of my arm to illustrate whatever point I was making. "Now, let me tell you about tonight." I related the meeting in the parking lot as neutrally as I could. He took it rather well, sticking out his lower lip and nodding at Dicky's confession, blanching at the knife at my throat, blinking his eyes as that nice police lieutenant distracted Norma. "And that's it," I concluded.

"Well, if you want my opinion . . ." But he cut himself off.

"Please. I'd like your opinion." I refilled his glass.

"Well, it seems to me that Norma is the key to the case," he said. "I mean, her brother seems awfully ineffectual. He might have carried out the actual murder, but I don't think he could have kept up such a detached front without some sort of encouragement." As he spoke, his voice became stronger, almost enthusiastic. "Listen, Judith, he went to pieces as soon as you put on a little pressure. And he's not terribly intelligent, right?

Well, I just don't think a man like that could stonewall it, not for the length of time he did. And why did she see fit to bring a knife along? She knew what a threat you were—and not just to her brother. Tell me, would she have risked your life out of sibling loyalty?"

"No," I said slowly. "I don't think so. She was pretty contemptuous of him."

"All right, so she's involved."

I nodded. But how? "Just one more glass of this stuff," I said.

"I think you've had enough."

"Not yet," I replied, "I'm still lucid."

"That's up to you," he sighed.

"But how is she involved?" I asked. "Dicky sort of said that she had told him to do the right thing or something like that, but I doubt if that makes her an accomplice. Unless she was the brains of the scheme and directed the entire production. But would she do that?"

"Well, you said Fleckstein kept all his affairs separate from his marriage, that he always behaved decently to Norma."

"Right," I acknowledged. "He was the perfect husband, loving, doting, calling her during the day to tell her how terrific she was."

"Right. What a phony. Then all of a sudden she finds out that this perfect husband was having a *ménage à trois* right in her living room—with her dog."

"Yes. She seems very attached to Prince."

"Judith, I'm serious."

"So am I."

He took a deep breath and then another sip of cognac. "Anyhow, all of a sudden this woman is face to face with the fact that her whole idyllic marriage is a fraud. Now, unless she was fairly blasé," he cleared his throat, "she couldn't help but be shocked at the affair—and at his sexual predilections. I mean, a lot of married men might fool around, but they don't record it for posterity. And they don't go in for animals and all that foolishness."

"Trite, maybe, but not foolish. If I were going in for a thing like that, I'd do something like Catherine the Great—a muscular black stallion with sweaty flanks."

"Judith! What kind of talk is that?"

"I don't know," I mumbled. "But why would Norma want him killed? Can you change from adoration to hate in a few minutes?"

"Perhaps. But unless she was really involved and feeling terribly threatened, why would she go all out to protect her contemptible brother—her husband's murderer?"

We tossed the same ideas back and forth for a few minutes, but no conclusions emerged. Then I yawned.

"Want to go to bed?" he asked.

I looked at him, not wanting to lose his goodwill again, but being so weary and so drunk that I knew I could not respond.

"Yes," I said finally. "I don't think I could manage anything else."

"That's all right," he said magnanimously, leaning over to kiss the top of my head. "Just one more thing."

"What's that?"

"Swear to me you'll never do anything like this again. Ever."

We stared at each other. "I can't," I whispered.

"Judith, no more. This was it. I won't permit it."

"Robert, how many more murders do you think I'll run across in my lifetime?"

"I don't know. But this was it, Judith. I want that understood."

"Bob," I began.

"Good night. Have a good night's sleep." He kissed me again, lightly, and we both undressed, not bothering to look at each other.

I slept almost immediately, but kept waking, fighting

to retain my portion of the quilt, feeling stiff and full of minor aches, as if I were about to get the flu. I don't remember dreaming, but each time I awoke, I felt anxious, uncomfortable, wanting to complete some unfinished business but too weary and confused to recall what it was—or what had to be done. At last, a little after three-thirty, I climbed out of bed and stumbled into the bathroom with a vague notion that aspirin might help. The mirror reflected a frowsy, bleary image, brown eyes circled with dark, sickly shadows, puffy lips with tiny cracks, like an enlarged finger print, all over their parched surface. God, I thought, what a picture.

And with that notion, I tiptoed from the bathroom out of the bedroom and downstairs to the den, where I called Sharpe's office. I held on for nearly ten minutes until he could come to the phone.

"Nelson," I said, my voice dry and croaking. "The photographs."

"What?" he asked. "Judith, you sound awful. Are you okay?"

"Fine. Don't worry. But listen to me. The photographs, they weren't at Dicky's, but if he and Norma were in cahoots . . ."

"I know. I thought of that too. There are two men at her house checking it now, but they've been there an hour and haven't found anything so far. And she's not giving an inch."

"She won't talk?"

"No. Her lawyer is with her, and he's screaming and jumping up and down, threatening to sue the whole world for false arrest. But we're holding her on an assault charge, and hopefully we can get the whole story from Dunck."

"Is he cooperating?"

"I think he will. It took us a couple of hours just to calm him down, but he's starting to open up. I have to get back."

"Okay," I said testily, in no mood to be fair. "I was just trying to help."

"I know."

"Would you call me if anything happens?"

"I'll try," he responded. "Otherwise, I'll have someone pick you up around nine-thirty. We need your statement, and after that I'll fill you in. Now get some sleep, Judith."

I stumbled back upstairs, took a couple of aspirin, and lay down, flat on my back. Who was watching Norma's children, I wondered? At that very moment, were the police ransacking their toy chests, looking for the photographs? Had anyone called Brenda to say, "Sorry, your husband won't be coming home tonight"?

"Bob," I whispered.

"S'okay," he mumbled and, still asleep, turned and put his arm around me. I shifted away from him and lay on my side, feeling his hand, hot from sleep, on my stomach. A few minutes later, I pushed it away and dozed off, thinking of Norma and her paring knife, Dicky and his shaved head, little stubs of hair rising out of his scalp after a long, dark night of interrogation.

Chapter Twenty

A uniformed policeman in an unmarked car picked me up at exactly nine-thirty. A young cop with sandy-colored hair and sandy-colored skin, he called me "ma'am" several times and asked how I was feeling after my "big night." I told him fine, but did not attempt to force my stiff, hungover muscles into a smile.

At headquarters, a couple of detectives interviewed me in what must have been the police equivalent of a presidential suite, a large beige room filled with leather chairs, glass-enclosed bookcases, and an automatic coffee machine. A nubby brown carpet replaced the regulation linoleum. One of them took notes while the other asked most of the questions. Had I, in any way, felt Mrs. Fleckstein's weapon piercing my body at any point?

"At any point in time?"

"No, Mrs. Singer. At any point on your, um, person."

"No." I lifted my chin to display my neck, unsullied, unscarred. We rehashed the evening until they seemed satisfied. The notetaker left, saying he would type up the statement.

"Where is Lieutenant Sharpe?" I asked the other, a tall, heavy-set man who wore his blond hair in a pompadour, like an aging leader of Hitler Youth.

"Just resting a few minutes. He said to call him as soon as we were finished."

"Did either of them talk?"

"I'm sorry, Mrs. Singer, but I'm not authorized to discuss the facts of this case with persons outside the department."

"That's okay." I asked if he was assigned to the homicide unit, but he told me he'd rather not say. My head throbbed, and I felt as though I had a great glob of foreign matter lodged in my throat. Finally, he suggested that we'd probably have an early spring and I agreed with him, just to put him out of his misery. A few moments later, the other detective returned with my statement. Although I never would have said "On or about March 7," it was accurate enough. I signed it. They examined my signature, which seemed to satisfy them, and asked me to wait. A few minutes later, Sharpe stuck his head in the door.

"Would you like some company?" he asked. His gray hair was disheveled, flatter on the right side, as if he had been napping on a rigid surface. I walked over to him and fluffed it with my fingers.

"What happened?" I demanded.

He sauntered into the room and motioned me to sit on the long leather couch; he sat beside me. "Dunck talked," he reported, taking my left hand and twisting my wedding ring around.

"Well?"

"Judith, I'm so tired. You have no idea."

"If you think you're going to put me off until you're well rested . . ."

"No. That would be cruel and unusual. Just let me get my thoughts together." We sat motionless for a few seconds until he kissed the palm of my hand.

"You're okay?" he asked.

"Yes. And you? If you're really too tired . . ."

"I'm all right. Should I tell you what happened?" I

336

nodded. "Well, the day before the murder, Dunck got a call from Fleckstein at about three in the afternoon. Fleckstein asked if he could drop by the printing plant for a few minutes to have a chat. Dunck said sure, thinking he might get even more information to give to the U.S. Attorney, to bury Fleckstein even deeper."

"He had no idea that Bruce was on to him?"

"None. Anyhow, Fleckstein wandered in there a little after four and began making small talk. How are things going? How's business? Dunck said everything was fine, and Fleckstein gave him this big shit-eating grin and said: 'You're lucky to be married to such a beautiful woman.' Dunck told us he smiled or said thank you or something and then Fleckstein repeated, 'a beautiful woman.' "

"What a bastard. Setting Dicky up like that."

"Wait till you hear the next part. Fleckstein said: 'You know, I came across some snapshots of Brenda today. Maybe you'd like to have them.' He reached into his pocket and took out a wad of Polaroids and scattered them over Dunck's desk." Sharpe's eyes were wide and animated, as if he were watching the scene being performed on a stage a few feet away. "Dunck glanced at them but didn't make the connection. He thought they were some new pictures that Fleckstein and his friends wanted printed. But then Fleckstein picked up a couple of them and held them right in front of Dunck's face and said: 'A beautiful woman, your Brenda.' Well, Dunck stared at them for a minute and then went bananas, crying and trying to punch Fleckstein, yelling that it wasn't really Brenda."

"But he knew it was," I interjected.

"Sure he did. He recognized her body, just like you did. Those two scars. Anyhow, Fleckstein's bigger, and he grabbed Dunck and held him in a tight grip. Dunck couldn't pull away. And Fleckstein said: 'Either you stop telling stories about me and my business associates

337

or I'll see these pictures get shown all over town.' Well, your friend Dicky finally calmed down enough and took another look at the photographs. He told Fleckstein that you couldn't see the woman's face, that nobody would believe it was Brenda. And do you know what Fleckstein said?"

"What?" I whispered, unable to locate my voice.

"He said he was sorry, but he forgot to bring all the pictures that afternoon that showed Brenda's face. And he sort of smiled at Dunck and said: 'Boy, if you think these are kinky, you should see the rest of them.' And so while Dunck just stood there falling apart, Fleckstein gathered all the photographs together and started to leave. Then, when he got to the door, he turned around and handed Dunck one of the pictures. Know what he said?" I shook my head. " 'Maybe you'd like a memento. Brenda's such a sweet girl—and a great animal lover.' And then he walked out, leaving Dunck with the picture."

"And then what?" I asked, turning to lean my head on his shoulder for a minute. He was wearing the same green sweater as the night before, and it felt scratchy against my cheek. Reaching under the sweater, I could feel his shirt damp with perspiration. His body had a strong, pungent odor. I began to rub his chest.

"Here?" he asked.

"You wouldn't dare."

"Try me."

"No. I mean, not here. Not now. What happened after that?"

"Dunck didn't remember how long he stayed in his office, but it was probably a half hour or so. He wanted to go home and confront Brenda, but he couldn't do it, couldn't think of what to say. So he sat there, staring at the picture, and suddenly realized that it had been taken in Fleckstein's house, by Fleckstein."

338

"You mean, he didn't connect the two of them before that?"

"No. He thought it had been taken by someone else, some stranger. So when it hit him that she was making it with Fleckstein . . ."

"You mean Prince."

"Well, she took turns. A very versatile lady. Anyway, when he realized this, he ran to his car and," he paused to glance at me, "drove right over to his sister's."

"To Norma's?"

"Right. Nobody was home, so he waited, pacing up and down the driveway, looking at the picture. It was really haunting him. Finally, Norma drove up— probably about five o'clock, with two of her kids. She saw Dunck as she pulled in, and said hello, but told him she had to make dinner and couldn't invite him in. Well, he told her it was urgent, about her husband, so she sent the kids upstairs or something and then asked him to come into the living room. And then guess who came trotting in to say hello?"

"Bruce?"

"Prince. Well, Dunck went to pieces completely and handed Norma the photograph. And do you know what she said?"

"What?"

" 'That's my living room.' " Sharpe grinned. " 'And that's Prince.' Dunck was crying by this time, and he told her: 'And that's my wife.' Well, Norma sat down and told him to get control of himself. Then she asked where he got the picture. And he told her."

I imagined Norma, amidst the jungle of green plants in her living room, neat and correct and trying to comprehend what was happening. "What did she do?"

"She took the photograph into the library, didn't say a word. Dunck just sat there, and every once in a while Prince would nuzzle him, wanting to be petted. Christ, that must have been awful."

I kissed him gently on the mouth. "You're so decent," I told him. "That's your best quality."

"*That's* my best quality? Judith, you of all people . . ."

"Then what happened?"

"She finally came back to the living room and seemed in absolute control. Dunck blurted out the whole story about how he was testifying against Fleckstein and that he was terrified about the pictures being spread around, but he was afraid of what the government would do to him if he didn't cooperate, and so on. All of a sudden Norma interrupted him and said: 'You'll have to get rid of them.' "

"Get rid of what?"

"That's what he asked her. He thought she meant the pictures, so he told her that her husband had the pictures. But she said: 'That's not what I'm talking about, Dicky. We've been humiliated.' "

"You mean she wanted him to kill Bruce *and* Brenda?"

"Yes."

"That's incredible. A middle-class Jewish woman with a Sicilian code of honor."

"She said that they had been humiliated, shamed, and it was time he behaved like a man and put a stop to it."

"Behave like a man," I repeated. "Poor Dicky. How did he react?"

"Well, to his credit, he said he tried to dissuade her. He even suggested they both get divorces. But she countered him. She said: 'Even if you got a divorce, could you ever go to your club and hold your head up high again?' "

I began laughing, less out of amusement than horror at her tortuous manipulations to keep up appearances. "What did he say?"

"Well, at first he refused. Then he said she should take care of Fleckstein. But she said she couldn't, that if a man is killed, they always suspect the wife."

"Is that true?"

"Sure. It's reflex. Then Dunck asked her: 'Won't they suspect me if anything happens to Brenda?' Norma conceded that and said they could take care of Brenda later. But Fleckstein had to go. She kept saying over and over that he had humiliated her, made a fool of her, and that Dunck could not allow that to happen to his sister."

"He really bought that?"

"Well, she laid it on thick, reminding him of how Fleckstein had humiliated *him* all those times, and asked just how much he would take. Remember, she's no genius, but she's light-years ahead of her brother. Anyhow, she told him that she would call him the next day at his plant, as soon as the coast was clear in Fleckstein's office."

"She'd be a lookout?"

"No, Fleckstein always called her a few minutes before he came home, to see if she needed anything. She told Dunck that she'd tell Fleckstein to wait, that she wanted to meet him in his office because she had a special Valentine's Day present for him."

I cocked my head and looked at Sharpe. "And then Norma would call Dicky and tell him to hurry over to Fleckstein's office?" Sharpe said yes. "But how come," I asked, "if the coast was clear, Marilyn Tuccio saw Dicky at the water fountain?"

"Well, I called her this morning and checked," he said. "She wasn't absolutely certain, but she thinks Fleckstein might have walked out of the room after he finished working on her, while she was coming out of the anesthesia. That's probably when he called his wife. He probably figured he'd be leaving in a few minutes anyway and wanted to save time."

I stood, stretched my legs and set out to pace around the room. After about six steps, I stopped and fell back onto the couch. My legs ached, my shoes pinched my feet. "Okay," I sighed. "Exit Marilyn, enter Dicky. Then what?"

"Dunck walked into the office. He claims all he wanted to do was talk with Fleckstein, to try and convince him to destroy the photographs."

"Do you believe him?"

"In a sense. I doubt if Dunck could have gotten it up to walk in there if he knew for sure that he was going to have to kill him. But as far as the law goes, he walked in there carrying a weapon—and that's murder one."

"Where did he get the weapon?"

Sharpe raised his eyes to the ceiling. "Wait till you hear this. I mean, I've dealt with a lot of murderers, a lot of sickies and mental defectives, but I've never come across a normal, middle-class killer as stupid as Dunck. He took the awl out of his plant foreman's tool box. I called the foreman this morning, and he said an awl had been missing, so he bought a new one. And Dunck approved the petty cash voucher for it. Christ, what a toad-load! Anyway, Dunck walked into the office with the awl in his pocket. He says Fleckstein seemed surprised to see him but was fairly cool, asking him how he was doing and if he had finally decided to get smart. Well, Dunck lost control and began crying, and guess what your boy Bruce said?"

"What?"

"He said, 'Stop acting like a woman, Dicky.' And then he grabbed Dunck's lapels and pulled him over and sort of sneered: 'But, then, Brenda tells me you always act like a woman, even in bed.' And he pushed Dunck away and called him 'stud' and 'big man.' "

"I guess that did it for Dicky."

"Sure. Well. He says that he went crazy when he heard this, but that's just a pathetic attempt to build up the basis for an insanity defense. I guess Dunck thinks that if he says he went crazy, the jury will understand and let him go."

"And that won't work?"

"No. There's enough premeditation in his statement to send him away for life five times over. Anyhow, Dunck pulled away from Fleckstein, took out the awl, and lunged for him."

"Did he die right away?" I asked.

"It took a few minutes. He says Fleckstein fell face down, and he turned him over to see if he was dead. But he wasn't quite dead, and Dunck said Fleckstein kept staring at him—for about five minutes."

A chill ran across my shoulders and down through my body. I rubbed my hands together as if the friction would be enough to warm me.

"Doesn't that disturb you?" I asked Sharpe.

"No."

"Oh." We sat there quietly for a few seconds. I began to feel a little warmer. Sharpe yawned. "Then what?"

"He broke the locks on the drawers and found one of them full of pictures. He grabbed them and stuffed them into his pocket, but of course he missed a few— the ones we found. Oh, by the way, he was wearing gloves the whole time, which probably adds weight to a premeditation charge. Anyway, he left and went back to Norma's."

"God," I said, shaking my head. Suddenly I looked at him. "Nelson, is there a cafeteria or something here? I couldn't get any breakfast down and now I'm starving. I mean, I know we have a lot of ground to cover, but if you have time . . ."

"Sure." He helped me on with my coat, and we left the building, walking a few blocks to a coffee shop, Maclyn's Luncheonette—Seating and To Go. Sharpe ordered eggs, bacon, toast, and coffee. I asked for orange juice and an English muffin.

He smiled at me and took my hand and said: "Judith, you'll never know how wonderful you are."

I smiled back. "I'm sorry I couldn't hold out, but my stomach isn't what it should be." I took a bite of the

343

marmalade-coated muffin. "What happened when Dicky got to Norma's?"

"Well, he gave her the pictures."

"That's right. God, how did I forget about them? Did you find them?"

"Finally, but it took almost four hours. She was pretty clever. Do you know where they were?" I shook my head. "Packed away in the basement, with all sorts of summer things. She had taken this inflatable sea horse that kids use and made a slit in it and stuffed the pictures in. Then she put a matching vinyl patch over it and blew it up. But one of the detectives is a very smart guy, and he noticed all the other toys were in various stages of deflation after hanging around all winter. He found it curious that this was the only one that was fully inflated."

"Not bad," I conceded. "But why did they want to hold on to the pictures?"

"*They* didn't," he replied, falling silent as the waitress approached. She poured him another cup of coffee and asked if I wanted a cup.

"You look like you could use it, honey," she commented. I consented.

"Do I look that bad?" I asked Sharpe.

"Yes," he said. I shifted uncomfortably, longing to reach into my bag for a mirror. "You look kind of yellow," he described, smiling. "But still beautiful. I like yellow. Look, do you want me to continue or do you want to go and powder your nose or something?"

"Go on." The waitress came and deposited my coffee.

"Well, Norma had persuaded Dunck to tear apart the office and find the photos. She told him she would take care of destroying them. When he came to her house, she had two questions: 'Is he dead?' and 'Did you get the pictures?' He told her the pictures were in his coat, and she took them. She put them in her pocketbook.

344

She told him to leave and she would light a fire and destroy them."

"That's fascinating," I said. "What could have motivated her to keep them? I mean, did she have some need to see them again and again? Or did she think she could use them for something, like blackmail?"

"Well, her motives were very complex, that's for sure. I mean, if the average woman found out her husband was carrying on like that, she'd either pack her bags or learn to live with it. But with Norma, the photographs gave her a hold on Dunck—and she used them."

"Tell me." I took a sip of my coffee. It was warm, not hot, and the cream had separated into pale little islands, floating on a dark black sea.

"Dunck says she took him aside before the funeral and told him she burned them. But that was before you came in."

"Me?"

"Yes. After you interviewed the Duncks, he called Norma and told her about you. She had a fit and ordered him to give you ' a warning.' Dunck said he didn't want any part of it, and that's when she told him he'd better toe the line—or she'd spread the pictures of Brenda around."

"So she was the one who told him to write the M.Y.O.B."

"Well, yes and no. She told him to give you a warning, but she wasn't specific. Apparently, when he told her what he had done, she blew up. Her idea of a warning was something a little more threatening."

"Well," I said, "it's a good thing she was so vague, otherwise you might have been introduced to me when I was laid out on a slab. You know, the minute I saw M.Y.O.B., I connected it with Dicky. Did she tell him to plant the awl at Marilyn's?"

"No. In fact, she never even asked him about the

weapon. The awl in the storm sewer was his own embellishment."

"I'm sure Norma was thrilled when he told her about it."

"Overjoyed. Do you know what he said? 'When I told Norma where I put the awl, she yelled at me.' "

I shook my head sadly. "Do you think he's a little off the beam? Or slightly moronic?"

"I don't think he's either. He's just a very ordinary guy who couldn't cope with the world he lived in and who remained a kid. There are loads of guys like him, but they don't get themselves mixed up with the grown-ups. But he was living in a very high-powered community, and he felt he had to keep in step."

"And Norma? She won't say anything?"

"Not a word. But we have enough circumstantial evidence to convict, I think—plus Dunck's testimony."

"When will the trial be?" I asked.

"I don't know." He took my hand. "Judith, now that it's over, I don't want it to be the end for us. Please. We have to talk. We have to come to some decision."

"Decision about what?" I asked softly. "Nelson, I'm not ready to decide anything right now."

"But you care about me, don't you?"

"Of course. But I can't give you a pledge of eternal passion and devotion, or anything else."

He crumbled a piece of bacon on his plate and then fixed his huge brown eyes on mine. "Do you love me?"

"You're talking to a woman with a hangover."

"I'm talking to the woman I love. A rich woman."

"What do you mean?" I asked.

"I spoke to the captain. We're going to recommend that you get the reward money. The Dental Association and Norma put up five thousand each, remember? I doubt if you'll collect from Norma, but the dentists will pay." He reached for my hand. "Now I can marry you for your money."

"No, you can't. But five thousand dollars will pay for

a lot of baby sitting. We can have some long, lovely afternoons together."

"And maybe more," he whispered, grinning.

"Maybe."